Rosie Goodwin is the author of a number of bestselling historical fiction novels. Having worked in the social services sector for many years, she is now a full-time novelist. Rosie's writing career began when her husband submitted a short story to *Take a Break* magazine, which was later published. Rosie lives in Nuneaton, the setting for many of her books, with her husband and their three dogs. *A Mother's Shame* is Rosie's twenty-first novel.

Visit www.rosiegoodwin.co.uk to find out more about Rosie and sign up for her newsletter. Or follow Rosie on twitter; @rosiegoodwin

The Mill Girl

Rosie Goodwin

corsair

CORSAIR

First published in Great Britain in 2014 by Corsair
This paperback edition published in 2015

A CIP catalogue record for this book
is available from the British Library.

ISBN 978-1-47210-175-4 (hardback)
ISBN: 978-1-47211-598-0 (ebook)

Typeset in Palatino by SX Composing DTP, Rayleigh, Essex
Printed and bound in Great Britain by CPI Group (UK) Ltd, Croydon, CR0 4YY

Corsair
An imprint of
Little, Brown Book Group
100 Victoria Embankment
London EC4Y 0DY

An Hachette UK Company
www.hachette.co.uk
www.littlebrown.co.uk

For Jane, my soul sister x

Part One
July 1850

Chapter One

'Ssh, don't wake him, lass,' Eve Meadows whispered to her daughter Maryann. 'He's worn out, bless him.' Her eyes were full of concern as she looked towards her husband, who was slumped in the bedside chair. 'And you must be an' all.'

Maryann was quick to reassure her. 'I'm all right, Mam, don't you get fretting over me.'

Eve Meadows was terrified of how her husband would cope if anything happened to her. John Meadows was a gentle man, and since his wife's illness he had become like a lost soul, which worried her considerably. What would become of the family, if she was no longer there to care for them? Her hand dropped to the mound of her stomach and she heaved a sigh. This last pregnancy had come as a shock, for she had thought she had left her childbearing days behind her. If truth be told, she had not wanted any more children – even though John had been thrilled at the prospect of a new baby. But from the day she had realised she was with child again, she had felt unwell, and also had this awful sense of foreboding – and now with this fever on top . . . She felt as if someone had lit a fire inside her that was consuming her. However, her biggest fear was not for herself but for her family. Maryann looked worn out. The lass was just seventeen, too young to be running a household and scurrying about after invalids – but she was powerless to help her.

'Why don't you take yourself off to bed now and get some rest?' she suggested weakly as Maryann plumped up her pillows and bent to plant a tender kiss on her mother's burning cheek.

'I will soon, Mam, but I fancy a bit o' fresh air before I turn in so I might go and stand out in the yard and cool down first.'

Once outside in the gloomy cobbled courtyard, the girl welcomed the slightly cooler air on her skin whilst trying to ignore the overpowering stench of the pigsty and the privy. Great fat bluebottles were buzzing about and she swatted them away tiredly. She was still standing there when Toby Jackson emerged from the door of the cottage across the yard. The pair smiled easily at each other.

'How are they?' He cocked his head towards the house.

'Violet seems to have turned the corner, but I'm still worried about me mam,' Maryann confided.

He patted her arm comfortingly. 'Happen she'll be on the mend soon,' he told her, but she wasn't so sure although she longed to believe him.

'She didn't have enough strength as it was,' she told him in a small voice and it was all he could do to stop himself from taking her in his arms there and then.

Toby worked at the mill with Maryann's father and so he knew how things were. John Meadows had been walking about as if he had the weight of the world on his shoulders

– but then that came as no surprise, knowing how much he thought of his wife. Unlike most of the chaps thereabouts, John's wages were tipped onto the table each week rather than finding their way across the bar in the local ale-house, and he was not ashamed to say how much he cared for his family. In fact, as Toby thought of it now he couldn't ever remember hearing a cross word sounding from the Meadows' house. Most of the women from the neighbouring cottages would sport a black eye come a Friday evening when their husbands staggered in drunk following a belly-full of ale, but Eve Meadows had never had to worry about that with John. He was a home bird, which from where Toby was standing only made the situation in which John now found himself all the more heart-breaking.

'I was just off for a stroll. Don't suppose you'd care to join me, would you?' he asked hopefully.

Maryann shook her head. 'Thanks, I'd love to but after I've cooled down I'm going to try and catch a bit of sleep in case me mam needs me during the night.'

He paused, wishing that there was something he could say to comfort her, but then giving up he strode away, leaving Maryann sagging limply against the wall.

Through the open door, Violet watched him go from her pallet bed at the side of the fireplace. Her expression was hard. It wasn't fair. She'd been fluttering her eyelashes at Toby for months but he never looked the side she was on; his sights were always fixed firmly on their Maryann. It was no surprise really though, she thought to herself resentfully. Maryann had always been the brightest and the prettiest. At least, that was the way she saw it. Maryann could do no wrong in their parents' eyes, whereas she always seemed to be in trouble for something or another. The girl didn't stop to consider the reasons why. The last time she had been scolded for instance, was because her mother had discovered she had been skiving off school and spending the penny a day it cost to send her there on fripperies, as Eve termed them, from the travelling tinker. How anyone could term ribbons and cheap pieces of jewellery as fripperies, Violet just could not imagine. Surely they were essential items to a girl if she was to look her best? And Violet liked to look her best.

Now her hand rose absently to touch her hair. It was lank after all the sweating she had done during her illness and she longed to give it a good wash, but although she felt much better now, she would not admit it just yet. It was quite nice to lie in bed and have Maryann wait on her, and when she did show an improvement no doubt Maryann would go back to work and it would be left to her to fetch and carry for their mother. She scowled at the thought. Violet was still finding it hard to forgive her mother for getting pregnant again. It was disgusting, the way she saw it, and for more than one reason. For a start off she considered her mother to be far too old to be having another child; she was suddenly no better than the other women in the courts, who bred like rabbits. And secondly, once the brat arrived she would no longer be the youngest, which was something she had taken full advantage of since the death of her other two siblings.

Seven-year-old Gertie and six-year-old Joe had died the year before from measles, which was probably why she had not been sent out to work as yet. Nearly all of the girls of her age that she knew had already been working for years, but Violet hated the thought of having to follow her father and sister into that dirty mill. Most of the people who worked there for any length of time ended up dying of the lung fever from the loose cotton fibres they were forced to inhale, and she had no intention of that happening to her! No, Violet intended to go into service when she had to – and not as a laundry maid either. She wanted to be a lady's maid at the very least. She had seen them occasionally when she had passed the posh houses, in their frilly lace caps and pretty aprons. A position like that would suit her just fine, for the time being at least. As she day dreamed she snuggled further down into the lumpy mattress and in no time at all she was fast asleep.

Maryann was just about to re-enter the house when a cry from her parents' open bedroom window had her springing through the door and up the stairs.

'Fetch Granny Addison right away,' her father ordered her as he gripped his wife's hand. 'I think the baby is coming.'

'But it's too early!' Maryann's hand flew to her mouth as she stared at her mother. Eve's face was distorted with pain. Her eyes were screwed tight shut and she had gone alarmingly pale. Without wasting another second, Maryann hoisted up her darned calico skirt and raced back down the stairs and across the yard where she hammered on Granny Addison's door.

One glance at the girl's terrified face told the woman all she needed to know, and without a word she followed Maryann back across the cobblestones.

'What's wrong now?' Violet complained as she struggled to sit up. She had been having a very pleasant dream, so was none too pleased to be woken so soon.

Neither Maryann nor Granny Addison bothered to answer her, and once they had disappeared up the narrow staircase Violet crossed her arms in a huff.

They found John Meadows leaning over his wife, and when he turned his face briefly towards their kindly neighbour, Granny Addison saw tears glistening on his lashes. Her heart went out to him. Both were aware that Eve was pitifully weak already, without having to face the strain of giving birth. However, it looked as if there was no other option now and she would just have to do what she could for her.

'Fetch me hot water an' towels, as many as yer can lay yer 'ands on,' she barked at Maryann as she threw off her old woollen shawl and rolled her sleeves up. 'An' you,' she addressed John, 'get yerself downstairs. The birthin' room ain't no place for a bloke.'

But John did not budge. 'I'm staying,' he answered with quiet determination, and so with a shrug she turned her attention to the poor soul on the bed who was gripped in a contraction.

'Well, don't say as I didn't warn yer.' Yet despite her words she felt a quiet admiration for him. Her Archie had been off to the ale-house as fast as a bullet from a gun when she'd started to birth each of her brood, an' he'd come home roaring drunk after it was over each time an' all.

Flicking aside the coarse blanket, she then unceremoniously hoisted Eve's nightgown up to her breasts and ran her hands across her swollen stomach as the woman groaned in agony.

'I reckon this little 'un is breech,' she mumbled worriedly to herself. Eve was in a bad enough way as it was without having to try and push out a babby that was upside down – but there was nowt she could do about it.

'That's it, you bear down now when yer feel the need to,' she soothed as she slid her hand into the woman's most private place. Eve screamed but Bertha continued to probe, hoping to get a hold on the child's feet.

John's skin already had the yellow pallor of most that worked in the mill, but now he was positively grey. He watched as sweat stood out on the midwife's forehead and began to run down her face like tears.

'C-can you feel it?' he whimpered.

'I can that, but feelin' it an' catchin' 'old o' the little sod

8

are two different things,' Granny Addison gasped as she withdrew her hand.

'Shall I send Benny for the doctor?'

'If you've a mind to – but can yer afford it?'

'If need be.' John Meadows would have sold his soul at that moment to get help for his wife.

Eve immediately dropped back onto the pillows as Granny Addison went on, 'I reckon we've a way to go yet, lad. This could take some time so, 'old fire till we see what's goin' on, eh?'

Maryann rushed back in then, clutching a bowl of hot water and with a number of clean towels folded across her arm. Like her father's, her face was fearful.

'She will be all right, won't she, Granny?'

The woman raised her eyes to the young girl's and wearily shook her head. 'I can't answer that, lass,' she said. 'It's all in God's hands now.'

The child, a perfectly formed little boy, finally slithered from his mother's body just as dawn was streaking the sky with soft purples and mauves. He was tiny, with downy chestnut hair the same colour as his big sister's, but he never took a breath and within minutes of his arrival his mother took her last too.

John Meadows stood in stupefied silence as he stared down at them whilst the rest of the family huddled together in the kitchen downstairs.

'I'm so sorry, lad,' Granny Addison said chokily as she pressed his arm. Dr Noble had been in attendance for the last two hours but even he had not been able to do anything. Now, the grim-faced doctor snapped his bag shut and rolled down his sleeves.

'I'll leave yer to say yer goodbyes, shall I, while I go an' get Maryann to make us a sup o' tea? Then I'll come back

9

up an' lay the pair of 'em out afore yer send fer Bill Roberts, the undertaker. I'll pay the doctor an' all, lad. Money in the tin on the mantelpiece, is it?'

John nodded numbly as he stared down at his beloved wife's face. Strangely, death seemed to have erased all the pain from it, and suddenly she looked like the bonny young girl he had fallen in love with, all those years ago.

With a last squeeze of his arm, Granny Addison shuffled from the room, closely followed by the doctor. Her heart was heavy and she was so tired that she could barely put one foot in front of the other, but her job wasn't over yet. Now she would have to tell the children – and it was a job she dreaded.

As she emerged from the small door leading to the stairs, she found three pairs of eyes all turned towards her; one look at her face told it all.

'Oh *nooo* . . .' Maryann began to cry as her brother, Benny, placed his arm protectively about her.

Violet whispered in stunned disbelief, 'Me mam – is she . . .'

Granny Addison nodded mutely.

'An' the baby an' all?'

The woman nodded again before crossing to the kettle and pushing it into the fire. She then paid the doctor who, after offering the family his condolences, pocketed the coins and sadly left. The kettle took only seconds to boil; Maryann had had it simmering all night, so now Bertha Addison crossed to the dresser, took down the heavy brown teapot and began to spoon tea leaves into it. It was one of the very rare occasions in her life when she was lost for words – for what could she say that would ease the suffering of the family left behind? Words seemed so inadequate at a time like this. She added the boiling water to the leaves then after placing the knitted tea cosy on the pot, she left it to mash and sank down onto one of the hard-backed chairs surrounding the table.

'Yer dad – he's taken it badly,' she forced herself to say eventually. 'So yer must all try to be strong fer 'im now. It's what yer mam would 'ave wanted, God rest 'er soul.'

His face ashen, Benny nodded. 'Will we be allowed to see her?' he asked brokenly.

Bertha sighed. 'O' course yer will. But why don't yer wait till I've washed an' changed 'er, once yer dad's said 'is goodbyes, eh?'

Maryann rose woodenly and taking a clean linen nightgown from the pile of ironing she had done that afternoon, she placed it on the table before asking in a small voice, 'Would you like me to help you?'

'No, pet. That ain't no job fer a young 'un. But yer could per'aps find me two pennies. Nice shiny 'uns if yer 'ave 'em.'

Crossing to the tin on the mantelpiece, Maryann extracted two coins with shaking fingers, and as she thought of what they were for, her heart broke. But then she pulled herself together with a great effort, and after fetching the jug of milk from the bucket of cold water in which she had stood it on the cold shelf in the pantry, she checked to see that it hadn't curdled. It was so hard to keep anything fresh in this heat, especially the milk, but thankfully it seemed all right and she prepared the mugs mechanically, feeling as if she were caught in the grip of a nightmare.

Their father joined them some time later, his eyes red and swollen. The tea had stewed by then and Maryann busied herself making a fresh pot. It had been the longest night of his life, but John knew he must hold himself together for the sake of the three young people who were dependent on him. He addressed their neighbour. 'Don't you need to get some rest, my dear?'

11

Bertha Addison gave a deep sigh. 'Thanks, lad, but I'd rather do what needs to be done first.' So saying, she lifted the pennies and the nightgown and slowly made her way back up the stairs, feeling as if she was climbing a mountain. Meanwhile, the children clustered around their father for what little comfort he could give them.

It was almost two hours later when Maryann asked, 'How are we going to afford to pay for Mam's funeral, Dad? There's only enough money left in the tin for the rent man, and enough food to see us through after paying the doctor till you get your next wages – and we haven't paid Granny Addison yet.'

'I'll not need payin', lass,' the warm-hearted woman assured her as she struggled out of the fireside chair. 'Yer mam did me many a good turn, an' that's payment enough.' She was so tired now that she could barely keep her eyes open and wishing to leave the family to grieve now that she had done all she could, she headed for home and the comfort of her old brass bed and Archie's snores.

Once the door had closed behind her, John pointed to the clock on the mantelpiece. It had been a wedding present and Eve's pride and joy, but he had his priorities.

'You can take that to the pawn shop soon as it's opened,' he told Benny dully. 'That should more than pay for a decent send-off.'

'But Dad . . . me mam loved that clock,' Maryann protested with a catch in her voice.

'Aye, I know she did, but it's either that or she lies in a pauper's grave – and I think she deserves better than that, don't you?'

Maryann's chin drooped to her chest as she watched Benny reverently lift the little ornate clock from the shelf. She doubted they would be able to afford a headstone with what the clock would fetch, but then that could always come later, and at least they would know where her resting place was. In the meantime, her dad could perhaps make a wooden cross.

'Will you be wanting her to be laid to rest with the children in Coton churchyard?' Her father nodded dumbly. 'Then perhaps you could call in and ask the vicar to come and see us when you've been to the undertaker's an' all,' she told Benny quietly.

Her brother paused in the act of carefully wrapping the treasured clock in a thin blanket. He made no objection, knowing all too well the necessity for speed. In this heat, the need to bury the dead was urgent, and he had no doubt the vicar would wish to do so within the next couple of days. Word had already spread through the courtyard, and when Benny stepped out onto the cobbles he saw that all the curtains on the other windows were tightly drawn and he had to blink to hold back his tears. He still couldn't quite believe what had happened, but somehow he knew that life as they had known it was about to change for each and every one of them.

Chapter Two

Two days later, Eve Meadows and her baby were laid to rest in Coton churchyard close to the grave of her beloved children. The night before, the weather had changed dramatically and as the family stood at the side of the open grave with bowed heads the rain came down in torrents, soaking them all to the skin.

'I shall be ill again at this rate,' Violet complained. A glare from Maryann silenced her.

Trust Violet to think only of herself on such a day, Maryann fumed. Thankfully she was young and fit and had survived the fever that had so weakened their mam, but there would be many funerals over the coming days, for the same fever that had taken their mother had swept through the town and claimed many lives. A vision of her mother in her coffin – of the two shiny pennies that had been placed on Eve's closed eyes before the undertaker had nailed down the lid – was dancing in front of Maryann, and she knew that she would never forget it. Even so, she was dry-eyed

– for now the pain she was experiencing went beyond tears. The same could not be said for her father, who was leaning heavily on Benny with tears pouring down his cheeks to mix with the rain.

'*We commit the body of our sister Eve Mary Meadows . . .*' The vicar's voice droned on, seeming to come from a long, long way away, but at last it was done, and after he had shaken John's hands and offered condolences, the man turned and hurried away to the warmth of the manse, his vestments flapping wetly about his legs. Only a few people had attended the funeral. Many could not and dared not take the time off work, so thankfully the family had not felt the need to offer refreshments afterwards. The fine ormolu clock had paid for the service and the burial, but there was little left in the kitty now and Maryann knew that it would be up to her to make every penny count if they were all to eat until the next payday. They turned as one and started for the lych-gate as the gravediggers moved in and began to shovel wet earth onto the coffin. The sound was like a knife piercing Maryann's heart.

By the time they turned into the cobbled alley in Abbey Street they were all miserable and tired, but as soon as they entered the kitchen Maryann drew back the curtains and placed the kettle in the heart of the fire. She would make them all a nice hot drink, hoping that once they had all changed out of their sodden clothes, they might feel slightly better. She went into the pantry to see what she might be able to cook them for tea. Life had to go on, and now that her mother was gone Maryann realised that she would have to take on the role of the woman of the house. She doubted Violet would be capable of it. Thankfully there were some green beans and carrots in the pantry, as well as some new potatoes and pickled beetroot. Some leftover apple tart and yesterday's loaf would help to make it filling. Once she had made the tea she then went upstairs to get changed, and soon they were all sitting around the table drinking the weak tea. The few remaining tea leaves they had were precious now.

'Right.' John cleared his throat and looked around at them all. 'I suppose we should talk now about how we are going to manage without— in the future.' His gaze rested on Violet and he told her quietly, 'I'm afraid you will have to start work now, Violet.'

'*What*?' The mug paused halfway to her lips as she stared back at her father in horror.

'Your mam and me have already kept you at school for far longer than most, but now without the money she brought in with the washing and ironing she did, we shall need another wage in order to stay afloat. I shall be having a word with the manager at the mill tomorrow. He'll no doubt be able to find you a place in the carding room.'

Violet slammed her mug onto the oilskin so hard that the contents slopped over the rim as all her hopes and dreams of becoming a lady's maid and wearing a fancy lace cap and apron began to disintegrate.

'B-but I don't *want* to work in the mill!'

Her father's head wagged from side to side. 'None of us wants to work there, lass, but needs must.'

'Well, I won't go!' She scraped her chair back and rose so suddenly that for a moment it was in grave danger of toppling over. 'If I must find work I'll ask about the big houses to see if any of them needs a lady's maid.'

John Meadows sighed. The last thing he needed today was confrontation, but knowing Violet as he did, there would be no use arguing.

'Very well then, I'll give you until the end of the week – but if you haven't found a position by then you'll start at the mill alongside me and Maryann next Monday.'

She stamped away upstairs as Benny and Maryann

16

exchanged an anxious glance. They both loved their younger sister dearly, but they also knew that she had been spoiled shamelessly, especially since the death of the younger children, so she would probably find the changes far harder than they would.

'I think we should all return to work tomorrow,' John said wearily as they all listened to Violet banging about upstairs. 'We will have to fit in the household chores and the cooking between us when we get home each evening. I know it won't be easy, but—'

'We'll soon get into a routine,' Maryann said quickly. He looked so sad, and yet there was nothing she could say that would ease his pain, and it had broken her heart all over again to hear him sobbing in his bed each night.

'Course we will,' Benny said strongly as their father stood up and made for the yard.

'I reckon I'll just go and have a smoke of me pipe,' he told them. Thankfully the rain had stopped although the skies were still heavy and overcast, reflecting their moods. Maryann was glad that it had rained in a way, for what could have been worse than to have to bury Eve Meadows in brilliant sunshine?

'There's a job going up at the big house in the stables, but I don't think I can go for it now,' Benny said in a hushed voice once they were alone.

Maryann glanced at him quizzically as she lifted the empty mugs to take them to the sink. 'Why ever not?'

He sniffed. 'I'd feel a bit like I were deserting a sinking ship.'

'Rubbish!' she scolded. 'We shall manage perfectly well once things settle down, and Dad wouldn't want you to miss this opportunity. We all know how much you hate going underground at the pit and how you've always dreamed of working with horses.'

'Well, I suppose I could always come back to help out with owt that needed doing on me days off if I *did* get the job. An' it goes without saying that I'd tip some of me wages up.'

'What you're forgetting is there'd be one less mouth to feed if you weren't living here, so we'd manage fine without your money,' Maryann pointed out.

Benny still looked unconvinced, but the thought of missing this wonderful chance was almost more than he could bear. But then he told himself it would be best to take things one step at a time. Today of all days was no time to be making decisions, and so for now he let the subject drop. The house felt so empty without his mam bustling about, and as it hit him afresh that he would never see her again he lowered his head and wept.

Chapter Three

Maryann, her dad and Benny rose at four thirty the next morning, and after a hasty breakfast of bread smeared with dripping and a mug of weak tea they went their separate ways, Benny to the pit and Maryann and John to the mill.

The rainclouds had disappeared as if by magic and it looked set to be a fine day, although none of them could find any joy in it. They had left Violet tucked up in bed, but Maryann hoped that she would rouse herself to go and look for some sort of job at least. Sadly, her younger sister was going to have to grow up now, but Maryann feared it was going to go mightily against her nature, knowing the girl as she did. Violet had adamantly refused to speak to any of them for the rest of the day following the funeral and had sulked in her room, venturing down only to eat the meal that Maryann had prepared.

'Haven't we even got a bit of meat to put in it?' she had asked as she stared down into her dish with a look of revulsion on her face.

'No, which is why we're going to need an extra wage,' Maryann had said quietly, sending Violet yet further into a dark mood. She had cleared her dish though, so Maryann supposed it couldn't have been that bad – and anything was better than having to go to bed on an empty stomach.

She and her father trudged silently through the empty cattle market in Queens Road then turned towards Attleborough and the mill. Eventually it loomed up ahead of them and Maryann suppressed a shudder as she did each time she approached it. Already they could hear the clamour of machinery from within, and the dark forbidding façade did nothing to lift her already dejected mood. The mill was built on the banks of the River Anker from where it drew the water to power the huge machines, and suddenly Maryann dreaded stepping inside it. Her nerves were stretched to breaking point and really all she wanted to do was find a quiet corner and cry her eyes out for the loss of her beloved mam. It was so hard to accept that never again would she return home to the smell of fresh baked bread and a stew bubbling on the range. To see her mam's gentle smile as she drew Maryann's shawl from about her shoulders and pressed the girl into a chair before passing her a mug of the hot tea she would have ready for her. Now all that her mam had done would fall on her shoulders, as well as trying to keep her job, and Maryann knew all too well how hard it was going to be, for she could expect little or no help from Violet.

The night before, when the rest of the family had retired to bed, Maryann had stayed up baking. Keeping busy was her way of taking her mind off things, and at least now they would have a meal to go home to after their long shifts, even if it was only one of bread and cheese. She had been taking the bread from the oven when a tap at the window had come. Opening the door, she had found Toby standing on the doorstep, twisting his cap in his hands.

'I err . . . thought I'd come an' see how you were,' he'd said awkwardly. 'I know what a difficult day it must have been for you all.'

Maryann had nodded shakily with her arms wrapped tight about her waist, and his heart had gone out to her. She was deathly pale apart from the dark shadows beneath her eyes, yet she still managed to look beautiful to him and he had never come closer to telling her how much he loved her, although he had opened his arms and she had gone into them willingly. And there, pressed against his warm chest, she had finally let out the flood of tears that she had held back as he stroked her hair and hugged her. The weeping had given her some release. She knew just as he did without any words being spoken that they would be together one day, and she was happy to bide her time. She also knew he wouldn't ask for her hand until he could provide her with a home of their own – somewhere far away from the cobbled courtyards infested with rats and flies where they had lived all their lives.

But now that she had lost her mam she wondered how she could ever leave her father and the family to cope alone. Still, at least Toby's presence had comforted her and now, squaring her shoulders, she followed her father into the dim interior of the mill.

Instantly the fine cotton particles that floated in the air caught in the back of her throat as she headed for the carding room, where she worked at feeding the cleaned cotton through the enormous carding machines. Her father meanwhile made for the spinning room.

Many of the women were already at work, their worn faces dull with exhaustion, and Maryann kicked off her wooden clogs and placed them against the wall before going to join them. The floor was always slick with oil in there and it was safer to go barefoot: there was less chance of slipping that way. Next she rolled up her sleeves for fear of

21

them being caught in the great metal teeth that snapped like giants at the cotton. Many a man and woman had lost their hands to the monsters, and even more children had been maimed when slithering beneath them as they collected up any cotton that floated to the ground.

By mid-morning, Maryann looked as if she had been out in a snowdrift. She was white from head to foot and the clogging cotton particles were thick in the air, shining like snowflakes in the shaft of light that poured through the one grimy window high up in the wall. She had become adept at shutting her mind to everything except the carding machine in front of her. It was easier that way, for otherwise she feared she might have died of boredom. Today, however, she found her mind wandering and struggled to concentrate.

Back at the small cottage in Abbey Street, Violet was preening in front of the cracked mirror that hung above the mantelpiece, adjusting her best bonnet and tweaking some colour into her cheeks. She had dressed carefully in her Sunday best and was now ready to approach some of the posh houses surrounding the town in the hope of finding work as a lady's maid. She stared at her reflection, wishing that she was slim and dainty like Maryann. She herself had always tended to be plump, and although she was quite aware that she was attractive, she knew that Maryann was beautiful. Her own hair was straight and a dull brown, whilst Maryann's was a wonderful shade of chestnut that gleamed with copper lights in the sunshine, and a mass of curls that no amount of brushing could tame. It was so unfair. Maryann would wash her hair and do no more than tie it back in a ribbon, whilst she, Violet, had to endure sleeping in rags to tempt her own hair into curls – and then they usually dropped out in no time at all. Sighing, she flicked at a speck of dust on her skirt before snatching up her basket and heading for the door.

I'll show them, she thought to herself determinedly. If they think I'm goin' to work in the mill they can think again! And off she went with her head held high.

She decided to begin her quest in Swan Lane, a better part of the town where doctors, shopkeepers and businessmen tended to reside, and where she was sure that she would find someone needing live-in help. Swan Lane consisted of rows of towering terraced redbrick houses that appeared enormous compared to the tiny two-up two-down cottage that was her home. Dotted amongst them were large, semi-detached properties and the largest and most impressive ones were all detached, set in their own enormous gardens.

At the first house, she paused to stare up at the three storeys and the snow-white lace curtains, then taking a deep breath she stretched herself to her full height, opened the gate and walked sedately up the tiled path to the front door. Here she lifted the gleaming brass knocker and jabbed it at the door. Almost instantly she heard footsteps approaching and seconds later a young maid, who looked to be no older than her, in a starched apron and white mob cap, peered out at her.

'I've come to see if there are any jobs going,' Violet told her imperiously and the girl thumbed towards a path that led up the side of the house.

'S'no good yer comin' to the front door then,' she answered, just as haughtily. 'Yer'd best go round the back an' ask fer Cook. Servants ain't allowed to use the front door.' And with that she closed the door firmly in Violet's face.

The girl flushed with anger. *Who does she think she is?* she fumed to herself as she set off in the direction the maid had indicated. After going through a high wooden gate she found herself in a large cobbled yard. Another maid was banging the dust from a carpet that was suspended across a line with a big metal carpet-beater as if her life depended on it, but she barely gave Violet a second glance. The girl headed for the open back door. Delicious smells of roasting meat and vegetables were wafting through it and her stomach rumbled; she had had nothing to eat that day.

As her frame blocked the light in the doorway a plump rosy-cheeked woman peered up from a big range where she was basting what appeared to be a whole leg of lamb covered in sprigs of mint. Violet's stomach rumbled again but she pasted a smile on her face before saying politely, 'I'm so sorry to trouble you but I was wondering if there were any jobs going?'

The woman rammed the roasting tin back into the oven and straightened before shaking her head.

"Fraid not, pet. Yer've just missed the boat. The missus set on a new parlourmaid only last week.'

The smile slid from Violet's face as she turned disconsolately away. The woman seemed to be very nice and she had an idea she would have liked working there.

'Thank you,' she muttered as she headed towards the gate, but then her spirits lifted. This was the first place she had tried, after all, and she was bound to have more luck further along the road.

By mid-afternoon she had tried every house on that side of the street and she was dispirited, tired and thirsty. Her feet were sore too as her Sunday-best boots were now at least two sizes too small for her and her heels were covered in angry red blisters. Her mother had been about to go to the pawn shop to try and get her a pair of better-fitting ones before she had taken ill. But I bet I'll have to wait a while now afore I get a new pair, Violet thought resentfully as she sank down for a rest in the shade of a large oak tree. They would be even shorter of money now that they didn't have the wage Eve Meadows had earned taking in washing and ironing. Yanking the offending boots off, Violet massaged the back

24

of her heels – but that only seemed to make things worse so she gingerly eased them back on again. For a while she sat enjoying the comings and goings of the carriages that rattled along the lane, many of them with well-dressed ladies inside reclining on the soft leather seats. No doubt many of them lived in the houses she had visited that morning and her heart swelled with envy that they should have so much while she had so little. *But I'll show them all,* she resolved, and with a new determination she hobbled off down the other side of the street. Someone, somewhere must need a maid surely?

When Maryann and her father entered the kitchen that evening after a long day in the mill they found it deserted and the fire almost dead.

'Violet must be out,' Maryann commented unnecessarily as she raked the fire and threw a few nuggets of coal onto it. Normally her mam would have been there with a steaming mug of tea and warm water all ready and waiting for them to wash in, and again they felt her loss as Maryann hung the kettle on the thick metal bracket and swung it above the flickering flames.

'Benny will be in soon,' she said. 'It's just as well I did some baking last night. There's fresh bread and I think we have some cheese and pickles left to go with it.' Secretly she was annoyed that Violet had cleared off and left them all to it, but then that was Violet. Maryann loved her sister but had long ago been forced to acknowledge that the girl was selfish through and through.

It was as she was slicing the bread that Violet appeared with a face as dark as a thundercloud. Throwing her basket down, she eased her boots off, complaining, 'These are far too tight for me now. When can I have some new ones?'

'When we have the spare money to get you some,' Maryann said more sharply than she had intended to. She had been walking about in wooden clogs for months but she hadn't complained. Then, hoping to lighten the atmosphere, she asked, 'Been looking for a position, have you?'

Violet sniffed and folded her arms across her chest. 'Yes, I have, as it happens. I tried every single house on either side of Swan Lane from one end to the other, but I've had no luck.'

'Never mind, it's early days yet,' Maryann soothed.

'Early days or not you'll start in the mill come Monday if you've found nothing,' her father said sternly.

Violet glared at him. Then, flouncing out of the chair, she headed for the stairs door saying, 'Oh, don't you worry, I'll find something 'cos I'm not going into the mill and that's an end to it.'

'Pay her no heed, she's just missing Mam,' Maryann said hastily as Violet disappeared up the stairs, then she hurried out to the well to draw water for their wash. It looked set to be a difficult evening.

It was as Maryann was clearing the table following their meal that Violet reappeared, saying, 'Is that all we've got for dinner? Bread and cheese? I've had nothing to eat all day!'

Benny was home from his shift down the pit by then and he stared at his sister in disgust. 'All the more reason for you to bring a few wages in to put in the pot an' all then, ain't it?'

Violet cut herself a thick slice of bread from the loaf. 'Oh, I'll be earning, don't you fret,' she responded cockily. 'But *I'm* going to get a live-in post so there'll be nothing of *my* money going in the pot.'

'All right, you two,' Maryann said. 'There's no need for squabbling. We should all be sticking together now more than ever.'

Benny had the grace to look ashamed but Violet merely tossed her head as she nibbled at the chunk of bread. Again

Benny was wondering if it was fair on them all for him to go and apply for the groom's job that weekend. But then even if he got it he had every intention of helping his family out, unlike Violet, who only ever seemed to think of herself. The girl quickly cleared the rest of the loaf and the remains of the cheese, then after helping herself to a mug of the now stewed tea she began to put her bonnet back on, saying, 'I'm going out for a walk. I need a breath of fresh air.'

Her father, who had barely said a word since arriving home, glanced up. 'I'd have thought you'd have had enough fresh air today.' Then, seeing her rude shrug, he held his tongue and let her go.

Once in Abbey Street, Violet turned in the direction of the Market Square and, just as she had hoped, she saw the carriage that had been parked there for the last few nights. Quickly smoothing her skirts and making sure that her bonnet was straight, she sauntered towards it, making a great show of peering into the shop windows as she went. She passed the barber's with its striped pole above the door, then Mr George Lashwood's, the tailor's, and moved on until she came to the doors of the gin palace, the Hare and Squirrel, owned by the local entrepreneur, Mr Ebenezer Brown. It was a popular drinking place for the miners and mill workers, and the person she had been hoping to see had been staying there on and off for the last few weeks.

The first time she had seen him, he had almost taken her breath away. It was one evening when she had been delivering the washing and ironing her mother took in back to her clients. He had been strolling along with a fancy-looking woman dressed in fine clothes at his side and Violet had envied her. He was so unlike the local men with their pale faces, and was tall, dark and handsome like the heroes in the romance novels she sometimes read in the free reading rooms. Ever since then she had made a point of taking a stroll past the Hare and Squirrel each evening, and when she was fortunate enough to spot him her heart would start to beat a wild tattoo. But tonight she had decided that she would do more than just watch him if she was fortunate enough to encounter him. She waited patiently and at last her patience was rewarded when he stepped through the doors of the gin palace and out into the square. He saw her almost instantly and the smile he flashed at her made her heart skip a beat.

'Hello, little lady.' He sauntered towards her, his fancy waistcoat shining all the colours of the rainbow in the failing sunlight. 'You're looking very smart tonight.'

Violet was suddenly pleased that she hadn't changed out of her Sunday best clothes as she simpered at him, her cheeks pink.

'I er . . . I've been out looking for work,' she told him. 'And if I don't find anything me dad says I've to start in the mill next week.'

On hearing this, he narrowed his eyes as he thoughtfully stroked his small, neatly clipped beard. 'Oh dear. Do I gather you're not overly keen on going into the mill then?'

She shook her head miserably and he suddenly held his arm out to her, making her heart go all a-flutter again.

'Let's go for a little stroll, shall we?' he suggested. 'I think I may just have the solution to your problems.'

Violet gulped, wondering what her dad would say if someone were to tell him that she had been seen walking arm-in-arm with a toff – a gentleman she didn't even know into the bargain! But then she thought about all the angry faces waiting for her back at home and swallowed her concerns. The man had only offered to take her for a stroll, after all. What harm could it do? When he gave her a winning smile, she tucked her arm into his and followed him like a lamb to slaughter.

Chapter Four

Maryann would have liked to visit the churchyard that evening to feel close to her mam and perhaps pick some wild flowers to place on the grave on the way, but there was too much to do at home. Because the cottage had been shut up all day it smelled foisty and damp, even though for once there were no wet clothes about. It was worse still in the winter when Eve had had no choice but to string the garments on lines from one corner of the ceiling to another, and only now did Maryann appreciate how hard her mam had worked. They regularly whitewashed the walls, but within weeks the tell-tale signs of damp would sneak up again and it was a never-ending battle to try and keep the place clean. Sometimes she wondered which was worse, the cold damp in the winter or the smells from the open door in the summer, but then they had always counted themselves lucky that they had a home and food on the table.

She was emptying the dirty water into the channel that

ran through the middle of the yard a few minutes later when her dad suddenly appeared at the back door. Her mouth gaped in surprise. He rarely ventured out of a night but she had no need to ask him where he was heading for he told her sharply, 'I'm off to the gin house. Happen a drop of ale will help me sleep the night.'

Maryann straightened with the tin bowl in her hands and stared at him incredulously. She had never known her father to drink before, ever – but seeing the look on her face he snapped, 'It's not a crime, is it?' And with that he strode off down the alley, leaving her staring after him.

'Don't get worritin', lass. Grief affects people differently. Happen a couple o' pints will 'elp to kill the pain.'

Maryann turned to see Granny Addison standing in her doorway. She supposed the woman was right, but they could ill-afford the pennies that the ale would cost, that was the trouble.

'As it 'appens I've got some eggs in 'ere that need usin' up,' the woman went on. 'Our Johnny dropped 'em off to me yesterday. He keeps hens on 'is allotments an' there's far too many eggs fer me an' 'is dad to get through. Yer'd be doin' me a favour if you could use 'em, an' there's a few broad beans and plums too.'

Maryann knew that the woman was being kind but she was in no position to refuse so she forced a smile and said, 'That would be lovely, Granny. Thank you very much.'

Her neighbour disappeared indoors and was back in minutes with the items in a tin bowl. In addition, she passed over a cracked jug full of flour.

'Yer could per'aps make some griddle cakes an' all,' she suggested. The girl swallowed to get rid of the lump that had formed in her throat. Whatever would she do without old Granny Addison, she wondered. Their friend really did have a heart of gold.

'Th-thank you,' she gulped, then overcome, she shot back into the kitchen.

The old woman shook her head sadly. She was a lovely girl, was Maryann, and it broke her heart to see her now have to become the woman of the house as well as hold down a job. Granny doubted there would be any help from young Violet. Now there was a little devil if ever there was one! Granny thought. There were times when she would have liked nothing better than to box her ears or tan her backside. Selfish as they came, was that one, whilst Maryann – well, she was like a little rough diamond. Granny Addison sometimes wondered how anyone from the courts could have turned out such a treasure, for in her eyes Maryann had it all. As well as being pretty, she was like a sponge when it came to learning, bright as a button, and kind and gentle too, and the woman had no doubt that if she had been togged out in the right clothes she could have been taken for gentry.

Her eyes then strayed to the alley down which John Meadows had just disappeared. Poor sod, to lose his wife and baby like that, after watching the two other little 'uns die. It was a bloody hard life, there was no doubt about it. No wonder he was feeling the need to drown his sorrows in a pint pot. Sighing, the old woman turned and went back into her own kitchen away from the stench of the privy and the pigsty.

In the quiet of her own home, Maryann placed the gifts on the wooden draining board then leaning heavily against it, she finally gave vent to her tears. Benny had disappeared immediately after their scant meal, her dad was at the gin palace and God alone knew where Violet had got to. She had never felt so alone. The terrible sense of loss at her mother's death was overwhelming. But feeling sorry for herself wasn't going to get the jobs done, so she wearily tied her apron on and set to work.

The candles were flickering and darkness was descending when Violet finally put in an appearance. Maryann was none too pleased with her.

'Where on earth have you been?' she asked sharply as Violet walked through the door looking like the cat that had got the cream. No one would have believed from her expression that she had lost her mother only days before.

'Out!' Violet answered shortly as she untied the ribbons on her bonnet and flung it onto the fireside chair.

'Well, thanks very much.' Maryann glared at her. 'A little help wouldn't have come amiss. I have been to work all day, you know!'

'And haven't I been out looking for work too?' Violet responded. 'My feet feel as if they're about to drop off.'

As Maryann strung the last of the washing she had done across the wooden clotheshorse her obvious frustration didn't seem to affect Violet at all. She appeared to be in her own little world.

'Is there anything to eat?' she asked as she dropped into her father's chair and kicked her boots off with a dreamy expression on her face.

'I've prepared a pan of porridge ready to warm up in the morning before we go to work. You could have some of that, as long as you leave enough for everyone else, or there's some cold plum tart in the pantry, help yourself,' Maryann said, before going upstairs feeling thoroughly hard done by. She could hear Benny's sobs from his bed in the downstairs parlour, her dad was out drinking for the first time she could recall and Violet was looking as if all her Christmases and birthdays had come at once. It felt as if the whole family was falling apart and there wasn't a single thing she could do about it.

Downstairs, Violet couldn't stop smiling as she recalled the time she had just spent with Jed Nelson, as he had introduced himself. He had explained that he owned businesses in London and had intimated that if she didn't find a position before the following week, she might consider coming to work for him. He had painted a very rosy picture of the gambling houses he owned and explained that she would live in the lap of luxury, only having to entertain the gentlemen for whom he catered for a few hours each night. He had described the beautiful gowns that his girls wore and her head was full of it. The girls were free to do as they pleased during the day, he had told her, and she wondered what it would be like to drive around London in a fine carriage. It sounded almost too good to be true, but she had to admit that she was sorely tempted. After all, what was there for her around here? She would probably end up marrying one of the local boys and then churn out a baby a year until she was old before her time. She shuddered at the thought before rising and going to help herself to something to eat. If she took Jed up on his offer she doubted that she would have to put up with such simple fare. All his houses had cooks, he'd said, and she would never have to lift a finger for herself again.

Violet glanced around the scantly furnished room, really seeing it for the first time. The two easy chairs on either side of the fireplace had come from the second-hand stall on the market, and heaven knew how old they must be. Violet certainly couldn't remember a time when they hadn't been there. Her dad had fixed crude wooden shelves along one wall which contained her mother's treasured pieces of china, only ever used on high days and holidays, but now as Violet studied them she saw that even they were mismatching. On the floor in front of the fireplace was a rag rug. It had taken Eve Meadows long months to make it from any old scraps of material that she could lay her hands on, but Jed had spoken of fine Turkish carpets and gilt-framed mirrors, a world away from the old cracked one that hung above the mantelshelf.

Deep down, Violet sensed how she would be expected to 'entertain' Jed's clients, should she choose to go with him, for although she had led a sheltered life she was not completely naïve and knew exactly what the women who stood in the Market Square late each night were at. She had heard Granny Addison speak about them. But surely even that would be a better way to earn a living than toiling in the mill? She sighed. It seemed that she would have a lot of thinking to do over the next few days.

The next morning when John Meadows arrived at work his head was aching fit to burst and his mouth felt like the bottom of a birdcage. But even so, after staggering home the night before he had slept like a baby so he supposed there was some compensation to alcohol.

'You're lookin' a bit rough this mornin', man,' a colleague shouted above the noisy whir of the machines, but then it was time to start work and they both scuttled away.

The day dragged slowly for Maryann. She was so tired that she felt she could have fallen asleep at her machine, but she was shaken out of her torpor when an accident occurred mid-afternoon. Little Tommy Briggs, one of the scavengers who crawled beneath the giant machines to collect the clean cotton before it hit the oily floors, suddenly let out an ear-splitting scream. Maryann instantly dropped to her knees to see him lying in a pool of blood. Without a thought for herself, she reached in, grabbed the waistband of his trousers and dragged him to safety just before the machine descended on him again. But the damage had been done. His right hand appeared to be hanging by a thread of skin and blood was pumping out of him at an alarming rate.

'I – I'm sorry,' he stuttered. 'I reckon I fell asleep an' toppled over.'

One by one the machines ground to a halt as Maryann snatched off her shawl and tried to stem the flow of blood.

'Get Mr Cooper to bring the cart round!' she screamed to anyone who would listen. 'This child needs to be taken to the cottage hospital or he's going to bleed to death.'

One of the women took to her heels and skidded across the slippery floor as Maryann rocked the little boy to and fro and crooned to him. But it soon became clear that the child was in shock. He was shaking violently and didn't seem to hear her. After what seemed a lifetime, the manager of the carding room raced across to her and lifted Tommy's convulsing form into his arms, telling them all, 'Get back to work, will yer! I'll deal with this now.'

'*Deal* with it?' Maryann screeched. 'The poor child should have finished work *ages* ago. Children below the age of twelve shouldn't work such long hours. He's been here since five this morning, the poor little lad. Just look at him! If he survives he'll be maimed for life. What job will he be able to do with only one hand?'

'I should worry about yer own job if I were you,' the burly manager snarled and stamped away, leaving Maryann to wring her hands in frustration.

'I'll go and speak to the gaffer personally the next time he comes in, you just don't see if I don't!' she muttered to no one in particular.

'I wouldn't waste me breath if yer know what's good fer yer, lass,' one of the older women responded. 'Since when 'as a gaffer worried about 'is workers? Little Tommy is just one o' many an' I've no doubt there'll be more maimed an' killed to line the gaffer's pockets.'

Maryann knew that she was right but all the same she was determined to put her point across – when Mr

Marshall the gaffer decided to put in an appearance, that was! The conditions the workers were forced to work in were appalling and it was time someone made a stand. The owner of the mill was known to be a very private man and he rarely visited the factory. But he would have to come sooner or later, and there and then she decided that she would be looking out for him. Maryann was fond of Tommy, and in the mood she was in, she was ready to do battle!

During their afternoon break, word reached the workers that little Tommy's life was hanging in the balance. He had lost a lot of blood and the surgeon had been forced to amputate his hand.

Seeing how upset she was about it, her father warned her, 'Now don't you get doin' anythin' silly, Maryann. We need our jobs and if you cause a fuss we could both be out on our backsides – an' then how would we pay the rent?'

They were sitting outside eating the bread and dripping she had packed for them that morning and although she knew that what John Meadows said was right, Maryann felt that she had seen too much of death lately.

It was much later that afternoon as Maryann was at work that the word went round that the master was in the mill. She instantly slowed her machine, risking a telling-off from the manager, and after straightening her skirt and tucking her hair behind her ears she stalked off in the direction of Mr Marshall's office. She was going to have her say about the conditions the children were forced to work in, even if it meant risking her own job.

Her father looked up as she passed him and guessing where she was going, he caught her arm, saying, 'Now please don't get doing anything you might regret, lass.'

Shaking her arm free she answered, 'Sorry, Dad, but I can't just stand by and do nothing.' And then she walked on through the whirring clatter of the machines. Mr Marshall's office was situated to one side of the mill and she could see him and the manager, Seth Brown, with their heads bent together over a large ledger, through the glass in the top of the door.

She marched up to it and rapped loudly, and both men looked surprised when they glanced up to see one of their workers standing outside. Seth always warned them that no one was to disturb him and the gaffer when Mr Marshall called in, so he was none too pleased as he threw the door open to enquire, 'What do you want? Can't yer see me an' the boss are busy?'

'Then I'm sorry to disturb you, but I'm afraid I need a word with Mr Marshall,' she answered boldly, and before he could stop her she had pushed past him and was staring at Mr Marshall across his desk.

'I'm so sorry, sir,' Seth stuttered, outraged, but Mr Marshall held his hand up.

'It's all right, Seth.' Then turning his attention back to Maryann, he asked politely, 'May I help you, miss?' It was clear that the girl was an employee from the state of her. She was covered from head to toe in loose cotton fibres that clung to her hair and shabby clothes, and yet there was a quiet air of dignity about the way she held herself and even in her untidy state she was quite beautiful.

'Well, it's not so much about helping me but about helping one of your young workers who was badly injured here this afternoon.'

Quite well-spoken too for a mill worker, he noted.

'Oh yes, and who would that be then?' He was quietly amused at the young woman's stance, for she looked as if she had come to do battle. Her hands were on her hips and her fine eyes were blazing.

'It was young Tommy Briggs, sir. He fell asleep beneath one of the machines and as a result of that he has had to have his hand amputated. The poor mite will never be able to lead a normal life again – that's if he survives – and I happen to know that his family are struggling financially already. He'd been in the factory working for over twelve hours, and he's only a little lad.'

The look of mild amusement instantly disappeared as Wesley Marshall stared at the manager. 'Is this true, Seth?' he demanded. 'And if it is, why wasn't I informed of the accident?'

'Well . . .' Seth squirmed. 'Aye, it is true – but if I were to tell you of every little accident that occurred I'd never be off your doorstep, sir.'

'Little accident?' Mr Marshall looked positively angry now. 'I would hardly call a child worker of mine losing his hand a *little accident*! And haven't I told you that I want no child under nine working more than nine hours a day?'

Seth glared at Maryann before shuffling from foot to foot, and now Mr Marshall addressed her again, asking, 'Do you happen to know where this child lives?'

'Yes, sir. He lives in the second court along Abbey Street.'

'Then I shall go and see his family as soon as I leave the mill,' Mr Marshall promised. 'And you may rest assured that I shall see to it that he is properly compensated.'

'And what about all the other children who work here and who are still doing far more hours than they should?' Maryann dared to ask.

'Why, I should sack you fer talking to the boss like that!' Seth growled but he was silenced by a glare from Mr Marshall.

'No one is going to be sacked for telling the truth,' Mr Marshall thundered, then looking at Maryann again he forced a tight smile as he asked, 'May I ask what your name is, miss?'

'Maryann Meadows, sir.'

It must have taken some guts to come in here and speak up for young Tommy Briggs, and the man admired her for it.

'Please leave the matter with me,' he said now. 'I can promise that there will be some changes made around here, starting immediately.' He looked sternly at Seth, who was quaking in his shoes. 'For a start, I want the names and ages of every child we have working here. But now, good day to you, Miss Meadows – and thank you for bringing this to my attention.'

Maryann nodded, all too aware that if looks could kill, the one Seth was casting at her right this moment would have felled her where she stood. But she merely stared coldly back at him then inclined her head to the master and turning about, she walked sedately from the office, hoping that justice would now be done.

'Good God, Maryann,' her father scolded her that evening. 'What made you do such a foolish, headstrong thing? You could have lost us both our jobs.'

'But we didn't lose our jobs, did we?' she said, ladling some rice pudding into his dish. 'What's more, Mr Marshall has promised to look at the hours the children work, so perhaps some good may come from poor little Tommy losing his hand.'

John Meadows stared at this beautiful daughter of his. She was so like her mother, in both looks and morals, that sometimes he could almost imagine his Eve was still with them. But of course she wasn't, and the knowledge made him push his dish away and hurry upstairs to get changed. He'd go and have a few pints of ale. It was the only thing at present that made him feel better.

Chapter Five

On their way home from work later that week, Maryann peeped at her father from the corner of her eye. He had the sickly pallor of all the mill workers but today he looked even worse than usual. She wasn't surprised really when she remembered the condition he had been in when he'd arrived home the night before. He had been so drunk that she had had to help him up the stairs to bed, and it had taken her all her time to rouse him this morning. But at least she hadn't had to lie listening to him sobbing into his pillow, so she could forgive him his temporary lapses. As long as it didn't become a regular occurrence, that was! They could ill-afford the pennies he had spent on ale, but then he had always been such a kind and gentle man that it was hard to stay angry at him for long.

When they entered the kitchen, Maryann looked about in surprise. Violet had the stew simmering away on the range and she had even tidied up.

'Ah, just in time,' the girl greeted them pleasantly. 'I've

just got to slice us some bread and the meal will be ready to serve. Do you want to wash first? Benny's already been in and had his, and he's upstairs getting changed now.'

'Yes, I think I will – thank you,' Maryann said, giving her sister a smile. Violet was often wilful and selfish but sometimes she could be kind, which made Maryann continue to love her. Once she was washed and changed and the family were sitting down for their meal she dared to ask cautiously, 'Did you have any luck with your job hunting today?' She had half-expected to get her head bitten off but Violet merely smiled as she ladled stew into the thick pot dishes.

'No, but I'm still not panicking yet. I'm sure something will turn up.'

Maryann and Benny exchanged a glance, but not wishing to spoil Violet's serene mood they continued the meal in silence.

It was as Maryann and Violet were carrying the dirty dishes to the sink a while later that Granny Addison burst in, saying, 'I hear that little Tommy Briggs is still in a bad way. Did yer see the accident?'

Maryann chewed her lip. 'Yes, I did – and it was awful. I've already spoken to Mr Marshall about it.'

'I don't reckon as that'll do much good,' Granny scoffed. 'I've heard tell Mr Marshall is a good man but he's rarely at the factory an' don't get to see 'alf o' what goes on there. 'E's 'appy to leave it all in the 'ands o' the manager fer the majority o' the time. 'E's a bit of a recluse by all accounts an' tends to keep 'imself very much to 'imself since 'e lost 'is wife about five years ago. I 'eard tell they 'ad a daughter but I ain't never spoken to anyone who's clapped eyes on 'er. She must be about six or seven years old now.'

'Well, he promised that he'd go and see Tommy's family, at any rate. He probably already has for all we know, so we'll just have to wait and see if he's as good as his word,' Maryann declared. She then began to bustle about collecting the dirty clothes before putting them in pails of water to soak. It looked like her day off this week would be taken up with washing!

It was almost eight o'clock that evening when Maryann's father appeared from the stairs doorway dressed in his Sunday best. Maryann's heart sank but she kept her voice light as she asked him, 'Off somewhere nice, are you, Dad?' She hoped he wasn't going to the gin house again. Her hair was sticking to the back of her neck, for she had scarcely sat down since the minute she got in from work and now she was so tired, all she wanted to do was to drop into bed.

Shamefaced, he lowered his head, and after crossing to the tin on the mantelpiece he extracted a few pennies from it before replying, 'Aye, I thought I might go and have a couple of tankards of ale to help me sleep, lass.' Seeing the way her face fell he added hurriedly, 'It won't be a regular thing, I promise you. It's just to get me over these first few days without your . . .'

Instantly Maryann's distress vanished, to be replaced by sympathy. She knew how much he must be missing her mother. 'Well, just don't get into the state you were in last night, eh?' was all she said. 'I had a rare old job to wake you this morning.'

Sheepishly he made for the door, and once he had disappeared through it she sighed as she placed a clean cloth across the bowl of dough she had been kneading and left it to rise.

Violet had long since gone out with a sparkle in her eye, all dressed in her best again, which Maryann found offensive, seeing as they had so recently lost their mother, and Benny had gone for a walk across Weddington Meadows as he did on many a night. He loved the outdoors, which was why it hurt Maryann to think of him trapped down in the bowels of the earth each day. But still, she consoled herself, come Sunday he would be going for his interview at the stables and if he got the job she knew he would be much happier. Deciding to take advantage of the peace and quiet for a few moments, she lowered herself into the fireside chair that had been her mother's and before she knew it, she had fallen sound asleep.

A noise woke her just as darkness was casting shadows across the courtyard. Jumping awake, she stared towards the door where a figure was blocking out the last of the light.

'Is that you, Toby?' she asked nervously. She lit a long paper spill from the fire and carried it to the table to light the candle there. And then as it began to sputter and flicker she exclaimed, 'Oh, it's you, Hugo! You gave me a rare old turn.'

Hugo was Toby's younger brother but they were as different as chalk from cheese and Maryann had never been fond of him. He was too full of himself by half although Toby adored him and was fiercely loyal towards him – not that Hugo appreciated it. He was jealous of Toby, Maryann knew, and always felt hard done by, insisting that Toby was their mother's favourite. He was even jealous of the fact that Maryann preferred his brother to him.

Grinning, he leaned against the doorpost and said cheekily, 'I thought yer might fancy a bit o' company, seein' as yer in all on yer own.'

There was something about this young man that always made Maryann feel nervous. However, her voice was level as she answered coolly, 'Who said I was in alone?'

He chuckled. 'I just saw yer dad in the gin 'ouse as I passed, an' Violet is walkin' the town wi' a bloke who was done up like a dog's dinner.'

43

'What do you mean?' Maryann scowled.

'Just what I said. Looked like a toff to me but your Violet weren't complainin'. She were clingin' onto his arm an' flutterin' 'er eyelashes at 'im fer dear life.'

Anger made colour flood into Maryann's cheeks as she said primly, 'Well, I dare say there will be a reason. Our Violet is a good girl.'

'That's why you're left 'ere doin' all the work then, is it?' Then, his face softening, he went on, 'It needn't be like this, yer know, Maryann.'

She inched herself around the table and placed it between them as he approached her.

'Thing is, I could take yer away from all this.' He spread his hands to encompass the small room. 'I know I'm a bit younger than you, but I earn a good livin' one way or another, certainly enough to get us a place out o' town, and yer wouldn't 'ave to go out to work neither. Yer dad an' the others 'ud get by wi'out yer, so whadda yer say? Shall we get married?'

Maryann's mouth gaped in amazement for a moment but then quickly clamping it shut again she told him firmly, 'I appreciate the offer, Hugo, but I don't love you.'

His face turned ugly then and leaning his knuckles on the table he ground out, 'No, an' that's 'cos you've got your sights fixed on our Toby, ain't it? Well, I'll tell yer now, if 'e were 'alf a man 'e'd take you out o' this, especially now yer mam's gone. Yer lookin' a gift 'orse in the mouth if yer turn me down fer 'im. 'E'll never make nothin' of 'isself, whereas I intend to go places an' you could come wi' me if you'd a mind to.'

'But I *don't* have a mind to, although I appreciate your offer,' Maryann told him frankly. 'And Toby and I have had an unspoken arrangement for some time. We care about each other and when the time is right we'll come together.'

'Then you'll wait a bloody long time,' he said sarcastically. 'Thinks 'e's too good to be true, that one does, an' 'e wants to do everythin' by the book!'

'That seems very sensible to me, and now, if you don't mind, Hugo, I have work to do.'

He seemed to swell in size as he straightened and glared at her. Hugo was used to getting his own way and her rejection of him was going sorely against the grain.

'So be it,' he said eventually. 'But you'll live to regret this day. You just see if yer don't, lady.' And with that he turned and, hiding his humiliation, he stormed away.

Maryann let out a huge sigh of relief. She hadn't meant to hurt him, but how else could she have rejected him? she asked herself.

Violet came in just as Maryann was preparing a pan of porridge for their breakfast. Her face was alight as she told her sister airily, 'I'm off to bed now then. G'night, Maryann.'

'You just wait up, young lady,' Maryann told her sternly. 'What's all this I hear about you walking around the market-place on the arm of a gentleman?'

Violet eyed her sister, unafraid. She should have remembered that gossip spread quickly around the courts. 'What's it to do with you if I was?' she said rudely. 'We're not all goody goodies happy to stay at home being the long-suffering domestic slave! I want more from life than this dump. I'm not going to get married to some pasty-faced mill worker who'll die before he's forty and turn out a baby a year till I'm old before my time. Jed, my friend, is a proper gentleman and he treats me like a lady. Look at these lovely ribbons he's bought for me! And what's wrong with that?'

'Oh, Violet,' Maryann said despairingly as the girl held out her gift to show her. 'You should be more careful who you mix with. This Jed could be anybody.'

At that, Violet's chin came up. 'Well, he *isn't* just anybody,' she argued. 'He's a well-off businessman from London. And now if you've quite finished, I shall get to bed. I have better things to do than stand here and listen to someone who has not a single ounce of ambition in their whole body.' And with that she turned and left the room, and all Maryann could do was watch her go with a sick feeling in the pit of her stomach. If only her mother were here!

By Sunday morning, Benny was experiencing a mix of terror and excitement as the time for his interview as a stable boy drew closer. On Maryann's advice he had said nothing to his father, although he would have dearly loved to. John Meadows continued to drink each night, staggering in from the gin-house at all hours much the worse for wear. Violet too was on edge, so needless to say the atmosphere in the cottage was fraught with tension. Even Maryann was snappy. Having to work all day in the mill then come home each evening to cooking and cleaning was taking its toll on her, although she did try her best to stay positive. After all, she told herself, things were bound to get easier when they established some sort of a routine. They had to, the way she saw it, for she didn't think she could keep it up for much longer.

Toby had taken to calling in each evening to see if there was anything he could do to lighten her load, and one evening he told her that Hugo had been in a terrible mood for days, although he had no idea why. Maryann kept his brother's visit and proposal to herself, having no wish to cause conflict between the two of them, but she dreaded bumping into Hugo now, since he would eye her malevolently and scare her. She had even taken to keeping the kitchen door locked of an evening. Rather suffer the stifling heat, the way she saw it, than risk him barging in.

Today, however, she was determined to keep the mood light for Benny's sake, and so as she cleared the dirty breakfast dishes into the sink ready for scouring, she asked Violet and her father, 'What are you two planning to do this morning?'

'I thought I'd spend some time in the vegetable plot and then take some flowers along to the churchyard,' John answered glumly. He was like a changed man since the death of his wife, and from what Maryann could see of it the change was definitely not for the better. Many of the men from the courts rented small plots of land in Abbey Green where they grew vegetables and salad stuff, but John seemed to have lost heart in his plot, which she supposed was understandable. But then she hoped the fresh air would do him good.

'That sounds nice,' she said encouragingly. 'If you could bring some broccoli and carrots back, I could cook them to go with the lamb shank I got from the butcher's yesterday for dinner, and if the birds have left any blackcurrants on the bush I could make you a pie for afters.' Fruit pies had always been one of his favourites although at present he was barely eating enough to keep a sparrow alive. He seemed to be existing on alcohol.

'I'm going to have one last try at getting a place,' Violet responded. The evening before, her father had reminded her in no uncertain terms that if she did not have a position by tomorrow morning, she was to start at the mill and the girl had been in a sulk ever since.

Her sister watched as Violet tied the ribbons on her bonnet and left without a word, and once her father had gone too and she and Benny were alone, she told him, 'This is it then. Go on and get yourself ready. It won't create a very good impression if you're late for your interview, will it?'

'I don't think I can do it,' Benny gulped nervously. 'What'll I say? I don't really know that much about horses, although I love the creatures.'

'That's a good place to start,' Maryann said. 'The right person for the job will be given the proper training, and if you just be yourself and show how much you love being around the horses, you're sure to win him over.'

Benny looked unconvinced, but went off to get changed all the same and within no time at all Maryann was alone again as she set about the household chores.

Her brother returned over two hours later, beaming from ear to ear.

'I *got* it,' he told her as he punched the air triumphantly.

She hurried across to hug him asking, 'And when do you start?'

'A week on Monday, after I've worked out my notice at the pit.' His face became serious again as he asked, 'But will you really be all right here without me?'

'I shall be fine, stop worrying.' Delighted at his good luck, she ruffled his hair as she had done when he was a little boy. She knew how much getting this job had meant to him and she was proud that he had got it. He then went on to tell her about what the job would entail and his living quarters, before she asked curiously, 'Did you get to meet Wesley Marshall?' It was strange to think that Benny would be working for the owner of the mill that she worked in.

He shook his head. 'No, I didn't, and Mr Carter says the family tend to keep very much to themselves.'

'Hmm,' she muttered, thinking of little Tommy Briggs. It was all around the town that the poor child had had to have his hand amputated following the accident at the mill, but it was also said that Mr Marshall had been true to his word. He had visited the family and not only paid for all of Tommy's medical bills but had also given the child a hefty compensation payment for his accident, so she was grateful for that at least.

Not wishing to spoil the mood, she told Benny, 'When Dad gets back you can tell him the good news – and don't look so worried. I'm sure he'll be as thrilled for you as I am.'

'I hope you're right,' Benny answered. 'And let's hope that Violet has some luck finding a job today as well. God knows how she'll cope with the conditions in the mill if she doesn't.'

Violet didn't have any luck as her long face told them the minute she set foot through the door. By then John had returned and been informed about Benny's new position and just as Maryann had prophesied, he was thrilled for his son.

'You'll do well, lad,' he beamed as he slapped the youth on the shoulder. 'I couldn't be more pleased for you. Let's just hope that this family's luck is turning. It's about time something nice happened after . . .' His voice trailed away and again they all looked towards Eve's empty chair. She had left a hole in their hearts that could never be filled, but they all knew that somehow they must go on without her, for what was the alternative?

'What's going on then?' Violet asked peevishly as she threw her bonnet onto the table that was neatly laid for dinner.

'Benny has been taken on at Windy Manor to work in the stables,' Maryann informed her. 'He'll be able to leave the pit now.'

Violet snorted. 'It's all right for some, isn't it?' she said spitefully.

'I take it that means you've had no luck with finding a position as a lady's maid then?'

'Huh! I haven't even been offered a place as a laundry

maid,' Violet griped. 'So whilst Benny goes off to play with the horses, I'll be forced to slave in the mill!'

'Only till you find something you'd rather do,' her father placated her but she was in no mood to listen and stropped away up the stairs as Maryann carried on with preparing the dinner.

Upstairs, Violet stood staring from the window as tears streamed down her cheeks. The thought of being forced to work long hours in the mill was just more than she could bear. The image of Jed's handsome face flashed in front of her eyes. The picture of the life she could lead should she choose to go with him was irresistible. He had told her of boat rides along the River Thames dressed in satins and silks and shielded by a fine parasol. Of sightseeing trips about London, visiting the Tower of London and other marvels she had only ever glimpsed in books. Of being pampered and adored by the gentlemen she would entertain . . . and suddenly she knew what she must do. Jed had promised that he would wait for her outside the inn in the marketplace until midnight, and if she chose to go to London with him she could work in one of his establishments and be treated like a queen.

The slight guilt that Violet felt at running away from her family was far outweighed by her fear of working in the mill, so going into her parents' room, she took a small carpet bag from under their double bed. It was made of tapestry but was so old that it had faded and split. It was also thick with dust, and she couldn't even recall when it had last seen daylight or even why her mother had bothered to keep it, if it came to that. But having no alternative, Violet quickly packed her few possessions inside before pushing it well under the bed she shared with Maryann in the second bedroom. Her mind was made up now.

That night, she lay tucked in against Maryann and

waited until her sister was sound asleep. Then, inching to the edge of the mattress, still fully clothed, she fumbled in the darkness for her bag, praying that Maryann would not stir. Finally she lifted her ugly, down-at-heel shoes from the end of the bed and on tiptoe she stole from the room. Downstairs, she found her father fast asleep in the fireside chair and crept past him to place the short letter she had written on the kitchen table. With luck it would not be noticed until morning – and by then she would be long gone. She frowned as the back door creaked when she opened it. Holding her breath, she paused – but her father didn't stir – and soon she was out in the cool evening air. Lifting her skirts, she slunk down the narrow entrance to the court. Only when she was out in Abbey Street did she stop to put her shoes on and then she began to run as if the hounds of hell were chasing her. She wouldn't be able to bear it if Jed left without her now, and she raced away from her home without giving it so much as a backward glance.

Chapter Six

John Meadows was already up and about when Maryann came down the stairs the next morning. He had made up the fire and pushed the pan of porridge into the heart of it to warm up.

'I'm sorry about last night again, love,' he humbly apologised. 'I know I've got to stop this silly drinking. And I've got to start sleeping in my own bed an' all.'

She squeezed his arm sympathetically. She could never stay annoyed with him for long. Then, glancing around the room, she asked, 'Has Benny already left for his shift? And where is Violet? She wasn't in bed when I woke up so I assumed she was already down here getting ready for her first day at the mill. I was quite impressed, to be honest. Knowing how much she's dreading it I thought I'd have to drag her out of bed. Is she out in the privy?'

'Probably. But I haven't seen her yet and I've been up and about for a good half an hour. I did see Benny leave though.'

As the first stirrings of unease started in Maryann's

stomach she stepped out into the yard and headed towards the privy, but as she neared it, it became apparent that it was empty.

Toby was just about to leave for his shift. Seeing Maryann's worried expression as he came out of his mother's cottage, he asked, 'Is everything all right?'

'Yes – no – oh, I don't know,' she blustered. 'It's just that we don't know where Violet is. She wasn't in bed when I woke up and Dad hasn't seen her either.'

'Well, she can't have vanished,' he told her soothingly. 'Come on, let's go back inside.'

They had barely stepped through the door when Maryann's eyes were drawn to the table and the sheet of paper propped up against the sugar bowl. Swooping on it she began to read, and as she scanned the page the colour drained out of her cheeks and she had to grip the back of the chair.

'What is it? What's wrong?' John asked, and after taking in a great lungful of air she began to read it aloud.

Dear Family,

By the time you read this I shall be far away, so please don't try to find me cos I shall be fine. I can't bear the thought of working in the mill so I've gone to London with Mr Nelson who's offered me a job there in one of his establyshments where I shall be treated like a lady. Don't worry about me. I can look after meself and once I'm settled I shall come back to see you all,

Till then,

Love,

Violet x

Of all of them, Violet had always been the worst at her lessons, but even ignoring the spelling errors in the short letter, she had made her intentions crystal clear and for now all they could do was gape at each other in amazement. The same thoughts were in all their minds. Who was this Mr Nelson? And what sort of establishment had he taken Violet to? And then John erupted with fear and fury as he banged the table, setting the crockery jiggling.

'The silly young fool!' he shouted. 'This fellow could be anyone! We have to find her straight away.'

Taking his arm, Toby pressed him into a chair saying, 'I'm afraid that might prove to be easier said than done, Mr Meadows. London is an enormous place and it would be like trying to look for a needle in a haystack.'

'But – but she's so young,' John spluttered. 'Who *is* this Mr Nelson she speaks of?'

'I think Hugo saw her walking with him one evening in the marketplace,' Maryann told them. 'He said he was dressed like a toff and our Violet was hanging onto his every word.'

'I'll *every word* him!' John ranted angrily. 'You can't just whip young lasses away from their homes without speaking to their families first!'

'But he hasn't just whipped her away, has he?' Toby pointed out sensibly. 'According to that letter, Violet has gone more than willingly, so from where I'm standing I reckon you're just going to have to wait until she decides to come home.'

John's shoulders sagged as he saw the wisdom of Toby's words. The young man had a good head on his shoulders and he supposed at the end of the day he was right. But oh, it hurt – so it did! His precious family was getting smaller by the day. First to lose his darlings Joe and Gertie, then his beloved Eve and their stillborn baby son. Benny would soon be off to live above the stables at the gaffer's house, and now Violet was gone too. There would only be himself and Maryann left, and when she and Toby finally came together as he had no doubt they eventually would, he would be quite alone. It was a terrifying thought.

'Look, I'm really sorry,' Toby said as he glanced at the cheap tin clock on the mantelshelf that had replaced the one they had pawned to pay for Eve's funeral, 'but if I don't get off now I'll be late for me shift an' I'm savin' hard so I can't afford to miss a day's work.'

He looked towards Maryann as he said it and she lowered her head shyly at the meaning behind the statement. When he had enough saved he would ask her father for permission to court her, she was sure of it – but how could she leave home now, with Benny and Violet going too? Then, deciding that now was not the time for such thoughts, she said, 'You're quite right. Dad and I must make haste too or we'll be late as well.'

Taking up their snap boxes they all left the house together. At the end of the entry, father and daughter parted from Toby and walked towards the mill in silence.

At a small coaching inn in Buckinghamshire, Violet was stretching luxuriously on a deep feather mattress. Jed had warned her that they could only afford to snatch a few hours' sleep if they were to board the next coach to London, but she didn't mind. Although modest compared to some inns, Violet had never known such luxury in her whole life and she was revelling in it. She had had a whole bed all to herself, and the night before on arrival they had eaten the most delicious meal she had ever tasted. It had started with tomato soup so thick that it stuck to the spoon, followed by roast beef and a selection of vegetables. To finish, they had been served with some concoction that consisted mainly of strawberries covered in meringue and topped with a thick whipped cream. Violet had been too embarrassed to ask what it was, but she had forced down every last spoonful and knew that she would never forget the taste of it for as long as she lived.

Now as she looked towards the chair where she had thrown her clothes, she wished that she had something finer to wear. But Jed had promised her that as soon as they got to London he would make sure that she was garbed from head to toe in the finest clothes that money could buy. She had no reason to doubt him, and as she scrambled out of bed and thought of him waiting for her in the dining room of the inn, her face was wreathed with smiles.

He was staring from the windows with his hands clasped behind his back when she entered the room, and he bowed to her, making her feel like a real lady.

'Did you sleep well?' he enquired as he led her towards the table and she nodded, conscious of the other guests' curious eyes on her. Even the maids who were waiting on the tables were better attired than her, but then again, it wouldn't be for much longer. Huge dishes full of all manner of delicious treats were placed in front of them, and despite the fact that she had told herself the night before that she would not be able to eat another single thing for at least a week, she tucked in. There were sausages and plump kidneys, slices of crisply fried black pudding and thick rashers of crispy bacon to name but a few and she tried a little of everything, washing it down with fragrant-smelling coffee with a layer of cream swimming on top of it.

At one stage, after she had taken a drink of it, Jed had laughed and, leaning across to wipe her upper lip with his napkin, he had teased, 'You have a frothy white moustache.'

Butterflies fluttered in her stomach at his touch, and she knew in that moment that she would walk through fire for the man if need be. She was more than a little in love for the very first time in her young life and her imagination began to run riot, although in fairness, Jed had never given her any indication that her feelings might be returned. Admittedly he was taking her to London to be his employee, but she was determined now that before they reached their destination she would make him fall in love with her and they would live happily ever after. She imagined a grand, big house with servants waiting on her. She would have her own carriage and so many fine gowns that she wouldn't know which one to wear each morning.

'Violet, my dear. Did you hear me? I asked have you had enough?'

His voice pulled her thoughts sharply back to the present and she rose from her seat and followed him trustingly out to the carriage.

It was nearing darkness the next day when the carriage bearing Violet to her new life drew up outside a tall Victorian terraced house in Greenwich. She had fallen asleep on the last leg of their journey but as soon as Jed gently shook her arm she sprang awake and knuckled the sleep from her eyes before peering from the window. If truth be told, although it looked enormous, the house was not as she had imagined it; in fact, it was somewhat of a disappointment. It was three storeys high and the red front door looked as if it was sadly in need of a lick of paint. Rusting iron railings ran along the front of it, with steps leading down to what she supposed must be the kitchen area. Three steps led up to two tall pillars with the front door set back behind them, but the curtains on the windows appeared to be all tightly drawn so there was little more to see.

Clutching her shabby carpet bag, Violet followed Jed down onto the pavement then waited patiently while he paid the coachman. He then took her elbow and guided her up the steps before lifting the heavy brass door knocker that was in the shape of a lion, and rapped loudly.

Chapter Seven

Footsteps sounded from within and the door was opened by a young girl in a frilly white apron.

'Evenin', sir.' She bobbed her knee and held the door wide without even glancing in Violet's direction, but the latter barely noticed. She was gazing in awe at the large entrance hall. It appeared to be almost as large as the cottage she had left behind her, and was very luxuriously furnished, which was a shock after the rather dull exterior. The walls were covered in a heavy red damask paper and on the floor was a rich red Turkish carpet. An enormous gilt-framed mirror hung on one wall, whilst a tall wooden coatstand with a number of coats hanging on it stood to the side of the door. Her eyes were then drawn to a number of gold-framed pictures, and colour flooded into her cheeks as she noticed that they were all of beautiful women in various stages of undress. For the first time she felt uncomfortable. Before falling asleep in the carriage she had found her first glimpses of London somewhat disappointing. Far from being paved with gold, the streets to her had looked grimy and dismal, teeming with people, and suddenly she felt a very long way away from home.

'Madame is in her room, sir,' the little maid told Jed as she took his hat and topcoat, and with a nod he clasped Violet's elbow again and propelled her past a number of doors. She could hear laughter coming from behind some of them and decided there was some sort of party going on. Her feet sank into the soft pile of the rugs and she suddenly wondered who 'Madame' was. Was she to be her new employer? Jed paused then and, opening one of the doors, he led her into a room where a woman was reclining in a deep chair.

'Jed, *darling*!' the woman gushed when she saw him, and she rose from her seat and came towards them. Violet's eyes almost popped out of her head. The woman was very plump, and her scarlet satin dress was so low-cut Violet was sure that her ample breasts were going to escape from it at any second. Her hair was curled into ringlets and was so black that the girl wondered if it was dyed, and her face was heavily made up with rouge. The woman embraced him then stepping back, she eyed Violet critically, saying, 'So this is the new recruit, eh?'

Violet shuffled from foot to foot under the woman's close scrutiny.

'Hmm, she ain't the prettiest I've seen,' she remarked as she walked around Violet as if she was viewing a beast she was thinking of purchasing at the cattle market. 'But then I dare say she'll do when we've got her into some decent togs an' done sumfink wiv her hair. An' she's the right age at least. The punters like 'em young.' Then leaning towards Violet she asked, 'How old are you, dearie?'

'I'm fi-fifteen, nearly sixteen,' Violet gulped. Her mouth had gone dry and she was wishing with all her heart that she had stayed at home.

'Good, good. I'm Ruby, by the way.' The woman held her hand out in a friendly enough fashion and Violet shook it, her own hand trembling.

'You needn't be afraid o' me, so long as you do as you're told.' The woman had picked up on Violet's nervousness and smiled, revealing a row of surprisingly straight, white teeth. Close up, Violet saw that she must be quite old: forty something at least if the lines on her face were anything to go by. The powder she had applied thickly was caked in them.

Violet looked at Jed enquiringly. Would she be working for him, or for Ruby?

As if he had picked up on her thoughts he told her then, 'Ruby manages this establishment for me, and whilst I am not here she will teach you what is required of you.'

'Oh!'

The sound came out as a little gasp but Ruby's attention was back on Jed now as, tucking her plump arm into his, she led him to the chair opposite hers, saying, 'I'll get Daisy to take the girl up to her room, and then you and me can have a little catch-up, sweetheart. I'm having a fair bit of bovver with the last one you brought me, I don't mind telling you. But forget about that for now. Did you manage to have a meeting with that young woman in Nuneaton?'

'I certainly did.' He gave a wide grin. 'And it went very well indeed. I think there may be quite a lot of money about to come our way.'

A feeling of disappointment spliced through Violet as Jed appeared so willing to go off with this Ruby. He seemed to have forgotten that she was even there – and yet the other woman was almost old enough to be his mother. Ruby's hands, she saw, were laden with rings containing stones of all different colours that caught and reflected the light from the heavy brass oil lamps that were dotted on small tables about the room. Violet watched as Ruby yanked on the bell-pull hanging at the side of the fireplace. Almost instantly, there was a tap at the door and another young woman entered.

This one was clearly no maid and was dressed almost as flamboyantly as Ruby in a blue crinoline gown with an embarrassingly deep plunging neckline. Her hair was a rich golden blonde and loose about her shoulders, and Violet was sure she had never seen anyone quite so beautiful.

'Come with me,' the girl told her with a smile, and with one last desperate glance towards Jed, Violet did as she was told. It appeared that he was too taken up with talking to Ruby to even notice that she was leaving.

As they stepped into the hallway Violet saw a well-dressed gentleman arrive and hand his silk top hat and cloak to the same little maid who had let her in. She then led him off down the long corridor as Violet followed Daisy up a sweeping curved staircase.

'You'll be sleeping on the second floor for now,' Daisy explained. 'But when you're ready to start work you'll be given a room on the first floor.'

Violet was so tired by now that she was sure she could have slept for a week; she was hungry too. They reached a long landing, at the end of which they climbed another, steeper set of stairs. These were bare wood and there were no pictures or mirrors on the walls, but Violet noted that it was still very clean.

There were a number of doors leading from the second-floor landing which was lit by two gas lamps placed on small tables along the way. Eventually Daisy stopped and pushed one of the doors open, and Violet stepped past her into a room that was easily twice as big as the one she had shared with Maryann back at home. It was quite sparsely furnished and as she squinted in the gloom Daisy hurried past her and lit a candle that was placed on a washstand to one side of an iron bed. The candle sputtered into life, throwing shadows across the bare walls as Violet looked about. The bedspread was faded but clean, as were the curtains that were drawn across the window, and she found that she was standing on bare floorboards which had been scrubbed until they were almost white. Other than the bed and the washstand the only furniture in the room was a straight-backed wooden chair, a small table and an old chest of drawers.

Daisy turned to her then and said, 'You'll find a chamber pot under the bed in case you need to – you know? And I'll get the maid to bring you something to eat shortly.'

Violet placed her small carpet bag on the bed. 'But can't I come down to eat?' she asked meekly as a little ripple of apprehension shuddered through her. And then before the older girl could answer, Violet's head snapped around. It sounded very much as if someone was crying in the next room.

'Oh, don't worry about that,' Daisy told her on seeing her anxious expression. 'That's just one of the other new girls who is having a bit of trouble settling in.'

'But why? And what job am I going to be doing exactly?' Violet challenged, although she had a very good idea.

'Jed will be up to see you all in good time to explain all that,' Daisy promised and then without another word she closed the door firmly between them – and to Violet's horror she heard a key being turned in the lock.

She ran across the room so quickly that she almost tripped over her skirts, but just as she had feared, when she reached the door she found it securely locked.

'*Let me out!*' she screamed as she began to pound on it with her fists. Anger had washed away her fear now and she was furious. How *dare* they treat her like this? It wasn't as if she hadn't come here by choice and she had no intentions of running away. Not until she knew exactly what was expected of her, at least.

Ten minutes later, as tears of frustration streamed down her cheeks, her hands dropped limply to her side. Crossing to the window, she swished the curtains aside to look out. The view almost took her breath away as she stared across the rooftops of London town. A smog was beginning to settle, giving the street far below an eerie appearance, and she saw immediately that there would be no escape that way. The cobblestones below were gleaming like dark jewels in the glow from the gas lamps. She suddenly realised that the crying from the next room had stopped, so crossing to the wall she hammered on it with her fist and shouted, 'Hello? Is anyone there?'

Silence greeted her, save for the muffled sounds of the horses and carriages on the street outside. With dragging feet she crossed to the bed and, still fully clothed, she clambered up onto it and curled into a ball. There was nothing she could do now but wait for Daisy or the maid to reappear.

Sometime later a gentle hand on her shoulder brought Violet springing awake. Disorientated, she knuckled the sleep from her eyes before looking up to see Jed smiling down at her. Relief followed by anger surged through her as she asked, 'Where have you been – and why did you let them lock me in?' She was still seething about the way he had greeted the woman called Ruby downstairs and annoyed with herself for falling asleep, but as he gently stroked her cheek her anger dissolved and she gazed up at him like an adoring puppy, dangerously close to tears.

'Why have I been locked in?' she demanded again.

'That's what I've come to explain to you.' His voice was soothing and she felt herself begin to relax. 'The thing is, this place is what you might call *a parlour* where gentlemen can come to escape their cares with a pretty girl after a hard day's work. But only very upper-class men mind,' he hurried on as he saw a frown on her forehead. 'Ruby is very particular about whom her girls entertain, and many of them have gone on to find themselves set up for life if they do as they're told.'

'What you mean is it's a knockin' shop,' Violet declared abruptly. She might have led a sheltered life but she still had ears, didn't she, and she had once heard Hugo bragging to his mates about visiting one of these places. Suddenly, everything was clear to her: the gentleman visitor, the way Ruby and Daisy were dressed. This place was a brothel just as she had suspected! But rather than be afraid at the discovery, she narrowed her eyes and peered at Jed more closely.

'What do you mean when you say some of the girls have been set up for life?' she enquired. 'The gentry don't marry girls below them in class, everyone knows that.'

'I didn't say they *married* them,' Jed pointed out. 'What I meant was, the girls can find themselves set up in a very nice little house somewhere where they need never worry about dirtying their hands again, waited on by servants and spoiled by their lovers. Doesn't that sound appealing? Far better that, than marry a lad from the mills or the mines and have a screaming brat each year and live in poverty, wouldn't you say?'

Violet had to admit that it did sound rather appealing, and after a moment she said in a wobbly voice, 'Exactly what would I have to do?'

Plastering his most charming smile to his face, Jed began to murmur in her ear.

Chapter Eight

There had been no word at all from Violet and Maryann was sick with worry, as was her father. John Meadows had been out every spare moment, asking everyone he passed if they had seen anything at all of Violet on the night she had run away – but it was as if she had vanished off the face of the earth.

And now the time had come for Benny to take up his new position at the stables. His son was standing in front of him with his few meagre clothes wrapped into a small bundle, and John's heart was heavy, although he was pleased that his lad had this chance. He just wished that Benny could have continued living at home. He and Maryann were going to rattle around like peas in a pod after today.

'Right then, lad. Have you everything you need?' John forced himself to sound cheerful although inside his heart was breaking.

'Aye, Dad, I have – but even if I've forgotten something I

can always come back to collect it on me first day off. I'll be coming back anyway to tip some of me wages up.'

'You will *not*,' his father responded indignantly. 'Me and Maryann will manage just fine between us. You save your money for when you meet a little lass and want to settle down.'

Benny couldn't see that happening for a long time but he wisely held his tongue and clamped his mouth shut. He'd make sure he slipped Maryann a bit on the side if he had to because he could be as stubborn as his dad when it came to it, and he knew they would struggle to pay the rent with just the two wages coming in.

The two men stared at each other for a moment then John suddenly pulled his son into his arms and gave him a rough hug, wondering when the lad had suddenly turned into a young man. He was as tall as John himself now and he could feel the lad's arm muscles straining through his thin cotton shirt.

'Make sure they give you enough to eat and treat you right,' John said gruffly as he stepped aside, and now it was time for Benny to say his goodbyes to his sister. She too hugged him to her with tears rolling down her cheeks.

'Take care of yourself,' she mumbled, and he nodded before turning to Granny Addison who had also come over to see him on his way.

She patted his hand as if he was still a young boy, too full to speak, and in her mind she was remembering the day she had delivered him into the world. A right strapping little baby he had been and he'd turned into a fine young man an' all. One anyone could be proud of.

'Be sure to come an' see me on yer day off,' she said thickly and Benny nodded before hoisting his bundle onto his shoulder and opening the front door. He turned once to salute them all, then strode away.

'I'd feel 'appier if he were goin' somewhere else to work,' she muttered. 'That mill owner might 'ave money but they're a right strange family from what I've 'eard of it.' She drew in her breath.

'That's just gossip,' John answered.

'Aye well, yer know what they say – there ain't no smoke wi'out fire!' Granny snapped, then she declared, 'Anyway, t'ain't likely to affect young Benny workin' out in the stables, is it? An' this ain't gettin' my dinner on, so I'll say good mornin' to yer both.' And with that she sailed out of the room.

Maryann and her father smiled at each other. They knew how much Granny loved a good gossip, but they were mildly concerned all the same, and both were hoping that Benny would be all right.

Benny meanwhile was marching along full of mixed emotions. It had always been his dream to work with horses, and now that dream was about to come true. But even so he wished that the timing for his new start could have been better, and he was racked with guilt about leaving his family when they had so much on their plate. They were all still grieving for his mam, and now with Violet going missing and all, he suddenly wondered if he was doing the right thing. Still, he told himself, he had agreed to take the job and he couldn't let Ted Carter down now, especially not when he knew for a fact that there had been so many others who had applied for the job. He would just take each day at a time and see how things went. And then if it didn't work out he could always go home and get his old job back again.

Feeling slightly better, he quickened his pace passing through the town and then on up the Cock and Bear hill, heading for his new home. Windy Manor, the residence of

Wesley Marshall, the mill boss, was perched high on the hill overlooking Bermuda village in the valley below. At last the walls surrounding it came into view. They were at least eight foot high, and set into them were two ornate metal gates, through which he passed. Beyond lay a tree-lined drive stretching away to the house, but ignoring the drive, Benny followed the wall round until he came to the back of the house where the stables were situated. A plump little woman with a very wrinkled face was in the yard hanging out washing with her mouth full of wooden pegs, but when she saw him she spat them out into her hand and gave him a big, welcoming smile that went a long way towards calming his nerves.

''Ello, lad, you must be young Benny Meadows,' she said, extending her hand. 'Ted told me to expect yer. I'm Nellie, his wife.'

Benny shook her hand solemnly as she nodded towards the stable block, saying, 'You'll find my Ted in there.'

Benny touched his cap. 'Thank you, Mrs Carter.'

'Eeh, lad, yer don't need to stand on ceremony wi' me,' she laughed. 'Nellie will do just fine.'

He thanked her shyly then turned and hurried towards the stable block scattering chickens in all directions, and leaving her to hang the rest of the washing out. The stables were in a large building, with living accommodation above. Downstairs there were four separate horse-stalls, all of which were full. The yard was cobbled and bordered by a wall with two high gates set into it, one at either end: one of them leading into a kitchen garden, and the other into a rose garden. Two other buildings, set a little apart, looked to be a laundry room and a dairy, but Benny doubted he would ever have cause to set foot into either one of them. A cinder path skirted the wall, and Benny supposed it would lead to the middens if the slight whiff coming from that direction was anything to go by. There was also a large barn that he guessed would house the hay for the horses, but then he had no time to take in any more, for he was inside the stable block blinking as his eyes adjusted to the dimmer light.

'Ah, you've arrived then, lad,' Ted greeted him. He was rubbing wax into what looked to be a fine leather saddle but he placed it down and came towards Benny, who was looking admiringly at the gleaming horse brasses hanging from the walls. Everywhere was as neat as a new pin and the place smelled pleasantly of fresh hay. It was apparent that Ted took great pride in the horses and the stables, and Benny was determined to do the man justice.

'Aye, I've arrived,' Benny told him with a grin. 'And now if you wouldn't mind showing me where I'll be sleeping I'll drop this bundle off and get straight to work.'

'O' course.' Ted led him past the stalls where the horses were gently snorting and pawing the ground, towards a ladder that led to the upstairs.

'You'll be sleepin' up here,' he told him, 'but you'll eat in the kitchen wi' me, Nellie an' our Cissie. You've no doubt already met Nellie me missus, an' Cissie is me granddaughter. Lived wi' us since 'er parents died when she were a nipper,' he confided. 'She 'elps the missus in the 'ouse, though bein' only the two of 'em an' Miss Lord, the 'ousekeeper, they can't keep it as they'd like.' He clucked his tongue. 'There were a time when this place were alive wi' servants an' the whole place shone from top to bottom. But all that's changed now since the young missus died an' we 'ave to settle fer doin' what we can.'

Benny eyed the older man curiously. Ted seemed nice enough and Benny thought he would enjoy working with him. He was stooped with age and his hair, which was silvery white, was sparse now. His face was heavily lined but he seemed spritely enough and he obviously cared deeply for the horses he tended, if the way they had tried to nudge him as he passed their stalls was anything to go by.

At the top of the ladder, Ted threw a door open and Benny stepped into what was to be his new home. The walls were sloping but for all that it was a large space and Benny was sure he would be comfortable there. An iron bed stood against one wall with a feather pillow and two grey woollen blankets that looked to be clean neatly folded on the bottom of it. A chest of drawers and a washstand with a jug and pitcher took up most of the other wall. Other than that, there was no other furniture, except for a small wooden table that leaned precariously to one side and a plain wooden chair.

'It ain't exactly a palace,' Ted apologised. 'But our Cissie come up 'ere an' gave it a good clean fer yer yesterday. She's a good girl, is our Cissie,' he ended.

Benny crossed to the only window in the room and gazed out of it. It gave a wonderful view of the back of the house, including down into the kitchen garden, but he was shocked at how overgrown everywhere looked.

'Bit of a mess, ain't it?' Ted said sadly, correctly gauging Benny's reaction. 'The gardeners 'ave been gone fer some long time. I do me best wi' it when I ain't workin' in 'ere, but there's only so much one body can do, lad. 'Ow would you feel about lendin' a hand out there?'

'I don't mind what I do,' Benny assured him good-naturedly. 'And the room is just fine, thank you.'

'That's good then.' Ted looked relieved and hoped that Benny would stay longer than most of the staff did. He seemed a pleasant lad and was clearly eager to please. 'Plonk yer bundle on the bed then an' we'll go over to the kitchen an' see if our Nellie's got a brew on, eh? Always ready fer a cup o' tea, I am.'

Benny did as he was told and followed the old man back down the ladder with a broad grin on his face. So far so good, he thought, hoping that the rest of the household would be as amenable as old Ted.

The two men crossed the yard towards an open doorway, and suddenly Benny found himself in the largest kitchen he had ever seen. It seemed to go on forever – and in the centre of it was an enormous scrubbed oak table where Nellie was busily rolling pastry for pies.

'I thought you'd be in,' she smiled, cocking her head towards a massive black-leaded stove. 'You'll find a pot o' tea brewin' over there, Ted, if you've a mind to pour it.'

'I think I can manage that, woman,' Ted said, and whilst he bustled away to collect some mugs Benny let his eyes stray around the room, wondering what Maryann would think of it. A huge fire was roaring up the chimney in a deep inglenook fireplace over which were suspended a number of gleaming copper pans of various shapes and sizes, and Benny felt another momentary pang of guilt, worrying how his father and Maryann would afford to pay for the coal now that his pit allowance was finished.

Six sturdy chairs were placed about the table, and on the wall next to it was a large wooden dresser with a collection of fine china displayed on it. Beyond that was a deep stone sink with a pump that connected to the well outside, and beyond the sink was an open door that he presumed must lead to a walk-in pantry. His eyes had no chance to roam any further, however, for at that moment a young girl appeared leaning heavily on a crutch with one hand whilst balancing a dish full of skinned rabbit for the pies in the other.

She had the bluest eyes he had ever seen and a heart-shaped face framed with thick golden hair – but it was the hand clutching the crutch he was drawn to. It was withered and ugly, and when she came forward he realised that one of her legs must be deformed too because she threw herself from side to side as she shuffled to the table. What a bloody

71

shame, Benny found himself thinking pityingly. She would have been a right bonny lass, had she not been so deformed. Even so she flashed him a friendly smile and he smiled back, doing his best now not to look at the crutch for fear of embarrassing her.

'This here is our Cissie,' Nellie introduced them as she took the dish from the girl, and Benny could see the pride in her eyes. 'And Cissie, this is Benny. Yer grandda is going to train him up to work in the stables. She's like me right hand this one is,' she went on.

'How do, Cissie,' Benny said politely and she smiled at him as she wiped her one good hand down the length of her thick apron, ready to shake hands. But then the niceties came to a sudden end when the green baize door leading into the main part of the house suddenly burst open and a finely dressed young woman with beautiful auburn hair barged in, her face contorted with annoyance.

'You're late with my coffee again,' she snapped, ignoring Benny completely. 'I've been waiting in the drawing room for over ten minutes now.'

Benny wondered who this was and how old she might be; he judged her to be somewhere in her late twenties to early thirties.

'Aye well, Miss Florence, I've only the one pair o' hands, an' as yer can see they're bein' put to good use at the moment, so happen you'll have to wait a while longer while I get the lids on these pies – unless you've a mind to make yer own, o' course.'

'*Really!*' Florence clenched her small, lily-white hands into fists and glared at Nellie malevolently. 'You'll go too far one of these days!' she hissed, and with that she turned about in a swish of satin skirts and strode out of the kitchen, slamming the door behind her so hard that it fair danced on its hinges.

72

Far from being alarmed, Nellie chuckled. 'There she goes again. That's the master's sister – and a right little madam she is an' all.'

Benny decided not to comment. It was a strange household from what he could see of it, although there had been no mention as yet of Mr Marshall's young daughter and he didn't like to ask about her.

Ted carried a brimming mug full of tea over for him then and as Benny drank it, he watched Cissie carry on with some household tasks. Ten minutes later he accompanied Ted back to the stable block. The old man showed him where everything was kept and the rest of the day seemed to pass in the blink of an eye.

He shared his evening meal with the Carter family in the huge kitchen, and it was the most delicious meal he had ever tasted. The pastry on Nellie's rabbit pie seemed to melt in his mouth. When he sat down at the table, he noted that there was another woman present – an older lady with a very stern face who barely said two words throughout the meal and left as soon as she had finished eating.

'That were the latest nanny fer Miss Fleur,' Nellie told him when she had gone. 'Though like the rest I don't reckon she'll stay long. None of 'em do.'

'Miss Fleur?' Benny raised a questioning eyebrow.

'Aye, she's Mr Marshall's young daughter, but you'll not get to see 'er,' Ted's wife confided. 'Kept to her room, she is.' Then seeing his expression she tapped her head. 'She's a bit funny up here if yer know what I mean so they keep her locked up, poor little mite.'

'What – you mean she's never allowed out, not even for a breath of fresh air?' Benny was appalled.

Nellie stared pensively towards the door through which the nanny had just left. 'No, never, but it ain't fer the likes of us to interfere, is it? We just do as we're told an' keep us gobs shut.' She sighed heavily, then changed the subject. 'And now how about a nice dish o' semolina puddin' to finish off, eh?'

'That sounds grand.' When Benny climbed the ladder leading to his little room above the stables some time later, he was full and content. Even so, as he snuggled down beneath the blankets on the ticking mattress, he couldn't help but think of his family – and he fell asleep praying that they were all right.

Chapter Nine

It was now two weeks since Benny had gone to work at Windy Manor and Maryann was alone, struggling to get the fire alight after her long shift at the mill, when a shadow fell across the doorway. She and her father could no longer afford the luxury of keeping the fire going throughout the day, now that they no longer had Benny's coal allowance, and this had given her yet another chore to do each evening.

'Do you need any help?'

Maryann's heart sank as she glanced up to see Hugo standing in the doorway. John Meadows had gone to visit the churchyard on his way home from work and she was uncomfortably aware that she was on her own and vulnerable.

'No, thanks,' she said shortly, hoping that he would take the hint that he wasn't wanted and leave. But Hugo could be very thick-skinned when he had a mind to be.

'You look tired,' he commented as he stepped inside without invitation.

Maryann snorted sarcastically. 'So would you, if you'd just done twelve hours in the mill. But then you wouldn't know what it's like to have to work for a living, would you?' She regretted the words as soon as they were said. There was no point in antagonising him, but it was too late to take them back now and she held her breath as she waited for his reaction. She needn't have worried – Hugo just chuckled.

'I'm still a sight better off than most hereabouts,' he bragged. 'Why use your brawn when you can live off yer brains, eh?'

The fire was flickering into life now and Maryann hastily threw some kindling onto it as she tried to ignore him. But Hugo had no intentions of giving in so easily. The lasses hereabouts usually dropped at his feet as soon as he smiled at them. Maryann was the only one who didn't – but that only served to make him want her more.

Once the kindling had caught, Maryann added a few nuggets of coal then rose wearily to prepare their evening meal. Thankfully there had been no shortage of fresh veg since Benny had started at Windy Manor. Each Sunday, he would arrive with a sackful fresh from the kitchen garden, courtesy of Mrs Carter – and the week before she had even sent them a fruit cake. He seemed like a different lad since starting his new job, happy and content – which was one worry off her mind at least. Tonight Maryann had stopped off at the butcher's and got them a couple of slices of belly pork to go with the vegetables, and she just hoped that she would be able to persuade her father to eat some of it. John seemed to be surviving mainly on alcohol at the minute. There had been no word from Violet and that, on top of everything else that had befallen the family, seemed to have tipped him over the edge. He was wandering around as if he was in a trance half of the time and his daughter was seriously concerned about him. He didn't even bother to tend his allotment any more, which was why Maryann was always so grateful for Benny's contributions.

Maryann had become so lost in thought that it was almost a shock when suddenly Hugo's arms circled her waist as she stood at the sink.

'Hugo! Stop it! When will you get it into your head that I'm not interested in you?' She dropped the potato she was peeling and turned on him, her eyes blazing. She hadn't even had time to wash or brush the loose cotton from her hair, but to Hugo she still looked beautiful and he felt himself harden at her closeness. Placing her hands firmly on his chest Maryann pushed him as far away from her as she could and she saw his lips set into a hard line.

'When are you gonna wise up?' he said. 'Here yer are, savin' yerself fer that brother o' mine, but has he ever actually asked yer to be his girl? Go on, tell me – has he?'

'W-we have an understanding,' Maryann stuttered as tears stung at the back of her eyes.

'Understandin' be damned. He's playin' yer along an' yer too thick to see it!'

'Well, if I'm so thick why are you bothering with me?' she shouted back and he clenched his fists in frustration before turning and slamming out of the door. Maryann let out a breath of relief. Toby had never *had* to declare his feelings to her: they both knew what they wanted . . . didn't they?

She swiped an angry tear from her cheek. Trust Hugo to try and plant seeds of doubt. Of *course* Toby loved her. And one day when the time was right they'd be wed. Yet strangely, that day seemed to be getting further and further away. What with losing their mam and then Violet going missing, how could she leave her dad all alone now – or even for the foreseeable future, if it came to that? As her shoulders sagged she lifted the small knife and continued preparing the meal.

Her father appeared soon after, his shoulders stooped and a faraway look in his eye, and Maryann hurried to fetch the kettle she had boiled so that he could wash. Just as she had feared, he ate little of his meal and disappeared off upstairs to get changed as soon as it was finished. No doubt he would clear off to the gin-house now, and the thought of it filled her with dread. She had pleaded with him to try and curb his drinking, but her words seemed to be falling on deaf ears.

It was whilst she was rubbing salt into the bottom of the big black cooking pot that Granny Addison appeared. Glancing round the kitchen, she asked, 'Yer dad not in again then, pet?' She plonked herself down at the table.

'He is at the moment, but I dare say he'll be off to the gin-house in a minute.' Maryann sighed heavily.

Granny Addison nodded. 'Well, 'appen that's his way o' copin' wi' things at present. Grief affects different people in different ways, an' if he can find solace in the bottom of a pint pot then yer can't begrudge it him fer now. He'll come through it.'

'I hope so.' Maryann dried her hands on the thick sacking apron tied about her waist then lifting the teapot from the hob she carried it to the table.

'An' still no word o' Violet, I take it?'

Maryann poured the tea into two mugs and sparingly added sugar. 'Not a word.'

'Ah well, at least yer know wherever she is she went willingly, and no doubt she'll be in touch when she's ready. An' on a brighter note, Benny seems happy as a sandboy, bless him! I noticed he had a right spring in his step when he called round last Sunday.'

'Yes, he does, thank goodness.' Maryann pushed Granny's tea towards her. 'So at least I don't have to worry about him.'

The woman fiddled with the edges of the tablecloth before saying cautiously, 'An' I couldn't help but notice young Hugo paid yer a visit earlier on. Is he botherin' yer, lass? 'Cos if he is, yer should have a word with Toby. He'd sort him out good an' proper.'

'I can manage Hugo all right,' Maryann said with a fiery glint in her eye. 'He'll get the message that I'm not interested sooner or later.'

'That's as maybe, but all the same I think yer should mention it to Toby,' her neighbour urged. 'Happen then he'd pull his socks up an' ask yer to court him properly.'

'He doesn't need to do that. We know how we feel about each other without having to do anything about it just yet. Toby wants to do things properly.'

'Huh! That's all well an' good, but after what you've been through I reckon yer could do wi' thinkin' o' yerself fer a change. Yer old enough to be wed an' I'd keep me eye on yer dad for yer.'

'That won't be necessary, thank you,' Maryann said tetchily. 'Even if Toby did ask me to marry him right now, there's no way I could leave Dad till he's over Mum and until I know that Violet's all right.'

Granny Addison shrugged. The way Toby was going about things was all wrong, to her way of thinking. It was all very well Maryann saying that they had an unspoken agreement, but the poor lass looked dead on her feet and she needed his support now, not sometime in the future when he decided that he had enough saved up. It would serve him right if some other chap were to snap Maryann up. She was a lovely-looking lass and the lads would be queuing up for her if they got the chance. Still, it was none of her business at the end of the day so she wisely held her tongue and slurped at her tea.

*

The following week, as Wesley Marshall visited the mill he saw Maryann sitting outside eating her dinner. He paused, trying to think where he had seen her before, and then it came to him. He frowned, wondering why her name was familiar before he asked politely, 'Didn't a relative of yours recently come to work for me at Windy Manor?'

'Yes, sir. It was my brother, Benny. He's working with Mr Carter in the stables.'

'Ah!' Wesley Marshall had heard a lot of good reports about Benny from Ted, his trusted servant, and he couldn't help but be impressed with the sister too. It must have taken some guts to come and speak up for young Tommy Briggs as she had done, and he admired her for it.

Maryann eyed him warily. In fairness the man had done what he had promised regarding little Tommy, and the younger children in the mill were now working fewer hours, but as far as she was concerned he was the boss and should have taken more interest in his business and his workers.

Her father came towards her then, his expression concerned, and Mr Marshall said uncomfortably, 'I shall leave you to eat your lunch in peace then. Good day, Miss Meadows.'

That night, as Maryann served their meal, her father scolded, 'I still don't think you should have gone and spoken to Mr Marshall as you did about young Tommy Briggs. You could have cost us our jobs and Benny's too.'

'But we didn't lose our jobs, did we?' she replied as she ladled some suet pudding into his dish.

John had no answer to that, and the conversation was dropped.

Part Two
September 1850

Chapter Ten

'Right, lad, Miss Florence is goin' visitin' today an' needs the carriage gettin' ready. Do yer reckon yer could give me a hand?'

'Of course,' Benny replied obligingly as he rose from the table. He was full of Nellie's delicious bacon and egg breakfast and felt ready to take on the world. Already after working in the fresh air for a while his cheeks had lost the deathly pallor of the miners who spent the majority of their lives in the bowels of the earth, and by now, Benny regarded the Carters almost as a second family. He rose early in the morning while it was still dark and fell exhausted into bed each night in his little room above the stables, but he wouldn't have changed his new life now for the world.

The sultry summer had turned into a cold and grey September and the nights were drawing in, but Benny didn't mind. He loved what he was doing, and the only thing that troubled him was constantly worrying about Maryann. He knew from his weekly visits home that she was having a rough time of it with his father. If anything, John Meadows' drinking was getting worse – to the point where he had even lost a few shifts at the mill recently. Everyone knew what a hard task-master Seth Brown was, and Maryann was living in fear that if it continued, her father would lose his job.

Since the day she had confronted Wesley Marshall about Tommy Briggs, neither she nor her father had been popular with the manager, and Maryann had confided to Benny that she feared he was only waiting for a chance to get rid of them both. God knew there were enough people desperate for a job to step into their shoes. Still, Benny consoled himself as he followed Ted outside, Maryann and Toby had agreed to pay a visit to Windy Manor on the coming Sunday afternoon and he could hardly wait. It would do his sister so much good to get away from home for a time and Mrs Carter had kindly told him to invite them. At first Maryann had refused the invitation, saying that she only had Sunday to do the main household chores in the cottage, but after seeing how disappointed Benny was she had changed her mind and agreed to come.

Soon Benny and Ted were in the tack room selecting the reins and harnesses needed for the carriage, and once they had them all to hand they went towards the stalls where the horses were restlessly pawing the ground as if they could anticipate the exercise to come.

Benny loved each and every one of them and it was clear from the way they nuzzled his hand as he stroked them and offered them a carrot each from the kitchen garden that his love was returned. In the first stall was Belle, Miss Florence's horse, a spirited pure white Highland pony. She was a feisty creature and Benny felt sorry for her because he knew that Miss Florence didn't give her nearly enough exercise. Even when she did, Belle would often come back to the stables all of a lather with the marks of the whip on her rump, and Benny often wished he could mete out the same punishment to her owner. Next to Belle was Storm, Master Wesley's thoroughbred. In contrast to Belle he was jet black and much bigger, although he was as gentle as a lamb. And finally in the last two stalls were Blaze and Bracken, the placid-natured Hackney horses used to pull the cart and the carriage. It was these he approached now, and after leading them out into the stableyard he and Ted began to harness them for the journey.

'I reckon after comin' along o' me today an' watchin' how it's done you could drive Miss Florence next time.'

Benny grinned from ear to ear. Up until now he had only sat next to Ted, and the thought of being able to drive the carriage himself was exciting.

'Where is Miss Marshall going?' he asked and Ted shrugged.

'Visitin' the nobs in the town again, no doubt,' he said with disgust as he spat out a wad of tobacco. He didn't have much time for Miss Florence and wasn't afraid to show it.

Soon after, Florence appeared in a gay bonnet and a very fine needle-cord costume in a dark green.

Ted was already in the driver's seat and as Benny helped her into the carriage she shouted, 'Swan Lane, Carter!' No please or thank you, but then none of them expected manners from this young woman any more.

'Has she always been this bad-tempered?' Benny whispered as Ted steered the horses down the drive at a trot.

Ted shook his head. 'No. The trouble started when the young master brought his French bride home. Miss Florence never took to her but then she were engaged to be married herself at the time, so none of us anticipated she'd be about for long. An' then just days afore the weddin' her fiancé suddenly cleared off an' jilted her. Married some lord's daughter so we heard – wi' a better dowry than Miss Florence, an' from that day on she turned into a shrew.'

'Blimey, that must have been hard for her,' Benny said, feeling an unexpected surge of sympathy for the woman.

'I dare say it was. He made a laughin' stock of her, there were no doubt about it, an' as far as I know, no other bloke's ever shown any interest since. From then on things went from bad to worse wi' the young mistress until . . . well, until the poor lass died to be honest. But in fairness it weren't down to young Amélie. She were a fragile little creature who wouldn't say boo to a goose.'

'How did she die?' Benny dared to ask, and for a few moments he thought that Ted wasn't going to answer him.

However, in the time that Ted had known the lad he had come to trust him, so he said quietly, 'She took her own life shortly after Miss Fleur were born. The baby weren't . . . well, you know. She weren't quite normal an' the young mistress took it bad. She couldn't love her 'cos she weren't perfect, like – so one night she climbed up into the attics an' jumped from the window. We found her sprawled out on the ground below the drawin'-room window, an' fer a time I thought the young master would go mad. It's no wonder he's become a recluse. Spends most of his time painting now, he does, an' his paintings are good an' all. I heard some of 'em have gone into an exhibition in London.'

'And does he have a lot to do with his little girl?'

Ted shook his head sadly. 'Never sees her from one month to the next. Per'aps she reminds him too much of her mother? That's why the poor little mite is kept locked up wi' only an' Miss Florence and a nanny to see to her.'

'Miss Florence?' Benny was surprised. He couldn't see her in the role of the kindly aunt somehow.

His instincts were proven to be right when Ted went on, 'Ah, but only so as she can check the child ain't up to no mischief. They keep her drugged up to the eyeballs fer most o' the time, an' to my knowledge she's never set foot out of the house since the day her mother died. We've had more nannies come an' go than I care to remember, but what can we do about it? At odd times Cissie an' Nellie have had to look after her till the replacements arrived, an' they both reckon the child could come on wi' a bit of encouragement. But there yer go, life's a funny thing whichever way yer look at it. I suppose she's better cared for here than she would be if she were stuck in an asylum.'

Benny was shocked to think that even rich people could have their problems. He had imagined that only poor people suffered. But it just went to show. As Ted said, life could be a funny thing.

On the way back from Swan Lane following Florence's visit, Ted allowed Benny to drive the carriage and he took to it like a duck to water.

'Capital,' Ted praised him. 'I reckon you're a natural when it comes to horses, lad.'

Benny was beaming like a Cheshire cat when he went into the kitchen some time later after putting the carriage away in the large Dutch barn and stabling the horses.

Cissie was kneading dough at the table, her pretty face flushed from the heat from the fire, and she smiled back at him. Benny's grin was very infectious.

'So what are you looking so happy about?' she questioned.

'Your dad let me drive the carriage back from Swan Lane and he reckons I did a good job.'

Benny helped himself to an apple from the dish and sat down at the table, marvelling at the way Cissie was handling the dough. He'd noticed that her lame leg and withered hand hardly stopped her doing anything. She never complained and was always cheerful, where many with her afflictions might have been bitter. It was a damn shame, the way he saw it. Cissie was such a pretty lass she could have had her pick of the lads, had it not been for her deformities – not that she seemed very interested. In fact, he'd barely seen her leave the house apart from the odd occasion when she went into market with her grandad on the cart. That was another thing he was feeling happy about. Ted had also hinted on the way back that he felt Benny was almost ready to start doing the trips to market on his own.

'Hoistin' all them sacks about is gettin' a bit much fer me now,' Ted had told him, and Benny was more than pleased to take on the job. In fact, he had turned his hand to many things since coming to work at Windy Manor, gardening being one of them, and already he had the kitchen garden looking a treat. He had weeded it from top to bottom when there was nothing to do in the stables, as well as digging fresh earth over and planting vegetables for next year. He had also begun to scythe down the long grass at the front of the house, and for the first time in years the grounds were beginning to look respectable again – not that there wasn't still a lot to do. But Benny was confident he could get it all ship-shape again, given time. He finished his apple and a mug of home-made cider that Cissie poured out for him, then whistling merrily he went back outside to see what else needed doing.

It was much later that afternoon when Florence appeared at the stables in her riding habit, telling Ted, 'Get Belle saddled immediately. I want to go for a good gallop. That ridiculous nanny has just handed her notice in, which means that I shall have to look after the damn halfwit again till my brother finds yet another replacement.'

'Yes, miss.' Ted touched his cap and with a nod at Benny to follow him he took Belle from her stall whilst Florence stood outside the stable block impatiently slapping her skirt with a riding crop.

It was Benny who led the pony outside and after handing the reins to Florence he told her, 'Go steady on her, miss. She's just had her oats so she'll need to let them settle. We didn't think you'd be wanting to take her out this late in the afternoon. It'll be dark soon.'

Florence stared at him disdainfully. 'I am quite capable of handling my own horse without any advice from the likes of you, and I certainly don't need to ask your permission to ride her. Now remember your place and help me to mount!'

As Benny helped her into the saddle, his mouth set into a hard line. No wonder no one is interested in her, he thought. She's a right tartar. And then she brought the crop down hard on Belle's rump and the horse reared and was off at a gallop down the drive.

'She'll break her bloody neck one o' these days!' Ted muttered from behind him and Benny could only hope for it to be true.

'Aye, you're right,' he agreed angrily. 'Either that or she'll break Belle's leg.'

It was well over an hour before Florence returned and her poor mare was foaming at the mouth.

Benny was disgusted as he rushed out of the stables to take the reins from her, and it must have shown because she snarled at him, 'I think you're feeding her too much. She's about as fast as the carousel horses at the fairground. See that you cut her meal down or you'll have me to answer to!'

'Yes, miss,' Benny replied through gritted teeth, and as she strode away with the feathers in her riding hat bobbing in the wind he stroked Belle and whispered to her soothingly, 'Come on, my fine girl. Let's get you rubbed down and settled, eh?'

He seethed as he saw the weal-marks on her rump. The whip had broken the skin in several places, and trickles of blood stood out starkly against her beautiful white coat. Ted was ambling towards him from the direction of the kitchen. He could afford to finish a little earlier now that he had Benny to help, but he saw at a glance that Benny was consumed with rage.

'D'you see what she's done to the poor beast?' Benny stabbed his finger towards the open wounds. 'Someone should take the whip and do the same to her.'

'Now then, lad.' Ted placed his hand on Benny's shoulder, feeling him tremble through his thin cotton shirt. ''Tis best to see all and say nowt if yer hopin' to keep yer job. Now let's get this girlie inside, eh? We'll soon have her cleaned up an' feelin' better.'

Benny's shoulders sagged with resignation as he did as he was bid. *But I'll have me day with that bitch, you just see if I don't*, he promised himself.

By the time Benny retired to his room that night he was in no better frame of mind as he thought of the cruelty Florence had inflicted on Belle. But his temper was somewhat restored after getting undressed and sliding into bed to find that Cissie had placed a hot brick wrapped in an old towel in there to warm the cold linen sheets for him.

He blew out his candle and pondered on the difference between the two young women. There was Cissie with nowt much, but with always a smile on her face whilst Florence had everything anyone could ever wish for – yet never had a kind word for anyone. The complexities and the unfairness of life baffled him, but never for a moment did he forget how fortunate he was to have got this position, nor how happy he was . . . and so finally he fell asleep with a smile on his face.

Chapter Eleven

Sunday was a grey dismal day but Benny didn't mind. He rushed through his jobs so that he would have time to spend with Maryann and Toby when they visited that afternoon. Nellie had made a large fruit cake for the occasion and had laid the table in the kitchen with a starched white linen cloth in preparation for her guests.

'I've no doubt a slice o' that an' a nice hot cup o' tea will slide down nice after their long walk,' she told him as she set out the plates, and he gratefully agreed.

Benny then hurried out to the pump in the yard to wash before going off to his room to change and at last he saw Maryann, Toby and Hugo picking their way through the chickens across the yard. He frowned; he hadn't invited Hugo as they had never really got on, but no doubt Hugo had talked the other two into letting him come along. Benny was so pleased to see the others that he decided to let it pass.

'Come on in and welcome,' Nellie said. She had got to

the back door before him and Benny stood to the side of the table as his sister entered with a wide smile on his face.

Maryann had made no secret of the fact that she hadn't wanted to come, but after such a warm welcome she began to relax, especially when Cissie hurried across to take her Sunday best straw bonnet and her shawl from her. She was amazed at the size of the kitchen, although Benny had tried to describe it to her, and felt as if she had stepped into another world.

In no time they were gathered around the table talking as if they had known each other for years. Nellie took to Maryann and Toby instantly, but she wasn't so sure about Hugo, as she was to comment to her husband later that night. She was a fair judge of character and sensed that he could be trouble. And she didn't like the way he was leering at their Cissie either, but she kept her mouth shut for fear of upsetting Benny.

'So,' Nellie said with a twinkle in her eye, 'young Benny here has been tellin' me how you sorted our Master Marshall out.'

'Well, not really.' Maryann blushed. 'I just pointed out that the young lad who had been injured should be compensated, and I told him about the atrocious conditions we have to work in. Thankfully, he listened and the children are already working shorter hours.'

'Good for you!' Nellie looked at her with approval. She was such a pretty, nice-natured lass and not afraid to speak up for what was right either by all accounts. Her young man seemed nice an' all, but she just couldn't take to his brother, who was having a good look around. I wouldn't trust that one as far as I could throw him, she found herself thinking, but she kept the smile plastered on her face and hastily poured out another cup of tea for everyone.

Benny then went on to tell Maryann how angry he had

been at Miss Florence's treatment of Belle. 'I could have throttled her with me bare hands,' he told them and Nellie tutted.

'Now, lad, there ain't no cause fer you to go sayin' things like that,' she warned, but then ended with a grin: 'Although I have to admit there's been many a time when I've felt like puttin' that little madam across me lap an' spankin' her arse fer her meself.'

They then went on to speak of the new railway that would be opening in the town the following year. The Irish navvies who had been drafted in to build the lines were a common sight walking about with their boots slung about their necks when they weren't working, and they had become popular with the local people – especially the local lassies, who couldn't get enough of their soft Irish lilt.

Nellie was chuckling about it when the kitchen door suddenly opened and Florence strode in, only to stop dead at the sight of so many people.

'I wasn't aware that I gave permission for you to have a party,' she said icily. 'Who are these people?'

Maryann's eyes popped at the sight of her fine clothes. The young woman was dressed for outdoors in a many-tiered dress, over which she wore a pardessus that buttoned to the waist before curving into a short skirt that flattered the wide dress. It was a deep lavender colour, all trimmed in lighter lilac ribbons that matched the ribbons on her bonnet, and Maryann had never seen anything like it apart from in pictures in the books that she had seen in the free reading rooms. At one time it had been her favourite place, but sadly since her mother's death she never seemed to have time to visit there any more.

'It's hardly what you'd term a party,' Nellie retorted. 'Just young Benny's sister and a couple of his friends who have called in.'

'Well, whatever it is I don't pay you all to sit about eating our food.' Florence's voice dripped spite. 'And I want the carriage prepared now!' She aimed the demand at Benny, who had blushed to the roots of his hair. However, it was Ted who rose from his seat at the side of the fire.

'It's Benny's afternoon off,' he informed her as he tapped his pipe out onto the hearth. 'So I'll see to the carriage fer you, Miss Florence.'

She was about to make another nasty remark when her eyes suddenly settled on Toby and lit up with interest.

'Oh, very well then, Carter,' she simpered. 'Will it take you long?'

'It'll be round the front waitin' fer you in ten minutes, miss.'

She nodded without taking her eyes off Toby then turned and walked sedately from the room.

'Why she keeps comin' into the kitchen instead o' ringin' for one of us I don't know. I reckon she just likes to keep a check on us,' Nellie grumbled. Then: 'Happen you've got yourself an admirer there, Toby me lad,' she chuckled as she cut some more slabs of fruit cake and loaded them onto their plates.

'Huh! Why would someone like her look at the likes o' me!' Toby had been totally unimpressed by the young woman's manners and could see now why she was so unpopular with the staff. No wonder no one stayed for very long. She spoke to them as if they were so much dirt beneath her well-shod foot.

Ted had left the room by then but for Maryann the visit was spoiled and she wanted to go home.

'Shouldn't we be thinking of getting back now?' she suggested to Toby. 'It'll start to get dark soon and I have to get an evening meal ready for Dad.' *Before he goes off to the inn*, she could have added – but she didn't.

Nellie immediately rose and scuttled off to the pantry, only to return with a basket laden with fruit and vegetables as well as a bag full of flour and another fruit cake wrapped in a piece of linen.

'You'll be doin' me a favour if you take some o' this,' she said tactfully as Maryann eyed the basket doubtfully. 'We've got more fruit an' veg than we can eat since your Benny arrived an' it will only go to waste.'

'In that case I thank you most kindly, Mrs Carter.' In her mind Maryann was already planning what meals she could cook with the gifts. There was enough fruit and veg there to last the pair of them for at least a week, although her pride would never have allowed her to admit it.

'You're very welcome, pet. An' don't leave it too long afore yer come an' see us again, eh?'

'Would you mind if I saw them part of the way home?' Benny asked and Nellie flapped her hand at him.

'O' course I wouldn't, lad. It's yer afternoon off, ain't it? But mind yer wrap up. The weather's turned now an' that wind out there is enough to cut yer in two.'

Benny bounded off to his room to fetch his coat while they all said their goodbyes, and minutes later he joined them in the yard.

Ted was already at the front of the house with the carriage all ready to take Miss Florence visiting, and they heard it rattle away as they followed the outer wall that led to the massive iron gates.

'So what do you think of them all?' Benny asked Maryann as they walked along. It was clear that he was very fond of the Carters and Maryann could see why.

'I thought Mr and Mrs Carter were lovely,' she told him sincerely. 'And Cissie too – and how pretty she is!'

Before she could say any more, Hugo piped up, 'Not 'alf! I wouldn't mind breakin' that little filly in. Shame she's a cripple though. Still, I dare say I wouldn't notice that in the dark.'

'That's quite enough of that talk, Hugo,' Toby said sternly, seeing the way Benny had been ready to leap to her defence. The last thing they wanted was for a pleasant afternoon to end in a fight.

Benny shoved his hands deep into his coat pockets and glared at Hugo, but for Maryann's sake he remained silent.

Eventually they came to the gates and paused to stare at the view. Below them in the valley was Bermuda village, and they could see the lamp-lighter walking along lighting the gas lamps. It made a pretty scene with the smoke pouring out of the chimneys of the cottages, but Maryann was keen to get home now. Her father had been very quiet and withdrawn that morning, and she didn't want to leave him alone for too long. She had even tried to persuade him to come with her but he had quietly refused, pecking her on the cheek and sending her on her way, insisting that a break would do her good.

Benny walked with them until they reached Heath End Road and then he took his leave, keen to get back to give the horses their evening meal.

'I don't think I've ever seen your Benny looking so well,' Toby remarked as he tucked Maryann's arm into his, taking the heavy basket from her with the other hand.

'He does, doesn't he? And I don't think I've ever seen him looking so happy either.'

They had come to the end of the road now and Hugo branched off towards the bullring, whistling merrily before telling them over his shoulder, 'I'm off then. I reckon I'll go an' sink a few pints in the Fleur De Lys.'

Toby merely nodded at his brother. He was still angry with him for his tactless comments about young Cissie and had a strong desire to knock his block off. He often felt that urge if truth be told, but Hugo was his little brother at the end of the day and so he endured him, hoping that he would settle down in time.

'I'm sorry about how rude Hugo was,' he apologised to Maryann. 'I thought Cissie was a really nice girl, and it's more than clear she's got a soft spot for your Benny. But you know Hugo don't mean any harm. His mouth just tends to run away wi' him sometimes.'

Maryann's eyes stretched wide. 'Do you really think she likes Benny?' She decided to ignore his apologies for his brother. Toby always defended Hugo although she didn't feel that he deserved it.

'No doubt about it, though I don't think Benny's clocked on to the fact yet.'

'Why, wouldn't that be wonderful?' Maryann was delighted at the thought of it. She had really taken to Cissie and couldn't think of anyone she would rather see Benny settle down with. She said as much to Toby, and he laughed.

'Hey, slow down. You'll 'ave them down the aisle in no time at this rate. You've got to stand back and let nature take its course. If it's meant to be, it'll be.'

Just for a moment, Maryann wished that Toby would state his intentions to her out loud. She was at an all-time low after everything that had happened and all too aware that the future was uncertain.

When she sighed, he looked at her searchingly. 'Is anything wrong?'

She shook her head. When Toby finally told her his plans for them she wanted it to come naturally, not because she had prompted him . . . and things were all right as they were for now, weren't they?

For the rest of the way home she thought of the chores she would need to do that evening before going to work tomorrow morning. As they walked down the long passage leading to the courtyard, the smell from the privy and the pigsty filled their nostrils although it wasn't quite so overpowering now that the weather had cooled down. Maryann couldn't help but compare their living quarters with those at Windy Manor. It seemed like another world there, surrounded by trees and grass.

She looked towards their cottage window and frowned. The place was in darkness and she wondered why her father hadn't bothered to light the oil lamp. It was certainly too early for him to have gone off to the inn, but perhaps he had fallen asleep in the chair. She hoped so; she knew that he hadn't been sleeping well.

'I'll just come in with you an' then I'll go an' start to get ready for work in the mornin',' Toby volunteered.

Maryann nodded. For some reason a sense of foreboding had come over her and she was glad of his company.

They entered the cottage and Maryann fumbled in the dark as she tried to light the oil lamp standing in the centre of the table. At last it lit and instantly threw dancing shadows about the room but her father's chair was empty and there was no sign of him.

'That's strange.' She looked towards the hook on the back of the door. 'Dad must be in 'cos his coat is still there.'

'Perhaps he went up to bed to have a lie-down?' Toby volunteered. 'I'll just pop up an' check on him for you, shall I, while you take your bonnet off?'

Maryann lit a candle for him and he strode towards the stairs door but he had gone up no more than two stairs when she heard him gasp.

'What's wrong?'

He reversed back into the room, his face ashen, then slamming the door shut again he choked out, 'Don't go up there, will yer, pet?'

'Why – what's the matter?' Before he could stop her, she

had pushed past him and yanked the door open again, and as she stared up the stairwell a scream rose in her throat as she was confronted with a pair of feet dangling in mid-air. For a moment she could only stare in shock, then as she realised what it meant she began to keen, 'No! *Nooo* . . .'

'Come away, there's nothin' to be done, lass.' Toby caught her in his arms just as his mother and Granny Addison burst into the room. They had heard Maryann's screams and were out of breath from running.

'What's up?' Granny asked, and as Toby jerked his thumb towards the stairs she glanced up and her face crumpled. 'God love 'im,' she gasped, then to Tilly Jackson she said, 'Run an' get your Matt, pet. 'E'll need to be cut down.'

She helped Toby to lead Maryann to the nearest chair and ordered him to, 'Put the kettle on, lad. We'll make 'er a cup o' hot sweet tea. It's good fer shock, though I wish we 'ad somethin' a bit stronger to 'and.'

Maryann was shaking like a leaf in the wind and Granny's heart went out to the lass. Hadn't she had enough to contend with lately, without this latest tragedy?

'Should I run fer the doctor?' Toby asked shakily but Granny shook her head, setting her chins wobbling.

'No, lad. 'Appen it's too late fer that. It's the undertaker we'll be needin' again.'

Moments later, Matt, Tilly's husband, appeared and after snapping his braces into place, he and Toby approached the stairwell, closing the door firmly behind them. Minutes passed until there was a dull thud on the stairs: the sound went right to the heart of Maryann. They had cut her father down. She heard them grunting as they manhandled his inert body back up the stairs to the room he had shared with his wife but did not see how gently they laid him on the bed. When they reappeared, their faces were grim.

And so as Maryann sat sipping at the hot strong tea that

someone put into her hand. With a heavy heart Granny Addison climbed the stairs to wash and prepare John Meadows for his last journey. Toby had been despatched to fetch the undertaker and a hush had fallen on the kitchen, broken only when Bill Roberts tapped tentatively on the back door a short while later. Once Tilly had admitted him he took off his cap and nodded towards Maryann then hurried away upstairs to take measurements.

Maryann felt as if she was in a deep fog. Nothing was clear and for some reason everyone seemed far away. She could hear them talking quietly amongst themselves yet their words didn't seem to be registering with her until suddenly a picture of Benny flashed in front of her eyes and she mumbled, 'Benny . . . we . . . we should let my brother know.'

'Of course. I'll do that. I'll go back there right now,' Toby volunteered instantly, then he said to Granny Addison, 'Will you stay with Maryann till I get back?'

'You've no need to ask.' She flapped her hand at him so after an anxious glance towards Maryann he hurried away into the darkness.

Bill Roberts came down the stairs a few minutes later. 'I'll have the coffin wi' yer first thing in the mornin', lass,' he promised. 'Would yer like me to get the vicar to call an' all, so as yer can arrange the funeral?'

Maryann nodded dry-eyed and so Bill departed, feeling sorry to his heart for the poor lass. She'd certainly had enough on her plate one way or another recently, that was a fact. It didn't seem like two minutes since he'd buried her brother an' sister – an' then her mam an' that poor little stillborn babby. But then that was life, or death, whichever way you cared to look at it.

Chapter Twelve

'I'm going to have to head off back to Windy Manor soon,' Benny told Maryann guiltily as they sat at the breakfast table the morning following their father's suicide.

Benny had returned home immediately the night before with Toby, with assurances from the Carters that they would square things with the master. But he didn't want to take advantage of their good will and he felt torn, for he didn't want to leave Maryann either. She had made them both some porridge for breakfast although neither of them had done more than touch it and now it lay in the dishes in front of them congealing. Neither of them had been to bed, but whilst Benny had sobbed for most of the night, Maryann was still dry-eyed. It was as if she had retreated into her own little world where no one could touch her. He knew that the undertaker would be calling soon to deliver the coffin so now he asked, 'Maryann, do you have enough money to cover the cost of the funeral?'

'Wh . . . what?' she asked in a daze. His words seemed

to be going over her head. She couldn't understand them.

'I said, do you have enough to cover the funeral expenses?'

'Oh!' She rose mechanically, fetched the tin on the mantelpiece then tipped the contents out onto the tablecloth. There was pathetically little there and Benny drew in his breath before delving into his pocket and adding the money he had to the rest.

'It's still not going to be enough, is it?' he said worriedly. 'Have we got anything that we could pawn?'

Maryann thought for a moment. 'I have Mam's wedding ring.' She had slept with it beneath her pillow every night since Eve had died, but this was no time for sentimentality, even if the ring was her most prized possession. It was the only piece of jewellery her mother had ever owned, and it had never been off her finger from the day she was wed until the day she had died.

Benny chewed on his lip, perplexed. He knew how much Maryann valued the ring – but what else did they have that was worth selling?

'In that case I could call into the pawn shop on my way back to Windy Manor,' he offered, and she rose and without a word went to fetch it. Whilst she was gone Benny stared vacantly at the window. Paying for the funeral was only the beginning of his worries – for what would happen to Maryann when it was over? She had never earned as much as their father at the mill – none of the women earned as much as the men – so how would she manage to pay the rent?

Deciding to tackle one problem at a time, he waited for her to return, reluctantly taking the ring when she held it out to him and tucking it safely down into his pocket.

'I feel really bad about leaving you,' he admitted gruffly. He was dressed for outdoors and not looking forward to the walk back at all, for it was drizzly and overcast.

'I shall be fine – but you will be back for the funeral, won't you?'

Hearing the trace of fear in her voice, he drew her into his arms and hugged her. 'Of course I shall. You don't think I'd miss me own dad's funeral, do you? And when it's over we shall have to decide what you are going to do. I'll ask Nellie if she knows where there are any live-in jobs going. You can't stay here all on your own.'

Maryann shrugged. At the present time she didn't much care what happened to her, but not wishing to distress him further she assured him, 'I shan't be on my own. Granny Addison is only over the courtyard and she is as good as family to us.'

'Aye, there is that,' he owned, but his heart was heavy as he left with promises to be back as soon as he could. He was troubled as he made his way back to Windy Manor and his mood was not improved by the weather. Only weeks before, the fields he was passing had been full of men, women and children harvesting, gathering up the stooks and placing them in neat rows along the fields. Now the stubble had been burned and the charred stumps looked dismal and grey, much as he was feeling. Shoving his hands deep into his coat pockets, he turned up his collar and with his head bent, he hurried on his way. Tonight, even the thought of returning to the horses that he had come to love could bring him no joy.

By noon the next day, John Meadows was lying in a coffin almost identical to the one they had buried his wife and baby son in, and following a visit from the vicar the funeral had been set for the following day.

It was the first time Maryann had been alone in the house since her father's suicide, and now she took a deep breath and slowly went into the parlour to say her last goodbyes.

Strangely, in death he looked far more peaceful than he had since her mother's passing, and Maryann was grateful to Granny Addison for tying a knitted muffler about his throat so that the terrible marks of the rope that had choked the life from him could not be seen. She could only hope that he and her mother were reunited now, for John had been a changed man since Eve's passing. Maryann could never remember him touching a drink before then, and yet since losing his wife he had taken to drinking every day to numb the pain.

It came to her as she stood there that Benny and Violet were all she had left now, and the tears she had held back finally flowed freely. Perhaps there was only her and Benny, for there had been no word from Violet since the day she had left – and only God knew where she might be.

At that moment in the Greenwich townhouse, Violet was happily transferring her new wardrobe of clothes down to a room on the first-floor landing. The last weeks had passed in a blur, and at first she had questioned whether or not she had done the right thing in running away with Jed. But now all her concerns had been put aside and she couldn't have been happier, although she dreaded to think what Maryann would have thought of her new way of life.

'This is it then. I hope you like it.' Daisy pushed a door open with a flourish and Violet stepped into what felt like another world. The walls were covered in a pretty crimson wallpaper, and in the centre of the room was a huge four-poster bed with what looked like real silk sheets on it. Gasoliers were studded about the walls and in between them were paintings of women in various seductive stages of undress, similar to the ones in the hallway. A large decorative mirror faced the bed. The drapes on the four-poster and the curtains were made of a luxurious velvet the same colour as the wallpaper, and Violet sighed with pleasure as she felt her calfskin day shoes sink into the Persian carpet.

Seeing the look of joy on the girl's face, Daisy felt a momentary pang of guilt. Violet was clearly fond of Jed Nelson, but then it was his charm and the promise of a better life that lured the girls here in the first place – herself included, although that felt like a very long time ago now. It hadn't taken Daisy long to realise that the only true feelings Jed had were saved for Ruby, the Madame of the brothel, which she found strange, for the latter was long past her prime. Still, she supposed that no one could choose where love might strike and she was contented enough for most of the time now. She just wished that all the young girls who came here could be as biddable as Violet. It would have made her life so much easier. Violet hadn't made a fuss, unlike young Meg Taberner who was becoming something of a liability now with her weeping and wailing and her refusal to let anyone near her. Only the night before, Daisy had overheard Ruby and Jed saying that if things didn't change very soon, Meg might need to be taken 'on a little walk'. By now, Daisy knew that the walk would lead her to the banks of the River Thames, but she never interfered in such decisions. It would have been more than her life was worth and she had no wish to join the unfortunates who didn't step up to the mark.

Jed had done his job well on Violet, coaching her in the art of lovemaking, and tonight she would entertain her very first client – the first of many, he hoped. He had showered her with silks and satins, and his smooth talking had convinced the girl that from now on, she would live a life of luxury, which was true up to a point – if she complied with the house rules. Daisy had chosen the man herself; he was an elderly judge well known for his harsh sentencing in the courthouse but with a fetish for young girls. Without the paint and powder that Violet had taken such a shine to, she still looked very young and naïve, and Daisy felt that she would suit the judge very well. In fact, she had high hopes that he might become one of Violet's regulars, for he was a very generous client.

Now, flinging an armful of her new gowns onto the bed, Violet clapped her hands in glee, telling Daisy, 'Why, it's just wonderful!'

'I'm glad you like it.' Daisy smiled indulgently.

Violet plonked herself on the edge of the bed and Daisy asked, her face serious now, 'Are you quite sure you've remembered everything I've told you?'

The girl nodded solemnly. 'Yes. I'm to wear no paint or powder and nothing but a nightgown. My hair must be loose and I must be waiting for him holding that teddy bear.' She pointed at the bear which sat like a king on a throne against the far wall. 'I must address the man as Uncle Teddy and I must cry when he first touches me and pretend to be frightened – but not *too* frightened – and when he caresses me *down there* I must tell him how much I love it and respond to him.'

'Very good,' Daisy said approvingly. 'And you must remember to never, ever argue with the clients: you must always do whatever they ask you to do. Ruby will be so pleased with you if you do well tonight; you are bound to be well rewarded. She might even let me take you on an outing to Regent Street tomorrow.'

Violet sighed happily as she stroked the skirt of her gown, a charming concoction of blue water-marked silk heavily trimmed with ribbons and lace, under which she wore a horse hair petticoat that made the skirt so wide she could barely get through the doorways. It was a world away from the drab clothes she had worn back at home.

Just for a second she thought of her family and wondered how they were faring, but then she was busy hanging her clothes away in the carved mahogany wardrobe and she forgot everything but how lucky she was to have met Jed.

On the morning of the funeral the sky was grey and overcast but Maryann barely noticed as she put on her Sunday best dress and straw bonnet. The dress was a faded blue – one of her mother's that Eve had altered to fit Maryann before her death. There was no money for a black one – no money for anything much, if it came to that, after paying for the funeral – but Granny Addison had placed a black ribbon around the rim of Maryann's bonnet for her – and that would have to do.

Benny had arrived early as he had promised he would and now brother and sister sat together waiting for the horse and cart that would bear their father's coffin to the churchyard.

'Seth Brown came to see me last night,' she informed him in a small voice, just when it seemed that the silence might stretch forever.

Benny frowned. 'What did *he* want?' He couldn't see Seth being the sort of man who would have come to offer his condolences, and he was proved to be right when Maryann said, 'He came to tell me that I no longer have a job at the mill.'

Benny's breath caught in his throat. This was the last thing they needed. 'Why not?'

'He says I've had too much time off and he's set someone else on in my place.'

'The bastard!' Benny had never sworn in front of his sister before but today he couldn't help himself and the words were out before he could stop them. 'But you've never lost time apart from when Mam was ill, and now.'

She shrugged. 'Seth has had it in for me and Dad ever since I confronted the gaffer about Tommy. I think he was just waiting his chance to get rid of me.'

Benny swiped his hand across his mouth. Now on top of everything else Maryann had no job to go to. Things seemed to be going from bad to worse. But before he could say any more, there was a tap at the door and Bill Roberts entered the room.

'Are yer ready, lass?' he asked gently. 'I've got the cart waitin' at the end o' the alley.'

Maryann nodded and watched as he and her brother disappeared into the front room to bring John Meadows' coffin out between them. As she waited for them, despair washed over her. What was to become of her now? But then with her usual resolve she raised her chin. This wasn't the time for feeling sorry for herself. Today she must be strong for her father and see that he was buried with the dignity he deserved.

Chapter Thirteen

'Are you ready, Violet?' Daisy asked that evening. 'I believe Judge Williams has arrived.'

'I'm ready,' Violet replied, suddenly nervous. Her sexual encounters with Jed had been very pleasant indeed. He was an experienced lover, but how would she feel having an older man paw her all over?

'Good girl, I'll go down and fetch him then. And don't look so worried, you'll be just fine if you do everything I told you.'

Violet nodded and lifted the teddy bear as Daisy left the room, closing the door quietly behind her. In the process she caught sight of herself in the mirror. Stripped of her paint and powder, with her hair loose about her shoulders and with nothing but a little cotton nightgown on, she looked about twelve years old. But then that was what Daisy had hoped for, so all Violet could do now was go along with it.

A short time later, she heard footsteps stop outside the

door and a man with a very deep voice ask, 'Are you quite sure that the child is a virgin?'

'Oh *yes*, sir,' Daisy replied convincingly. 'She's as pure as the driven snow. Jed brought her here especially for you and would allow no one to touch her until you came.'

'Hmm . . . good, good. Then come along.' The man licked his lips in anticipation, and when Daisy opened the door and he saw Violet he was not disappointed.

'Good evening, m'dear.' He looked her over hungrily as Violet clutched the teddy and stared back at him. He was a short man, and from what she could see of it almost as far round as he was high. Even so, she saw at a glance that the heavily embroidered waistcoat that strained across his stomach was of the very finest quality, as were the rest of his clothes. She also caught a peep of a very fine gold watch chain before her eyes went to his face. He had a bulbous nose, likely through a love of fine wines and too much port, and his thick lips looked wet and slobbery. He was a far cry from handsome Jed, but Violet had her sights set on becoming rich, and she sensed immediately that if she played her cards right, she might be in for some rather nice presents. Daisy had informed her that Judge Williams could be very generous to the girls that pleased him.

'I shall leave you now then,' Daisy told him, nodding towards a bottle of wine and two glasses that the maid had placed on the bedside table. 'Please ring if there is anything that you require, sir.'

'I certainly will.' But even as he spoke he was already removing his coat.

An hour later, Violet lay with her head on his chest as he leaned back against the headboard sipping the wine with a broad smile on his face.

'Are you all right, m'dear?' he enquired and she nodded,

her small rounded breasts resting on his naked expanse of stomach.

'Oh yes, Uncle Teddy,' she simpered. 'I was frightened when you first came in but you've been so kind to me, I'm not scared any more.'

Thankfully the sexual act had been over in seconds, for by the time he had undressed her and run his hands across her firm young body he had hardly been able to contain himself. The tiny bag of pig's blood that Daisy had made her insert inside her tight little fanny had broken immediately he thrust inside her, and the sight of what he thought was virgin blood on the silk sheets had inflamed his senses all the more.

'I'm pleased to hear it,' he boomed. 'Now why don't you be a good little girl and go and fetch Uncle Teddy a cigar from his coat pocket, eh?'

As she slid from the bed he watched her naked bottom wobble as she hurried off to do as she was told. Instantly his cock began to harden again but he knew his limits. Once a night was about all he could manage now, but even so there would be lots of other nights for he had quite taken a fancy to this little filly. She was very obliging.

'How about if Uncle Teddy were to come and see you again tomorrow with a nice little present?' he suggested.

Violet lowered her head coyly, causing the ringlets that Daisy had teased into her hair to fall across her face.

'I – I'd like that. But what sort of a present?' She fluttered her eyelashes innocently.

'Hmm . . . well, now then, let me see.' He cut the end expertly from the cigar, and once he had got it alight he dragged deeply on it before saying, 'How about a pretty bracelet? Most little girls like jewellery. What's your favourite colour?'

'Blue, I think.'

'Ah, blue to match your eyes, eh? Then Uncle Teddy will go out and buy you some sapphires tomorrow. But now come here and let me stroke you.'

Violet knelt obediently on the bed as he nipped at her pert breasts, amused to see the way her nipples stood to attention for him. He had already decided that he wanted to keep this one exclusively to himself – until he tired of her, at least – and he knew that Ruby would oblige him. This was no back-street whore-house but an upper-class place, which was why he frequented it, and no one seemed to mind his fetishes here. He did enjoy giving the girls a good spanking – not that he had tried that on Violet yet – but he would, given time, and if she behaved herself she would be well rewarded.

His breath was coming fast now and he told Violet, 'Stroke this for Uncle Teddy, pet, there's a good girl.'

Violet instantly took his semi-flaccid member in her small hand and began to play with it, and in seconds he had spent himself for the second time – which was a rarity.

She smiled secretly to herself as he closed his eyes in ecstasy, and a feeling of power surged through her.

Maryann rubbed at the blisters on her heels, keeping a watchful eye on the kitchen window. It was now Friday evening and despite the fact that she had spent every waking minute for days traipsing from one place to another trying to find work, she had had no luck at all. And now the tallyman was due for his rent. As she gazed at the meagre pile of pennies on the table, her stomach turned over. After paying the funeral expenses she had only enough to give him half what she owed, and she knew what he was going to say. But what could she do? Her parents had always prided themselves on paying their dues and demands on time, but things had been different then. And then the knock she had been dreading sounded on the door. Lifting the coins from the table, she went to open it and held out her hand.

The tallyman looked at the collection of coins and tutted. His eyes fastened on Maryann's chest straining against the old dress that was far too tight for her. 'Now this will never do, will it?' he said softly.

Maryann had always had a deep dislike for the fellow. He was well-known thereabouts for taking advantage of women who couldn't pay their rent, but she had no intention of letting him have his way with her. She would enter the workhouse before that!

Even so, she kept her voice level as she pulled her shawl more tightly about her slim shoulders, telling him, 'I'm sorry, sir, but my father passed away earlier in the week and I've had to find the money for the funeral.'

'Aye, so I 'eard. 'Anged hisself, didn't he?'

His callous words stabbed at Maryann's heart, but ignoring them she assured him, 'I should be able to make up the difference by next week. I'll be working again by then.'

'Let's 'ope you are,' he said slyly. 'Otherwise we'll 'ave to come up wi' another way fer you to pay me, shan't we?'

Maryann abruptly shut the door in his face and rushing to the tin bowl that stood on the wooden draining board she was promptly sick into it – not that there was much to fetch up. She had barely eaten for days, for the food seemed to stick in her throat. Swiping the back of her hand across her mouth she then went to sit in her father's chair, and as she rocked herself to and fro, she asked the empty room, 'Dear Lord, what is to become of me?' She had never felt so lonely in the whole of her life, and for the very first time she was truly afraid.

Out in the courtyard, Granny Addison had just waylaid Toby who was arriving home after his shift at the pit. She

113

had heard what the tallyman had said to Maryann and she was desperately worried for the girl.

'Toby – 'ere, lad,' she hissed urgently from her kitchen doorway, not wishing Maryann to hear.

'What's the matter, Granny?' he asked.

She cocked her thumb towards the Meadows' cottage. 'It's Maryann,' she said. 'The tallyman just called an' the poor lass hadn't enough brass to pay 'im 'is rent in full. Everyone knows that you an' she 'ave an agreement an' she's no one else to look out fer 'er now – so ain't it about time yer wed 'er, lad?'

Toby frowned, feeling as if he was being backed into a corner. He thought the world of Maryann and always had, but he had nowhere near enough savings put by to think of getting wed just yet.

'Yer could move into the cottage wi' 'er,' Granny pushed. 'An' then once she finds work again, you'll both be fine.'

Toby shook his head. 'No disrespect meant but I've no intentions of living here when I get wed,' he told her firmly. 'You know as well as I do that once I did that, the babies would start to arrive an' then we'd be stuck here forever. No, don't worry, Granny. When we do get married I intend to take her to a fine house somewhere. An' Maryann *will* find work – somethin'll turn up, you'll see.'

'Hmm.' She glared at him, feeling nowhere near as optimistic as he did – but what more could she do but hope that now she had sown the seed, he might at least consider marrying the girl? Dreams were all well and good for those that could afford them, but the way she saw it, Maryann was in a corner at the moment with no way out of it, poor lass.

Later that evening, when Toby had washed and eaten the meal his mother had prepared for him, he crossed the courtyard and tapped on Maryann's door. What Bertha

Addison had said to him was weighing heavily on his mind and he needed to clear his conscience.

Maryann opened the door and he stepped past her into the room, saying without preamble, 'Granny Addison collared me on me way home from work, Maryann. She's worried about yer, an' the long an' the short of it is, she reckons that I should ask yer to wed me.'

When she looked taken aback, he hurried on, 'I know I've never actually said it out loud but I want yer to know I've always thought of you as my lass. But the thing is, I want better than this fer us.' He spread his hands to encompass the sparsely furnished room. 'That's why I don't go out drinkin' like other chaps me age an' why I'm savin' every penny I can get me hands on. But the thing is, I ain't got enough saved up yet, though I'll gladly give yer some of me savin's to tide you over till you get another job.'

'There'll be no need for that,' she told him as her pride rushed to the fore. 'I'm sure I shall find a position soon and I quite understand why you don't want to get married yet. We're far too young anyway.' Deep down she knew that this wasn't true. There were many girls her age from the courtyards already married with babies, but she couldn't bear the thought of Toby marrying her just to get her out of trouble.

'So . . . you understand then?'

She nodded. 'Of course I do. But now if you don't mind I've had a really long day and I'm ready for my bed.' She might not have a lot but she still had the principles her parents had instilled in her, and she didn't want to set the neighbours' tongues wagging about her and Toby being alone in the house together.

'Oh yes – yes, o' course.' Looking mightily relieved, Toby backed towards the door then paused to ask, 'But you will say if yer need anythin', won't you?'

Again she nodded and then he was gone. Maryann leaned heavily on the back of the chair for support as she asked herself, would she have married him if he had asked her to tonight? And the answer came back, yes, yes she would because the loneliness she was feeling was almost unbearable. The cottage had always been her home, her sanctuary, but now it had become a place of sad memories, full of dark shadows. If Toby proposed, she wanted him to do so because he was in love with her and was ready to get wed, *not* because he felt obliged to take care of her. Until that time came, she would survive somehow – she had to.

Late that evening up at Windy Manor, Benny went out to perform his last duty of the day, to shoo the chickens into their coop. It was a task he had willingly taken over from Cissie, for he knew she struggled to bend with her lame leg. They had lost a lot of the birds to foxes lately and he was just shooing the last of them into the coop when he heard a commotion from inside the kitchen. It sounded like Miss Florence shouting, and he wondered what had upset her now. It didn't seem to take a lot – but then he'd come to the conclusion that even if the house had been heaving with servants she would still have found something to complain about.

When all was safe in the hen-house, he warily crossed to the kitchen and peeped through the window. He usually shared a glass of hot milk with the Carters before he retired, now that the nights had turned colder, but tonight he decided that he'd forgo that pleasure if the master's sister was on the warpath. Thankfully, everything seemed to have quietened down but he opened the kitchen door cautiously and stuck his head round it just to be on the safe side.

'Eeh, you'll never guess what's happened now,' Nellie

116

said, gesturing for him to come in and shut the door. She didn't want him to let all the cold air in.

'Miss Florence has only gone an' sacked that poor child's nanny again!' she rushed on. 'She ain't been here for more than a couple o' weeks neither.'

'What's caused all this, then?'

'Huh! Likely the poor woman complained about the child's treatment, like most o' the rest of 'em have.' Nellie sucked her breath in and shook her head in annoyance. 'Our Cissie's just offered to take over the care o' the little mite till they employ someone else but her ladyship won't hear of it. No surprise there though – she's probably worried the child would get to hear a kind word. I've got all the time in the world fer the master – till it comes to the welfare of his daughter. He just don't seem to care what happens to her one way or another an' just leaves it all up to his sister.'

'Oh dear.' Benny crossed to the table and sat down, taking his cap off and watching as Cissie pushed a pan of milk into the heart of the fire. He felt sorry for the child in question but his head was so full of his own worries that he didn't give the matter much more thought until later that night.

He entered his room above the stables to find one of the cats that lived at Windy Manor curled up fast asleep on his bed. This one – Ginger, as he had taken to calling him – seemed to have adopted him and followed him about like a shadow, sneaking up the ladder into his room whenever he could. As well as the horses, there were a number of cats and dogs and, coming from a family that couldn't afford to have pets, Benny had taken a shine to all of them. Ginger and the rest of the cats were very good at catching rats and were therefore fat and contented.

Benny crossed to the bed and stroked the purring animal. He noted that Cissie had been up to place a hot brick in his bed again and had removed the pile of dirty clothes from the only chair the room boasted. She was a good lass, was Cissie, bless her. No doubt his clothes would reappear in a day or two, all laundered and pressed, and he was grateful for it and often told her so. She did so many kind things to make his life as easy as she could.

Once more, his main thoughts returned to his sister and what was to become of her. It seemed that Maryann was heading for the workhouse, but Benny knew that he could never allow that to happen. He would take to the road with her before he would witness that, finding work and shelter wherever they could. And it was then that the solution to their problems came to him in a blinding flash. It was staring him in the face! The more he thought of it, the more sense it made. But he would have to put his idea to the master first before the idea could become a reality, and it was too late at night to trouble him now.

Sighing with frustration, Benny undressed and clambered between the cold cotton sheets, glad of the brick Cissie had placed there, and eventually he slept, dreaming of happier times when the family had been all together.

Chapter Fourteen

When Benny appeared in the kitchen half an hour early the next morning, Nellie, who was raking out the fire, raised an eyebrow.

'What's this then? Couldn't you sleep?' she teased.

'Oh yes, I slept all right but I was wondering if you could tell me what the best time would be to have a word with the master?'

She sat back on her heels looking amazed. None of them saw much of Mr Marshall, apart from when they served his meals, so she wondered what it could be about. She just hoped that Benny wasn't going to leave. They had all got used to having him about the place now and he did the work of two men, which had taken a lot of the load from her husband's shoulders.

'I dare say straight after breakfast, round about eight thirty,' she told him, and it was then that Cissie appeared from the small room she occupied that led off from the kitchen. She was yawning and although she was fully dressed, her hair was still loose about her shoulders.

Benny looked at her in astonishment. Her hair, which she normally wore in a thick braid that hung almost to her waist, was quite beautiful. It was so fair it was almost white and it shone in the light from the candles, making him long to run his fingers through it. She'd be a real stunner if she wasn't crippled, he found himself thinking, then immediately felt guilty. Cissie couldn't help the way she had been born and she was a lovely lass for all that.

Feeling a blush rise to his cheeks he averted his eyes, telling Nellie, 'Right then, I'll go an' check on the horses an' let the chickens out.'

'Aye, you do that, lad.' As Nellie placed some kindling on the fire she was thoughtful. She had seen the way Benny had looked at her granddaughter, and if she hadn't been much mistaken he had been admiring her. She had also seen the way Cissie's eyes would follow him about and had a sneaky suspicion that the girl had a soft spot for him, but . . . silently scolding herself and hauling herself up, she went to wash her hands before starting on the breakfasts.

Once Cissie had served Miss Florence, Miss Lord the housekeeper and the master with their meals and prepared a tray for Miss Fleur, which her aunt would take up for her, the Carters and Benny sat down to a hearty meal of bacon and eggs. However, today the food stuck in Benny's throat as he wondered what his sister would be eating.

'Not hungry, lad?' Nellie's voice was full of concern as she looked across the table at him. He had suffered so many heartaches recently that it was no wonder he was off his food.

'Not really – although it's delicious,' he assured her, not wanting to hurt her feelings.

The bell at the side of the green baize door tinkled and

Nellie told Cissie, 'That'll be the master ready fer his second pot o' coffee. Take it through, would yer, pet?' Then to Benny, 'Give 'em another ten minutes or so then I'll go in an' ask the master if he'll see yer.'

Benny nodded and gulped nervously but at last the time passed and Nellie pottered away to have a word with her employer.

'He says yer to go through to the library,' she told Benny on her return. 'It's where he does his paintin'. Our Cissie will show yer the way.'

Benny thanked her and followed Cissie from the room. Once out in the enormous hallway, his mouth gaped open. He had never ventured beyond the green baize door before and it was like stepping into another world. A huge staircase with an intricately carved balustrade led up to a beautiful galleried landing, and landscapes in heavy gilt frames were dotted about the walls.

'The master painted most o' these,' Cissie whispered as she saw him admiring them and he was impressed. He had had no idea what a talented artist the master was.

'Sadly, me an' Grandma can't keep it as nice as we'd like to 'cos the place is so big. We just have to do the best we can,' Cissie told him regretfully.

'It looks fine to me,' Benny told her kindly as she led him past a number of doors.

'This here is the day room, an' that's the door into the dinin' room.' She pointed them out to him as they moved along. 'An' that there is the sittin' room an' here's the library. Will you be all right now?'

He nodded, suddenly so nervous that the words seemed to be lodged in his throat.

Cissie squeezed his arm reassuringly. 'Don't be afraid o' the master. He's a lovely man. It's Miss Florence an' Miss Lord yer have to watch out for,' she whispered, then she limped away as Benny raised his hand and tapped on the door.

Almost immediately a voice called, 'Come,' and taking a deep breath Benny opened the door and walked inside. The room almost took his breath away. There were floor-to-ceiling shelves bulging with the weight of books bound in leather, as well as a huge leather-topped desk with a matching leather chair at one end. Then his eyes were drawn to the deep bay window where a large easel was positioned to catch the light. Mr Marshall stood there, cleaning a number of paintbrushes. There seemed to be canvases everywhere he looked, some of them blank, some of them partly finished. Mr Marshall had donned a large linen smock that was splattered with oil paints all the colours of the rainbow and now he asked politely, 'Was there something you wanted to see me about, young man?'

Before Benny could answer, Wesley Marshall added: 'I hear from Ted that I have a lot to thank you for. He tells me that you have worked tirelessly since coming here. Not only in the stables but within the grounds as well.' His eyes strayed to the window and he sighed. 'There was a time when the house and grounds were immaculate,' he confided as if he was talking to someone of his own class. 'But sadly, since my wife . . . well, let's just say I have somewhat lost heart in it all now. But never mind that, I'm rambling on. What was it you wished to speak to me about?'

Benny nervously cleared his throat and then blurted out, 'Sir, I heard that Miss Fleur's nanny has left an' I wondered if you had anyone in mind to take her place yet, 'cos if you haven't I think I might know just the right person for the job . . .' His words trailed away as he saw Mr Marshall frown.

'And who would that be then, Meadows?'

'M-my sister, sir. Maryann.'

'Hmm.' Mr Marshall peered at him thoughtfully. 'Ah yes. She is the young lady who came to inform me about the boy Tommy Briggs' accident at the mill.'

Benny's heart sank. He very much doubted the master would consider Maryann now that he had realised who she was. After all, there were very few people who would have dared to confront him as she had. They were all too afraid of losing their jobs.

'Er, yes, sir, that's right.' Benny shuffled uncomfortably from foot to foot. Suddenly this didn't seem like such a good idea after all and he was hoping that he wouldn't get his marching orders too.

'But surely she is still working at the mill?'

Benny shook his head miserably. 'No, sir, she isn't. Our father died, you see, and she had to have time off to bury him, so Seth Brown sacked her and now she's out of work with no way to buy food or pay the rent.'

Mr Marshall placed a clean brush carefully on a table that was loaded with artist's materials.

'But haven't you recently lost your mother as well?' he enquired.

Benny angrily blinked to stop the tears that had sprung to his eyes from falling. 'Yes, sir,' he said hoarsely. 'We have.'

Mr Marshall tutted. 'And you say that the manager sacked her for having time off to lay your father to rest?'

When Benny silently nodded, unable for the moment to speak, Mr Marshall then asked, 'Does your sister have any experience of being a nanny?'

'Well . . . no, sir. But she did help a lot with our younger brother and sister until they died and she has a way with children, always has had.'

'You have lost siblings too?' Mr Marshall looked appalled. He thought for a moment then said, 'Do you think your sister would be prepared to come and speak to me?'

123

'Oh yes, sir. I'm sure she would,' Benny replied with hope shining in his eyes.

'In that case, I am giving you permission to go and see her and tell her to present herself here to me at four o'clock this afternoon. Could you do that?'

Benny nodded emphatically then with a slight bow he backed towards the door, saying, 'Thank you, sir. I'm sure you won't regret it.' Once in the corridor, he punched the air with glee then, after getting his bearings, he raced back towards the green baize door eager to tell Nellie and Cissie his news.

Since Benny had burst into the cottage earlier in the day with the news that she was to report to the master, Maryann had passed the day in a state of anxious anticipation. At three o'clock sharp, she left for the walk to Bermuda village with her heart pounding in her ears. She had brushed her hair and polished her old boots until she could see her face in them, but there wasn't much she could do about her clothes. As she left the town behind she breathed deeply, enjoying the fresh air. Already a few leaves were fluttering from the trees and she gazed with pleasure at the thistles and the elderflowers in the fields and beneath the hedges. Cows and sheep were grazing contentedly in the fields and she began to understand why Benny loved working outdoors so much. It was wonderful to escape from the smelly, close confines of the courtyard and walk with the grass beneath her feet, and she began to feel a little better. After all, she asked herself, what did she have to lose? The worst Mr Marshall could do was refuse her the post.

When she came to the gates of Windy Manor she followed Benny's directions round to the back of the house. Benny had been rubbing Blaze down in the stableyard, but as soon as he saw his sister, he tethered the gentle creature to a ring on the stable door and hurried to meet her.

'All ready then?' he smiled.

Maryann nodded bravely, some instinct telling her that what happened in the next few minutes could change the course of her life – forever.

Chapter Fifteen

'Here she is then,' Benny said proudly as they entered the kitchen.

Nellie was kneading dough on the table and Cissie was peeling potatoes in the deep stone sink, but both women instantly wiped their hands on their aprons and hurried to meet Maryann with welcoming smiles on their faces.

'It's good to see yer again, pet.' Nellie gave her a quick hug then glancing at the clock that stood on the thick oak beam across the inglenook she asked, 'How would yer like a nice sup o' tea afore you go in to see the master an' Miss Florence? You've plenty o' time an' I dare say yer feelin' a bit nervous.'

'I am a bit,' Maryann admitted as she sat down on the chair that Cissie had pulled out for her. 'I left home allowing myself plenty of time to get here. I didn't want to be late.'

Cissie hurried away to pour some tea and Maryann drank it gratefully. It was the first tea she had tasted for some days, and yet Benny seemed to take it for granted now.

The hands on the clock ticked by interminably slowly, but at two minutes to four the door from the hallway opened and Miss Lord appeared with her hands clasped firmly at the waist.

'Ah, so you are here then.' She eyed Maryann as if she were a dirty smell. 'I suppose it's commendable that you can at least be on time for appointments. I wasn't sure that you would be able to tell the time.'

Maryann opened her mouth to tell the woman that in fact she was quite well educated, but a stern glance from Benny made her clamp it shut again. This, she supposed, must be the housekeeper and Benny had warned her how objectionable she could be. Had she not known differently, Maryann could have been forgiven for thinking that she was the mistress of the house as she had so many airs and graces.

Placing her empty cup carefully on the table, Maryann rose, and after smoothing her worn skirt down she followed the woman sedately from the room. As she passed through the door Nellie winked at her and Maryann grinned back. Much as Benny had been, she was taken aback at the size and opulence of the entrance hall but her face betrayed nothing as she trotted along behind Miss Lord's stiff back.

At the door to the library the woman paused, and after giving Maryann one last withering glance, she tapped and entered, saying, 'Miss Meadows to see you, sir.'

'Ah, thank you, Miss Lord. Do show her in.'

The woman stood to one side of the doorway and inclined her head at Maryann, and as the girl stepped past her she leaned back as if fearful of catching something contagious. The door clicked shut and once again Maryann found herself standing in front of Mr Marshall. He was positioned before a lovely marble fireplace where a fire burned brightly, but as she took a step towards him she saw that he was not alone. Miss Florence was sitting in a velvet upholstered chair to one side of the fireplace and she looked about as pleased to see her as Miss Lord had done. She was dressed in a becoming gown of soft green in a fine wool material with a wide skirt that pooled on the floor about her feet like silk, and instantly all the confidence that Maryann had managed to muster flew right out of the window as she glanced down at her own shabby clothes.

'So, we meet again, my dear. Do come in.' Wesley Marshall extended his hand and Maryann hesitantly took it as Florence looked on disapprovingly.

'I believe you have come to apply for the post of nanny to my niece,' she stated imperiously and Maryann nodded.

'Yes, miss.'

'Florence, I believe that it should be me who conducts this interview and—'

Wesley Marshall was silenced by a wave of his sister's hand.

'*Do* leave this to me, dear,' she said condescendingly. 'After all, I am the one who knows Fleur's needs *far* better than you do. May I remind you that you only see her on high days and holidays?'

'But that is only because you have informed me that it would be detrimental to her health to leave her room more often than that,' he objected as a faint colour rode up his neck and flooded into his cheeks.

'So . . .' Florence kept her eyes firmly fixed on Maryann as if he had not spoken. 'What references are you able to offer us and what qualifications do you have?'

Maryann gulped. This was the question she had been dreading. 'I have none, ma'am, but I do have a way with children, so I am told.'

'Huh! Are you aware that Fleur is not like other children?'

'Yes, I have been led to believe that Miss Fleur is not well,' Maryann answered tactfully.

128

'Fleur is an imbecile,' Florence informed her coldly. 'And I really believe that it would be far beyond your capabilities to care for her satisfactorily. After all, you are merely a mill girl, are you not?'

Before Maryann could answer, Mr Marshall objected, 'Now hold on, Florence. I think that is rather unfair and I think I *should* take over from here.'

Florence stood and glared at him and he seemed to crumple in front of Maryann's eyes. Wesley was usually so biddable, his sister thought crossly – and yet here he was, showing her up in front of a cheap little trollop from the courts.

'Wesley . . . have you forgotten that this is the very girl who confronted you about the accident at the mill? She has cost you dearly,' she spat. 'Now kindly leave this to me! *I* will decide who shall or shall not be nanny to Fleur!'

The man made to object and tell her that she hadn't done too good a job of it up to now but then thought better of it and bowed his head. The slight confrontation had obviously affected him badly, and after sinking into a chair he said no more.

In full control again, Florence eyed Maryann from head to toe, taking in her shabby clothes and her down-at-heel shoes. She pointed to a chair and Maryann plonked herself down.

'The thing is,' Florence began, 'Wesley's wife was a very . . .' She seemed to be struggling for the right words here as Maryann kept her eyes trained on her. 'Shall we say she was highly strung and really rather frail, so she didn't find her pregnancy easy. Then when Fleur was born it was immediately apparent that there was something not quite right with her, and Amélie found that very difficult to deal with. Because of this she never really showed any affection to the child. We brought in a wet nurse from the village for the first few months of her life, and Amélie saw very little of the baby. She never fully recovered from the birth and then, unfortunately, she . . . died.'

She glanced at Wesley before hurrying on, 'With the aid of a nanny I then took over the care of the child. She too is of a very nervous disposition, which is why I keep her in her room for most of the time so as not to distress her. She also has a heart problem, so of course she needs constant attention. Have you had any formal training in tutoring children? Fleur doesn't have a tutor, so part of her nanny's job would be to teach her basic English and mathematics. But then – no, of course you wouldn't have!'

'No, I haven't had any formal training,' Maryann said as her chin lifted proudly. 'But I have had younger siblings and the education side of it would be no problem. I can read and write fluently. In fact, Miss Emmett, the teacher at the school I attended said that I had the ability to go on and become a teacher myself if I so wished.'

Her back straight now, she looked challengingly at Florence as the woman sat looking thoughtful. Every instinct she had was warning her that it would be foolish to employ this girl. After all, she had been brought up in the courts and was a lowly mill worker. And yet for all that, surely she would be better than no one until someone more suitable came along? It would certainly take a weight from her shoulders. The girl had spirit, as her confrontation with Wesley about Tommy Briggs had proved, and today she was at least neat and tidy, her hair shining with no signs of the headlice that seemed to be so prevalent among the women at the mill. Her clothes were worn but she could see that they were washed and pressed, and she held herself with a quiet dignity.

Suddenly making a decision she asked, 'Would it help if you were to meet Fleur?'

'Yes, miss, I think it would.'

Florence pondered for a moment. Then: 'Very well, follow me.'

Maryann followed her from the room, along the hallway and up the sweeping staircase. The sheer size of the house was like nothing she had ever seen, but she tried not to stare about too much, and as they walked along the landing her heart began to beat faster. She had heard so many rumours about Mr Marshall's daughter. Some said that she was violent, others that she was a monster, so she had absolutely no idea what to expect.

At last at the very end door Florence paused, and after taking a key from the pocket of her gown she inserted it in the lock and turned it.

Maryann's breath caught in her throat as she entered a room that was as dark as night. The curtains were firmly drawn and for a while she could see nothing until her eyes began to adjust to the gloom.

'Why is it so dark in here?' she dared to ask as she made out the shape of a bed against one wall.

'The child becomes too excitable in bright light so I keep the curtains closed,' Florence answered unfeelingly.

'I see. Well, could you draw them just long enough for me to meet her?' Maryann asked. It was as quiet as the grave in there and she shuddered to think that anyone could be kept in total darkness. What a terrible existence the poor child must lead.

With an impatient sigh Florence crossed to the window and swished the heavy drapes aside, allowing the light to flood into the room. As she did so Maryann's hand flew to her mouth.

A small shape lay huddled beneath the bedclothes with just one tiny hand showing which was tied securely by a long cord to the bedpost.

'Is she kept tied up *all* the time?' she asked, horrified.

'Yes. She tends to try and escape if we don't do that.'

'And why is she still fast asleep at this time of the day?'

Florence pointed to a small bottle of clear liquid on the bedside table. 'I find it best to keep her sedated for most of the day so that she doesn't try to hurt herself or get too excited.'

Maryann thought there was little chance of that happening as she looked about the room. There was not a single toy visible and she wondered how the little girl managed to keep herself amused. And then suddenly the child stirred and as Maryann watched, a headful of the most beautiful platinum-blonde hair emerged from beneath the covers – or at least Maryann was sure it would have been beautiful if it hadn't been flat to the child's head with grease. There was an unhealthy stale stench about her, and Maryann wondered how long it had been since the little lass had been washed. And then she found herself staring into a pair of intensely blue slanted eyes and she gasped. They appeared to be unfocused and had a faintly oriental look about them; what's more, the child's head seemed slightly too large for her small body. Her mouth hung slackly open but then as her eyes settled on Florence she whimpered and blinked.

'Hello, Fleur,' the woman said, looking distinctly uncomfortable.

The child held her arms out to her but to Maryann's amazement Florence backed towards the door, clearly finding her repugnant. How strange, since Florence was supposed to be so devoted to her niece. Maryann immediately remembered another child who had lived in the courts with features similar to this one. The little boy had died quite young, sadly, but she could recall how the other children had teased him unmercifully and called him names.

'So, Miss Meadows, what do you think? Do you still feel you would be able to care for her?' Florence's acid voice pulled her thoughts sharply back to the present and Maryann nodded, badly shaken.

Anger and pity vied for first place as she continued to stare at the child. How could Fleur be expected to thrive, being kept in a darkened room tied to a bed and sedated all day? Why, even the barefoot child from the courts who had died so young had been better off than this poor little mite. At least he had been allowed out to play on the cobbles. It would have been cruel to keep an animal in these conditions, let alone a child.

'Yes, I'm sure I could,' she forced herself to say. She had every intention of speaking to Mr Marshall and asking him if she might make changes in the way Fleur was treated should she be given the job, but she was wise enough not to mention that just yet. She instinctively knew that Florence would never agree to it.

When Florence raised a quizzical eyebrow, Maryann rushed on, 'You clearly do not deem me suitable, but I'm sure that I could do it.'

Florence shrugged and gave in. If this foolish girl was willing to try, then so be it. 'Very well. We shall give it a try if you are sure that you feel capable of coping.'

'I am,' Maryann said firmly. She smiled at Fleur but the child simply stared back at her vacantly, her slack mouth drooling spittle all down the front of her grubby nightgown.

Florence moved to close the curtains again then, and although Maryann was tempted to ask her to leave them open, she decided it was best not to push her luck. Once back out on the landing, Florence securely locked the door again and as they stood there the child began to wail pitifully. Maryann's heart felt as if it was breaking but Florence seemed to be used to it.

'This is why I keep her sedated, apart from mealtimes and lesson times,' the woman said coldly. 'And now shall we go and discuss when you might start and your wages? My brother will deal with that side of things. Oh, and that door there next to Fleur's is where you will sleep.'

Maryann would have liked to take a peep at it but was too afraid to ask so she moved on, and with the cries of the little girl echoing in her ears, they made their way back downstairs.

Once back in the library Mr Marshall dared to ask her, 'When do you think you might be able to start?'

It appeared that Florence was at least content to let her brother take over now, and she left the room in a swish of skirts.

'As soon as you like.' As far as Maryann was concerned, it was a case of the sooner the better. There was nothing to keep her in the courts now.

'Then I suggest we start you on four pounds a year. You will have every Sunday afternoon off and of course you will live in. There is a room right next door to Fleur's where you will sleep, as my sister has probably told you. You may eat with Fleur or in the kitchen as you prefer, and of course we shall have to find you some new clothes. Does that sound acceptable?'

'Yes, sir.' It sounded more than acceptable. 'And I could start first thing tomorrow if you like.'

'Excellent.' Mr Marshall extended his hand and Maryann shook it timidly before backing towards the door.

'Until tomorrow then.'

Maryann couldn't help but stare at him. What sort of a man was he, to leave his child in such dire conditions? But of course she realised that it wasn't her place to ask him.

'I shall be here at seven o'clock sharp, sir,' she said instead, but he had already turned back to the canvas he was working on and taken up a brush, so she bobbed her knee and let herself out in a daze.

Chapter Sixteen

It was almost teatime and the light was already fast fading as Violet came out of her room dressed in a fine silk peignoir heavily trimmed with feathers. She nearly collided with Daisy and Jed on the landing. They were supporting Megan between them, and Violet noticed that the other girl looked strange and sleepy. Violet had been entertaining her gentlemen clients until the early hours of the morning and so had gone for an afternoon nap before getting ready for the coming night, but now she raised a finely plucked eyebrow and asked, 'What's this then? Is Megan not well?'

Daisy flashed an anxious glance at Jed who instantly smiled disarmingly before saying, 'Actually, we've decided to let Megan go home. She hasn't taken to this way of life at all, as you know – not like you, our little star, who is fast becoming in great demand!'

Violet flushed prettily at the compliment. She was well aware that she had quickly become a favourite of Ruby's and took full advantage of the fact. Jed went on, 'We thought it would be kinder to let her go back to her folks, but you go on with what you were doing. Off down to the kitchen for a cuppa, are you?'

'Yes, I was, as a matter of fact,' Violet responded, as she stared at Megan. She was sure that Megan would have fallen, had it not been for Daisy and Jed supporting her, and she didn't look well at all. But then at least they were letting her go now and Violet wasn't surprised. Megan had done nothing but cry since she had arrived and it was clear that she was very unhappy. She for one certainly wouldn't miss her. The girl couldn't see a good thing when it was handed to her on a plate, but then to be fair, this way of life wouldn't suit everybody.

'Goodbye, Megan,' she chirped as she skipped off down the stairs. Already she was thinking of her first client that evening – Judge Williams. He had become a regular visitor to the house now and already Violet had leeched a small amount of very expensive presents out of him, including a lovely emerald and diamond bracelet that was set in pure gold. Her wardrobe was heaving with fine silk gowns and bonnets of varying designs, as well as soft leather shoes and boots. Of course, she still had to clutch her teddy to her every time he came and do her little girl act, but she could stand that when he came bearing gifts. Even the spankings he was so keen on inflicting on her didn't seem so bad when she thought of the lovely surprise he would present her with at the end of it. As she frequently told herself, it was worth having a tingling red arse for a few hours!

In the kitchen she found two of the other girls sipping tea as Cook and Fanny the little maid bustled about preparing the evening meal. That was another thing Violet loved about living there. Hunger was a thing of the past now. The walk-in larder had great smoked hams hanging from the beams wrapped in muslin and the shelves were heaving with home-made preserves and pickles that ensured none of them ever went hungry. Her old life in the courts seemed a million miles away. Admittedly she did miss her family from time to time, but she had no doubt they would have adjusted to life without her now and she had no regrets whatsoever.

'I've just seen Jed and Daisy bringing Megan down. They've given up on her now and have decided to let her go home,' she told the other two girls as she helped herself to tea in a fine china cup and saucer.

Mirabelle, a petite blonde, and Georgia, a fiery redhead, had been there much longer than her; she saw them exchange a glance.

'It's good that she's going home, isn't it?' Violet enquired innocently, and keeping their eyes down they nodded.

Violet frowned. Usually the other girls were very chatty but suddenly the cat seemed to have got their tongues. Not that she was overly concerned for her head was too full of the coming evening and the clients Ruby had booked for her. First there was 'Uncle Teddy' as he still liked to be called. The old fool still believed that Violet was exclusively his, but the way she saw it, what he didn't know about wouldn't hurt him. Then there was Francis Bartholomew, a tall, dark, handsome sea captain who had visited her the week before. Just the thought of him made her heart flutter. A glance from his deep brown eyes could turn her legs to jelly and she could hardly believe that she was actually being paid for entertaining such a man. Sadly, his ship was due to set sail for Amsterdam from Rotherhithe docks the following day. Still, there would be plenty of other men until he returned, she consoled herself as she drained her cup and headed back up to her room. The maid would have prepared a scented bath for her by now and she would lie and soak in it in front of the fire before dinner.

She was halfway up the stairs when something occurred to her: Megan had had no luggage with her. Odd. But then perhaps Jed had already carried it down into the hall? It was really no business of hers at the end of the day, and she hurried on her way, her thoughts fixed on what trinket Judge Williams would present her with that night. She had dropped broad hints about a gold locket set with a fiery ruby that she had seen on one of her shopping expeditions with Georgia in Mayfair, and the prospect of adding it to her collection of treasures made her eyes gleam greedily.

'I think that's about it then,' Maryann said as her eyes scanned the familiar room. 'Please take what you want, Granny. Mam would have liked that and then the rest can be left for the new tenants. I've no doubt they'll be grateful for them.'

'I'll do no such thing.' Granny Addison glared at her. 'First thing tomorrer I'll fetch in Will Stubbs from the second-'and stall on the market. He'll take everythin' an' then I'll save whatever he gives me fer it till the next time I see yer, pet. You ain't in no position to be so generous. What'll 'appen if yer don't like it up at the 'ouse, eh?'

'I suppose you're right.' Maryann sighed as she looked around again. It was strange to think that this was the last time she would ever sleep in this cottage. It might not be much but it was the only home she had ever known, and until recently it had been a happy one, which only made leaving it all the harder.

Granny meanwhile was simmering with anger. She was pleased that Maryann had got the position, for God knew the girl needed it, but she was finding it hard to forgive Toby for not rescuing her in her hour of need. After all, would it have been so bad if he had been forced to stay in the courts for a while? As far as she was concerned, dreams were all well and good for those that could afford them, but from where she was standing Maryann needed him now – and he wasn't there for her!

'I should go on 'ome an' let you get to bed,' she said then as she struggled out of the chair. ''Appen you'll be wantin' to get off early in the mornin'?'

Maryann stretched her arms in an affectionate hug around the woman's considerable frame. 'Yes, I will – but don't worry, Granny. I shall be back to see you very soon.'

'I should 'ope so an' all.' The woman sniffed to stem the tears that were threatening. 'An' just you remember, there'll always be a home wi' me an' Archie waitin' fer you if things don't work out.'

'And you *will* tell Violet where I am if she turns up?'

''Ow many times do I 'ave to tell yer? O' course I will.' Though she seriously doubted *that* little madam would ever do any such thing – unless she was in some sort of trouble. Bertha Addison often wondered how two such different girls could have come out of the same womb, for they were as different as chalk from cheese.

She waddled off towards the door then, afraid that she might break down if she stayed any longer, leaving Maryann staring into the empty fireplace, alone with her thoughts.

She was still there an hour later when Toby knocked on the door and came in.

'So you got the position then?' he said awkwardly, taking a seat opposite her. 'And Granny tells me that you'll be off first thing. It'll be strange not to see you pottering about the court, but we'll still meet up regularly, won't we?'

She nodded. 'Yes, I get every Sunday afternoon off so I'll see you when I come back to visit Granny Addison. Or perhaps you could even come to visit me sometimes? I'm sure Mrs Carter wouldn't mind.'

'I'll be there.' He suddenly reached out and grasped

her hand, and it was almost her undoing. She had always respected Toby's wish to better himself – even admired him for it – but at that moment she just wanted him to ask her to marry him – *now*, not some time in the distant future.

'I read in the paper tonight that the cholera epidemic that started in Ireland after the potato crops failed is spreadin' like wildfire,' he said unexpectedly and Maryann stared back at him blankly. She usually loved to hear about what was happening in the world, but tonight she was too full of her own imminent future to care. Why wasn't Toby telling her that everything was going to be all right?

Sensing that he had said entirely the wrong thing, he stood up and said sheepishly, 'Well . . . good luck for tomorrow then, lass. An' I'll see you on Sunday, shall I?'

For a wonderful moment she thought he was going to kiss her but then he strode towards the door, and after smiling briefly at her was gone. She wrapped her arms around herself as she muttered to the empty room, 'Oh Mam, Dad, what's to become of me?' But the only sound was the ticking of the clock, and it came to her then that for now at least she was truly alone in the world.

The following morning, bright and early, Maryann set off for Windy Manor. She had locked the door to her home for the final time and posted the key through Granny Addison's door. The old lady would pass it on to the tallyman. *At least I won't have to see that little weasel again*, the girl consoled herself as she stepped out through the town. There were quite a few people about, making their way to their workplaces, and their wooden clogs rattled on the cobbles as some of them raised their caps to her. All she had with her was a pillowcase holding her few meagre possessions. Violet had taken the only carpet bag they possessed when she ran away but Maryann was not overly concerned. Mr

Marshall had told her at her interview that she would be supplied with new clothes.

When she finally reached the gates of Windy Manor following a brisk walk she paused to stare down at Bermuda village nestling in the valley far below her. A watery sun was burning off the mist that had settled and she stared in wonder at the cattle and the sheep contentedly grazing in the lush green fields. No wonder Benny loves working here so much, she thought to herself. The air away from the pit chimneys and the cloying cotton particles that belched out of the mills was clean and fresh, but it was the quiet that impressed her the most. In the mill, people had to shout to make themselves heard above the clatter of the machinery, but here all that could be heard was birdsong and the lowing of the cattle. She rested until she had got her breath back then turning towards the gates, she braced herself and moved on. There was no going back now.

When the house came into view Maryann paused again to admire it, since she had never really studied it closely before. The sun was shining on the many long windows and she suddenly realised just how huge the Manor was. It was so old and weathered, and blended so well into its surroundings that she could almost have believed that it had grown from the earth beneath it. A profusion of ivy and Virginia creeper had climbed to the roof as if wrapping the house to protect it, and curved stone steps ran up to two huge arched oak doors. She noticed a large brass bell, sadly tarnished, hanging at the side of them. The porch that shielded them was supported by two massive marble pillars, and in front of that was a large gravelled area where carriages could turn. It felt strange to think she would be living in such a beautiful house, if only as a servant, and Maryann briefly wondered what her mam and dad would have made of it. But then it wouldn't do to be late on

141

her first day, so she hastened unobtrusively round to the kitchen yard and there she tapped on the door. Nellie Carter opened it almost instantly with a broad smile on her face and ushered her inside.

'Ah, so you're here then, lass,' she greeted her warmly. 'You've just missed Benny. He popped in fer a cup o' tea but he's out workin' in the kitchen garden now wi' our Cissie. Never mind, you'll see him later, no doubt. Miss Florence informs me you're to eat in here wi' us or up in Miss Fleur's room.' She lowered her voice then and glanced towards the green baize door before adding, 'I should watch yerself wi' that one, if I were you. It's clear she don't really want yer here but I reckon yer her best option at present – no offence meant, o' course. From where I'm standin' it's the best thing that could have happened fer that poor little soul up there. I'm sure you'll treat her a sight better than her aunt does – but then that wouldn't take much doin', atween you an' me.' She cocked her thumb towards the ceiling as if to add emphasis to her words.

'But why does Mr Marshall allow his child to be treated like that?' Maryann asked. 'From what I saw of her, the treatment she receives borders on cruelty and I intend to make a few changes! An animal shouldn't be kept in the dark as she is.'

'Aye well, happen he don't see the half of it,' Nellie said stoically in her employer's defence. 'His head's been all over the place since Miss Amélie died, an' Miss Florence has never encouraged him to have anythin' to do with the little lass.' She stopped talking abruptly as the woman she was referring to suddenly strode into the room.

Florence eyed Maryann disdainfully up and down before saying unnecessarily, 'So you decided to come then?'

Maryann stared back at her calmly, refusing to be intimidated. 'Yes, I did.'

'When speaking to me you will address me as *miss*!' Florence snapped, but still Maryann stared steadily back at her. Her heart was thudding but she sensed that if she showed the woman she was afraid of her now, all would be lost.

'Very well . . . *miss*!'

Two spots of colour rose in Florence's cheeks and she turned about sharply in a rustle of lavender silk, saying, 'Follow me, girl. I shall show you to your room, and once you have changed you can begin your duties in Fleur's room.'

'I'm afraid I have nothing to change into,' Maryann informed her as they proceeded along the hallway. 'Mr Marshall told me that I would be supplied with some new clothes.'

'I see.' Florence wrinkled her nose as she stared at Maryann's faded dress. 'In that case the clothes you are wearing will have to do for now. You look about the same size as me so when I go into town to see my dressmaker this afternoon I shall ask her to run you up a couple of dresses and other necessities. Don't get expecting anything fancy, mind.'

'Thank you.'

They were climbing the stairs now and once again Maryann could not help but be impressed at the size of the place. Under other circumstances she supposed she could have been very happy there, yet some niggling little voice inside her warned that Florence would be out to make things as difficult as she could for her. They had certainly not taken to each other but even so Maryann was determined to carry out her role as nanny to the best of her ability.

When they eventually reached the door adjacent to Fleur's, Florence pushed it open and ushered her inside before handing her a key.

'That is the key to Miss Fleur's room,' she told her icily. 'You will find her medication on her bedside table. She should sleep until shortly before lunch when you will go to the kitchen and bring up a tray for her. Then once she has eaten you will give her another spoonful and she should sleep through until teatime. After her last meal you are to administer two spoonfuls and that should make her sleep through the night.'

'May I ask what the medicine is for?' Maryann asked boldly as she laid her few possessions on the bed.

'It is to keep her calm – not that it's any of your business,' Florence hissed. 'Just do as you are told if you wish to keep your post, and should you need to ask anything then come and find me.'

'Very well . . . *miss*.'

As Florence swept out of the room without giving her so much as another glance, Maryann stuck her tongue out at her retreating back in a most unladylike manner.

144

Chapter Seventeen

Now that she was alone, Maryann looked about the room and was pleasantly surprised. It was much bigger than the room she had shared with Violet and dear little Gertie when she was alive, back in the cottage, and there was even a wardrobe and a large chest of drawers in there. At home she had hung her clothes on a nail knocked into the back of the door – not that she had had many clothes to hang. The thought made her look down at her drab skirt, and her spirits lifted as she remembered the dresses Miss Florence was going to have made for her. She had no doubt they would be very plain but even so they were bound to be smarter and better-fitting than the rags she was wearing now. She might even be able to afford a new bonnet once she had saved some of her wages.

Crossing to the window, she flicked aside the curtain and was delighted to see that her room was at the back of the house overlooking the stable block, which meant that she might be able to glimpse Benny going about his business now and again. She would see him at mealtimes too, so that was an added bonus. At that moment she saw Cissie come out of the kitchen door and disappear into what she supposed was the laundry room, toting a huge basket of washing. Admiration warmed her. Cissie was such a nice girl and she worked so hard. But it was time to start work herself.

After hastily taking off her bonnet and her shawl, Maryann tidied her hair in the small mirror that hung on the wall above the chest of drawers and quickly put her things away. Then when she was certain that the room was tidy, she took up the key Miss Florence had given her and unlocked the door to Fleur's room. The acrid smell of urine and sweat met her and she had to swallow the bile that rose in her throat. She glanced towards the bed, but as she had expected, the only thing to be seen was a slight mound beneath the blankets. Fleur was fast asleep.

Maryann stood uncertainly for a moment but then making a decision she strode to the window and swished aside the curtains, allowing light to flood into the room. Dust motes floated in the air, and as she looked around she saw that the room was none too clean. In fact, she could have written her name in the thick dust that had settled on the furniture. *This will never do*, she told herself, and after again checking that Fleur really was fast asleep, she let herself out onto the landing, relocked the door and hurried down to the kitchen to get some cleaning things.

'Could I have a scrubbing brush, some soda crystals and a bucket of hot water and some cleaning rags?' she asked Nellie, who looked up in surprise at her entrance. 'Miss Fleur's room is really dirty, and seeing as she's asleep I may as well set to and clean it. I can't just sit by her bed fiddling my thumbs all day.'

'That's what all the rest o' the nannies the mistress has set on have ever done,' Nellie said wryly. "An' as fer her bein' asleep . . . huh! I'd rather say the poor little soul is drugged till she's near-unconscious.'

Maryann had secretly thought the same but deciding not to comment just yet she held her tongue. She would form her own opinion as the days wore on. Soon after, she made her way back upstairs laden down with cleaning materials. As luck would have it, it was as she reached the landing that Miss Florence appeared, dressed in a fine navy-blue riding habit.

'Whatever have you got there, girl?' Her voice was scathing but Maryann refused to be intimidated by her.

'I'm going to clean Miss Fleur's room while she is asleep. It doesn't look as if anyone else has bothered to do it for some time.'

Florence's lip curled in a sneer. 'Well, I suppose skivvying is more in your line of work than being a nanny,' she retorted. 'So you may as well earn your keep doing what you're used to.'

Again Maryann controlled her temper as she smiled at her sweetly and moved on, but inside she was seething. I haven't even been here a day yet and I've made an enemy already, she thought, but even so she was determined not to rise to the bait. Florence might eventually stop taunting her if she didn't respond, and as long as the woman was satisfied with her work, her position there would be safe.

Once back inside Fleur's room, she crossed to the huge sash-cord window and wrestled with it until at last she managed to open it a few inches. Fresh air poured into the room. *That's better*, she told herself, then set about the furniture with a large damp rag, attacking the dust and sending it swirling into the air. The rest of the morning flew by until just before lunchtime when Maryann looked towards the bed and became aware of two large blue eyes peeping at her above the blankets.

'Ah, Fleur, you're awake.' She smiled as she placed the scrubbing brush back in the bucket and swiped her grimy hands down the front of the large apron Nellie had lent her. 'How are you today?' She rose from her knees and began to approach the bed, but as she did so the child shrank away from her, her eyes appearing to become bigger by the second.

'I'm Maryann, and don't be afraid, I'm your new nanny.'

Still the child looked terrified so Maryann halted and pointing towards the window, said, 'I thought you might like a little fresh air. The room smells much nicer now, doesn't it?'

The child briefly glanced towards it before returning her frightened eyes to Maryann.

'It will be lunchtime soon,' Maryann chattered on, keeping a safe distance. 'And then I thought we might do some spellings. How would you like that? Or would you rather we just had a story today?' But it struck her then that whilst cleaning the room she hadn't come across a single storybook, and she was saddened as she thought back to cold winter nights when her own family had all gathered snugly around the fire while their father read to them. Pushing the painful thoughts away, she rushed on, 'Can you smell the beeswax polish? It's nice, isn't it?' Sadly, all the polish in the world would not take away the smell issuing from the bed and there was nothing she would have liked more than to bathe the child and get her into clean nightclothes. But she was wise enough to know that this would have to come when the child began to trust her – if she ever did, that was.

She could feel Fleur's eyes burning into her, although every now and again she would glance towards the window.

She was obviously used to being kept in the dark, which to Maryann's mind was cruel.

'Right then,' she said chirpily, 'I think I'll go down and get your lunch for you now. I'm sure it will be ready and I seem to recall Mrs Carter was preparing rice pudding for afters. You'll enjoy that, won't you?'

There was still no response from the bed, so gathering the cleaning things together, Maryann headed for the door, saying, 'I shall be back in a minute. Would you like to sit up ready?' Without waiting for a reply, which was not forthcoming anyway, she left the room, locking the door firmly behind her – although she wondered why she needed to. The poor child was firmly tied to the bedpost, so how far could she go?

'Good grief, lass. Look at the state of you,' Nellie laughed when she entered the kitchen. Maryann's face was smeared with dirt and wisps of hair had escaped their pins and straggled about her face.

'I suppose I must look a sight,' Maryann responded apologetically, 'and I'm afraid I've really dirtied your apron, Nellie, but the floor was filthy. God knows when it was last scrubbed.'

'Hmm, well, that's 'cos Miss Florence wouldn't let us in there an' the other nannies that have been here were too idle to wipe their own arses half o' the time. Still, things'll look up for that poor little soul now that you've arrived. Lord knows it's time someone showed her a bit o' kindness. I mean, it don't cost nowt, does it? An' she can't help bein' as she is. But here's me prattlin' on and I've got her tray ready here. Not that she usually eats much, if I'm honest. Miss Florence allus makes me send thin gruel or somethin' equally unappetisin' up to her, sayin' anythin' else'll upset her stomach, but today I've done her a nice bit o' roast lamb an' some mashed potatoes. There's a dish o' rice puddin' there an' all, bless her – she'll think it's her birthday. Will you be comin' back down here to eat wi' us? Cissie is just servin' the others in the dinin' room but ours should be ready soon.'

'Sounds lovely and yes, I will be down when I've seen to Fleur,' Maryann promised as she took up the tray. Once she was outside Fleur's bedroom door she cursed and had to lay the tray on a small table whilst she unlocked the door again. It all seemed so unnecessary, and she determined to have a word with Mr Marshall at the first opportunity. Anyone would think there was a wild animal behind the door instead of a little girl, and to Maryann's mind it was ridiculous. She wondered briefly why Miss Florence should be so hard on the child, but then hurried inside intent on getting Fleur's meal to her while it was still hot.

The child was still lying in exactly the same position as Maryann had left her in but after a little coaxing she cautiously pulled herself up in the bed and Maryann placed the tray across her lap. She then flitted away to replace the bits and pieces she had dusted so as not to distract the child, and when she turned back to her she was pleased to see that Fleur had eaten a few mouthfuls at least.

'Good girl,' Maryann praised. 'We'll soon have you nice and strong if you eat all your dinners up. Now just try and eat a little more and then you can have your pudding, eh?'

Fleur did much better than a little more and almost cleared her plate before starting on her rice pudding, which she ate in seconds.

'Well done.' Maryann smiled at her warmly but then the smile slid away as the child slipped out of bed to perch on a chamber pot that was placed at the side of it where she did her toilet.

That's my next job this afternoon after I've eaten, Maryann promised herself. She would take the chamber pot to the midden to empty it and give it a thorough clean: though she couldn't imagine why the child shouldn't be allowed to use the bathroom. Surely lying in bed all the time and being allowed no exercise whatsoever couldn't be good for her! What was her father thinking of?

Fleur was back in bed by this time and Maryann saw her glance towards the bottle of medicine resignedly. She was clearly used to taking it after each meal, but when Maryann pulled out the cork and sniffed it she almost gagged. It smelled like laudanum to her and she was horrified that this was the method Florence had used to keep the child quiet.

Making a decision, she poured out half a spoonful. She would have liked to leave it off altogether, but it was far too soon to risk incurring Miss Florence's wrath. The woman clearly didn't like her as it was.

'I think we'll halve this for now,' she told Fleur as she firmly replaced the stopper, 'on condition that you promise me you'll be a good girl and sit there quietly while I go and have my dinner. If you make a noise, your aunt will be back in and no doubt she'll make you take it. Will you do that for me?'

When the girl nodded in agreement, Maryann felt a little thrill. So she did understand what was being said to her, after all which just went to show she couldn't be as backward as her aunt had painted her to be. Maryann poured her out a glass of water from the jug at the side of the bed, then taking up the tray she said, 'I shall be back very soon, and if you've been good I'll tell you a story, eh?'

She hurried from the room and once in the kitchen she related what had happened to Nellie over their meal. Ted, Cissie and Benny had joined them and they listened intently as she said, 'I'm sure that child could be much more active if she was given the chance. Why does Florence keep her locked up like that?'

'Hmm, well, I've got me own thoughts on that,' Nellie confided, then leaning over the table she muttered, 'I reckon Miss Florence wants her out o' the way. Fleur's next in line fer inheritin' the house if anythin' should happen to the master, see? There were a right stink when the old master passed away, God rest his soul. Now there were a lovely man if ever there was one! Miss Florence reckoned he should have left the house equally between her an' the young master, but everyone knows it allus goes to the son. She weren't having it though and kicked up a right ruckus. Then o' course her fiancé jilted her just after the young master had come home from France wi' a young wife, which lowered her chances of ever gettin' her hands on it even more.'

Maryann frowned. Poor Fleur. It seemed that Miss Florence would be happy to see the back of her niece – but it wasn't going to happen if she could help it!

Chapter Eighteen

When Maryann descended the stairs early that evening to fetch Fleur's dinner, she overheard heated words coming from the dining room.

The master and his sister were in there waiting to be served, and as Maryann passed the door on her way to the kitchen she heard Florence screech, 'That slut Meadows has already begun to change the routines that I have laid down for Fleur! Why, she doesn't even know the child *or* her needs yet!'

'Now calm down, my dear,' Maryann heard Mr Marshall say. 'What has Miss Meadows done?'

'Well, she's cleaned her room from top to bottom for a start, inferring, I believe, that it wasn't to her *satisfaction* – and when I peeped in this afternoon, Fleur was awake with the curtains wide open. Meadows also informed me that she only gave Fleur half her medication after lunch without consulting me! She also had the nerve to ask me to have some toys and books delivered to Fleur's room!'

'Perhaps the lowering of her medication is only to be a trial to see how Fleur responds to it?' the man suggested in an obvious attempt to appease her. 'If it doesn't work, surely we can quite easily raise the dose again? And as for books and toys – well, Florence, all I can say is I am shocked to discover that they are not available to my daughter already. I presumed that they were in her room.'

'They were for a time,' Maryann heard Florence say defensively. 'But they got her too excited, which as you are well aware is very bad for her heart.'

'Even so, I shall instruct Ted to take some to her room this evening. I'm sure Miss Meadows will make sure that Fleur does not overly exert herself – and what harm can reading her a story do?'

'Huh! Since when does a common trollop from the courts have the medical knowledge to decide what is good for the child?' At this, Maryann flushed angrily. 'And since when have *you* become such an expert on how to take care of an infant, Wesley?'

'I'm sure Miss Florence is right, sir,' Maryann heard Miss Lord pipe up smarmily, obviously eager to stick up for her mistress. 'Miss Florence has done such an *excellent* job of caring for Miss Fleur up to now.'

Maryann nearly snorted out loud on hearing this. Not wishing to be caught eavesdropping, she hurried on to the kitchen where Nellie was spooning vegetables into silver dishes ready to be served in the dining room.

'Miss Florence and her brother are having a terrible argument,' Maryann confided to her.

'I know, pet, we can hear 'em all along the hallway. But Miss Fleur's tray is ready fer you over there – look. I've done her some nice ham, some o' me fresh crusty bread an' a big slice o' me sponge cake. There's a glass o' milk fer her on there an' all. I can make sure she gets some decent food now that you are servin' her instead o' the slop her aunt always insisted she had.'

Maryann lifted the tray and headed back to the door again.

'Be sure to come down fer yours when you've seen to the little 'un,' Nellie shouted after her and Maryann smiled and went on her way, scuttling past the dining-room door as fast as she could. The argument was obviously continuing from the amount of shouting that was going on but she didn't hang about. She had had more than enough confrontation for one day. But at least Mr Marshall had taken her side, which she supposed was something at least. Perhaps he wasn't entirely heartless, after all?

Fleur was still awake when she entered her bedroom and for the first time she didn't shrink away from Maryann as she placed the tray upon her lap.

'Look at this lovely tea Mrs Carter has made for you,' Maryann beamed. 'And later on, Mr Carter is going to bring some books and toys in for you too.'

Although she still said not a word Maryann was encouraged when the child lifted a slice of bread and bit into it without being cajoled. As the afternoon had ticked by and the effects of the medication had worn off, Fleur had become much more alert, and Maryann was now debating whether or not she should leave off the final dose too. She decided that she would – but if Fleur had a bad night she would administer a dose as normal the following night. The worst she risked was a disturbed night's sleep, after all.

Downstairs, Cissie had just returned from the dining room in a huff. 'Miss High an' Mighty wouldn't let me serve 'em again,' she told her mother. 'Miss Lord's taken over that role an' all now.'

'Well, it's one less job fer you to do,' Nellie pointed out

as she stirred a pan of thick creamy custard that would accompany the apple turnover dessert.

'They're all in a right old mood,' Cissie sighed, straightening the lace-trimmed mob cap and apron she wore when serving meals. 'Yer could cut the air in there wi' a knife.' But then she brightened instantly as Benny entered the room and tossed his cap onto a chair. The smile on her face was not missed by her grandmother, who chewed on her lip anxiously as she strained the custard into a jug.

It was more than obvious with every day that passed that Cissie had really taken to Benny, and Nellie hoped that there wasn't heartache ahead for her girl, for up to now apart from being as friendly as the day was long, the lad had shown no inclination to take their friendship any further. Still, it's early days yet, she thought, and then grinned as he said, 'By, somethin' smells nice. I'm that hungry I could eat a horse.'

'Not one of ours, I hope. You'd better not let my Ted hear you say that,' she warned teasingly and he chuckled as he took a seat at the table.

Once Cissie had taken the pudding into the dining room she changed back into her work apron and they all sat down to their meal. There was the fresh bread and ham, as well as cheese and a great pat of butter, and Benny tucked in as if he hadn't eaten for a month. He'd found that his appetite had increased since he'd been working out in the fresh air, and Nellie was pleased to see that he had filled out. She just hoped that Maryann would do the same, for the girl wasn't as far through as a line-prop.

Maryann joined them halfway through the meal, smiling as she pointed to the almost-empty plate on Fleur's tray.

'She did really well with her meal,' she informed them with satisfaction.

'I'm not surprised,' Nellie said. 'The muck Miss Florence made me send up to her was not much better than pigswill.

Happen the poor little lass thinks she's in heaven now that you're in charge.' Then, cutting some bread from the loaf, she waved the knife at her husband, telling him, 'Oh, an' that reminds me – you're to go up an' take some toys an' books out of the schoolroom and into Miss Fleur's room after we've eaten.'

She then went on to tell him how Maryann had overheard Mr Marshall agree to decreasing Fleur's medication to see how she went on, and Ted whistled through his teeth.

'Well, good fer you, lass,' he said, addressing Maryann. 'It's about time he started takin' an interest in the little soul. I swear Miss Florence wants shot of her.'

'That's exactly what I were sayin' earlier on,' Nellie agreed. 'Though I have to say I reckon you might be in fer a few bad days, pet. Miss Fleur must be addicted to that medication now an' happen she'll take it hard, coming off it.'

'Well, all I can do is see how she goes on,' Maryann agreed thoughtfully. She hadn't thought of that possibility. What if she was careful and lowered the doses slowly? Yes, that's what she'd do, she decided. Tonight she would give Fleur half a spoonful, and the same again in the morning and see how she went on.

Once the meal was finished, Maryann began to carry the dirty pots to the sink but Nellie flapped her hands at her and ushered her away.

'No, no, lass,' she objected. 'This ain't your job. Yours is to see to Miss Fleur. Me an' our Cissie'll manage this. You're a nanny now, though I have to say you don't look like one, dressed like that. No offence intended, o' course.'

Maryann smiled. 'None taken. I know exactly what you mean, Nellie. Miss Florence has ordered her dressmaker to run up two new gowns for me, so I'll soon look more respectable. But now if you're sure you don't need any help, I'll get back up to Miss Fleur.'

'Yes, an' I'll come along with yer an' get those toys an' books you've asked for,' Ted told her obligingly as he scraped his chair back from the table.

'There's just one more thing,' Maryann said then, looking towards Nellie and Cissie. 'Fleur really does need a bath. Do you think one of you might be able to help me carry some water up tomorrow and help me to bathe her?'

'I'll do that,' Nellie volunteered. 'It's a bit too much for our Cissie, trying to lug pails o' water up the stairs an' manage her crutch at the same time. We'll do it mid-mornin', eh? When I ain't took up wi' cookin'.'

And so it was arranged and Maryann went off feeling quite pleased with how her first day had gone.

That night, Maryann read a story to Fleur from one of the beautifully illustrated books Ted had fetched from the schoolroom and the child listened to her entranced, although as yet she still didn't offer to talk to her. *But then there's plenty of time*, Maryann assured herself. *She has to learn to trust me first*.

When the story was finished she drew the curtains against the cold night then after administering half a spoonful of the revolting medicine she tucked the blankets around the child, assuring her that she would be back later to check on her.

Fleur stared up at her from guarded eyes but made no effort to respond so Maryann slipped from the room and headed down to the kitchen to share a last drink with the Carter family and Benny.

As she passed the drawing-room door, which was slightly ajar, she glimpsed Miss Lord and Miss Florence sitting either side of the fireplace with crystal glasses in their hands, but she flitted quickly past, not wishing to make her presence known.

'Ah, now that's what I call good timin',' Nellie greeted

her as she entered the kitchen. She was just lifting a large pan of hot milk from the stove ready to make their evening cocoa.

'Miss Lord and Miss Florence are in the drawing room,' Maryann told Nellie, and the older woman looked baleful.

'Ain't nothin' new there. They'll be drinkin' the master's wine, no doubt.' She shook her head. 'That Miss Lord starts first thing in the mornin',' she confided. 'It's no wonder the master's wine bill is allus so high. Not that I'm allowed to see the books, mind. I just pass over a list o' what I need each week to Miss Lord an' she manages the bills. An' that's about all she does do, an' all,' she ended scathingly. Then on a lighter note she asked, 'An' how is the little 'un?'

'Going on what you said I've just given her half a dose of her medicine this evening. We'll have to see how she goes through the night but she loved the story I read to her.' Maryann felt tears gather in her eyes. 'I think it's so cruel, the way she's kept tied up like an animal.'

The family nodded in agreement and Maryann went to take a seat at the side of Benny as they sipped at their steaming mugs. Her first day at Windy Manor was almost over.

Chapter Nineteen

As Maryann sliced through the cord that bound Fleur to the bedpost she stifled a sob. The child's wrist was raw from where the cord had dug into it. Once it was off, she walked purposefully towards the fire, then paused. She longed to throw the cord into the flames, but knew that this would only cause trouble.

'That would be the best place for it,' she said angrily. 'And poor Fleur won't have to be tied up for much longer if I have my way. There need to be some drastic changes in here!'

'It's right glad I am to hear it,' Nellie agreed.

A tin bath full of warm water was ready in front of the fire and now all they had to do was persuade Fleur to get into it.

'Come on,' Maryann urged gently as she walked back towards the bed where the child was cowering against the headboard rubbing her sore wrist. 'Let's get your hair washed and make you all nice and clean, eh? Then you can have a fresh nightgown and be comfy.'

Much to her amazement, she had discovered when she opened the wardrobe that it was full of nice clothes, which made it all the more ridiculous that the child was kept in bed all the time.

Between them, Nellie and Maryann managed to coax the child from the bed but she wobbled dangerously as they led her towards the bath.

Her eyes full of compassion, Nellie glanced at Maryann over the child's head. 'She's weak from lack of exercise,' she said gravely and Maryann choked back a sob of agreement.

Gently, Maryann began to lift the nightgown over Fleur's head, and as she did so the breath caught in both of the women's throats. The little girl's frail body was covered in bruises all the colours of the rainbow.

'Who did this to you, pet?' Maryann asked, horrified, but the child simply stared back at her without saying a word.

'Eeh!' Nellie's eyes leaked with sympathetic tears as she helped the mite climb into the water and then between them they began to wash her hair.

'Whoever has done this to the poor little lass should be horse-whipped an' the master should be informed,' Nellie murmured in disgust.

'Don't worry, he *will* be,' Maryann assured her, but then they concentrated on washing her and no more was said. Already Maryann had formed the opinion that Fleur would be capable of doing much more than she was allowed to, and she intended to speak to Mr Marshall as soon as she felt the time was right – even if it meant upsetting Miss Florence again. Not that she thought he would take much notice. He didn't seem to care what happened to his own child.

Once Fleur was clean, Maryann sat her before the fire wrapped in a large towel whilst she rubbed her hair dry, then she tenderly slipped a clean nightdress over her head. The child was transformed.

'Why, just look at you! You're as pretty as a picture,' Nellie said admiringly, and was sure she saw a smile twitch at the corners of her small mouth. 'But now I'd best get back downstairs else there'll be no dinner ready for that lot an' there'll be blood on the moon. Leave the bathwater, Maryann, an' I'll help you empty it after dinner.' And with that she patted the child's shining hair affectionately and hurried from the room. She was nearly at the top of the stairs when she saw Miss Florence marching towards her with a thunderous expression on her face.

'What's this I hear about the child having a bath?' Florence barked. 'I didn't give my permission!'

'Seems to me *nobody* should need permission to be clean,' Nellie quipped caustically. 'An' from what I understand, Maryann is in charge o' the little 'un now.'

Florence's cheeks flared up and she clenched her hands into fists. Nellie had always been rude to her, safe in the knowledge that Wesley would never sack her. The Carters had been with the family for far too long. But the same did not apply to Maryann Meadows and Florence wanted her out of the house as soon as possible. She realised that she had made a grave mistake in employing her. When *she* was mistress, Florence vowed to herself there and then, she would make sure that the Carters got their marching orders too, every last one of them!

'As it happens,' Nellie went on steadily, 'when we undressed the child, we found that she's covered in bruises. I don't suppose yer can shed any light on that, can yer?'

Florence was so angry that she looked as if she was about to erupt. 'I hope you are not daring to suggest that it was me! It was probably the last nanny that caused them. I told Wesley that she wasn't suitable when we took her on. No more than the new one is actually.'

Nellie shook her head calmly. 'No, you've no need to fear

this one hurtin' the child. Young Fleur's quite taken wi' her, as it happens.'

Florence opened her mouth to reply but then promptly snapped it shut again, refusing to get into a confrontation with one of the servants.

'Go about your duties – that is what you are paid for,' she spat, and then stormed on towards Fleur's room.

Drat! she thought. Now that the bruises had been discovered she would have to tell Wesley about them. Of course, she'd lay the blame on the previous nanny but she must get to him before Nellie or the trollop did. But first she would confront her. When she flung the door open, she was astounded to see the child looking as neat as a new pin sitting in the chair by the window as Maryann collected up the soiled towels. Fleur was cuddling one of the lovely dolls Ted had brought from the schoolroom for her, but the instant she saw Florence she threw it down and raced unsteadily back to the bed where she hid beneath the blankets.

Maryann watched in amazement, and then as the implications of what this might mean sank in, she glowered at Florence, saying, 'Did you want something, *miss*?'

'Yes. I want to know just what you think you are doing by changing the girl's routine so drastically. Tie her back up at once!' Florence commanded.

Maryann continued with what she was doing for a moment as outrage surged through her veins. From Fleur's reaction it seemed that it was her aunt who had been responsible for those spiteful bruises, and at that moment there was nothing Maryann would have liked better than to inflict a few on her. Even so, she was fully aware that Miss Florence was just waiting her chance to get rid of her, so she answered politely, 'As you can see, the change of routine doesn't seem to have had an adverse effect on your niece

– quite the opposite, in fact. Even so, Miss Florence, I will replace the tie if you feel it is necessary. And now, if that is all, Miss Florence, I would appreciate being left to get on with the job I am being paid to do.'

Put well and truly in her place, Florence seemed to swell to twice her size before stamping from the room. 'And see that you lock this door after me,' she said as a parting shot. 'We don't want *that thing* running riot around the house!'

Maryann paused to stare after her. *That thing!* she had called Fleur. It made her blood run cold. She dropped the towels in a heap then approaching the bed she whispered, 'It's all right, darling. She's gone now. You are safe with me, I promise.'

Seconds passed, but then those two startlingly blue eyes appeared above the blanket. Maryann refastened the tie onto her wrist, although it broke her heart to do so.

At that moment in the townhouse in Greenwich, Daisy was leaning across Violet and gently sponging the open weals on her pert backside.

'Ouch,' Violet protested, but then as her eyes fell on Judge Williams's latest offering she didn't feel quite so bad.

'I'm afraid the judge got rather carried away with his reprimanding last night,' Daisy remarked as she wrung the bloody cloth out in a bowl of cool water. 'I can't see you working for the next couple of nights.'

'Of course I shall,' Violet answered airily. 'It'll take a bit more than a raw backside to keep me from me clients.'

Daisy shook her head. Violet never ceased to amaze her. She actually seemed to enjoy what she was doing, whereas most of the girls simply tolerated the men who pawed them, particularly the fat, older ones. It was no wonder that Violet was so popular. The men loved the way she fawned over them and she was fast becoming the most sought-after. So much so that she was even having clients in the afternoons now.

'Well, if you're quite sure.' Daisy smoothed some arnica cream into the wounds then stood to dry her hands, saying, 'There's not much more I can do for you now, but you're going to be sore for a few days, I guarantee it.'

'I can always sleep on me belly,' Violet laughed as she reached for her silk dressing gown, another present from one of her clients. Daisy left the room and crossing to the window, Violet looked down into the street below, suddenly wondering how her family were faring. She still thought of them from time to time and had even considered going back to Nuneaton to pay them a visit. But how would she explain away her fancy clothes and expensive jewellery? Her father was a kind, generous man but she knew that John Meadows would die of shame, should he discover how she was earning her living. It was then that a thought occurred to her. Even if she couldn't go and see them, she could write to them again and send them some money. She could certainly spare it and if she didn't put her address down they need be none the wiser. *Yes, that's what I'll do*, she told herself, and hurrying across to the small escritoire she dipped a pen into the inkpot and began her message. There was no time like the present and it might go a little way towards making her feel a wee bit less guilty about the way she had upped and left them all.

Benny was rubbing down one of the horses later that afternoon when he saw a figure crossing the kitchen yard. He patted Bracken and put down his brush then walking towards the visitor he asked bluntly, 'What brings you here then?'

Unaware that he had been spotted, Hugo started. 'Matter 'o fact I just thought I'd come along an' see how Maryann is settlin' in.' He stared back at Benny cockily and Benny frowned.

'For what business it is o' yours, she's settling in just fine. But I don't reckon the master will take too kindly to you just turning up whenever you feel like it. Maryann's afternoon off is on a Sunday so you'll have to wait till then to see her. *If* she wants to see you, that is,' he ended sarcastically.

Hugo squared his shoulders. He and Benny had never really got on, probably because Benny couldn't abide the way Hugo strutted about as if he owned everything in sight. Hugo's first reaction was to tell Benny to mind his own business, but then thinking better of it, he smiled smarmily before asking, 'Mistress o' the house about, is she?'

So that was it, Benny thought. 'Matter of fact I haven't seen her today,' he answered testily. 'But you're setting your sights a bit high there, Hugo. Why would Miss Florence look twice at the likes of you?'

Hugo had no time to respond, for at that very moment the person they were talking about suddenly strode across the yard in her riding habit, eyeing him suspiciously.

'Meadows, saddle Belle immediately.' When he had gone, she asked imperiously, 'And who are you? Are you aware that you are trespassing on private land?' Almost before the words had left her mouth she suddenly recognised him. This was the brother of the trollop's young man. She had seen him once in the kitchen. Pity it wasn't his brother who had called, she found herself thinking.

Hugo bowed gallantly before saying, 'Pardon me for intruding, miss. I was passing and just thought I would call in to see Benny here and find out if there were any odd jobs going.'

It was a long time since Florence had seen such open admiration in a young man's eyes and despite herself she felt herself responding to him. After all, her confidence had taken a severe knock when her fiancé had jilted her, and it was nice to know that she was still attractive to the opposite sex, even if it was only the working class. Now that she studied him more closely, Florence saw that Hugo was actually a very attractive young man. Common as clouts admittedly, but then all men – and women, for that matter – were the same when they were undressed.

Feelings that she had long since subdued began to awaken in her as she stared at him haughtily and said, 'I could have you escorted from our land, you know.'

He smiled at her saucily. 'I dare say yer could, but I hope yer won't?'

Slightly flummoxed at his boldness, Florence stuttered, 'D-did you say you were looking for odd jobs?'

Hugo leaned against the stable wall and crossed his arms. 'I did that. Why, did you have somethin' in mind?'

Her thoughts were racing. It was more than clear what was on *his* mind and shockingly, she found that she wasn't averse to the idea. At breakfast Wesley had informed her that he would be spending the day at the mill tomorrow and Benny and Ted would be going to market. She could quite easily send Elizabeth Lord off to the dressmaker's to see if her new gown and the dresses she had ordered for the nanny were finished, and then apart from the rest of the staff, who rarely ventured into the main house, she would have the place to herself.

'As it so happens, the wardrobe door in my room needs attention.' She was trying to maintain her dignity but a dull flush had crept into her cheeks. 'It – it's almost hanging off the hinges, so I suppose if you were to call at, shall we say, eleven o'clock tomorrow morning, you could perhaps repair it?'

'I reckon I could manage that.' His eyes were twinkling.

'An' happen if yer think of anythin' else that needs seein' to, I could manage that an' all.'

He's quite blatant with it, she thought, and yet suddenly she didn't care. What Wesley didn't see wouldn't hurt him, and she was entitled to some fun, wasn't she?

'Very well then. Come to the front door and I shall let you in. And make sure that you are prompt.' She swept past, the feathers in her riding hat bobbing in the breeze. She could feel his eyes burning into her back but when she emerged from the stables some minutes later, she was relieved to see that he had gone.

Benny had led the horse out behind her and now as he helped her to mount, she saw the disapproving look on his face and she was mortified to realise that he had probably heard every word that had been said.

'Stand *back*!' she snarled, then brought her riding crop sharply down on the poor beast's flanks and Belle reared with pain before setting off at a gallop that almost unseated her.

How *dare* that scum look at me like that, she thought as anger made her urge the horse to go even faster.

Benny meanwhile was watching her progress with a deep frown on his face. It looked like she was going to take her frustrations out on the animal, so God alone knew what state poor Belle would be in when that bitch brought her back. But her frustrations would only last till tomorrow, for then he had a feeling that Hugo would be giving her relief. Benny was unimpressed. And her a so-called lady and all!

Chapter Twenty

'Ah, so you did not forget,' Florence said the next morning as she opened the door to admit Hugo. She was trying her utmost to appear calm but the trembling of her hand gave her away and he grinned.

'As if I would,' he muttered as he stepped into the entrance hall. And then he forgot everything for a moment as he took in his surroundings. His eyes instantly settled on a fine figurine on a small table and mentally he was calculating its worth. It looked expensive and was surely worth a bob or two.

Bloody hell, he gulped deep in his throat. There must be hundreds of pounds' worth of knick-knacks in here alone.

'Would you err . . . care to come and look at the job?' she croaked, praying that Cissie or Nellie would not appear from the kitchen.

His thoughts snapped back to the present and with a cheeky grin he nodded and followed her up the stairs.

Once in the sanctuary of her room he glanced at the

wardrobe, which as he had expected looked perfectly fine, before slowly removing his jacket and laying it across a gilt-framed chair. Then he approached her and without a word he began to undo the row of tiny buttons up the front of her dress before gently peeling it from her shoulders. She stood quite still, her back as straight as a broom, making no objection as the dress pooled about her ankles. Next he slid her petticoats down to join them, maintaining eye-contact all the time.

He trailed his finger across her breasts before loosening her stays, and all the while she remained as still as a statue without saying a word until she stood quite naked before him.

His breathing was becoming heavier by then. She had a fine figure, there was no doubt about it, and he could feel himself responding as he then began to strip off his own clothes. When they had joined hers on the floor he leaned and took one of her nipples into his mouth and to his delight it instantly stood to attention before he led her to the bed.

He caressed her flat stomach before fondling and licking her nipples again, and then as she arched towards him his fingers lowered to the triangle of hair at the top of her legs and slid inside her, making her gasp with pleasure as he felt her wetness.

Suddenly the grand lady was gone as she began to play with him, making him moan with pleasure. They rolled together, enjoying the sensation of skin on skin until he could bear it no more, and pushing her legs apart, he thrust inside her; they moved together as one until at last they climaxed. Her legs were wrapped about his waist and she clung to him as if she might never let him go. Eventually they lay side by side and she ran her fingers through the thatch of dark hairs on his chest.

'You're very virile for a little boy,' she said languorously and he laughed.

'Here, not so much o' the little,' he retorted as he felt himself hardening again. 'An' you ain't so bad yerself.' And then he began to fondle her again and before they knew it, the time had flown past.

'I think you ought to be going now,' she said eventually after glancing at the clock above the mantelpiece. 'It would take some explaining if Wesley were to come home and see you coming out of my room.'

Leaning up on his elbow he traced his finger sensuously around her nipple, causing it to stand to attention again as he murmured, 'Fair enough. But when will I see yer again?'

'How about Saturday afternoon in the barn behind the stable block?' she suggested. It would be asking for trouble if she were to invite him into the house when her brother was at home.

'I'll be there.' He slid out of bed and she lay admiring his muscled young body as he reached to the floor to retrieve his clothes before she too got down from the bed to struggle back into her own.

They tiptoed through the house and she opened the front door as quietly as she could before whispering, 'Until Saturday then.' He might be little more than a boy in age, but Hugo had certainly proved himself to be a man in bed and she could visualise many happy hours together – until she tired of him, that was. She always did in the end.

Hugo's mind was going ten to the dozen as he strolled whistling down the drive. He recalled the numerous treasures he had spotted in the house, especially the jewellery box that stood on Florence's dressing table. No doubt it would be bulging with gems and his hands ached to get hold of them. But not yet. He would bide his time. The opportunity would come eventually and when it did he would take enough to

171

get him out of the area forever. He'd always fancied London, and if he could get his hands on her jewels and pawn them, the life he craved suddenly seemed much closer.

'You are in a remarkably good mood this evening, my dear. Have you had a good day?' Wesley enquired as they sat at dinner that evening.

Florence smiled privately before replying primly, 'Oh, rather quiet really. But Elizabeth fetched the new gown I ordered from the seamstress for me today and it's really quite stunning. It's just a shame that we don't have dinner parties any more or I'd have the chance to wear it and show it off.'

Wesley dabbed at his lips with a napkin before pushing his unfinished meal away. That damn griping pain was back in his stomach again and yet he had eaten no more than a few mouthfuls – and Miss Lord had assured him that she had chosen only the choicest beef from the silver platter for him. It was so tender that his knife had sliced through it like butter, but nowadays it seemed that anything he ate upset his stomach. Secretly he could not understand why Elizabeth Lord had taken over the serving lately. To his mind, Cissie had always done it perfectly well, but it was another of Florence's whims and he just wanted an easy life so he rarely argued with her.

Seeing that Florence was looking for a reply he said quietly, 'You know that I do not feel ready to start entertaining again yet. It would seem . . . disrespectful.'

'What nonsense! We are well out of our mourning period for Amélie now, Wesley – as you well know. I get so lonely stuck here with nothing to do – especially since that creature Meadows has taken over the care of Fleur. Why, she even had the audacity to practically accuse me of inflicting bruises on the child!'

'I'm sure she didn't mean to insinuate that,' Wesley said quickly, sensing that one of Florence's tantrums was about to erupt. Then looking over at the sideboard he said, 'Perhaps I might try a little of that soufflé, Miss Lord. But just a little.'

'Of course, sir.' Elizabeth Lord glanced towards her mistress before going to the sideboard where she turned her back on them whilst she measured a small amount of the dessert into the bowl.

'Oh, I almost forgot.' Florence's lips set in a line. 'Elizabeth also collected the dresses I ordered for Meadows. At least she won't walk about the place looking like a vagrant any more – although I do believe the saying goes, "you can't make a silk purse out of a sow's ear".'

Wesley sighed as he pushed his dish away and rose from the table. He had spent a long day at the mill, where many changes were in progress. He had listened closely to Maryann's complaints about the conditions the mill workers were forced to labour in and live in, and he fully intended to do something to improve things for them. Her words had made him realise that he had been unfair to his workers and had ignored his duties for too long. But now the last thing he wanted was to sit and listen to his sister in one of her contrary moods.

'If you will excuse me,' he said and strode from the room without another word.

When he had gone, Florence looked questioningly towards Miss Lord, and when the woman gave a slight nod she said sweetly, 'Perhaps you wouldn't mind taking the dresses up to her room, Elizabeth. I have a headache coming on so I might go and lie down for a while.'

'Of course,' the woman simpered. 'I have to work on the accounts this evening anyway.'

Some minutes later, she carried the dresses up the stairs.

After tapping on Maryann's bedroom door and finding that she wasn't there, she continued to Fleur's room. She tapped again, and when Maryann opened the door, the housekeeper was astounded to see Fleur contentedly sitting in front of the fire looking at the pictures in a beautifully illustrated book. Her hair was shining in the firelight and she was smiling; in fact, she was shocked to see that the child looked almost pretty.

'Miss Florence asked me to bring these up to you,' she said coldly. 'I'm afraid if they need any alterations you will have to do them yourself.'

Maryann's face lit up with pleasure as she took them and she thanked the woman profusely. She held up the gowns to admire them. They were very plain and simple, and identical admittedly, but even so she had never owned garments of this quality before in her whole life. The material was a very soft dove grey wool with little pearl buttons reaching from the waist to the chin, where the dresses had been trimmed with a pretty lace collar. The sleeves and the skirt were full, and suddenly Maryann could hardly wait to try one of them on. There was also a bag which she saw contained a number of petticoats and undergarments too, as well as a pair of soft leather house shoes and a pair of button-up boots for outdoors. Florence had clearly had to guess her size, but when Maryann slipped her feet into them she found that they fitted like gloves.

'Oh, just look at all these wonderful new clothes, Fleur!' she exclaimed with delight as she waltzed around the room with one of the dresses held out in front of her.

Fleur looked up from her book, and seeing the obvious pleasure on Maryann's face she smiled and stuttered, 'P-pretty.'

Maryann stopped dead in her tracks and gazed towards the child in shock. This was the first word that Fleur had uttered since she had been there, and she sensed that this was a major step forward.

'Yes – yes, they *are* pretty and I shall wear one of them tomorrow,' she told her. The child smiled again before turning her attention back to the book and suddenly Maryann was very happy to be there, even if it did mean having to suffer Miss Florence's spite.

Later that evening when Fleur was tucked up in bed fast asleep, Benny carried the tin bath upstairs for her. Maryann lugged some buckets of water up to her room and bathed herself from head to foot, as well as giving her hair a thorough wash too. She then sat in front of the fire and when her hair was dry she plaited it and twisted it into a neat bun at the nape of her neck, securing it with pins. Then it was time to try on her new clothes, and as she slipped into them she even forgot the heartaches of the last few months for a while as she revelled in the feel of the soft cotton petticoats against her skin. Finally she slipped on the house shoes and then demurely made her way down to the kitchen, feeling like the bee's knees.

'What do you think?' she asked as she entered the kitchen and gave them a twirl. Benny was sat at the table reading with Cissie. Ted was sitting at the side of the fire smoking his pipe, and Nellie was darning some stockings. Her mouth dropped open.

'Well, I'll be!' she uttered. 'Yer look more of a lady than Miss Florence, so yer do, pet.'

'Huh, she ain't no lady,' Benny muttered, but thankfully no one heard him. They were too intent on staring at Maryann.

'I can't believe how well everything fits,' Maryann chuckled and Nellie was touched. It was nice to see the lass looking so happy for a change.

'You look really beautiful,' Cissie whispered enviously,

and as Benny looked across at her he wished he could buy her a new dress too. She certainly deserved one, the way she worked. Perhaps he could save up and get her one made for Christmas? He was sure Maryann would help him with this.

'Well, seein' as we're all in such a good mood, I reckon we should have a drink, don't you, Ted? Cissie, go an' get that jug of ale out o' the pantry fer the men an' I reckon I've got a drop o' sherry tucked away in the dresser somewhere that were left over from Christmas.' Nellie hurried across to the dresser and began to rifle about in the cupboard beneath it as Cissie limped off to do as she was told, and soon they each had a drink in their hand. Maryann had never tasted alcohol before and eyed the ruby liquid apprehensively, but Nellie told her in a cheery voice, 'Go on, lass. Just try it. That drop won't hurt yer. It'll warm yer cockles.'

And so she did, and to her surprise she found that she quite liked it, although she refused a second glass in case Fleur might need her in the night. The first one had made her feel quite light-headed.

As she snuggled down in bed that night after checking that Fleur was still fast asleep, Maryann felt more positive than she had done in some time. More than ever now she realised how fortunate she and Benny had been to find a position here at Windy Manor. There was nothing she could do about the loss of her parents, and she knew that they had left a hole in her heart that no one else would ever be able to fill. Of course, she was still worried about Violet and prayed daily that she would turn up again like a bad penny, but it would soon be Sunday and she would see Toby . . . and the thought made her glow with pleasure.

On Friday morning Florence entered the kitchen just as Benny was about to start work to tell him, 'Have the carriage brought round to the front as soon as possible, Meadows. Miss Lord is going to Bedworth on an errand for me. And saddle Belle too. I'm going for a gallop.' There was no please or thank you but then the staff never expected civilities from the mistress.

'Right away, miss.' Benny nodded and once she had left the room Nellie looked thoughtful.

'I wonder what it is she's sendin' her to Bedworth for? Ted's been takin' her every few weeks fer the last few months now. Seems strange that the miss can't go herself. An' Miss Lord allus made Ted wait fer her while she went off to do whatever it is she's goin' for.'

Benny shrugged. It was no business of his and he was always glad of a chance to drive the carriage. The horses didn't get near enough exercise to his mind so the outing would do them good.

He and Maryann rose from the table at the same time and again Benny was struck at the change in his sister's appearance. In her smart dress and with her shining hair coiled neatly at the nape of her neck he reckoned she looked every inch the lady.

'See you all later,' he called cheerfully across his shoulder.

It was then that an idea occurred to Maryann. If both Miss Lord and Miss Florence were going to be out, it would be the ideal opportunity to speak to Mr Marshall about Fleur.

She thought of Fleur, who was sitting upstairs in bed. As the effects of the medicine she had been given early that morning had worn off she appeared brighter, and now more than ever Maryann was convinced that the child might be capable of so much more. Coming to a decision she asked Cissie, 'When Miss Florence and Miss Lord have gone out, would you mind staying with Fleur if I pop down and have a word with the master?'

'Of course I wouldn't mind,' Cissie answered good-naturedly.

'And would you also mind going in and asking him if he would just give me a few moments of his time?' she implored Nellie.

The kindly woman was busily baking scones, one of the master's favourites, for his afternoon tea, but she nodded and after removing her apron and wiping her hands she crossed to the window to watch Benny's progress. When she was quite sure that both the women had gone she then said, 'Wait there a minute, pet. I reckon he'll be in his library.'

Maryann impatiently strummed her fingers on the table but Nellie was back in no time to tell her, 'He is in the library paintin', but he says yer to go straight in.'

Maryann smiled her thanks at her then swept along the hallway feeling much more confident than she might have done had Miss Florence been at home.

After knocking lightly on the door she entered the library intent on what she wanted to say, but then words failed her as her eyes were drawn to a painting of a young woman that hung above the marble fireplace. The woman was so beautiful that she took Maryann's breath away and she was unaware of the master who had come to stand beside her in his painting smock.

The woman's blonde hair was piled high on her head and teased into ringlets that framed her delicate face, and her blue eyes were exactly the same colour as Fleur's. There was an ethereal quality about her that made it difficult for Maryann to look away. She was dressed in a low-cut blue silk ballgown that showed off her slim shoulders to perfection. About her neck was an exquisite diamond and sapphire necklace that exactly matched the colour of her eyes.

Wesley, meanwhile, was struggling to come to terms with

178

Maryann's new look. He barely recognised her! Her hair was quite magnificent and he imagined trying to capture the colour of it on canvas. She was like a beautiful butterfly that had just emerged from a chrysalis.

But then, pulling himself together, he informed her, 'That is Amélie, my late wife. I painted that shortly after we were married.'

His words caused Maryann to blush and stammer, 'I – I'm so sorry, sir. I didn't mean to stare, but she's so . . .'

'Beautiful?' He nodded as Maryann struggled to find words. 'Yes, she was, but sadly she was very fragile and . . . Anyway, I'm sure you didn't come here to talk to me about my late wife, Miss Meadows. How may I help you?'

Pulling her eyes away from the portrait with a great effort she said, 'Actually I wanted to speak to you about Fleur.'

'Why? Is she being difficult?'

'Oh no, sir, quite the opposite,' she hastened to assure him. 'In fact, so much so that I wondered if you would give me permission to lower her medication even further and untie her.'

'Untie her?' The man frowned. 'But I thought Florence only tied her wrist at night so that she wouldn't wander about and harm herself.'

'No, sir. She has been kept in a darkened room and tied at all times, and the level of medication she was on was so high that it ensured she only woke to eat. She is getting no exercise whatsoever – and surely that can't be good for a child?'

'But my sister informed me that she keeps her that way so as not to overtax her. She has a heart condition, as we told you when you applied for the post.'

'Even so, I still feel that a little exercise and fresh air would be beneficial to her, so do I have your permission to reduce the dose further as a temporary measure to see how she responds to it? She appears to be much more alert since I have halved it.'

He hesitated, tapping the brush he was holding in the palm of his hand, and as she saw his lips set into a thin line her confidence wavered. Had she overstepped the mark too soon? After all, she hadn't been there that long. Or could it be that he genuinely had not been aware of the atrocious conditions in which Fleur had been kept?

But then he said, 'Very well. You may certainly untie her, but I'm not sure about lowering her medication. Perhaps we could get the doctor's opinion on that? I shall ask him to call at his earliest convenience.'

Maryann nodded her agreement, delighted with his reaction.

'And was there anything else, Miss Meadows?'

'Just one more thing, sir. I was wondering if, when Fleur has built her strength up a little, I might be allowed to take her for little strolls about the garden?'

'Again I think we might ask the doctor's opinion about that,' he answered, and satisfied, Maryann bobbed her knee and headed for the door.

As she left the room Wesley Marshall found himself thinking about her. She was just a slip of a girl but she obviously wasn't afraid to speak out for what she considered to be right, as she had proved to him yet again. Even so, her requests had sounded alarm bells in his mind. He had always left the hiring and the firing of Fleur's nannies entirely in his sister's hands, and when there was no nanny present Florence herself had seen to the child's needs. Now he was forced to question the care of his child. Admittedly he had been grateful to leave it to someone else. He had found it too hard to look at the little girl, for every time he did so, he was reminded of the look of horror on his wife's face the night Fleur had been born. It had been

180

immediately apparent that something was not quite right with her, and from that moment on Amélie had steadfastly refused to so much as look at her. It had been the beginning of his wife's downfall, for from that moment on her nerves had deteriorated and she had locked herself away from everyone but himself.

Is that why I have never really played any part in the child's life? he questioned himself. It was the first time he had allowed himself to admit it, and guilt sharp as a knife stabbed at his heart. But at least he could make things a little easier for her now, even if it would mean a terrible confrontation with Florence. Crossing to his easel, he stared unseeingly at the half-finished canvas. Here was Maryann, a virtual stranger, going against all the rules his sister had laid down for his daughter, and not afraid to ask for what she wanted. More surprising still was the fact that Fleur seemed happier than she had ever been under Florence's strict regime. In fact, now that he came to think about it, he could not recall hearing the child cry once since Maryann had been caring for her. The only problem he had with her latest request was that, should he allow Fleur to come downstairs, he would be forced to see her – and this was always painful for him. But now he acknowledged that things must change and he must start to put his own feelings aside.

Chapter Twenty-One

'So did yer get to see where Miss Lord nipped off to?' Nellie asked nosily when Benny returned later that morning.

'I'm afraid not, Nellie. She made me stop on the edge of the Market Square and nipped off like a whippet, and I just had to sit there and wait for her to come back, so I have no idea where she went. Then soon as we got back, the master asked me to go straight out again to ask the doctor in Swan Lane if he'd call at his earliest convenience to see Miss Fleur. The doctor's wife promised that he'd be here later this afternoon. She's not ill, is she?'

'Far from it. In fact from what Maryann says, the child is doing really well. So much so, that your sister feels it would do her good to get outside now. That's why the master wanted the doctor to check that she's well enough before he gives permission.'

'I see.' Benny tapped his lip thoughtfully. 'Don't Miss Fleur's grandparents ever come to see her?'

Nellie snorted. 'Huh! There's fat chance o' that happenin'.

Mr Marshall's parents have passed away, as yer know. When the mistress, Miss Amélie that is, died, her parents did come over from France for the funeral but when they saw that Fleur was . . . well, as she is, they couldn't get away quickly enough, an' far as I know, they ain't been heard of since. That left her to the tender mercies o' Miss Florence an' more nannies than I care to remember. Mr Marshall brought in a doctor from London once to examine her, an' he said she was a . . . Now what was it he called her?' She stared off into space as she chewed on her lip for a moment before saying, 'Ah – a Mongole, or somethin' like that, I believe it was. It's a medical condition by all accounts and all the people that are born with it have the heads that look slightly too big for their body and the slanty eyes like Fleur's. Miss Florence prefers to refer to the child as an imbecile, but if what Maryann is sayin' is right, she's far from one o' them. She's already got her countin' up to five in a matter o' days, so what could she be capable of, eh? I reckon Miss Florence has just kept her drugged up for peace an' quiet.'

'Hmm, it sounds like you could be right,' Benny agreed. But then he had a list of chores as long as his arm waiting for him and so he rose quickly and headed for the door, saying, 'I'll see you later, Nellie.'

Once outside, he paused to do his coat up. There was a nip in the air and he thought he could smell autumn fast approaching. The first job on his list was cleaning out the stables, so he headed for the barn. He was loading some clean hay into a barrow with a pitchfork when he heard a muted sound from the hayloft above him and paused in his task. It had sounded like someone giggling, a woman if he wasn't very much mistaken. The sound came again after a few seconds and he knew then that he had not imagined it. But who could it be? Nellie was in the kitchen, Maryann was upstairs with Miss Fleur and he had passed Cissie busily feeding clean sheets through the mangle in the washhouse on his way to the barn.

Glancing up, he caught a flash of blue silk and his face hardened. He had seen Miss Florence in a dress that colour that very morning, but who could she have up there with her? Deciding that what he didn't know couldn't hurt him, he hastily finished filling the barrow and wheeled it away. He then led the horses into the paddock behind the stables to graze and the next hour was spent emptying the stalls and swilling them out. Then whilst they were drying he filled another barrow with the dirty straw and headed for the huge compost heap at the side of the barn to dump it. It was a dirty smelly job, yet Benny didn't mind. And he always got a little thrill when he led the horses back into their clean stalls.

After emptying the first barrow he paused to wipe the sweat from his brow and as he did so he saw a figure emerge from the barn. It was Miss Florence, and after she had looked furtively first one way then another to check that there was no one about, she lifted her skirts – showing a very shapely pair of ankles – and slipped across to the Manor. Thankfully, she had not seen him so he stood quite still, waiting to see who else might emerge. Within minutes Hugo appeared, picking the loose straw from his trousers. As he rounded the corner of the barn and spotted Benny, he halted abruptly. For a moment the two men stared at each other but then Hugo grinned.

'Now that were what yer call a nice roll in the hay,' he smirked shamelessly. 'A right hot-arsed little bugger she is, that mistress o' yours, Benny. Yer should try 'er out sometime. But not till I've 'ad me fill of 'er, eh?'

As Benny's lip curled with disgust, Hugo laughed. 'What's up? Did yer think the gentry were above that sort o' thing? Well, let me enlighten yer, she's better than most

184

o' the doxies I've paid for in the past, an' she's grateful fer it an' all.' Then shoving his hands deep into his pockets he sauntered away whistling merrily without a care in the world.

Later that afternoon, after placing his stethoscope on Fleur's chest and listening carefully, Dr Piper straightened and smiled at Maryann.

'Her heart is certainly no worse than the last time I examined her, so I see no reason why a gentle walk should do her any harm,' he said. 'But mind you don't overtax her. Heart problems in people with Fleur's medical condition are common, so easy does it, eh, young lady?'

'Oh, I promise I won't let her overdo it, Doctor,' Maryann assured him. Then drawing him away from the bed she lowered her voice to ask, 'How bad is her heart, sir?'

'Hmm, now that's a difficult question.' Looking towards the bed he stroked his chin. 'It's very hard to say but what I should warn you is that many people with this disability do not reach adulthood. Of course, with tender care, Fleur could be an exception to the rule. On the other hand, she could go just like that.' He clicked his fingers, making Maryann jump, before placing his stethoscope back in his bag and snapping it shut. 'But all in all, I have to say she looks better than I have seen her for a long time. Your care of her must be exemplary, my dear, and you are to be commended.'

Maryann blushed at the praise. 'And you are quite happy with me reducing her doses of medication?'

'Absolutely. I only prescribed the medication because Miss Florence was finding her difficult to cope with. And now I must be off to see my next patient, but I shall have a word with Mr Marshall on my way out and try to put his mind at rest. Goodbye, my dear.'

'Goodbye, sir, and thank you.'

Maryann hurried across to the bed and kissed Fleur's soft cheek soundly once the doctor had left, greatly reassured that Fleur would suffer no ill effects from the treatment she was receiving. Already she was growing very fond of the little girl and now, more than ever, she was determined to do right by her despite the resistance from her aunt.

Downstairs, Gideon Piper studied the landscape Wesley Marshall was painting before saying gravely, 'Are you aware, Wesley, that Fleur has quite severe bruising to her body? Admittedly these blows must have been inflicted some time ago as the bruises are fading now. Who could have done this to her?'

Wesley said gravely, 'Yes, I was aware of them. Florence told me about them a few days ago and we can only assume that her last nanny did it.'

'Hmm, well, thankfully the girl you have employed doesn't seem the sort to let it happen again. I was very impressed with her. She seems quite devoted to Fleur.' He then went on, 'The other concern I have is the dosage of medicine she was on before the new nanny reduced it. Good Lord, Wesley, the child was on enough to knock a racehorse out! Whoever made her take so much?'

'I'm afraid that was Florence,' Wesley said. 'She thought it would be in Fleur's interest to keep her calm.'

'Keep her calm! Why, the dose she was on could have killed her! In fact, it would have done before very much longer,' the doctor said angrily. Then in a softer tone: 'She's not a monster, you know, Wesley. She's just a little girl with a disability, and if you allowed yourself to spend a little time with her, you might actually find you enjoyed it.'

He knew how hard it had been for the man to lose his wife, but all the same he hated to see him turning into a semi-recluse. As far as he was concerned, it was time

Wesley started living again. And as for that sister of his . . . had she been there, Dr Piper would have told her that she was very lucky indeed to still have a niece after the amount of medicine she had been tipping down the child's throat. Thank goodness the new nanny had arrived when she had, otherwise it might have been another corpse he had been coming to examine today.

He could still clearly remember the day he had been called to the house following Amélie's accident – if it had been an accident. They said she had fallen from the window, and by the time he got there, all he could do was sign the death certificate. She must have died the second her body hit the ground if the horrific injuries she had sustained were anything to go by. And yet strangely, he had felt no surprise. Amélie had always been of a very nervy disposition. From that day forward, Wesley had shut himself away, ignoring his daughter and rarely venturing further than his factories occasionally. To Dr Piper's mind it wasn't healthy but now he asked himself, what could he do? He could only help those who were prepared to help themselves.

Sighing heavily, he buttoned his greatcoat and lifted his bag, then gently placing his hand on Wesley's arm he said softly, 'Think about what I have said, man. I have served you, and your mother and father before you, for many years, and it hurts me to see you so lonely and unhappy. Good day.'

Once the doctor had left the room, Wesley stared unseeingly at the canvas as guilt again settled about him like a cloak. The doctor was right: he had not done right by his daughter and yet it wasn't her fault she had been born as she had. She was the innocent victim in this whole sorry mess.

Lowering his head into his hands, he began to weep. 'Oh Amélie, I'm so sorry!' he sobbed to the empty room, and the secret he was forced to keep pressed down on him like a lead weight.

*

On Sunday afternoon, while Cissie looked after Fleur, Maryann hurried to her room to wash her hands and face and brush her hair. She then wrapped her warm old shawl about her shoulders and raced downstairs, intent on not wasting a single moment of her afternoon off. She had reached the hallway and was heading for the kitchen when Mr Marshall came out of the library.

Smiling at her kindly, he asked, 'Off into Nuneaton, are you, Miss Meadows?'

She nodded, her face radiant, and again he found it hard to take his eyes off her. She looked very smart in her new dress, but it was a shame about the old shawl she had draped about her shoulders and her straw bonnet. They looked quite out of place now with the rest of her neat clothes.

'You might find you need a coat on,' he suggested. 'I'm afraid it's turned very cold and drizzly out.'

'Oh, I shall be fine in this, thank you, sir.'

When she lowered her eyes it suddenly occurred to him that the shawl was probably the only outer garment she owned, and he cursed himself silently for embarrassing her.

'Very well. Off you go, and do have a good afternoon.'

She bobbed a curtsy and he stared from the window. His first thought was to ask Florence to choose a suitable cape and bonnet for her but he dismissed that idea almost instantly. Florence had made it abundantly clear that she had no time for Maryann whatsoever, so she would probably choose something totally unsuitable, out of spite. This left him with a problem. It would not be fitting for him to be seen buying clothes for his daughter's nanny. That would set the gossip-mongers' tongues wagging good and proper – and then it came to him and without stopping to think he raced up the stairs.

It was Cissie herself who opened the door to Fleur's room to him, and he suddenly felt foolish and wondered if this had been such a good idea, after all.

'Why, hello, sir.' He could see the surprise in her eyes as she held the door wide and invited him in, and he was fully aware that he would appear even more foolish if he didn't go in now.

Just inside the doorway he paused and looked around in astonishment. The room smelled pleasantly of beeswax polish, and a cheery fire was burning in the grate. Fleur was sitting cross-legged on the hearthrug nursing her dolly, and at the sight of him her face broke into a smile that made his heart turn over. Her eyes and hair were exactly the same colour as her late mother's, but there any similarity ended. Even so he noted that she was wearing one of the pretty dresses he had had sent from London for her, and there was a blue ribbon in her shining blonde hair that exactly matched the colour of her eyes.

Quickly turning his attention back to Cissie, he blurted out, 'Cissie, I was wondering if you would do a great favour for me.'

'Why, sir, o' course I will if I'm able to. What is it?'

He tugged at the collar of his shirt, clearly uncomfortable, as he rushed on, 'I just saw Miss Meadows leave the house and I realised that although I have supplied her with house clothes I have not provided her with suitable outer garments. So . . . I was wondering, if next time you went into the market with young Benny, you might choose her a bonnet and cape for me. It wouldn't do for the nanny of my daughter to be seen walking about in an old shawl, and I thought you might have some idea of what she might like and what would be suitable?'

Cissie's smile broadened as she told him, 'I'd be delighted to help sir, an' I know just the shop to go to get 'em. They

189

have some lovely things in there an' I often have a peep in when I go into the market.'

'Excellent.' Looking relieved, he withdrew his wallet and counted out some coins to her. The girl stared down at the three golden guineas in her hand.

'And I would be very pleased if whilst you are choosing a cape and a bonnet for Miss Meadows, you might purchase cloth for a suitable gown for yourself too,' Wesley went on. 'You and your family work very hard for me and I'd like to show my appreciation.'

'Oh, sir, I couldn't,' she breathed, although in her mind's eye she could picture the sprigged cotton material she had been admiring in the shop the week before. She and her gran could make it up in no time.

'I will be most disappointed if you don't,' he told her sternly. 'But will you have enough money there?'

'Lordy, more than enough an' I'll bring yer some change, sir,' Cissie breathed.

'I'm not worried about that,' he said dismissively, very aware that Fleur was now ambling towards them. And then she was there in front of him, clutching Cissie's hand and looking up at him from those curious blue eyes and making his heart flutter.

He forced a smile whilst backing towards the door and then without another word he was gone, leaving Cissie to scratch her head in bewilderment.

Chapter Twenty-Two

'Ah, so here you are then, pet. An' looking right bonny an' all. Eeh, I hardly recognised yer all done up in yer fancy togs. But I thought Toby were comin' up to the Manor fer tea today?'

'He is,' Maryann said breathlessly as she flew into Granny Addison's outstretched arms. 'But I thought if I came to meet him, we could walk back together and then I'd get to see you too. He hasn't already left, has he? I've run all the way.'

'Well, I ain't seen him go by the winder,' the woman answered as she smoothed the damp curls that had escaped their clips from Maryann's forehead. 'Why don't yer just go an' let him know yer 'ere before yer both set off back while I make yer a nice hot drink, eh? Then yer can tell me 'ow yer settlin' in.'

Maryann hurried away to do as she was told and by the time she came back, Granny was straining tea into two heavy mugs.

'Toby will be here in a minute,' the girl informed her as she took a seat at the oak table, and then she went on to tell the old lady all about her first days at Windy Manor.

'I don't like the sound o' that Miss Florence,' Granny said when she'd done. 'Yer'd best watch yer back wi' that one. It sounds like she's out to get rid o' yer. Oh, an' by the way, I've somethin' 'ere fer yer. It came yesterday.' She pottered across to the mantelpiece and returned with an envelope addressed to Maryann's father. When the girl looked at the handwriting, she paled. It was from Violet, but of course she could have no way of knowing that their father had passed away, nor that they no longer lived in the cottage.

'The woman who lives in your old place now passed it on to me,' Granny said, then tutted. 'Ten kids she's got an' all crammed into that little place. I tell yer, the yard 'as turned into a children's playground an' they're poor as church mice by the look of it. Still, they seem pleasant enough. But go on, open the letter. Let's see what she has to say for 'erself.'

Maryann carefully slit the envelope with her thumb, noting the quality of it before extracting a single sheet of paper,

Dear Dad,
I hope this letter finds you, Maryann and Benny all well. I just wanted to let you know that I've now settled very well into my position in London and I am enjoying it very much. It's so different living in a city to a small town but I love the hustle and bustle. I have enclosed a small amount of money for you that I hope will be useful. I do think of you all and one of these days I shall come home for a visit.

In the meantime I remain your affectionate daughter and sister,

Violet xxx

Maryann delved back into the envelope then gasped with shock when she withdrew two banknotes.

'There's *two pounds* here,' she croaked as she looked up at Granny Addison. 'But however could she have earned this much? And why has she still not given us an address or told us what her job is?'

The woman had her own thoughts on that, but deciding to keep them to herself for now she merely said, 'Happen she will tell yer when she feels ready to, but at least yer know now that she's all right. An' the money will certainly come in 'andy.'

'I don't want her money,' Maryann said as tears flooded into her eyes. 'I'd much rather know where she is and what she's doing. I can't even let her know about our father.'

'Then why don't yer just put it away safe fer a rainy day, eh? An' while yer at it, yer can add this to it an' all.' She picked up a jar at the side of the deep stone sink then placed it in Maryann's hand, telling her, 'There's just over a pound there. I sold as much of yer furniture an' beddin' as I could, an' I left the rest fer the new tenant, as yer said. It ain't much, I know, but every little 'elps, don't it, lass?'

'Oh, Granny!' Maryann was deeply touched at the woman's kindness yet reluctant to take the money. 'Why don't you keep that for all the help you've given to our family over the years?'

'I'll do no such bloody thing!' Granny retorted indignantly. 'Just put it away an' we'll say no more about it.'

Maryann shook her head. Here she was with over three pounds when only a few weeks before she had been struggling to find enough money for food and rent. All the money in the world couldn't make up for the loss of her family, of course. Even so, she was grateful and she tucked the letter and the money deep into her pocket. Toby came in shortly after, and while he was talking to Granny, she sneaked ten shilling coins back out and slipped them behind the teapot. She hoped Granny and Archie would treat themselves to something nice with it.

She left soon after, with promises to come back again soon, and as she and Toby strolled along she told him about Violet's letter.

'Well, at least you know she's well now and doing all right by the sounds of it,' he pointed out. It appeared that Violet had left of her own free will, he said, and all Maryann could do now was wait until her sister was ready to forward an address on to her.

Toby pulled Maryann's arm through his and they strolled along, soon passing the workhouse on the Bullring. Old people who were past working for their keep were sitting outside on chairs, their eyes vacant and staring, and Maryann shuddered. One old man was coughing blood into a piece of ragged huckaback whilst another sat there with half of his nose eaten away. *There but for the grace of God*, Maryann found herself thinking, but then her spirits rose again as Toby spoke.

'I checked me stash under the mattress the other night an' I reckon in another year or so I'll have saved enough to buy me own cottage outside o' the town.' He squeezed her hand and she knew what he was inferring with no words being said. 'An' our Hugo's got his tail up good an' proper at the moment an' all,' Toby went on. 'I reckon there's a new lass caught his eye.' He chuckled. There were times when he could have cheerfully strangled his irresponsible younger brother, but at the end of the day he loved him just the same and would have walked through fire for him.

Maryann felt a surge of relief. If Hugo had his eye on someone else he would leave her alone, which was something to be grateful for. Then she felt Toby stiffen as he pointed ahead.

'Wasn't that our Hugo I just saw turnin' off towards the Blue Lagoon?'

Maryann followed his finger. The Blue Lagoon was a disused quarry that was now full of crystal-clear water. The local people liked to swim there in the summer, but it was highly unlikely that anyone would be wanting to swim in it in this weather.

'I didn't see anyone,' she said.

Toby shrugged. 'I thought I spotted his coat. Brand new it is, though where he got the money for it, God knows.'

They talked of this and that until the high walls surrounding the Manor came into view, and it was then that Toby said thoughtfully, 'I wonder why it's called Windy Manor?'

'I wondered the same thing, but according to Nellie it was named that because it's high on the hill so even on the calmest of days it still catches the breeze.'

As they walked through the gates he then commented, 'I must say the grounds are looking a lot better kept since your Benny started here.'

'The inside is too, because when Fleur is having her naps I help Cissie about the house. I don't have to, of course, but I don't like to sit about and be idle. I actually took her for a stroll in the rose garden yesterday and her little face was a picture. She's been cooped up inside for so long that I think it was a rare treat for her.'

Hearing the affection in her voice for the child she was caring for gave him a warm glow inside. Maryann would make a wonderful wife and mother when the time was right, and now more than ever he could hardly wait for that time to come.

They had just turned into the stableyard when Miss Florence came towards them leading her horse by its reins, but instead of glowering at Maryann she simpered prettily at Toby.

'Good afternoon. Come to visit our little nanny, have you?' she asked sweetly.

'Aye, I have,' Toby said tartly. The woman could be as nice as she liked, but after hearing how she treated his Maryann when he wasn't present he had no time for her. Benny came up behind her then and after he had helped her up into the saddle she galloped away.

'Poor bloody horse,' Benny muttered. 'I wonder where she's off to in such a hurry?'

'Perhaps she's gone to meet her secret lover?' Maryann suggested with a grin.

Well, if she is I've got a good idea who it will be, Benny thought, but he didn't say anything. Instead they followed him into the kitchen where Nellie was just spreading jam and cream over a batch of scones fresh from the oven.

Ted was sitting at the side of a roaring fire sucking contentedly on his pipe and Cissie was making tea while Fleur had her afternoon nap. The next hours passed pleasantly as they spoke of this and that, but all too soon it was time for Toby to leave.

'It seems such a long wait until next Sunday,' Maryann said regretfully. She had walked with him to the gates, but now it was time for her to get back to Fleur.

'It'll be here afore yer know it.' He leaned forward and gave her a chaste kiss on the cheek and just for a moment Maryann felt annoyed. This unspoken agreement they had was all well and good, but just sometimes she wished that Toby could forget his principles and give her a proper passionate kiss.

She watched him swing merrily away before turning and hurrying back to the house.

'The master has barely touched his meal again,' Nellie lamented that evening as she and Cissie cleared the dinner dishes from the dining room. 'I reckon it's high time he went to see the doctor. He looks as if a penn'orth o' God help him would do him good.'

Ted chuckled. 'I reckon you just like to have sommat to fret about, woman,' he teased, but Nellie was genuinely worried all the same. This stomach complaint of his was lasting just a little too long to her way of thinking.

When Cissie and Benny returned from the market the following Wednesday, Cissie hurried excitedly into the library to show the master her purchases. Whatever painting he was working on he obviously didn't want her to see, for he hurriedly turned the easel away the instant she entered the room.

'I got what you asked for, sir,' Cissie told him, and she drew a fine navy-blue cape with a paler blue lining from the largest parcel. It had a hood and looked warm and practical as well as being very attractive.

'I went for a thicker one seein' as it's turned so cold,' she explained. And when he smiled approvingly, she then produced a bonnet in the same colour. Its brim was trimmed with ribbon, and she could hardly contain her excitement as she showed it off to him.

'And do you think Miss Meadows will be pleased with your choice?'

'Oh yes, sir. I reckon she'll be over the moon with 'em,' Cissie said happily.

He looked at her mock-sternly then. 'And I hope you also treated yourself to the material for a new gown?'

'Yes, sir, I did – an' it's really lovely. Thank you so much. I have some change for you here.' She laid the money carefully on a small table but he barely glanced at it.

'Thank you, Cissie. Now can I trust you to see that Miss Meadows gets them?'

'Oh yes, sir. I'll take 'em up to her right away.' Cissie curtsied as best she could with a crutch stuck beneath her arm, then snatching up the purchases, she hobbled from the room at a rare old pace. She was longing to see Maryann's face when she saw the items.

Wesley, in turn, was surprised to realise that he cared what she thought of them too. Irritably he turned the easel back and gazed at the portrait he was painting. It was Maryann. He had spotted her walking in the garden one day with Fleur scampering ahead of her. The sun had been turning her hair to burnished copper and he had been unable to get the image out of his mind.

Pull yourself together man, he scolded himself. *She's just a girl and your daughter's nanny into the bargain*. Even so, the image remained and taking up his brush he began to work on the portrait again.

Chapter Twenty-Three

Upstairs, Maryann twirled happily in front of the mirror in Fleur's room in her new cape and bonnet.

'Oh Cissie, it's just perfect!' she exclaimed. 'You chose so well! But why would Mr Marshall want to spend his money on me?'

''Cos he's a kind man, that's why. But are yer quite sure yer like it, Maryann? They did say in the shop that it could be changed if you didn't.'

'It's what I would have chosen myself,' Maryann assured her as she tied the ribbons of the navy-blue bonnet beneath her chin and turned to admire herself again. 'Not that I could *ever* have afforded to buy anything like this,' she ended. Fleur pottered over to her smiling broadly and gently stroked the material of the cloak. 'Pretty,' she said and both the young women laughed. 'Pretty' was fast becoming the little girl's favourite word.

'Yes, it is pretty, sweetheart – just like you. And now we shall both be snug and warm when we go for a walk, won't we?'

At mention of the word 'walk', Fleur's ears pricked up. Weather permitting, Maryann took her for a short stroll every afternoon now and it had fast become the highlight of the child's day. Maryann marvelled at the way everything she saw was new and magical to her, which must be due to the fact that Fleur had never been allowed outdoors before.

'I'll tell you what,' she said now, 'I'll go down with Cissie and fetch you your lunch up, and if you eat every scrap like a good girl we'll go out early today so that I can try my new cape and bonnet out. How does that sound?'

Fleur nodded vigorously as she hopped from foot to foot in anticipation, and Maryann reluctantly took off her smart new garments and placed them carefully across the chair before following Cissie down to the kitchen.

'Do you think I should go and thank Mr Marshall?' she asked Cissie as they passed the library.

'Thank Mr Marshall for what?' A voice cracked like a whiplash from behind them. The girls whirled about in fear to see Miss Florence bearing down on them.

Maryann squirmed uncomfortably. 'The master kindly got Cissie to fetch me a warm cape and a bonnet from the town,' she muttered.

'He did *what*!' Florence looked as if she was about to burst a blood vessel with temper as she turned about and thumped towards the library, her skirts swirling madly about her. Maryann and Cissie scuttled off to the kitchen whilst the going was good.

'Whatever were you thinking of, Wesley?' Florence demanded, as hands on hips she confronted her brother. 'You'll be the talk of the town when people learn that you are sending a servant to buy the nanny new clothes!'

'She needed a warm cape,' he answered defensively. 'It

wouldn't be seemly for Fleur's nanny to be walking about in an old shawl.'

His sister said in exasperation, 'So why didn't you get *me* to buy one for her?'

'Because you make it more than obvious that you detest her, and I didn't think you'd want to.'

'Detest her! Huh! That's an understatement if ever there was one. We were all doing fine till that common little piece came here, but now she's got you under her spell.'

'Don't be so ridiculous, Florence. And as for us doing fine – how can you think that? You only have to look at Fleur to see that she's thriving, so Miss Meadows must be doing something right!'

Bitterness surged through the young woman as she stared back at her brother, whose anger had now mounted to meet her own. It had been years since Wesley had stood up to her, but now . . .

Deciding to try a different tack she took a tiny lace handkerchief from the pocket of her dress and dabbed at an imaginary tear on her cheek. 'How can you say that to me,' she choked, 'when I have done my very best for the child all these years?'

His anger subsided as quickly as it had come. 'I know you did what you thought was right for her, and I appreciate it,' he said quietly. 'But now you can have some time to yourself again. In fact, why don't you go to the London townhouse for a few weeks and enjoy yourself? Go to the opera and the theatre. It would do you good.'

'It wouldn't be much fun on my own, would it?' she said peevishly.

'Then take Miss Lord with you,' he urged. 'I'm sure we could manage here without her for a time, and you haven't been to London for a while.'

Now that he had planted the seed, Florence was tempted.

It did seem like an awfully long time since she had had any fun, apart from with Hugo that was, and she was tiring of him already. After all, he was little more than a boy at the end of the day, and he was no more than a peasant too.

'I'll think about it,' she answered, then turning about she flounced out of the room leaving him to shake his head and hope she would take him up on his suggestion. A little break from each other might be just what they both needed.

'So what do you think of the idea, Elizabeth?' Florence asked that evening as the woman was helping her to dress for dinner.

'Well, you know how much I love London and so the thought of going again is very exciting. But what about . . .'

When her voice trailed away, Florence looked at her in the mirror. 'It has been started and just a couple of weeks shouldn't make any difference.'

'In that case, should you decide to go I should love to accompany you.' Elizabeth Lord fastened a rope of pearls about her mistress's neck then stood back to admire her. Florence was actually quite a striking-looking woman and who knew? In London she would have her mistress all to herself and Florence might decide that they would be happier living there permanently. Elizabeth would love that, for it meant then that she would no longer have to live in this little back-of-beyond place. She had never been able to understand Florence's obsession for Windy Manor.

'In that case I shall give it some serious consideration. Now do you have everything ready, Elizabeth?'

Miss Lord patted the pocket of her dress and nodded smugly. 'Oh yes, miss. Now shall we go down to dinner?'

*

'While I was up at the Manor this afternoon, Maryann was saying that Miss Florence and that lady's maid-cum-housekeeper of hers are going off to London for a while later this week,' Toby told his family conversationally over tea that evening.

Hugo almost choked on the piece of fruit cake he had been chewing and turned an alarming shade of red as his mother leaped up from her chair and began to pound his back.

'What have I told yer about chewin' yer food properly afore yer swallow it?' Tilly Jackson scolded, but Hugo's attention was firmly fixed on Toby and he flapped her away.

'An' when was all this decided?'

Toby shrugged. 'Just recently, I believe, but from what I can see of it they'll all be glad to see the back of her for a while; Maryann especially. She's a right tyrant.'

Hugo scowled as he pushed his plate away. Only the day before he had arranged to meet Florence in the barn but although he had waited for over an hour she had failed to turn up. Now he knew why. She was probably too busy packing for her trip to bother with him. His mouth set in a grim line and beneath the chenille tablecloth that Tilly kept strictly for Sundays his hands bunched into fists. Well, Miss High and Mighty needn't think she was going to get rid of him that easily! He was no toy that she could fling aside when she tired of him, as she'd discover to her cost if she tried it. He hadn't done with Miss Florence yet, not by a long shot.

'So whereabouts in London are they goin' exactly?' he asked now, trying to keep his voice calm.

Toby frowned, his cup halfway to his lips as he tried to remember.

'Mayfair, I believe they said – Grosvenor Square, if I remember correctly. Apparently they keep a skeleton staff on there in case Mr Marshall ever has to go there on business. An' from what I could make of it, Miss Florence used to go there quite regularly an' all till lately.'

The talk then moved on to other things and as soon as he could, Hugo left the table and went out into the yard where he prowled around, thinking deeply. Mayfair, eh? Quite a posh area so he understood, and he quite fancied a little break in London. How to get there was the problem. The few coins in his pocket wouldn't get him very far. And then it came to him and he grinned. He had just thought of the perfect solution.

'Goodbye then, my dear. And do have a good time,' Wesley told Florence as he handed her up into the carriage that would take her to the railway station. Elizabeth Lord was already seated looking as excited as a child. It had been nearly a week since Florence had made the decision to go, and the days had flown by in a flurry of preparation and packing.

'I shan't be gone longer than a few weeks at most,' Florence promised, suddenly wondering if this had been such a good idea, after all. Had it not been for that girl arriving her plans to become the mistress of Windy Manor would have been so much more advanced by now. But then Wesley slammed the door and Benny urged the horses on, and they were off, rattling away down the drive.

Wesley Marshall watched the carriage until it was out of sight, slightly ashamed to admit that he felt a great sense of relief. And then he turned and walked back into the house to resume his painting.

'So where's Hugo then?' Toby asked his mother as he sat down to his evening meal. His limbs ached after a long shift down the mines and already the thought of his bed was calling him.

'Your guess is as good as mine,' Tilly said tartly. 'The young devil ain't showed his face all day. He'll get a right old tongue-lashin' off me when he does decide to put in an appearance, you just see if he don't! He went off all dressed up like a dog's dinner shortly after breakfast.'

Toby grinned, wondering what his brother was up to, but didn't really give the matter a lot more thought. They were all used to Hugo's comings and goings by now. Once Toby had eaten his meal he settled down by the fire to read the newspaper with his father, but before long he yawned and told his parents, 'I'm off to bed then. Tell Hugo not to disturb me when he comes in, 'specially if he's roarin' drunk!'

'He hadn't better be else he'll get a clip round the ear, big as he is,' his mother threatened, and laughing, Toby disappeared up the stairs.

The following morning, his mother shook him awake, saying, 'Toby – Toby, wake up, son. Yer brother ain't been home all night.'

'What?' Glancing across at Hugo's neatly made bed, Toby rubbed the sleep from his eyes. 'Well, it ain't the first time is it, Mam? He's no doubt tucked up in some young lass's cot somewhere.'

'Dirty young bugger,' Tilly grumbled as she tossed Toby's work trousers onto the bed for him. 'Come on, yer breakfast will be ready in no time.'

When Toby returned from work that evening he fully expected to see Hugo there, but his mother greeted him with, 'He still ain't back, Toby. Where do yer think he could have gone? He ain't got enough money to go far.'

It was then that alarm bells began to clang in Toby's mind – and without even waiting to take his pit boots off – much to his mother's disgust – he raced upstairs and upturned his mattress, sending the sheets and blankets scattering all across the floor.

'Whatever are yer doin, lad? Whatever's come over yer?' Tilly cried as she puffed up the stairs after him.

Ignoring her, Toby thrust his arm deep inside the hole he

had made in the underneath of his tick mattress and then as he thrust it this way and that, he groaned.

'Aw no! I don't believe it. The little toad 'as made off wi' all me savin's!'

Tilly's hand flew to her mouth. 'No – no he couldn't – he wouldn't,' she said in disbelief. 'Surely he'd not steal from his own brother!'

'Our Hugo would steal from God Himself if he could get away with it,' Toby ground out. As much as he loved his brother, he was all too aware of his weaknesses.

'Get out o' the way an' let me 'ave a look,' Tilly commanded as she pushed past him. She knew how long and hard Toby had worked to save that money. Right since the day he'd started work he'd saved, and she couldn't accept that it had been stolen. But minutes later she was forced to accept the fact that he was right. There was not so much as one penny piece still remaining.

'Perhaps it weren't Hugo as took it,' she said faintly, unwilling to believe that her youngest could be so cruel. But even as she uttered the words she knew deep down that it could have been no one else, and so did Toby.

Her son was sitting with his head bowed now and she felt tears stab at the back of her eyes.

'I had almost enough saved to get me an' Maryann a little cottage, Mam,' he whispered brokenly. 'An' now it's all gone.'

Covering the short distance between them she wrapped her arms around him and they cried together as all his dreams crumbled to dust. It would take him years to save up again, but that was not the worst of it. Only days before, he had led Maryann to believe that in the not too distant future they could finally start their life together. What was he going to tell her now?

Chapter Twenty-Four

As Hugo alighted from the train at Euston station his eyes were popping out. He had never seen so many people in one place in his whole life before; had never dreamed that there *were* so many people in the world, if it came to that, and he was feeling slightly out of his depth.

The noise of the trains pulling in and out of the station was deafening, and as he stood there he was jostled this way and that. He saw there were well-dressed women in colourful crinolines on the arms of gentlemen in smart jackets and silk top hats, and he suddenly felt like a country yokel, even if he was wearing his best new jacket. But then he patted the pocket of his trousers and as he felt the wad of money nestling there his confidence returned somewhat. He didn't give a thought as to how Toby might be feeling if he had discovered all his savings were gone. All he had to do now was find out what direction Mayfair was in, so he strode along the platform towards the entrance with his head held high.

Outside, it was even busier than the station had been and he gazed about in amazement. The streets were teeming with horses and carriages, and beggars sat holding their hands out as they pitifully begged for pennies. A flower-seller holding a basket full of heather hopefully held a bunch out to him as he passed and on a whim he took a penny from his pocket and bought it. All women loved flowers and he might as well get off on the right footing with Florence when he finally tracked her down. There seemed to be pigeons everywhere and he was surprised to see that their mess covered almost everything that stood still. Oh well, he was here now and was just going to have to make the best of it.

'Could you tell me which direction I 'ave to take to get to Mayfair?' he asked an elderly man who was passing by, and the man turned on him.

'Piss orf!' The old fella scuttled on as Hugo flinched in shock. It was certainly not the best of starts, that was for sure. He attempted to stop a few more people to ask for directions but they hurried past him eyeing him suspiciously, so eventually he gave up and decided to get something to eat. It had been a long time since he had had any food and his stomach was grumbling ominously now. As he strolled along Euston Road he came to a stall selling jellied eels and so he bought himself a portion. He had never tried jellied eels before and after the first mouthful was sure that he never would again.

'New round 'ere, are yer, guv?' the stall-holder asked pleasantly.

'Yes. I've just arrived as it so 'appens.'

'Then let me give yer a word of advice, young man. Keep yer 'and on yer wallet 'cos this place is full of pickpockets and they're so good at what they do that when they rob yer, yer don't feel a thing.'

'Really?' Hugo's hand rested on his pocket as he stared about him suspiciously before giving up on the jellied eels and tossing them onto the ground for the pigeons, who immediately began to fight over them. They clearly were not fussy what they ate. 'I reckon I'll try your pease puddin' instead,' he said, fishing out some more change, and the man laughed jovially.

'Jellied eels are an acquired taste, I 'ave to admit. Most folks either love 'em or hate 'em.'

The pudding was much more to Hugo's taste and when he had finished it he asked, 'Could you tell me which way I 'ave to go to get to Mayfair?'

'Well, I could,' the man answered obligingly, 'but the streets are like rabbit warrens round 'ere so if yer take my advice you'll flag down a cab. It ain't that far away an' it shouldn't cost yer much.'

'Right, I will. Thanks, mate.' Hugo watched what other people were doing then held his hand up and sure enough a carriage pulled up next to him.

'Where do yer wanna go, squire?' the driver asked him as Hugo clambered inside.

'Grosvenor Square, if you please,' he called, then slamming the door he settled back in the seat wrinkling his nose as the smell of the stale straw on the floor filled his nostrils. The horses set off at a trot and soon they were bowling through the streets at an alarming rate, narrowly missing other cabs that seemed intent on cutting in front of them.

It's like takin' yer life in yer 'ands, travellin' in one o' these contraptions, Hugo thought as he clung to the edge of the seat for dear life. He was tired now, having spent the whole of the night before hiding in the waiting room at Trent Valley railway station back in Nuneaton, waiting for the first train to London. And he still had to locate which house Florence was staying at in Grosvenor Square, he thought miserably. Darkness was falling and a smog was settling across the cobbles, making him feel cold and dejected, but he had come this far and he had no intentions of going back now. He wasn't ready to face Toby's wrath just yet, if ever!

By the time the carriage drove into Grosvenor Square, Hugo's chin had drooped onto his chest and he was almost asleep.

'Whereabouts in the square did yer want droppin', mate?' the cabbie shouted from his seat perched high above the horses' heads.

'What?' Hugo blinked and stared out of the window, then gasped with dismay. The square was absolutely huge. There was a large park in the centre of it and it was bordered with houses on every side. The trouble was, he had no idea which one Florence was staying in.

'Er, here will do fine, thanks,' he told the man as he tumbled out of the carriage and quickly paid him. The cabbie doffed his cap then clicked his tongue and the horses set off again, leaving Hugo standing there. A lamp-lighter was doing his rounds and as he passed Hugo he stared at him curiously before moving on to the next lamp. A fine drizzle had started to fall and that, combined with the smog that was floating across the park, made the air feel chilly.

Hugo's spirits sank as he stared along the rows of houses. He turned his coat collar up, although it did little to keep out the cold. He wasn't sure what to do next. It could take him the rest of the day to knock on each door trying to locate Florence. But then what other option did he have?

Resolutely, he climbed the steps to the nearest house. It was huge and towered above him but he rang the bell and minutes later was rewarded when a young maid opened the door.

''Scuse me, miss.' He hastily took his cap off. 'I were

wonderin' if yer could tell me which 'ouse belongs to the Marshall family.'

'No, I could not. Now clear orf,' she said rudely and promptly closed the door in his face.

He got a similar reception at the next six houses. By then the rain was soaking through his clothes and he was feeling thoroughly miserable as the futility of his task set in. The square was deserted, apart from the odd carriage that rattled past, so he headed towards the park hoping to find somewhere he could shelter from the rain while he decided what to do. Eventually he stumbled across a bandstand and he slipped inside. The sides were low but at least it had a roof on which would shelter him from the rain, but he was still bitterly cold. Huddling down he wrapped his arms about himself. He supposed that he should go and try to find somewhere to stay for the night, a cheap lodging place perhaps? But then he had no idea what direction to go in so he decided to stay where he was for the time being at least until he felt a little more rested. The lack of sleep the night before and the long journey had caught up with him now and almost before he knew it he had nodded off to sleep.

The sound of a dog barking early the next morning roused him, and stretching painfully he peered over the side of the bandstand to see a girl in a maid's uniform exercising a small spaniel.

He yawned, then glancing down he noticed his handkerchief lying on the wooden floor near his feet. The night before he had stuffed it down into his pocket to stop his money from falling out, so how the hell had it ended up down there? And then a sinking feeling churned in his stomach as he delved into his pocket, only to find that it was quite empty. Suddenly the stall-holder's words echoed in his mind. *Keep yer 'and on yer wallet 'cos this place is full of pickpockets.*

'*Aw no!*' Hugo leaped up feeling strangely light-headed and frantically began to search around, but the money had vanished into thin air. He had been robbed whilst he slept.

Panic set in then. What would he do if he couldn't find Florence? He was in a strange city with no way of letting anyone know where he was and no way of getting home. Taking a deep breath of air he tried to calm himself. Then he suddenly remembered something. When he had paid the cab driver, he had dropped some change into his other pocket. He felt for it, quickly, sighing with relief when his hand closed around some loose coins. It wasn't much but it might be just about enough to get him home on the mail train if he travelled in one of the mail vans that delivered the post to different towns along the way. More than ever now he knew that he must find Florence. If only he could do that, all his troubles would be over.

Hugo's legs felt wobbly as he set off across the park and he realised that he had caught a chill, but that was the least of his worries for now. Once he came to the square he began to saunter along watching closely as people left their houses. Either Florence or Miss Lord was bound to venture out eventually, he reasoned, and when they did he would be home and dry.

By mid-morning his stomach was rumbling ominously again and his throat was parched but he daren't risk spending any of his little remaining money on food or drink. Every halfpenny was precious now so he walked on. He had done four laps of the entire square when suddenly just ahead of him he saw a smartly dressed woman descending the steps from one of the houses, and as he sped towards her he could have cried with relief when he saw that it was Elizabeth Lord. She was with a tall, good-looking man in a top hat and smart jacket, and something about him looked vaguely familiar. Hugo strived to remember where he might have seen him before. And then it came to him: he was the toff that he had seen in the marketplace back at home, round about the time Violet had gone missing. He shrugged, thinking nothing of it. He had more pressing things on his mind at present and his first instinct was to shout to Miss Lord – but then he thought better of it. Florence might want to see him alone before coming up with an explanation for Miss Lord as to why he was there so he loitered, relieved to see that once she reached the bottom of the steps she was setting off in the opposite direction.

He bided his time until the woman was a safe distance away before approaching the house and looking up at it. There were railings along the front of it with steps leading down on one side to what he supposed was a kitchen area, and he noted that heavy velvet drapes were hanging at the tall upper windows. The steps leading to the front door looked as if they were marble. It was a very impressive residence, and he glanced down with dismay at his travel-stained clothes. Even his new jacket was damp and crumpled now, and he knew that he must look a sight. As a wave of dizziness overcame him, he reached out and held on to the railings for a moment. He was shivering with cold and yet strangely his forehead was burning and he had a headache.

Still, he consoled himself, *I'll soon feel better with a nice hot cuppa tea and a good breakfast inside me*. He waited for the dizziness to pass then climbed the steps to the front door and lifting the brass lion-head knocker, he rapped loudly.

Moments later, the door was opened by a young girl dressed in a frilly white apron and cap over a grey dress.

'Sorry, no beggars allowed.' She began to close the door on him but he put his hand out and pushed it open again.

'I ain't a beggar,' he told her with what dignity he could muster. 'I'm 'ere to see Miss Marshall.'

'Oh!' She looked astounded as she eyed him up and

213

down suspiciously and he rushed on, 'Tell 'er Mr Jackson is 'ere to see 'er. Mr Hugo Jackson.'

She hesitated for a second then said doubtfully, 'Very well, step inside and wait here while I go and ask the mistress if she will see you.'

He swiped his cap off and looked about as the little maid bustled away. It was certainly a nice place with fine Oriental carpets scattered about on the immaculate tiled floor.

Within seconds the maid was bustling towards him again. 'Follow me,' she said and he was only too grateful to do just that. 'Miss Marshall is in the morning room.'

He stifled a grin. Morning room indeed! What with those and drawing rooms and studies and libraries and dining rooms, he wondered that the folk as lived in them didn't get lost. Back in the court where he lived there was just one small cramped room that served as both the kitchen and the sitting room. And more often than not the larger families would have some of them sleeping in there and all. This lot didn't know they were born.

The maid paused in front of a pair of double doors and after opening one of them she ushered him inside without another word and closed it quietly behind him.

Florence was standing in front of a blazing fire waiting for him. She was dressed in a very becoming high-necked gown of lilac satin and her hair was neatly braided around the crown of her head. He gave her a saucy grin but before he could open his mouth to say anything, she attacked. 'Just what the *hell* do you think you are doing here? Are you intent on making me a laughing stock?'

He muttered uncertainly, 'B-but I thought yer'd be pleased to see me, Florence.'

'My name is Miss Marshall to you,' she informed him coldly. 'And whatever made you think that?'

'Well, we've been havin' a good time together, ain't we?

214

So I just thought why should it stop while yer in London?'

'Then you thought wrong!' Her eyes were like chips of ice. 'How dare you come here embarrassing me like this! And how would I have explained your presence to Miss Lord, had she been here?'

Hugo's temper began to rise as he gripped the back of a chair. 'I saw her go out with a fancy-looking chap so I knew she weren't in – and yer didn't feel so embarrassed when we was rollin' about in the hay together an' yer drawers were round yer ankles, did yer!'

'Get out this instant!' He could see her trembling with rage and hoping to turn things around he tried to look contrite.

'Look – I'm sorry if I've upset yer,' he told her. 'I just couldn't stand the thought o' not seein' yer for a while. An' so I . . . well, I'm ashamed to say I stole me brother's savin's to follow you here an' surprise yer, but then I got 'em all stolen when I slept in the park last night. I'm skint – broke – an' I don't even know 'ow I'm goin' to get back home.'

'That is not my problem,' she said scathingly. 'And now please leave or I will be forced to get someone to escort you from the premises.'

'But Flo . . . Florence.'

Turning about, she strode over to the bell-pull hanging at the side of the fireplace and asked threateningly, 'Do I really have to have you forcibly evicted?'

He could see that she meant it and suddenly all his hopes of having a lazy holiday in London disappeared in a puff of smoke. He'd imagined bowling around in a fine carriage seeing all the sights he had only ever heard about. But now he didn't even know if he had enough money to get him home in a mail van, and he felt so ill.

'So is this really all I mean to you?' He spread his hands but her face remained hard.

'You stupid boy!' she sneered. 'You mean absolutely nothing to me and you never did. Do you really think that a stupid fumbling child like you could ever hold the attention of someone like me for more than a short time? You were simply an amusing diversion but it's over now, so in future kindly keep your distance.'

Total humiliation washed over him like a bucket of ice-cold water. Throwing the withered bunch of heather he had bought for her the day before to the ground he turned, and with as much dignity as he could muster he marched out of the room slamming the door so hard behind him that it danced on its hinges.

'Bloody stuck-up old cow!' he swore, much to the little maid's amazement as he stamped towards the front door. How dare she think she could use him like that? And now it was crystal clear that this was exactly what she had done. But she'd pay for it, he vowed as he took the steps leading down to the road two at a time. Oh aye, he'd make sure the bitch paid for it if it was the last thing he ever did!

Chapter Twenty-Five

From the window of the library, Wesley Marshall watched Maryann and Fleur strolling about the lawn – at least, Maryann was strolling and Fleur was skipping ahead, showing interest in everything she saw. Occasionally she would pick a weed or a flower and carry it to Maryann for inspection and he saw how patient the girl was as she explained to the little girl what it was.

Everything was so new to her! It was as if the child had been freed from a prison, and with a start he realised that in a way, she had been.

He turned his attention back to the canvas he was working on and a small smile twitched at the corner of his lips. He had captured the colour of Maryann's hair perfectly and he was pleased with the portrait so far, although it hadn't been easy to paint without her sitting for him.

It was later that afternoon as he was making his way to the drawing room for his afternoon tea that he was shocked to see Maryann down on her hands and knees, scrubbing away at the hall floor.

'Miss Meadows.' He halted and stared at her in amazement. 'Whatever are you doing?'

She grinned up at him. 'Fleur is having her afternoon nap, sir, so I thought I'd give Cissie a hand with the cleaning. I often help out when I'm able to. This is a big house for her and Nellie to try and keep clean on their own, especially now that the weather has turned cold and they have all the fires to see to as well.'

'Good heavens.' He had never given the matter much thought before as Florence had fired the staff one by one, but now he felt guilty at how hard Cissie and Nellie must be forced to work.

'Do you think I should employ someone else to help them?' Somehow he trusted this young woman's judgement. She seemed very sensible, as well as being extremely kind to Fleur.

Maryann sat back on her heels for a moment before answering. 'Well, a maid who could help out with the cleaning and the laundry would certainly take a great weight off their shoulders, sir.'

'Yes, yes. I think you are right,' he agreed as he thoughtfully tapped his chin. 'But even if I were to advertise for one, who would interview them with Miss Florence away? I usually leave the hiring and firing to her.' For some reason that he couldn't explain, he didn't like to see Maryann doing such menial work, although she clearly didn't seem to mind. In fact, she must have volunteered to do it.

'I'm sure Nellie would be happy to conduct the interviews in Miss Florence's absence,' Maryann told him. 'After all, she must know exactly what type of person would be most suitable for working here.'

His face lightened and he was impressed. She was such a capable young woman.

'Very well, I shall advertise for one straight away. But do

we need this person to live in?' He clearly didn't have a clue.

'If it was someone suitable from the village they could perhaps come each day and work set hours, then go home?' she suggested, and seeing the sense in what she said he nodded, trusting her implicitly.

'Thank you, Miss Meadows. Leave it with me.' He began to walk away but then suddenly paused to ask, 'Are you having dinner with Fleur in her room this evening?' He had noticed that she had taken to doing that of late, and judging by the sound of laughter that was regularly to be heard coming from the room it was obviously pleasing Fleur.

When Maryann nodded he flushed before rushing on, 'Would you mind very much if I joined you? I find it rather lonely dining alone with my sister away.'

For a moment it would have been hard to say who was the most shocked, he for asking her, or she because he had.

'Well, I err . . .' She glanced down at her plain grey dress. It was the best she had ever owned, but certainly not the sort of thing ladies would have dined in.

He guessed exactly what she was thinking and before he could stop himself he blurted out, 'We wouldn't need to stand on ceremony and get changed. I was going to suggest a picnic outside during the day but it's rather too cold for that, isn't it?'

Maryann looked at him doubtfully, but then sensing his sincerity she said gently, 'I'm sure Fleur would love it if you joined us, sir.'

'Right, I shall go and ask Nellie straight away if she would mind bringing my meal up there too then, if you are sure it won't be imposing?' On seeing her smile, he turned and hastened away in the direction of the kitchen.

A six thirty prompt, Mr Marshall tapped on Fleur's

bedroom door and was instantly admitted by Maryann. Fleur was sitting in front of the fire with one of her dollies clutched in one arm whilst she turned the pages of a fairy-story book with the other. She was wearing a charming dress with a blue ribbon tied in her gleaming fair hair and her father realised that she was actually quite pretty when she smiled – which she was cautiously doing now. After nodding a greeting to Maryann, he crossed to her and, bending down to her level, he returned her smile.

'Say hello to your papa, Fleur,' Maryann encouraged.

Fleur swallowed before saying shyly, 'He – hello, Papa.'

At that moment a tap came on the door and Nellie entered bearing a heavy tray.

'Phew, them stairs are steeper than I remembered,' she puffed as she placed the tray on the table that Maryann had laid ready.

'Enjoy your dinner, an' just give us a shout if there's owt I've forgotten.' And with that she bustled away with a broad smile on her face, thinking how wonderful it was to see the master finally taking an interest in the little 'un and spending some time with her. Perhaps things were looking up?

Maryann meanwhile had started to serve the food and they all sat down at the table together.

There were juicy lamb cutlets served with freshly made mint sauce and a selection of vegetables from the cottage garden, and Mr Marshall was astounded when he saw the way Fleur was enjoying her food. Her appetite had definitely improved and she even had some colour in her cheeks now. He found Maryann easy to talk to and in no time at all they were chatting away together with Fleur, much to his amusement, chipping in now and again.

When the meal was over, Fleur drifted away to play

with her toys again before it was time to get ready for bed. Maryann and Mr Marshall sat watching her.

'I don't think I quite realised what I was missing,' he said unexpectedly, more to himself than anyone else, and Maryann felt a little thrill of satisfaction. And then he amazed her when he said, 'I was wondering if I might ask another favour of you, Miss Marshall.'

'But of course.' She folded her hands neatly in her lap as she waited for him to go on.

Eventually he said, 'I was wondering if you would mind very much – when you have time, of course – if you would mind packing up my late wife's clothes for me. I'm sure that Cissie would be willing to help you.'

The girl realised how hard this decision must have been, to finally take a step towards getting rid of his late wife's clothes, and she smiled at him compassionately.

'I could certainly do that for you, sir – if you're quite sure that is what you want.'

'It is!' Strangely, now that he had made the decision he felt a surge of relief. Amélie's room had remained as a shrine to her for quite long enough. It was time to say goodbye to the past. 'Perhaps you could get Cissie to direct you to her room when you have the time?'

'And what would you like us to do with the clothes once they are packed?'

'I can get Ted to take them up to the attic for me,' he replied. 'But please, if there is anything that you or Cissie would like, do help yourselves.'

Maryann nodded, then not wishing to dwell on it she turned the conversation to other things until it was time to get Fleur ready for bed.

'Night night, Papa,' the child said as he was leaving the room and Maryann watched different emotions flit across his face before he smiled and replied, 'Night night, Fleur.'

The very next afternoon, whilst Fleur was happily playing with her dollies, Cissie led Maryann towards Amélie's suite of rooms with the key to them clutched in her hand.

'Fancy that, the master havin' dinner wi' you an' Miss Fleur,' she giggled. 'I wonder what Miss Florence would think o' that? Happen she'd have a dicky fit!' Inserting the key in the lock she turned it. At first it squeaked in protest and then they entered a dark room.

Cissie hurried across to the window and swished the curtains aside; instantly the cold autumn light flooded in. Maryann looked around her. There was still the faint scent of perfume in the air and the room was cold and felt slightly damp after being shut up for so long.

'It's lovely, ain't it?' Cissie whispered, as if she feared disturbing the woman who had once slept there. 'But look at the dust everywhere. Yer could write yer name in it.' To emphasise her words she trailed her finger along the fancy dressing table, leaving a line in the dust. 'That door there leads to Miss Amélie's sitting room,' Cissie went on. 'She spent a lot o' time locked away up here alone. An' that door there leads to the master's room an' his dressing room. She never allowed him to sleep in here wi' her from the day they returned from their honeymoon in Paris. Strange, ain't it? I mean, you'd think newlyweds wouldn't be able to get enough of each other. But then, wishin' no offence to the dead, Miss Amélie allus were a bit strange. Beautiful . . . but strange.'

'How do you mean – strange?' Maryann asked curiously as she looked towards a beautifully carved four-poster bed.

'Well, what I mean is, she were a great one fer lockin' herself away. She hated dinner parties an' such, an' her an' Miss Florence never saw eye to eye from the day she arrived. Between you an' me, I reckon Miss Florence were jealous of her, an' with Miss Amélie bein' such a nervous little thing she made her life hell.'

'Poor soul.' Maryann ran her hand across the superb silk counterpane. It too was thickly coated in dust, as was everything else in the room, but it was clearly of a very high quality. 'It's just as I always imagined a princess's room to be,' she confided and Cissie smiled.

'She were a bit like a princess in her ways. She was the only daughter of very wealthy French parents an' I reckon they'd pampered her shamelessly. She didn't even know how to wash her hair or have a bath on her own, and she had a maid who waited on her hand and foot. Her parents soon changed their tune after she died though and they came to see Miss Fleur. As soon as they realised she weren't quite normal they took to their heels an' to my knowledge the master ain't never seen 'em nor heard from 'em since either.'

'How sad, and yet if everyone would just give Fleur a chance they would see that behind her disability is a normal little girl who is craving to be loved.'

Cissie nodded in agreement as she limped towards the armoire saying, 'I reckon you're right there, Maryann, but now let's get on wi' what we came for, eh? There's bound to be somethin' here that you'll like, although I dare say everything will be old-fashioned by now.'

She flung the doors open and Maryann gasped at the array of gowns hanging there. They were all the colours of the rainbow and she was sure she had never seen anything quite so beautiful.

'These were her evening gowns,' Cissie confided. 'An' that armoire on the opposite wall is full of her day dresses. Eeh, she knew how to dress, did the mistress. But now, which ones do yer fancy? The master did say we were to 'elp ourselves.'

'I really don't know.' Maryann was completely spoiled for choice as she stroked the material of one dress after another. 'I'm sure all of these are far too fancy for the likes of me.'

'Rubbish. Why, you're beautiful if you did but know it. An' I was only sayin' to me gran the other day that you conduct yourself like more of a lady than Miss Florence.'

Maryann blushed at the compliment as Cissie withdrew a gown in a beautiful shade of emerald green. The neckline was heavily trimmed with guipure lace and quite low-cut, and the skirt was full. Thankfully because the clothes had been stored behind closed doors they were remarkably clean. The moths hadn't got into them either, luckily.

'Try this one,' Cissie urged. 'I reckon this would be just right wi' your colouring.' Maryann reluctantly began to undress and soon after the girl slipped the dress over her head and laced it up the back. She then stood back and eyed her critically before saying, 'Just wait there. It needs a few more petticoats underneath to do the skirt justice.' She went over to the other wardrobe and took out an armful. Maryann stood patiently whilst Cissie secured them about her waist. She felt as if she was confined in a sea of silk and laughed in disbelief as Cissie took her hand and drew her towards a tall cheval mirror.

'Just look at you,' Cissie sighed admiringly. 'You're like a rough diamond that's been polished and has come to life.'

Never in her wildest dreams had Maryann imagined that she could look like this. Cissie was rummaging around in a cupboard to try and find some satin shoes to complement the outfit. When she finally located a pair that were just the right colour, she carried them over to her, and as Maryann slipped her feet into them she found that they fitted like a glove.

'Didn't I tell yer that this one would be perfect?' Cissie said smugly.

Maryann agreed. But as beautiful as the dress was, she didn't want to wear the clothes of a dead woman, although she wished that Toby could have seen her in the green gown. 'Yes, you did, and you were right, but I would never get an opportunity to wear it, although it was lovely to try it on. Now, is there anything that you fancy, Cissie?'

The other girl chose to keep a cherry-red day dress that she said her gran could alter to fit her, along with some other bits and pieces, and then side by side the two young women carefully folded the clothes into the huge trunks that Ted had carried down from the loft for that very purpose. Eventually the task was done and the lids were closed.

'I'll ask Ted and Benny to take them up to the attics tomorrow,' Maryann said. 'And maybe one day soon, when we've both got time, we can give these rooms a thorough going-over. A blast of fresh air would do them a power of good.'

Chapter Twenty-Six

'OK, laddie, 'fraid this is as far as I can take yer,' the friendly farmer informed Hugo. 'We're at the top o' the Griff Hollows now an' I'm headin' fer Stockingford, but you ain't got far to go into town.'

Hugo groaned as he pulled himself up from between the wooden crates full of squawking chickens. He had been fortunate enough to scrounge a lift on the back of the horse and cart from Coventry where the mail train had dumped him earlier in the afternoon. He'd only got that far because the ticket-inspector at Euston had taken pity on him. Hugo could still recall the humiliation he had felt when he had offered his ha'pennies and pennies to the man.

'Huh!' the ruddy-faced fellow had snorted. 'There ain't enough there to even get yer halfway to Nuneaton.' But then noting the sweat that stood out in glistening beads on Hugo's forehead, he had relented. 'Come on then, mate, give it 'ere,' he'd said wearily. 'An' tell the guard in the mail van that I said yer could travel as far as Coventry.'

The lad looked so ill the man had half-expected him to topple over in a pile at any minute, but Hugo had toddled unsteadily off to spend an uncomfortable journey on the bags of mail at the back of the train. Thankfully, the guard just happened to have a son of Hugo's own age, and seeing the state he was in he'd brought him a cup of weak tea mid-afternoon, saying, 'Get that down yer, son. Yer look like yer could do wi' it.'

The tea was tepid and unsweetened but Hugo was sure that nothing had ever tasted so good. He had drained the mug thirstily. Once alighting at Coventry he had seemed to walk for miles until at last, as he reached the Foleshill Road, he had managed to flag down the farmer who had given him a lift for the rest of the way.

Dizzy with fever, he stood on the road now as the farmer snapped his reins, telling him, 'Get yerself home an' into bed, laddie. Happen you'll feel better come tomorrer.' And with that he set off again, leaving Hugo to stare miserably after him.

Up until now, his anger at the way Florence had treated him had kept him going, but now he had something more immediate to concern him. What reception was he going to get when he reached home, if Toby had realised his money was gone? He shuddered with a combination of fever and fear. Had he had somewhere else to go he would have given his home a very wide berth, but he hadn't – and he couldn't bear the thought of another night out in the cold. It was October now and the nights had turned bitterly chilly as he had learned to his cost the night before. It would be the death of him. So thrusting his hands deep into his pockets, he set off down Coventry Road, the golden leaves that were fluttering down from the trees in the biting wind crunching beneath his feet.

He stumbled beneath the Coton Arches and on until

he reached the cattle market, every step an effort. He was almost home now.

And then he was entering the court where he lived and his stomach turned over as he tentatively took hold of the back-door handle.

His mother was just ladling rabbit stew into dishes whilst his father sat at the side of the fire and they both looked up as he entered, but neither of them smiled and he knew then that they had discovered the theft.

Glancing fearfully towards the stairs door, his mother said croakily, 'So . . . you're back then. I wouldn't like to be in your shoes when yer brother gets his hands on yer. An' yer know what, Hugo? This time I can't blame him. You've done some bad things in yer time but I never dreamed that you'd stoop to stealin' off yer own.'

'What you on about, Mam?' he asked, hoping to bluff his way out of it, but then the door leading from the stairs opened and suddenly the two brothers were face to face.

Hugo was shocked to see the look in Toby's eyes. He had always been able to wrap his big brother around his little finger and he'd lost count of the many scrapes from which Toby had rescued him. But now Toby was looking at him as if he hated him.

'What's up, man? What yer lookin' at me like that for?'

Toby was advancing on him and Hugo had never seen him look so menacing.

'You low-life little bastard!' Toby ground out as Hugo swiftly put the table between them.

'I say again, what you on about? I don't know what yer talkin' about,' Toby said desperately.

'No? So it weren't you who took all me money from beneath me mattress then?'

'O' course it weren't. Why would I do that?'

'So where yer been then?'

'I err . . .' The hesitation was Hugo's undoing. He hadn't thought to come up with a plausible excuse and this spoke volumes. And then suddenly everything seemed to happen at once as Toby leaned across the table to grab him. Hugo leaped out of the way but Toby upended the table and the precious pots went crashing to the floor, spewing stew all over it as their mother let out an ear-splitting scream.

Matt jumped out of his chair and made to get between his sons but not before Toby's bunched fist had found its mark on Hugo's chin. The younger man spun backwards but as his spine connected with the wall, Toby thumped him again, knocking him flat on his back.

'Stop it, Toby! You'll kill 'im,' their mother pleaded as she clung to his arm.

'That's just what I intend to do,' Toby hissed, and that was the last thing Hugo remembered before a comforting darkness settled over him.

Pausing in front of the dining-room door, Maryann smoothed her skirt before tapping and entering. Mr Marshall was standing with his back to her staring into the heart of the fire, and when he turned and saw her he smiled.

'Sorry to disturb you, sir, but I just thought you'd like to know: Cissie and I packed your wife's clothes up as you requested, and Ted and Benny have now placed them up in the attics.'

'Thank you, I appreciate it.'

Her heart went out to him and on an impulse she suggested, 'Why don't you come and have your dinner with me and Fleur again, sir? She so enjoyed it, and I know she'd be delighted if you'd join us.'

'I would enjoy that, Miss Marshall, thank you very much.'

'Could you not call me Maryann just for tonight if we

are to dine together again?' Maryann asked and he bowed gallantly.

'Of course. And you in turn must call me Wesley.'

She thought that might be rather hard to do but she nodded anyway. It seemed so silly for them to stand on ceremony with each other, particularly as Miss Florence wasn't there to disapprove. And so it was decided.

When Nellie came into Fleur's room that evening bearing the first of the silver salvers containing their dinner, she winked cheekily at Maryann before asking, 'Would yer like me to serve yer, ma'am?'

Maryann flushed. 'Oh no,' she said hastily. 'I can do that, Nellie. With your permission, of course, sir – I mean Wesley,' she ended, addressing the master who was looking highly amused.

He inclined his head. 'Of course.'

Nellie scuttled from the room with a big grin on her face, happy to leave the three of them to it. When Nellie had departed, Maryann lifted the lid of the first dish saying, 'Ooh, roast beef. It was my father's favourite although we couldn't afford it very often.'

She clamped her mouth shut and coloured then as she remembered who she was talking to, but Wesley said easily, 'Yes, it's one of my favourites too and Nellie has a way of cooking it that makes it melt in your mouth. I just hope I shall be able to do it justice this evening. I've been suffering from rather an upset stomach lately and seem to be losing my appetite, although I must admit I feel slightly better today. Perhaps it's thanks to my charming dinner companions?'

His eyes twinkled as he winked at Fleur, and Maryann felt herself begin to relax. Mr Marshall was actually a very nice, kind man and quite good-looking too. Nowhere near as heartless as she had first thought him to be.

Once their plates were full and Fleur was happily tucking into her dinner he asked, 'So do you have any hobbies, Maryann?'

'Oh yes, I love reading when I have the time.'

'Oh? anything in particular?'

'Most anything I can get my hands on, really. I particularly like to try and keep up with the latest news in the newspapers. I read last week that until recently, a large number of crimes carried the death penalty, but now the criminals will face transportation instead, which is a major step forward, don't you think?'

'I do indeed,' he agreed, enjoying himself enormously. It made a nice change to speak of things that did not involve the latest fashions from Paris, which was usually all he managed to get out of Florence. 'As it happens, I read the same article and I believe the government are trying to do away with the death sentence for every crime, apart from murder. Long overdue, as far as I'm concerned.'

They then moved on to speak of the potato famine in Ireland and the cholera epidemic that had broken out over there before discussing the plans that Prince Albert had of opening an exhibition in London the following year.

'I was also fascinated to read that the Duke of Devonshire's friend and gardener, Joseph Paxton, has come up with the idea of a vast glasshouse that will cover over nineteen acres. Once built, it will be able to contain more than two hundred rare plant exhibits, and already *Punch* magazine has christened it "The Crystal Palace",' Wesley said.

'And you might also be interested to hear of some of the changes I have been making at the mill,' he went on. 'I now have an up-to-date register of every child working there, and I think you will be pleased to learn that I have shortened their hours and improved their working conditions.'

'More – meat, please,' Fleur demanded just then, and the conversation was halted as her father loaded more onto her plate and cut it up into bite-sized chunks for her.

It soon became apparent to him that although Maryann had never travelled beyond her home town she was very well read and abreast with world events. The time seemed to disappear as quickly as the food in front of them, for when he glanced down he was shocked to see that he had cleared his plate for the first time in months.

The main course was followed by one of Nellie's delicious home-made apple pies covered in thick creamy custard, and Fleur managed to get it all over herself, much to their amusement. Finally Maryann pushed her empty dish away, dabbed at her mouth with a napkin and declared, 'That was absolutely wonderful, si— Wesley. But I'm afraid I have made rather a pig of myself and I couldn't eat another mouthful. I shall be running to fat at this rate.'

He chuckled. 'Never. You work far too hard for that – speaking of which, I have placed an advertisement in the local paper for a maid.'

'Oh, that's wonderful! Nellie and Cissie will be so pleased. Believe me, they both work far harder than I do. Most of my time is spent caring for Fleur and that's no hardship at all. She really is such a lovely little girl and she's coming along in leaps and bounds, aren't you, pet? Do you know, she can almost recite the alphabet all the way through now, *and* she can count up to twenty.'

'Already?'

'Yes.' Suddenly serious, Maryann led Fleur away from the table to carry on with a jigsaw puzzle on a table near the fire. Once the child was out of earshot, she returned to her place and said quietly, 'I'm sure she would do even better if she were to get some encouragement from you. She knows that you are her papa even if she doesn't see you often, and she has so loved spending time with you.'

Wesley visibly bristled, and he gripped the cut-glass goblet he was holding so tightly that Maryann feared it might smash in his hand. Had she gone too far? Was he thinking: how *dare* she have the audacity to say such a thing to him? Was she inferring that he had neglected his daughter? And then he suddenly seemed to shrink, right in front of her eyes. She was right, he was thinking. He *had* neglected the child: there was no running away from the fact. *And why?* he asked himself desperately. The answer came back loud and clear. *Because she is* your *child and she isn't perfect – and that knowledge led to your wife's death. All these years, you have blamed that innocent little soul.* He had been utterly and thoroughly selfish, but perhaps it wasn't too late to put things right? Thanks to this inspiring young woman, hadn't he already made a start?

'We do our lessons between eleven o'clock in the morning and twelve,' she told him. 'And then again from two until three in the afternoon. It would be wonderful if you could spare the time to come and see for yourself how bright your daughter is.'

'I . . . I'll try,' he gulped, on the edge of tears if she did but know it, and even though there had been no promises made, Maryann felt as if she had achieved another major victory.

All too soon she told him, 'Thank you so much for joining us, but it is past Fleur's bedtime now and she'll be tired.'

'Of course.' He stood up and gallantly held her chair while she rose from the table then as he was walking towards the door he said, 'I have enjoyed this evening, Maryann. Perhaps we could do it again?' He found himself hoping that Florence would prolong her stay in London. His sister would be apoplectic, were she to discover that he had been dining with Maryann and Fleur in the child's room.

233

As if she could read his mind, Maryann simply smiled at him. 'Goodnight, sir,' she said.

Once again, they were employer and employee – and he wondered why it should bother him so much.

Chapter Twenty-Seven

'Ah, so yer back with us in the land o' the livin' then are yer, lad?'

Hugo groggily opened his eyes and tried to focus, but everything was blurry. And then someone lifted his head and trickled some water into his mouth and he choked.

'Just a sip at a time now.' He recognised his mother's voice, which seemed to come from a long way away, and then someone else said, 'He should be all right now that the fever has broken, Mrs Jackson. Give him lots of rest and beef tea, and nature should do the rest.'

'Thank you, Doctor. My husband will pay you on your way out.'

Hugo groaned. Every bone in his body ached and his chin was sore too. What had happened to him? And then it all slowly began to come back to him and he shut his eyes again, wishing he could slip back into the darkness. It was too painful in the light.

'Wh-where's Toby?' he croaked through dry cracked lips.

'He's at work.'

'B-but I remember . . . we had a fight.'

'That was three days ago,' Tilly told him as she straightened the blankets on his bed. 'You've been very poorly indeed. In fact, for a time there we didn't think you were going to pull through. But you're over the worst now, an' in another week or two yer should be right as rain again. Not that yer deserve to be, me lad! What yer did to yer brother were unforgivable an' you asked for all yer got, so you'll get no sympathy from me.'

'Did Toby do this to me?'

'No, he did not,' she snapped. 'You caught a fever, though I admit he whacked you a couple o' times. An' I have to say yer deserved it an' all. Eeh, whatever made yer make off wi' all his hard-earned money, lad?'

He shrugged. 'I wanted to go to London,' he said feebly and she snorted.

'Oh aye? Thought the streets would be lined wi' gold there, did yer?'

He nodded miserably, seeing no need to mention Florence. What his mother didn't know wouldn't hurt her, and things were bad enough as it was.

'I suppose I did, but the first night there I got robbed.'

'Yer mean someone took all o' Toby's money?'

When he nodded again, her eyes filled with tears and trickled down her cheeks. She angrily swiped them away with the corner of her apron. Half of her wanted to berate Hugo whilst the other half was just relieved that her son was going to recover.

'Well, happen you'll have to grow up now an' find yerself a proper job so as yer can start payin' yer brother back,' she said as she sponged his forehead with a damp cloth.

He looked horrified. 'But it'd take me *years* to do that on the wages they pay round 'ere!'

'Perhaps yer should 'ave thought o' that before yer stole from him,' she said bluntly. 'Trouble is, you've allus been jealous o' Toby – an' everythin' he has, you want. Well, it stops now, I'm tellin' yer straight – else you'll find yerself out on yer ear!'

Hugo shut his eyes in despair. If it hadn't been for that bitch he had gone chasing after he wouldn't be in this position now. It was all *her* fault – and somehow he was going to make her pay!

Violet was taking some undergarments from the drawer in her room when her eyes fell on the clean rags that she used for her monthly courses. Now that she came to think of it, her course was late. In fact, it was *very* late. She began to calculate the weeks since it had appeared, and her stomach lurched. But then the delay could be due to anything, she tried to convince herself – although she was normally as regular as clockwork and Ruby usually booked her clients around it. She'd noticed that her breasts had become quite tender over the last couple of weeks, and for some reason she had not been able to face breakfast. *But it can't be*, she told herself. *I've religiously used the methods that Ruby and Daisy told me about to avoid an unwanted pregnancy.* Her hand unconsciously dropped to her stomach. Was it her imagination, or was it ever so slightly swollen?

She shook her head to try and clear it of the terrifying thoughts and yanked out her lace-trimmed bloomers from the drawer. Even so, after being brought up in the courts she had seen more pregnant women than she cared to remember, and the symptoms they displayed. They tended to breed like rabbits there and she was suddenly afraid. She loved the life she was living now and couldn't begin to imagine how awful it would be if she had to go back to the old one. Especially if she was having a child. What would her family say?

No, she told herself firmly, *I'm just letting my imagination run away with me*, and she turned her thoughts to her first client of the day, an elderly accountant who had become one of her regulars. Like Judge Williams, he always arrived bearing a gift and she wondered what he might bring today.

As Fleur and Maryann sat with their heads bent over a book, Maryann found herself glancing every so often towards the door. She had hoped that Mr Marshall would look in that morning whilst Fleur was at her lessons, but so far there had been no sign of him. Still, she knew she shouldn't expect too much of him, too soon. He had never actually been involved in his daughter's life until recently, and he would probably need a little time to get used to the idea.

'Fish!' Fleur said triumphantly as she pointed towards one of the brightly illustrated pictures in the book spread out before her.

'Very good,' Maryann praised her. 'Now shall we see if we can spell the word? Which letter does it begin with?' She pointed down to the alphabet letters she had cut out of coloured paper and placed in a line above the book, and Fleur narrowed her eyes in concentration as she looked along them before pointing to the letter D.

'Not quite,' Maryann told her patiently. 'Shall we try again?'

Fleur turned her attention back to the letters, and when she stabbed her finger at the right one, Maryann hugged her.

'Clever girl. You're getting really good at this now, sweetheart. At this rate you'll be reading and writing in no time.'

It was then that she heard the door open and turning her head she was thrilled to see Wesley hovering there. He looked as if he were about to take flight at any minute, but as though it was an everyday occurrence for him to be there, she said lightly, 'Come and see how clever Fleur is getting with her letters.' The last thing she wanted to do was make him feel uncomfortable and frighten him away.

He cautiously approached the table and, delighted to see him again, Fleur pointed to the picture.

'Fish!'

'Very good, my dear.' He had a lump in his throat as he stared at the girl's shining hair. Fleur dashed away from the table then to fetch her dolly, which she proudly presented to him.

'My baby,' she said, holding it out, and he gently took it from her and pretended to examine her.

'She's very pretty.'

As he handed it back she solemnly repeated, 'Very pretty!'

She seemed happier than he had ever seen her. But then that was no wonder. Maryann really was doing a remarkable job with the child.

'I was thinking that once she's got a little more fluent with her letters and her numbers, you might consider bringing in a tutor just for a few hours a week,' Maryann suggested to him then. 'I can teach her the basics but I don't profess to be a teacher.'

'Well, from what I can see you appear to be doing remarkably well,' he said. And then suddenly Fleur reached out and took his hand, and shock registered on his face. It came to him that he had never actually touched her before, and yet the feel of her warm little hand in his was actually quite pleasant.

'See Teddy.' She began to haul her father towards the chair next to the window where a number of dolls and teddy bears were sitting, and Maryann was thrilled when she saw that he didn't pull away.

This might be just the beginning for them, she found herself thinking, and she offered up a silent prayer that she was right. Next, she decided, she would ask Wesley if he would care to take a walk with them one afternoon.

She was still very mindful of what Toby had told her the Sunday before, that within a year he could be in a position to buy his cottage. There would be nothing to stop them getting wed then, and if by that time she had managed to build up a loving relationship between Fleur and the little girl's father she would be able to leave with a clear conscience. Suddenly everything was falling into place and she contentedly watched Fleur and Wesley solemnly examining her family of toys.

Sunday morning dawned grey and overcast, and by the afternoon the rain was pouring steadily down from a leaden sky.

'Will you come away from that winder, lass, an' sit yourself down,' Nellie scolded. 'Toby'll be here, I guarantee it, if he said he was comin'.'

Maryann had been like a cat on hot bricks ever since lunchtime and was concerned that the gusty wet day might put him off.

From his seat at the side of the fire, Benny grinned at her. Everybody was so much more relaxed with Miss Florence away, and they were all hoping she wouldn't rush back any day soon.

And then Maryann gave a cry of joy and tugging the back door open she was off across the yard, only to return some minutes later hauling a rather bedraggled-looking Toby by the hand.

'Let me take your coat, it's wet through, then go and sit by the fire while I fetch you a nice hot drink,' she ordered bossily, and meek as a lamb Toby did as he was told.

Nellie scowled as she looked across at him. The lad wasn't

his normal chirpy self at all, and she sensed that something was badly wrong. He looked as if he had the weight of the world on his shoulders.

Maryann chattered away happily to him as he drank his tea, but she got the impression that he wasn't really listening to her. And then suddenly he blurted out, 'Maryann . . . I need to tell you something.'

'If you need to talk in private yer can both go into the drawin' room, seein' as Miss Florence ain't here,' Nellie said tactfully.

'Thanks, Nellie.' He gave her a weak smile. 'But you'll all find out about it soon enough, so you may as well hear it now.' He sighed heavily avoiding Maryann's eyes as he stated quietly, 'I'm afraid our Hugo stole me savings at the beginnin' o' the week. Every last penny is gone.'

'*What!*' Maryann was horrified. 'But why would he do that?'

'Seems he had some hare-brained scheme about runnin' off to London an' makin' his fortune, but the first night he got there he was robbed while he was asleep an' he had to come home on the mail train as far as Coventry, then hitch a ride on a farmer's cart back into Nuneaton. He'd caught a fever an' all, after stayin' out in the cold all night, an' fer a time we thought we'd lose him.'

'Oh, Toby, I'm so sorry.' Maryann could feel his pain, and placing her arms about his shoulders she hugged him. She of all people knew just how hard Toby had worked for that money. Since the day he had left school he had scrimped and saved and gone without any pleasures so that he could buy a home of his own, away from the courtyards. And now he was telling her it was all gone, just like that, in a single stroke.

Benny, who had been listening closely, asked, 'Why did he say he was going to London?'

241

'Seems he thought he could make something of himself there.'

'Hmm, well, it sounds like a bit too much of a coincidence to me.'

'What do you mean?' Maryann raised her eyebrows.

'Well . . .' Benny pondered on whether he should say anything or not for a moment, but then deciding that there was nothing to be gained by remaining silent he went on, 'The thing is, I saw Hugo comin' out o' the barn a while ago, shortly after Miss Florence had come out, an' judgin' by the state o' the pair of 'em, it didn't take much guessin' about what they'd been up to. In fact, Hugo went to great pains to let me know that they were . . . well, yer know.'

'Hugo an' Miss Florence?' Nellie gasped incredulously. 'Surely not, lad? Hugo's only a kid compared to her.'

'He may well be. But I know what I saw, an' what Hugo told me. He was openly braggin' about the fact that he and Miss Florence had just had a romp. So going on that, don't you find it rather strange that he should suddenly disappear off to London at the same time as her?'

They all gazed at each other as a stunned silence settled on the room.

Chapter Twenty-Eight

'I'm so sorry about what's happened, Toby,' Maryann told him when she had walked him to the gates of Windy Manor early that evening. 'I know how hard you've worked to save that money up.'

'Aye, I did.' He gazed down at the lights of Bermuda village in the valley below them. 'An' now I'll have to start all over again,' he ended bitterly.

Maryann was feeling heartsore for him, but she suddenly blurted out angrily, 'I can't believe that Hugo would do this to you. Surely now you will see him for the selfish person he is!'

But Toby wouldn't met her eyes. 'Happen you're right, but he's still me little brother, ain't he?'

'But this means it will be *ages* before we can be together!' Suddenly she had had enough of waiting for Toby to declare his feelings for her and *do* something about it! Two high spots of colour appeared in her cheeks.

'Can't be 'elped, can it?' He shuffled from foot to foot and

Maryann had the feeling that he wanted to get away, rather than discuss their future. Yet strangely, although this latest development would mean a long delay before they could be together, she wasn't as disappointed as she had thought she would be. After all, she was happy at the Manor and it would mean she could stay on longer with Fleur, of whom she had become very fond. The leaves were fluttering from the trees like rose petals at a wedding as they stood there, and it was bitterly cold, but wrapped up in her fine new cloak Maryann felt warm and snug.

'I suppose I'd best get off then,' Toby said eventually. 'An' when I get back, Hugo's goin' to have some explainin' to do. Whatever was he thinkin' of, messin' about wi' the master's sister, eh? Surely he knew nothin' could ever come of it. People like them don't care much for the likes of us.'

'That's not entirely true,' Maryann said, quickly coming to the master's defence. 'Mr Marshall is a good, kind man – and from what he's told me he's been making a lot of improvements to the working conditions for the people at the mill. I admit that Miss Florence isn't so nice though,' she ended lamely.

Toby looked at her oddly for a moment. She was very quick to take Mr Marshall's side. But then he shrugged and after squeezing her hand he set off without another word. Maryann watched him go for a while and then turning about she slowly made her way back to the house in a frustrated mood. Hugo was a bad apple, there were no two ways about it, but even after what he had done, it seemed that Toby was prepared to defend him.

Over the next week, Mr Marshall made two visits to the mill, much to Seth Brown's disgust. The master was turning soft, taking such an interest in his employees' welfare all of a sudden, and he had a good idea why and all, as he voiced to some of the other foremen one lunchtime.

'It's ever since that Meadows bitch moved up to the Manor,' he confided with a knowing wink. 'Have yer seen the way she struts about the town in her fancy dresses an' her fine cloak an' bonnet? Makes yer think, don't it? She's taken him in, that's what she's done, an' I wouldn't mind bettin' she's a sight more than just a nanny to his imbecile brat.'

As gossip was prone to do in such a small community, word soon spread and the following Sunday on her afternoon off when Maryann visited the court to see Granny Addison and Toby, the woman greeted her with a concerned expression.

'I ought to tell yer that there's talk that the master o' the mill has taken yer as his mistress,' she told Maryann, watching closely for the girl's reaction.

Maryann's shocked face told her all she needed to know – not that she'd ever believed there was any truth in the rumours.

'What?' Maryann was horrified. 'But Mr Marshall has never behaved as anything other than a perfect gentleman to me,' she gasped.

Granny shrugged. 'Well, I suppose wi' Miss Florence clearin' off to London an' you bein' alone up there with him, it's set folks jumpin' to the wrong conclusions.'

'But I'm *not* alone with him,' Maryann objected hotly. 'Benny and the Carters are all living there too, and they'll all tell you that there's no truth in what's being said.'

Granny held her hands up as if to ward off Maryann's anger. 'All right, lass. Calm down. It ain't me as yer have to convince. I dare say people have seen yer walkin' about all dressed up to the nines all of a sudden an' they've put two an' two together an' come up wi' five.'

Undoing the clasp of her cape, Maryann threw it over the

back of a chair and began to pace agitatedly up and down the small confines of her old neighbour's kitchen, her skirts and petticoats whirling about her as if she had been caught in a gale.

'You just can't do right in this town,' she said fiercely. 'You're condemned if you're poor and you're condemned if you try to get on. I'm just doing an honest job. Why do people have to read more than that into it?'

'That's just how folks are,' Granny answered shrewdly. 'But I shouldn't let it worry yer. While they're talkin' about you they'll be leavin' some other poor devil alone.'

'I'm afraid that's not much consolation. What if Toby were to hear it?'

'Matter o' fact he already has, but you've no worries there. He knows you better than that, pet.'

Maryann's anger dispersed as quickly as it had come and her shoulders suddenly slumped. She had begun to think that things were looking up for her, but now she had all this tittle-tattle to deal with, when all she really yearned for was a quiet life.

'Come on now,' Granny said cajolingly. 'There ain't nothin' to be gained by gettin' yerself in a state. Truth be told, I was in two minds whether to tell yer or not, but I didn't want yer hearin' it from someone else as you no doubt would have. You just go out there an' hold yer head high. You've done nothin' wrong so just let it die down. They'll have someone else to gossip about in no time, you just see if I ain't right.'

'I suppose so,' Maryann agreed pensively. Her biggest concern now was whether the rumours might reach the master's ears. Would he dismiss her if they did? But then deciding that there was nothing much she could do about it, she finally sat down and let Granny fuss over her until Toby eventually arrived.

When he did, his glum expression decided her. She had been toying with an idea ever since the week before, and now she felt it was time to put it to him. But not yet. She would wait until he was walking her back to the Manor and they could speak in private.

And so early that evening as they battled the cold October wind, which was threatening to blow her bonnet away, she said cautiously, 'Toby, I've been thinking . . .'

'Oh yes, what about?'

'Well, the thing is . . .' She clung on to his arm and took a deep breath before rushing on, 'I wonder if we shouldn't just get married now and be done with it.'

'What?' He stared at her as if she had lost her senses. 'But we've got no savings – nothin'! How would we live?'

'Probably a lot more comfortably than most,' she said stoically. 'You've still got your wages coming in each week and I could have a word with Mr Marshall and ask him if I could still work there with Fleur during the day. With my wages coming in too we could rent somewhere temporarily and still manage to save a bit.'

He shook his head. 'No.'

Maryann felt let down again and humiliated. Was having his own place really more important to him than them being together?

'But – but there are rumours flying around about me and Mr Marshall!' she protested.

Toby waved his hand dismissively. 'So what? You and I know there's nothin' in 'em so let 'em talk. We'll get wed when I feel the time is right an' not a day before.'

'But what about when I feel the time is right?'

He forced a smile and squeezed her hand. 'It'll happen if yer just be patient. Like I've always told yer, I don't want to end up like most folks round here, doin' a dirty job fer the rest o' me life wi' a rook o' kids round me neck. No, we're gonna wait an' do this properly. It'll be worth it in the end, you'll see.'

At this, Maryann felt a little surge of resentment, and not for the first time. Why did Toby seem to think it would be *him* making all the sacrifices? She loved her job at the Manor, but even so she would have given it up in a sigh if need be, in order to be with him. Her parents had always been as poor as church mice but they had been happy and content to be together – so why was Toby being like this?

He confused her further then when he said, 'Oh, an' by the way, I shan't be able to see yer for the next couple o' Sundays. Now the weather's turned so cold they're doin' Sunday shifts at the pit an' I've put me name down for 'em.'

'But Sunday afternoon is the only chance we get to see each other now,' she objected weakly.

'I know, but needs must.'

Silence settled between them then until they reached the gates of the Manor, where Maryann told him shortly, 'You needn't come any further. I'm sure you'll want to get back and rest if you're going to be working extra shifts.'

Ignoring the sarcasm in her tone he simply nodded and after giving her hand another squeeze, he turned about and marched back in the direction they had just come in. Maryann didn't watch him go today as she normally did, but set off for the house with her lips set in an angry line.

November swept in almost before they knew it. Fleur was spending a little time down in the kitchen with Nellie and Cissie now that the weather was too cold to venture outside, and the women spoiled her shamelessly. The child was blossoming before their very eyes, and the atmosphere was light with no Miss Florence or Miss Lord to spoil it. The master looked a lot better too lately, Nellie commented one day. His appetite had returned and he had lost the pallor that had been worrying her for a time. The only problem they seemed to have was that some of their suppliers were asking to be paid now and Miss Lord normally saw to that.

'Well, I'm sure if I was allowed to look at her account books I could settle the bills,' Maryann volunteered and so Nellie had a word with Mr Marshall and he willingly gave his permission.

The very same night when Fleur was tucked up in bed all warm and cosy and fast asleep, Nellie got the key to Miss Lord's room and she and Maryann entered it to fetch the account books.

'I know she keeps 'em all in that little desk over there by the winder,' Nellie said as they lit the oil lamp.

In no time at all Maryann had located the one she needed and she told Nellie, 'I may as well come and go through it in the kitchen where it's warm, if you don't mind?'

Nellie was only too happy to oblige, since Maryann was like one of the family now. 'I'll just go an' get my order book an' all so yer can see what's what,' she said and bustled away to fetch it.

Soon Maryann was engrossed as she made lists of all the suppliers that needed paying. Nellie had marked down everything she had ordered in her own book so that Maryann was able to then enter it neatly, along with the outgoing amounts, into Miss Lord's ledger. But soon she was frowning.

'Nellie, have we ordered a lot less meat from the butcher this month than we normally do?' she asked. She supposed it was quite possible, with two fewer people in the household to feed – but then there did seem to be an enormous difference in the amount compared to the previous months.

'Slightly less, I dare say, but not so much as you'd notice,' Nellie replied, glancing up from the sock she was darning at the side of the fire.

Maryann nodded before moving onto the bills for the everyday items. Again, the amount of money spent on candles and oil was much higher than the bill that Nellie had presented her with – and yet surely the earlier bills should have been *less* for the summer months when the nights were lighter?

Meticulously she worked through the small pile of bills and it soon became apparent that there was a significant discrepancy somewhere. Some of the bills Miss Lord had entered in the ledger were double the amount of the ones that Nellie had presented her with. But why? Maryann wondered – and then as the answer came to her, a sick feeling started in the pit of her stomach.

'Nellie, would you mind coming over here?' she asked quietly, and when the woman obliged, Maryann went on to show her the huge difference in the amounts.

'Bloody hell!' Nellie gasped, stabbing a finger at the accounts for September. 'She's entered two whole pounds fer candles there, but I happen to know that I didn't need more than ten shillings' worth that month. Look, I've got it written down in me book somewhere.' Sure enough, she pointed to an amount that was a fraction of what Miss Lord had recorded, and the two women stared at each other for a moment.

'Who actually pays these bills?' Maryann asked, wondering what she had got herself into.

'Why, Miss Lord does, o' course.' Nellie fidgeted nervously. 'I enter the amounts I've spent in me book then pass the bills on to her. Then when she's brought the accounts up to date she takes the book through to the master an' he gives her enough to pay 'em all.'

'Hmm.' There was a silence.

'She's been creamin' money off the master right, left an' centre, ain't she?' Nellie croaked eventually.

'It does appear that way,' Maryann nodded solemnly. 'But what do we do about it?'

'There's only one thing we *can* do from where I'm standin'. You'll have to take the whole lot through to him an' let him see fer himself, lass.'

Aware that she was about to stir up a hornets' nest, Maryann shuddered. Even so, she knew that Nellie was right. The master needed to be made aware of what was going on right beneath his nose, and there was no time like the present. She slammed the books shut, Nellie's and Miss Lord's, and tucked them beneath her arm, then with a last apprehensive glance at Nellie, she headed purposefully towards the library.

Chapter Twenty-Nine

Half an hour later as Wesley Marshall straightened from leaning across the books she had spread out on his desk, Maryann saw that his face was flushed.

'She has inflated every single bill that Nellie ever presented to her,' he said with ominous calm.

Maryann remained silent. What could she say? The facts spread in front of them spoke for themselves.

'I blame myself,' he muttered. 'I should have asked for the actual bills to be presented to me – not just believed what she cared to write down in the damn book.' He glanced apologetically at her then and began to pace up and down with his hands clasped behind his back. 'Excuse my language, Maryann. I know everyone thinks I am a soft man, but I am not a fool. How long did Miss Lord think she could get away with this?'

Maryann bobbed her knee and made a hasty exit, mumbling, 'I'm so sorry, sir.'

'So what did he say then?' Nellie asked anxiously the

second Maryann set foot into the kitchen. 'He didn't think this fiddlin' were owt to do wi' me, did he?'

'Not at all,' Maryann assured her. 'But he is very angry with Miss Lord and he's going to write to Miss Florence and request that they both come home as soon as possible.'

'Oh no!' Nellie rolled her eyes heavenwards. 'That's the end of our peace an' quiet then.'

'The good news is that Mr Marshall has asked if you will interview someone tomorrow who has applied for the post of maid here. And that's not all – he's going to set another man on to help with the gardens and all the outside work.'

'Thank the Lord fer that,' Ted piped up. 'Even wi' young Benny here doin' the lion's share now, it takes us all our time to keep on top of it. Another pair o' hands will be greatly appreciated.'

'So how much do yer think Miss Lord has fiddled then?' Nellie asked, returning to the main topic of the evening.

'I honestly don't know,' Maryann said. 'But Mr Marshall almost had a fit when he saw how much she wrote that she had paid to the wine merchant. I have an idea it could run into an awful lot of money.'

'Do yer reckon he'll bring the authorities in?'

'No, but from what he said I think there's a good chance she'll get instant dismissal without a reference.'

'Serves herself right,' Nellie said righteously. 'Me an' mine have worked for the Marshall family for more years than I care to remember, an' I can say hand on heart that never once have I taken a penny that weren't mine. But there you are. It takes all sorts I dare say.'

Florence and Miss Lord arrived back in the middle of the following week and instantly the atmosphere in the house changed.

'Where is my brother?' Florence barked at Cissie as she flung her hat and coat at her, then before the girl could answer: 'Get Meadows to fetch our trunks in immediately.'

'The master is at the mill, miss. He goes in at least three days a week now. I'll fetch Benny right away.'

'See that you do, and then bring Miss Lord and me some tea in the drawing room. We've had a long journey, though why Wesley should insist we should rush back so soon, I really do not know. It's most unreasonable of him.'

Nothing would have delighted Cissie more than to tell her exactly why, but she wisely held her tongue and limped away on her crutch to do as she was told.

Nellie instantly flew into a panic. 'Trust her to turn up wi' no warning,' she grumbled. 'I were only planning on having Maryann an' the master to cook for tonight. I shall have to get that joint o' beef I were counting' on roasting tomorrer out o' the larder now.'

Maryann meanwhile was chewing worriedly on her lip as she glanced towards Fleur, who was busily rolling out some pastry that Nellie had saved for her to play with, on the kitchen table. She had rolled it out and then squashed it into a ball so many times that it looked grubby now but she was obviously enjoying herself enormously.

'I'll try and sneak Fleur back upstairs while you serve Florence her tea in the drawing room,' she whispered to Cissie. She shuddered to imagine what the woman's reaction would be, should she bump into the child in the hallway. But then her plans went awry when Miss Lord suddenly strode into the kitchen in her usual manner with her nose in the air. She clearly had no idea why she and Miss Florence had been summoned home. Now she stared at Fleur in disgust.

'What is *that* doing in here?' She pointed a gloved finger at the child and Fleur instantly dropped the rolling pin and hurrying over to Maryann, buried her face in her skirts.

Ah well, thought Maryann, may as well get it over with, and drawing herself up to her full height whilst keeping a protective arm about Fleur's slight shoulders she told her calmly, 'Miss Fleur often comes down to the kitchen now.'

'She does *what*?' The woman looked at her incredulously.

'And before you tell me that too much activity is bad for her I should inform you that not only is Dr Piper fully aware of her new routine, but he is fully in favour of it too, so if you have any objections regarding my care of her, perhaps you would like to take it up with him?'

'I rather think Miss Florence will do that! The routine she had set for the creature had always worked perfectly well – until *you* turned up.' And with that, Elizabeth Lord stamped away to her room.

'She won't be so cocky when the master gets in,' Nellie grinned. 'How the mighty are fallen, eh? An' that one will have a long way to fall.' And with that she bustled away to get Fleur a nice jam tart fresh from the oven, hoping to cheer her up again.

As the master was handing the reins of his horse over to Benny in the stableyard early that evening, Benny informed him quietly, 'Miss Florence and Miss Lord are back, sir.'

'Oh!' The smile instantly faded from the man's face. He had been looking forward to a quiet dinner with Maryann and Fleur that evening, but he couldn't see that happening now that his sister was home. She would never countenance him dining with them, not if he knew her. She had clearly taken an instant dislike to Maryann the very first day she had set foot through the door, and knowing Florence as he did, he couldn't imagine her changing her opinion, especially when she saw the changes that Maryann had made to Fleur's care. He imagined that she wouldn't be any too pleased either to discover that he was finally spending time with his daughter! Even so, he had more pressing things on his mind at present than his sister's notorious tantrums. Miss Lord!

He began to walk away, slapping his riding crop against the side of his leg, before he remembered his manners and paused to say, 'Thank you, Meadows.'

Benny inclined his head before leading Storm away for a good rub-down.

Nellie looked up in surprise when Mr Marshall entered the kitchen through the back door. They rarely saw him in there but before she could greet him, he said shortly, 'Would you or Cissie mind going to tell Miss Lord that I wish to see her immediately in the drawing room, please, Nellie.'

'O' course, sir. I think she's in her room.' She nodded towards Cissie who instantly grabbed her crutch and hopped away to do as she was bid. Nellie then asked, 'Is there anythin' I can get for yer, sir? A cup o' tea perhaps?'

'No, thank you, Nellie. Maybe later.'

She watched him leave the kitchen with a heavy heart. Wesley Marshall was a gentle man and she guessed how hard the confrontation ahead was going to be for him. But then what option did he have? He couldn't have those who worked for him fiddling him left, right and centre, now could he? She sighed. Elizabeth Lord obviously hadn't known how well off she was working for him, but Nellie had a sneaky suspicion she was going to find out now – and sooner rather than later, judging by the expression on the master's face.

As Maryann was returning Fleur's dinner tray to the kitchen an hour later, she saw Miss Lord storm into Florence's room with tears streaming down her cheeks. The woman left the door swinging wide open behind her, and not wishing to appear to be eavesdropping, Maryann halted uncertainly.

'He's found out,' Elizabeth sobbed and Maryann bit down on her lip. Should she go back to Fleur's room, or continue? If she did the latter, she was bound to be seen.

'What do you mean, he's found out?' Florence was changing for dinner.

'He had all the account books – everything! That bitch he employed to look after Fleur looked at them whilst we were away and noted the discrepancies,' Elizabeth wailed. 'And now he has dismissed me. What are we going to do?'

Maryann heard Florence's sharp intake of breath, then, 'You didn't tell him that I was involved in this, did you?'

'Of course not!' Elizabeth cried. 'But that money was for our future together. What shall we do now?'

'And what about . . . *the other thing*, in London?'

'He has no idea about that.'

Maryann wondered what 'the other thing' could be, but then Florence went on with a note of panic in her voice, 'I must talk to him. Don't cry, darling. Things will be all right, you'll see. I have always been able to wrap Wesley around my little finger. Now come here.'

When there was a silence Maryann hastily moved on, but as she scurried past the room she glanced inside and what she saw made the colour drain from her face. Florence and Elizabeth were locked in each other's arms and they were kissing as only lovers could.

She was so shocked that she almost stumbled, but she forced herself to descend the stairs calmly, and only when she reached the bottom did she pause to place the tray down on a small table. Her hands were shaking as she tried to make sense of what she had just seen. Miss Florence and Miss Lord lovers? Yet only a few weeks before, Benny had informed them all that Florence had been seeing Hugo. That was why he had stolen Toby's money and raced off to

257

London, to try and find her. It just didn't make any sense and yet she couldn't dispute what she had just seen.

At that moment she became aware of someone coming down the stairs. She started, then breathed a sigh of relief when she saw that it was Wesley Marshall.

'Ah, Maryann . . .' He paused. She looked as if she had seen a ghost. 'Might I have a word? We could go into the drawing room.'

She nodded, too shocked to speak, but followed him meekly. Once the door was closed behind them he asked, 'Are you all right? You look very pale.'

'Y-yes, sir. I'm fine,' she managed to mumble.

'Oh. Good. Well the thing is, you are probably aware that Florence and Miss Lord are home.' He shook his head, obviously agitated. 'I confronted Miss Lord about the account books and she could not deny that there was a considerable amount of money missing. And so unfortunately I had no alternative but to dismiss her. She is probably telling her mistress about it right now.'

She certainly is, Maryann thought, but she remained tight-lipped as she stared back at him steadily.

'I have told her that I want her gone by the end of the week,' Wesley continued. 'It's most disagreeable but I cannot employ staff who are not trustworthy. The other thing is . . .' He looked decidedly uncomfortable now. 'I know we were all going to dine together this evening, but under the circumstances—'

'It's quite all right,' Maryann assured him hastily. 'I understand that it would not be appropriate to do so now that Miss Florence is home, and I don't mind, really I don't.'

'Thank you.'

Managing a polite smile she backed towards the door and in a second she was gone, leaving him to stare after her feeling strangely bereft.

Chapter Thirty

'Put that down and get out, you useless cripple!' Florence screeched at Cissie shortly afterwards as she carried some of the silver serving dishes containing their meal into the dining room.

'Yes, miss,' Cissie said with a tremor in her voice, and after dropping the dishes onto the sideboard she limped in ungainly fashion from the room as fast as her crutch would allow her to.

'Lordy, she's screamin' at the master in there at the top of her voice,' she told Nellie when she came back into the kitchen.

'I know – we can hear 'em even from in here,' Nellie said. 'Best leave the rest o' this food where it is till things have calmed down a bit. Miss Lord came in, lookin' very sorry for herself, I might add, to tell me that she wants her meal served on a tray in her room.' Glancing towards the remaining dish, she grumbled, 'All the trouble I went to an' all. It'll be stone cold at this rate.'

'Ah well, no point in us goin' hungry an' all, is there,' Ted piped up. 'Let's have ours an' leave 'em to it, eh?'

They all sat down to their meal but noticing that Maryann made little attempt to eat hers, Nellie eyed her worriedly, asking, 'Are you all right, pet? Yer as white as a sheet. Has that bitch had a go at you an' all?'

'Not yet,' Maryann said ruefully. 'But I'm sure she will at the first opportunity.' She was still reeling from the shock of what she had witnessed and wondered if she should tell them, but then she decided to wait a while. Things were quite bad enough as it was without her adding fuel to the fire.

'I'm takin' Blaze an' Bracken to the blacksmith to have new shoes fitted tomorrow,' Benny said conversationally as he tucked into the tender meat on his plate, and he and Ted then began to discuss the horses, one of their favourite topics, as the women picked at their food and fell silent.

'I'm telling you, Wesley. I cannot do without Elizabeth,' Florence stormed. 'That creature must have been mistaken. Elizabeth would never steal from you!'

'I'm afraid the evidence that she did just that is written down in black and white, and in the circumstances she should think herself very lucky that I haven't called in the authorities and had her sent to prison – where she might well have been sent to the colonies!' her brother said as calmly as he could. Florence in one of her tantrums was a force to be reckoned with, but this time he was determined not to give in to her. He had allowed his sister free rein in the household for long enough, but now it was high time to remind her who was the master there.

She was pacing the room like a woman possessed, and now she rounded on him again to ask, 'But who will take over the housekeeping and act as my lady's maid if Elizabeth goes?'

'We can appoint another one. Someone we can trust next time,' he answered firmly.

Florence was panicking now and she began to cry. She had been able to turn the tears on like a tap since a very early age and it usually never failed to work.

'Wesley, I beg you to reconsider,' she sniffed. 'Surely if I paid back the money you think she has taken, we could put this behind us? You could stop it out of my allowance. I'm sure it is nothing more than a genuine misunderstanding and I promise she will never do such a thing again. I would miss her so, should she be sent away. She is my only friend since my fiancé deserted me so cruelly . . .'

Seeing him waver she hurried on, 'Please, Wesley! I beg you not to send away my only friend.'

His mouth worked indecisively for a moment before he said, 'If I allowed her to stay – and I only say *if* – then there would have to be changes. For a start I would only allow her to stay on in the role of a lady's maid to you. I shall ask Nellie if she could be in charge of checking the household accounts each week until I appoint a new housekeeper, and I would no longer permit her to dine with us.'

Florence instantly opened her mouth to object but then thinking better of it she quickly clamped it shut again. If Wesley would only agree to Elizabeth staying, there would be time to work on him about the dining arrangements at a later date.

'Very well,' she answered meekly, although inside she was still seething. This was all that girl's fault! She had been nothing but trouble since the day she had entered the house, and now more than ever, Florence was determined to get rid of her.

Truthfully, she would not have cared if she never set eyes on Elizabeth again. She had simply been a diversion, much as Hugo had been. Florence had discovered long ago at finishing school that her sexual needs could be sated by either sex. But that had not been the main reason why she had kept Elizabeth in her employ. The woman was so gullible, willing to do anything she asked, believing that when Wesley and Fleur were gone she would live happily ever after in Windy Manor with her female lover. But to Florence, Elizabeth was just a means to an end, and once Florence had achieved what she wanted, she would drop her like a ton of bricks, or better still, have her disposed of. She was well aware that there were people in the town who would do anything for money – even make a person disappear without trace. But not yet – for now Elizabeth was still essential to her plans. And so she stared at her brother imploringly until at last he relented.

'Oh, very well,' he said. 'She may stay, but only on the terms that I have just laid down.'

'Oh, thank you,' his sister whispered, blinking back the tears prettily. 'I shall make sure that you don't regret this, dear, and I shall keep a very careful eye on her from now on. But now shall we eat?'

'I find I have no appetite,' Wesley answered tartly, striding towards the door with his mouth set in a grim line, and with that he was gone.

Breathing a sigh of relief, Florence dropped down onto the nearest chair. That was the first problem resolved; now she must think of a way to get rid of the girl! Her fingers played on the tiny glass vial in her pocket but she wouldn't worry about that for now. There would be plenty of time to continue with the next part of her plan tomorrow.

The house soon settled back into some sort of routine, but everyone seemed slightly subdued. During Miss Florence's absence the place had rung with Fleur's laughter and the sound of her footsteps echoing along the corridors. But now she was closely confined to her room again, and she had become a little fretful. The bitterly cold weather had made it unwise for her to venture outside and she would stare from the window of her room longingly, like a little bird that was trapped in a cage. Whenever Miss Florence was out, Maryann would sneak her down to the kitchen, but for the rest of the time she was forced to entertain the child as best as she could in her room.

Before they knew it they were into December and Fleur was enchanted one morning to see that the landscape was sparkling with frost.

'Look – everything has been painted white,' she told Maryann excitedly as she pointed across the lawns. Her father had slipped in to see her before leaving for the mill, as he often did now, and she was bored.

Maryann stroked the child's hair affectionately. 'Yes, it's pretty, isn't it? It's called frost and soon we might have some snow.'

Fleur instantly scampered away to fetch a book with a picture of a snowman in it.

'That's right, snow,' Maryann told her indulgently, but there was no time to say any more for just then they heard a shout out on the landing and the next minute the door was flung open and Florence stood there.

'My ruby brooch is missing. Do you know anything about it?' she asked accusingly.

Maryann's hand flew to her breast as Fleur covered her eyes with her hands.

'No, I do *not*,' she replied indignantly.

Florence sneered, her eyes cold and condemning. 'Then you won't mind if I search your room, will you?'

Maryann almost choked with indignation. 'If you feel you must, then go ahead – but I assure you, you will not find it there. And I want someone present whilst you do it,' she added, not trusting Florence an inch.

'Very well. Go and ask Nellie to come upstairs immediately.'

Maryann looked down at Fleur before saying gently, 'You stay here, sweetheart, and look at your book. I won't be long.'

She and Florence left the room then and she walked past the woman with her head held high. She had just reached the bottom of the stairs when Wesley appeared through the front door. Spotting her he told her, 'Storm just threw a shoe so I've had to come back.' Then noting her expression, he asked, 'Is something wrong?'

'Actually there is, sir, as it happens.' Maryann had to fight very hard to swallow the tears that were threatening. 'It appears that a brooch of Miss Florence's has gone missing and she's insisting on searching my room. She asked me to fetch Nellie to watch while she did it.'

He scowled, then throwing his hat down he told her, 'There's no need to disturb Nellie. I shall come, although I don't believe for a single moment that we will find it in your room. Come along.'

When they got upstairs they found Florence standing outside Maryann's room with a smug expression on her face. She looked mildly surprised to see her brother but when he told her why he had been forced to return, she shrugged.

'Perhaps it's as well you're here to see for yourself what sort of a person we've employed to look after your daughter,' she said acidly. 'Shall we go in and start?'

Cissie, who had been busily washing the insides of the windows on the long landing, lifted her bucket and went back downstairs without a word before they entered the room, wondering what the mistress was going to come up with next. She was a nasty piece of work; there was no doubt about it.

Deeply humiliated, Maryann stood with her hands clasped tightly together as Florence made a great show of flinging one of the drawers open. Wesley looked embarrassed too but they both remained silent as the woman then went on to the next drawer.

'Nothing there,' she commented eventually, as if she was greatly enjoying herself. She then checked the wardrobe as colour burned in Maryann's cheeks.

'And nothing there!' Crossing to the bed, she swished aside the blankets on the neatly made bed, scattering them into a heap on the floor. The pillows then followed, but even that wasn't enough for her.

'It seems there is only one place left to look now, doesn't it?' With a satisfied smirk on her face she heaved aside the mattress but then her face fell when there was nothing beneath it.

'Are you quite satisfied now?' Wesley said from between clenched teeth. 'It appears you owe Miss Meadows an apology, Florence.'

'B-but . . .' Florence was speechless but her brother had had quite enough.

'I suggest you now put everything back as you found it,' he said sternly. 'And I am still waiting for that apology!'

'I refuse to apologise to the likes of her,' the furious woman spat. 'She is just a servant and I most certainly will not put anything back. I'm sure she took it and nothing will make me think otherwise.'

'This is ridiculous,' Wesley said angrily. 'Let us go and check your jewellery box. You must have missed it.'

'Fine! And then perhaps you will believe me when I say that it's been stolen.' Florence threw a malevolent glare at Maryann as she marched past her and slowly she and Wesley followed her along the landing.

Once in her room, she waved towards her jewellery box,

265

saying, 'Go on then. See for yourself. My ruby brooch is missing and I know it was there yesterday. I wore it to go into town and put it safely away last night.'

She smirked as Wesley crossed to the box and opened the lid, but then her mouth fell open when after a moment he lifted a delicate gold brooch in the shape of a leaf set with a large ruby to ask, 'Isn't this the one you are talking of, Florence?'

'B-but it can't be! I tell you it wasn't there earlier on. She must have returned it.'

'This nonsense has to stop!' Wesley's nerves were stretched to the limit now. 'You merely overlooked it, so all this upset and accusation was for nothing. I suggest you are more careful in future.' And with that he took Maryann's elbow and led her from the room, closing the door firmly behind them and leaving his sister in no doubt whatsoever of how angry he was.

'Maryann . . .' he said falteringly once they were back outside Fleur's room. 'I don't know what to say to you. I can't begin to tell you how appalled I am at my sister's accusation, and I can only apologise profusely for her behaviour.'

She shrugged. 'I assure you, sir, I have never stolen a single thing in my life and I am not about to start now.'

'Believe me, I never thought for one single moment that you had.' It was obvious that he was greatly distressed. She was suddenly addressing him as 'sir' again, yet during Florence's stay in London they had been on first-name terms.

'I . . . I think that it might be best if I tendered my resignation,' she said then. 'Miss Florence is never going to accept me and I fear that I may be coming between you now.'

'You'll do no such thing!' He was horrified at the very

thought. 'I would rather send *her* away than you,' he ended, and he was astounded to realise that he meant it.

Maryann said nothing but silently let herself into Fleur's room and as he stood there, the truth suddenly hit Wesley like a blow between the eyes. The reason why he was so upset was that somehow, somewhere along the way, he had fallen in love with her, for what good it would do him!

Chapter Thirty-One

'Where is Cissie?' Maryann asked once Fleur had settled for the night and she had gone down to the kitchen.

Nellie crossed to hug her. 'She's just popped over to put a hot brick in young Benny's bed but she told us about what happened earlier on,' she said grimly. 'It seems that Miss Florence tried to set you up, lass, but luckily Cissie happened to see what was goin' on.'

'What do you mean?'

Taking her hand, Nellie led her to a chair and made her sit down. 'Our Cissie were cleanin' the windows on the landin' earlier on when she happened to see Miss Florence goin' into your room. She immediately sensed somethin' fishy afoot so she crept along and peeped inside, just in time to see her lift yer mattress and put something beneath it. O' course, she daren't let the missus spot her so she waited till she'd gone an' then went into your room to see what it was. That's when she found the brooch. She instantly guessed what that bitch

268

were up to, so she took it back to her room an' placed it back in her jewellery box.'

Maryann was so grateful to Cissie for protecting her, and stunned that anyone could stoop to such depths. 'She must really hate me,' she shuddered, and Nellie could only nod in agreement.

'Happen you're right, but at least now we're aware o' what she's capable of.'

'Cissie isn't going to tell the master, is she?' Maryann whispered fearfully. The way she saw it – it could only make things ten times worse.

'She bloody well should do,' Nellie said angrily. 'He needs to know in case the little madam tries anythin' like this again.'

'No, he mustn't know – and neither must Benny. He doesn't, does he?' And when Nellie shook her head, Maryann breathed a sigh of relief. She dreaded to think what he might do if he learned what Florence had been up to. 'Please promise me that you won't tell him, or the master,' she implored, and Nellie nodded reluctantly, although personally she thought Miss Florence deserved everything she got.

'All right then,' she agreed. 'But I can't see why yer should cover up for the likes o' her.' And she then went off to take her frustrations out on whipping the batter for the Yorkshire puddings.

Much later that evening when Maryann was finally tucked down in bed, she gave way to the tears that had been threatening all night. As she sobbed into her pillow, she knew that she would never forget, not if she lived to be a hundred, the humiliation she had suffered while she had been forced to stand by and watch Florence search her room as if she were a common thief. She felt sorry for Wesley too. He had looked so helpless and upset, and she had sensed that he didn't believe in her guilt – which, she supposed, was something.

269

The house seemed so depressing again now, and she found herself remembering the pleasant meals she and Wesley had shared together with Fleur. Of course she knew that this could never happen again, but he had been good company and they had found that they had a surprising amount in common. Her thoughts turned to Toby and she screwed her eyes tightly shut. She had only seen him twice during the last month. He was working every spare minute that he could to try and save again but she was still stinging from his rejection and hadn't missed him nearly as much as she thought she would. The only bright spots in her life at the moment were the Carters, who had made her feel as if she had a family again, and little Fleur, who was fast developing into an adorable little girl. Maryann found that she could look beyond Fleur's condition now to the mischievous little imp within, and she felt herself growing closer to her with every day that passed. She suspected that Wesley did too. He was a frequent visitor to Fleur's room now, much to Florence's disgust, and the child was loving every minute of it.

If only Florence hadn't come back, everything would be perfect, Maryann thought and then instantly felt guilty. The woman had every right to be there. It was her home, whilst Maryann was merely a servant, as Florence gleefully pointed out at every opportunity.

Turning on her side, she waited for sleep to come.

'Benny.'

'Yes, sir?' Benny took his cap off and waited while the master strode across the stableyard to him.

'I know you have a lot of horse-feed to pick up today from the market, but whilst you're there do you think you'd have room on the cart for a couple of Christmas trees as well?'

'I could make room, sir,' Benny beamed as Mr Marshall took some money from his wallet and handed it to him.

'Excellent, then we'll have one as tall as you like and perhaps a slightly smaller one for Miss Fleur's room. I think she'd like that, don't you?'

'I think she'd love it, sir.' Benny's smile died momentarily as he remembered happy Christmases spent at home with his family. This would be the first one without his parents. But then he took the money and swung himself up onto the cart, and after touching his cap he urged the horses on. Cissie was in the seat beside him, all dressed up against the cold, and she giggled.

'Ooh, fancy that, eh? I don't think we've had a Christmas tree in the house since Miss Amélie died.'

Benny asked curiously, 'Exactly how *did* she die, Cissie? No one seems to talk much about her for fear of upsetting the master.'

Cissie pursed her lips before telling him, 'She died falling from one of the windows in the attic, but to be honest everyone seemed to agree that she jumped rather than fell.'

'What – you mean she took her own life like my dad?'

Cissie nodded. 'Yes, it looked that way although of course the doctor recorded a verdict of accidental death to spare the master's feelings.'

'It must have been awful for him,' Benny commented, thinking of how he had felt after his father had hanged himself.

'It was.' But then wishing to change the subject to happier things Cissie said, 'One of the kitchen cats is due a litter any day now, and I was wondering if Miss Fleur might like one. She makes such a fuss of them when she comes down to see us, and having a pet of her own might do her good. What do you think?'

'I think it's an excellent idea, provided Maryann wouldn't mind clearing up after it in her room,' he added.

Cissie chuckled. 'I can't see Maryann minding that. She's made of stern stuff, is your sister. I don't mind admitting she's made that little girl's life worth living and done marvels with her. Between you and me, I reckon she'd have died under Miss Florence's care if Maryann hadn't come along when she did. And worse still, I think Miss Florence would have been glad.'

Benny glanced at her and noticed that the cold air had made her cheeks rosy. She seemed more relaxed too, probably because her workload had been reduced with the arrival of Polly Perkins, the village girl that Nellie had interviewed and set on while Miss Florence was in London. Polly had taken on the role of general maid and didn't seem to mind what she did, from clearing out the fireplaces to helping Nellie prepare the meals. She was a plump, cheerful girl, with a mop of dark hair, laughing blue eyes and an easygoing nature, and they had all taken to her. All apart from Miss Florence that was, who had questioned her brother on why they should need to pay out yet another lot of wages. True to his word, Mr Marshall had also taken on another outside help, Dennis, who was proving to be a godsend to Benny and especially Ted, whose arthritis was worse in the cold weather. Dennis Weaver was also an easy chap to get along with and they had all watched with amusement as his eyes lit up each time they settled on Polly.

'You just mark my words, there'll be a romance blossoming there in no time,' Nellie would say whenever she saw them together, and none of them doubted it.

When Benny returned from market later that day and lugged the Christmas tree he had bought for Fleur into her room, the little girl was beside herself with excitement. She had never had a tree of her very own before.

'I'll go an' fetch a bucket of earth up now for you and set it up,' he told Maryann, and the tree soon had pride of place at the side of the fireplace.

'We'll cut out some pretty paper decorations to put on it this afternoon,' Maryann promised, and now that his job was done Benny left to return to his normal chores.

'Eeh, I've had some wonderful news this mornin',' Nellie told Maryann when she went down to the kitchen later that afternoon to fetch Fleur her milk and biscuits. 'The master's just been in to inform me that Miss Florence an' Miss Lord are goin' to London again the week afore Christmas, an' they won't be back till early in the New Year! Seems there's some play the miss wants to see. Just think on it – that means we'll all be able to enjoy the holiday now wi' them miserable pair out o' the way. Oh, an' Benny informs me that the ginger cat had her litter this morning. She's nursin' 'em over in the barn an' Benny reckons they're lovely. I just sent her a dish o' meat over, she'll need extra food wi' kittens to feed. Miss Fleur can pick which one she wants when she's ready, but o' course they won't be able to leave their mam till they're eight weeks or so old.'

'That's good news,' Maryann agreed. Every time she saw Miss Florence or Miss Lord now a picture of them clasped in each other's arms would flash before her eyes and she avoided them as much as she could. It was good news about the kittens too and she could hardly wait for Fleur to see them – but not yet. She would leave the mother in peace with her babies for a time. She didn't want her rejecting them.

After leaving the kitchen, she took Fleur her afternoon snack, then when she was sure that the child was occupied, she went back downstairs and tapped on the library door, guessing this was where the master would be. Since the incident when Florence had accused her of stealing her brooch she had only seen him when he visited Fleur in her room, but today she had a favour to ask of him and she was feeling quite nervous about it.

'Come in,' he called, and when she entered he looked quite flustered. He was putting the finishing touches to the portrait on the easel but he walked away from it and smiled a welcome before saying, 'There's nothing wrong with Fleur, I trust?'

'Oh no, sir, she's fine,' she assured him hastily. 'But I have a request to ask of you.'

'Then ask away.' His eyes sparkled kindly and Maryann felt a little easier.

'The thing is,' she began, 'my afternoon off as you know is on Sunday, and I was wondering if I could change it to Saturday this week so that I can go into town and buy some Christmas gifts. Unfortunately all the shops are shut on Sunday. Cissie has offered to watch Fleur whilst I'm gone. I've already asked Nellie and she doesn't mind.'

'You're quite right, the shops are closed,' he agreed amiably. 'And of course you are welcome to have Saturday instead. Now . . .' He looked self-consciously towards his easel as if he were trying to come to a decision about something and then suddenly making up his mind he said, 'I wonder if you would care to see my latest portrait?'

Her eyes lit up with pleasure and he led her towards it, watching intently for her reaction. As he turned the easel towards her, she gasped and her hand flew to her mouth.

'B-but it's *me*!'

'I hope you don't mind,' he said anxiously. 'You see I was watching you when you were in the garden with Fleur one day in the summer and I couldn't resist catching you on canvas.'

274

'It's really beautiful,' she told him as she stared at it in awe. Surely she didn't look like that? She was leaning down to pick a flower with the sun glinting on her hair, turning it to gleaming copper. It was so lifelike that it almost took her breath away and she could think of nothing else to say.

He looked visibly relieved when he saw that she wasn't offended. 'I am quite pleased with it myself,' he confided. 'But I realised once I had started it that I should have asked your permission first.'

'It doesn't matter.' She was unable to tear her eyes away from it. 'But what will you do with it now that it's finished?'

'A friend of mine owns an art gallery in Birmingham and he's asked if I would do an exhibition of my work there in the spring. If you are agreeable, I'd like this to be included – and of course I would wish you to attend the exhibition with me. I thought we could take Nellie along too – she doesn't get out much, does she – and I'm sure Cissie could hold the fort while we're all gone.'

'But what about . . .'

As her voice trailed away he smiled. 'Were you going to say, what about Florence?'

She nodded.

'She'll just have to accept it, won't she?' he answered stoically and suddenly they were both smiling at each other like two children caught up in a conspiracy.

Chapter Thirty-Two

On Saturday afternoon Maryann set off for the town to do her Christmas shopping, but she had gone barely halfway down the drive when Benny drew the carriage to a halt at the side of her and the master popped his head out of the window.

'Are you off into town?' he enquired pleasantly and when Maryann nodded he held the door wide. 'Then please allow me to give you a lift. It's silly for you to walk when I'm going there too. You got me thinking that I ought to get some of my Christmas shopping done as well. You could perhaps assist me in choosing something for Fleur. You obviously know what she likes better than I do.'

Maryann chewed on her lip. The offer of a lift was very tempting, admittedly, but people were gossiping about them as it was. Surely it could only make things worse if she were seen to be shopping with him? But then it would look very childish if she refused so she allowed him to take her hand and help her into the carriage. Let the gossipmongers do their worst, she decided. She knew that it was all just spiteful speculation and so did the master.

She noticed that Wesley, as she now thought of him, was looking pale again. 'Are you feeling unwell again, sir?' she asked, concerned. 'You look a little under the weather.'

'Oh, it's just this damn stomach of mine playing up again,' he told her dismissively. 'It tends to come and go. I just hope it settles down so that I can enjoy Christmas. Nellie always does us proud over the holidays.'

'Perhaps you should see the doctor?' she suggested, but he shook his head.

'I'm sure it's nothing. It will probably sort itself out, given time. But now what do you think I should get for Fleur?'

They spent the rest of the way into town discussing what they might each buy the little girl for Christmas, and by the time the carriage drew to a halt in front of the livery stables they were both in a festive mood.

'I'll come with you to help choose Fleur's present first and then I'll do my own shopping and go and see Toby – if he isn't at work, that is,' Maryann told him, failing to notice the way his face fell.

Lucky chap, that Toby, Wesley found himself thinking. But then they were strolling through the marketplace glancing in the shop windows and the sombre moment passed. Eventually, in the only toy shop in town they chose Fleur a new doll with long blonde ringlets and a china face as well as a tiny perambulator for her to push it about in.

'She will love it,' Maryann promised him, as excited as a child herself, and after paying for the purchases he asked the shopkeeper to wrap the items, telling him that his groom would be along to collect them shortly.

Once outside again they stared about at the busy

marketplace. People intent on doing their Christmas shopping were scurrying about like ants and there was a festive feeling in the air.

'I don't suppose I could tempt you to a nice hot toddy in the Bull Hotel to keep out the cold, could I?' he asked hopefully, unwilling to let her go.

She opened her mouth to refuse but then on a whim changed her mind. 'That would be very nice, thank you.'

He made to take her elbow but then thought better of it and instead they set off walking a sedate distance apart.

Once in the hotel he led her to a corner table next to a roaring fire before hurrying away to order their drinks and then he rejoined her, thinking how well the bonnet and cape Cissie had chosen for her suited Maryann.

'I have to admit I've missed the little dinner parties with you and Fleur,' he told her and she saw that he meant it.

'We've missed you too,' she replied, and almost gasped when it suddenly hit her that she really had. She had the urge to stand up and leave then, although she had no idea why, but a maid was placing their drinks in front of them. Taking hers, she gulped at it to avoid having to look at him. *What am I doing sitting here with him?* she asked herself. *We're the subject of gossip already and this will only add fuel to the fire!* Even so, she forced herself to remain calm as she glanced across at him, noticing the way a lock of his dark hair had fallen across his forehead. He really was a very attractive man and the fact that she had acknowledged it to herself only added to her confusion. She and Toby had an agreement, didn't they?

Drinking her hot toddy as fast as she could, she then stood and said politely, 'I hope you don't mind but I still have all my shopping to do and I want to leave a little time to spend with Toby before I have to get back, so I should be getting on.'

He looked crestfallen but then forced a smile as he said, 'Of course. I perfectly understand.'

Leaving his unfinished drink, he stood and escorted her back into the street where he said, 'Have a good afternoon, Maryann. Goodbye.'

'Goodbye, sir.' She watched him walk away for a moment before turning about and soon becoming lost amidst the throng of shoppers scuttling about the market stalls.

She was loaded down with packages and it was beginning to grow dusk as she turned into the court late that afternoon, but as always she received a warm welcome from Granny Addison who was sitting toasting her toes in front of a roaring fire.

'Well, bless my soul. I didn't expect to see you the day, pet. You've just missed our Archie. I thought yer afternoon off were Sundays?'

'It is,' Maryann grinned, gratefully dumping all her shopping onto one of the chairs. 'But the master let me change it this week so that I could get my Christmas shopping done.'

'Ah, well, now yer here it's a good excuse fer a nice hot cup o' tea,' Granny said, thrusting her chilblained feet back into her sturdy lace-up boots.

Maryann meanwhile was rummaging amongst the bags and after a while she held one up. 'Ah, here it is,' she said happily. Then proffering it to Granny, she told her, 'This is for you. I doubt I'll get to see you on Christmas Day, so you may as well have it now, with my love.'

'Eeh, yer shouldn't have gone spendin' yer money on me, lass,' the woman scolded, but she opened the package excitedly all the same. And then when the contents were revealed, her eyes welled with tears. The bag contained a beautiful woollen shawl, heavily fringed, in a lovely autumn gold colour, and it was clear from the look on her face that she absolutely loved it.

'Why, would yer just look at that,' she breathed, throwing it about her shoulders and going to admire herself in the pitted mirror hanging above the mantelshelf. 'I ain't never seen such a beautiful shawl in me whole life. Thank you, pet.'

She gave Maryann a big hug and the girl felt a warm glow inside. The shawl had cost over a week's wages, but as far as she was concerned it had been worth every penny of it. Granny Addison deserved it for all the kindness she had shown to her and her family across the years.

Just once, as she glanced across the yard at her old home while she was sipping her tea, did grief overwhelm her at the memory of Christmases past, but then she blinked her tears away, consoling herself with the knowledge that, wherever they were, her mam and dad were together again. Reunited in death.

'I don't suppose there have been any more letters for me, have there?' she asked hopefully, thinking of Violet, but Granny shook her head.

'Not as yet, but if yer thinkin' o' that sister o' yours, I'm sure she'll be in touch soon wi' it nearly bein' Christmas.'

'Yes, of course she will,' Maryann agreed with a forced brightness.

After a while, she rose and, slipping her warm cape on again, she told Granny, 'I'm just going to see if Toby is in.'

'Yes, you leave yer bags there fer a while an' do that,' Granny encouraged. 'I'm sure I saw 'im pass the winder just before yer arrived, so I don't think he's at work.'

Toby's mother answered the door, and when she saw Maryann standing there she caught her by the arm and drew her into the cosy little room, saying, 'Why, our Toby will be right pleased to see you, luvvie. He's upstairs gettin' changed. Go an' tell him Maryann is here would yer, Hugo?'

Glancing across Tilly's shoulder, Maryann saw Hugo

grin at her as he rose from his seat. Maryann felt a surge of resentment spread through her. If it weren't for him, she and Toby might have been getting wed sometime in the coming year, but she kept a tight rein on her feelings as she stared coldly back at him. As her mother had been fond of saying, there was no point in crying over spilled milk; they just had to make the best of things now.

'So what brings you here on a Saturday then?' Toby asked when he appeared from the stairs door, and after she had explained, he suggested, 'Well, how about we take a stroll round the park till it's time for you to go back? I'll walk you home then.'

'I'd be grateful of that so you can help me with my shopping bags,' Maryann chuckled. 'I think I got a bit carried away and I'll never manage them all that way on my own.'

In no time at all they were strolling along the banks of the River Anker in Riversley Park. The branches of the leafless weeping willow trees were bent low across the water and hoar frost on the grass twinkled like diamonds; Maryann was shocked to see that ice was forming on the river too.

'I reckon we're in fer some snow soon,' Toby commented, sniffing at the air. 'Per'aps we'll 'ave us a white Christmas, eh?'

Maryann nodded, hoping he was right. She had never known him to be wrong before when it came to forecasting the weather, and she knew that Fleur would love it.

'Nellie says you can come and have tea with us at the Manor on Christmas Day if you like,' she told him. 'Miss Florence is off to London again and won't be back till after the New Year so it should be a good day.'

'Huh! Let's just hope that Hugo doesn't take it into his head to try and follow her again this time,' he snorted. 'But I'd like to come to tea,' he added, giving her hand an affectionate squeeze. 'I can give yer yer present then.'

'And I can give you yours.' She was really looking forward to it and could hardly wait for the special day to come round.

'I see what yer mean about carryin' all this lot back,' Toby grumbled as they slithered about on the icy paths on the way home. 'Me arms'll be down to me knees at this rate.'

Maryann chuckled. 'It's good for you, so stop moaning,' she teased him.

He walked her all the way to the kitchen that day, gratefully accepting a hot drink and a slice of cake from Nellie before setting off for home again. Maryann accompanied him to the gate where he put his arms about her in an uncharacteristic show of affection.

'I'm sorry if I've been a bit short wi' yer lately, lass,' he said gruffly.

'It's all right, I understand,' she answered. She knew how hard he had worked for the money that Hugo had stolen and how badly he had taken it.

'But I'm goin' to make it up to yer, I promise,' he went on as she nestled against his chest. She could feel his heartbeat through their thick layers of clothes and wished that they could stay there like that forever.

'You don't have to make anything up to me. Things will come right in the end, you'll see,' she whispered optimistically, and then he kissed her full on the lips and all was right with the world. When he left she floated back to the kitchen on a blissful cloud and Nellie grinned, pleased to see the girl looking so happy.

Florence and Elizabeth Lord left for London the week before Christmas and instantly the atmosphere in the house lightened.

'Why is she going again so soon?' Maryann asked Nellie

curiously later that day as she watched Fleur licking the spoon with which Nellie had just stirred the cake mixture.

The woman shrugged. 'I've no idea, to be honest, but I did overhear her say summat about a business matter to Miss Lord when I passed the drawin' room t'other day. Whatever it is that draws her there, long may it continue. The house is certainly a happier place wi'out her here an' that's a fact.'

Maryann nodded in agreement then fetched a cloth to try and get all the cake mixture out of Fleur's hair.

The snow finally fell in the night two days before Christmas, and Maryann woke to an eerie grey light filtering into the room through a slight gap in the curtains. When she twitched them aside and peeped out to discover a glistening white world she gasped with pleasure. Thin ice had formed on the inside of the window, creating a cobweb of patterns, and snatching up her old dressing gown she raced next door to Fleur's room without even waiting to get dressed.

The child was just stirring as Maryann cried, 'Fleur, come and look at this!'

Tumbling groggily out of bed, the child staggered across to join Maryann at the window then screamed with excitement.

'Snow,' she breathed, her eyes wide.

Maryann laughed. 'Yes, sweetheart. It's snow, and if you're very good I may wrap you up warmly and let you go outside to throw some snowballs later on.'

It was then that the door opened and Maryann was embarrassed to see the master standing there.

'Ah, I see you've already beaten me to it,' he chuckled. 'I was coming to show Fleur the snow.' His heart beat faster as he looked at Maryann. Her glorious hair was tumbling about her shoulders in loose curls and he was sure that he had never seen anyone look so beautiful even in her modest nightclothes.

'I was just telling Fleur that she might be able to go out in it and throw some snowballs later on,' Maryann mumbled, drawing her old dressing gown tighter about her.

'Oh, I think we can do better than that.' Wesley winked at Maryann conspiratorially before going on, 'I'm sure there's an old sledge that Ted made for me when I was a boy still knocking about in the barn somewhere. I'll get Benny to have a scout about for it, eh? Then we can see what Fleur thinks of sledging.'

Fleur didn't actually know what a sledge was but she hopped across to her father to hug him all the same, and Maryann was touched when she saw him return the hug. Father and daughter were finally becoming close and it did her heart good to witness it.

'Right, I'll go and have a word with Benny straight away,' Wesley said then, appearing almost as excited as Fleur was. 'And we'll go out straight after lunch. How does that sound?'

'It sounds wonderful,' Maryann told him and was amused to see him go off with a spring in his step. Perhaps this wasn't going to be such a bad Christmas, after all.

Chapter Thirty-Three

'Violet, Ruby would like a word with you downstairs,' Daisy said to the figure lying huddled on the bed.

Violet lifted her head to stare at her as her stomach did a somersault. This was the moment she had been dreading, but now that it had come she was keen to get it over with.

'Tell her I'll be down in a minute,' she muttered, feeling very sorry for herself. She rarely ventured downstairs into the kitchen before lunchtime now and even then it was usually late afternoon before the awful sickness subsided and she could eat something.

Dragging herself out of bed she groaned as she caught sight of herself in the mirror. There were dark circles beneath her eyes and her skin had a sickly pallor to it without her powder and paint on. Still, there was no time to do anything about it now, so taking a deep breath she pulled her feather-trimmed peignoir on over the stays that she had taken to wearing all the time now and made her way downstairs.

She found Ruby reclining on the couch in the morning

room eating sweetmeats and Jed standing with his legs apart and his arms behind his back in front of the fire.

'Ah, so you're here then,' Ruby remarked unnecessarily as she licked the chocolate from one of her fingers. Then frowning she asked, 'Is there anyfink yer want to tell me, ducks?'

Very aware of Jed watching her closely, Violet flushed, wishing the ground would just open up and swallow her.

'About yer monthlies, I mean,' Ruby probed. 'Or should I say the lack of 'em?'

When Violet lowered her head in shame she went on, 'When did yer last bleed?'

'Just before I came here, I suppose,' the girl muttered.

'Hmm, I thought yer were puttin' a bit o' weight on.' Ruby tapped her lip with her finger as she studied her solemnly before asking, 'Yer do know what this means, don't yer?'

Violet nodded.

'Did yer not take the precautions like I advised?'

The girl's head snapped up then. 'Oh I did, honest I did,' she babbled as tears threatened. 'I used the sponges just as you showed me before every client.'

'Well, sadly it appears that somewhere along the road yer slipped up.' In her mind Ruby was calculating how far along Violet might be. 'Seems to me that yer must be around four months gone. Question now is, what are we gonna do about it?'

'There's only one thing we can do,' Jed said then, speaking for the first time. 'Violet'll have to go. She ain't gonna be able to work for much longer, is she? She's showin' slightly already, and the rules are: catch the pox or get pregnant an' you're out!'

In actual fact, beneath her tightly laced stays Violet was showing more than 'slightly' but she didn't tell him that, of course.

'Now just hold yer horses a minute,' Ruby addressed him sharply. Violet was very popular with the punters so she didn't want to make any rash decisions. There'd be no point in cutting her nose off to spite her face. Narrowing her eyes, she peered at Violet then before asking, 'Would yer be prepared to give this babby up when it arrives?'

'Oh *yes*,' Violet assured her quickly. 'I don't even want it.'

'Hmm, then perhaps we can salvage sumfink from this mess,' Ruby said thoughtfully. 'Have you anywhere yer could go to have it and leave it?'

Violet nodded again. She could always go home and have the baby then clear off and leave Maryann to look after it. She was daft enough to do it if she knew her sister. She'd always been good with children, unlike Violet who couldn't stand the snotty-nosed little beggars.

'Look, Ruby, I really don't think this is such a good idea,' Jed butted in worriedly. 'Yer know the owner o' this place won't take kindly to pregnant whores.'

Violet was confused. Jed had led her to believe that *he* was the owner of the brothel, but perhaps that was how he encouraged all the girls there?

'Shush a minute, Jed, I'm finkin',' Ruby said irritably, then peering at Violet again she made a decision. 'I'll tell yer what I'll do. Yer can work fer a bit longer till yer get uncomfortable, then I want yer to disappear fer a while an' come back when it's all over – an' that'll be an end to it. Now I can't say fairer than that, can I?'

'No, you can't. Oh thank you, Ruby,' Violet said gratefully as the tears finally gushed down her cheeks. Then after glaring at Jed, she rushed from the room breathing a sigh of relief. She had long since got over the crush she had had on Jed but loved her job and was grateful to him for bringing her to Greenwich. It was just a shame that she was going to have to leave for a while, but it couldn't be helped.

The way she saw it, she should be able to work for another couple of months if she laced her corsets even more tightly, then she would head back home and stay there until after the birth. As yet she had no idea what story she would come up with for her family as to how she had got into this position, but she would worry about that later. For now she was just relieved that she would be allowed to return to the brothel. It was a way of life to her now and she loved every minute of it. And when she did come back she would take extra precautions to ensure that this never happened again.

'Here it is then,' Wesley said proudly that afternoon as he dragged a rather bedraggled-looking sledge across the snow to where they were all assembled on the lawn. 'She might look a bit the worse for wear but she's still sturdy. Ted made her to last and there's years of wear in her yet.'

'You ain't jokin' about the "worse for wear",' Nellie chuckled. The paint had long worn off it and there were chips out of the wood here and there, but as he said, the sledge did still look sturdy.

'If you think that's bad, you should have seen the state of it when I found it,' Benny piped up. 'It was covered in years of cobwebs but I've dusted it off and given it a bit of a clean.'

'Well, I'm leavin' yer to it,' Nellie stated, shivering. The snow was falling steadily and she certainly couldn't see any fun in standing out in it. 'I'm off to sit by the fire, but be careful. We don't want any broken legs or anythin' just before Christmas.'

'So who's going first?' Wesley asked and Fleur instantly plodded through the snow and sat down heavily on the seat. She had so many layers of clothes on that she was almost as round as she was high, and as Benny and Wesley started to tow her along, her delighted laughter echoed across the grounds.

Cissie was finding it particularly hard going to keep up with them, with her crutch to contend with, but even so she struggled along gamely, determined not to miss out on any of the fun. When Fleur eventually got tired of the sledge they made snowballs which they threw at each other, then Benny and Cissie showed the little girl how to make a snowman. Time passed and before they knew it, the light was beginning to fade.

'We must have been out here for at least two hours,' Maryann said, stamping her feet to try and get some feeling back into them. 'It's high time we got Fleur back inside now. She must be worn out.'

Benny and Cissie set off towing the sledge behind them in the direction of the barn while Wesley and Maryann each took one of Fleur's hands and led her back towards the house.

'Don't *want* to go back in yet,' Fleur stated petulantly. 'Want to play with the snowman!'

It was a measure of just how much the child had enjoyed the afternoon and Wesley chuckled as he told her, 'Don't worry. The snowman will still be here tomorrow and we'll come out to see him again then, but he needs to have a rest now. Mr Snowman is tired.'

Slightly mollified, she yawned widely and pottered along obediently between them as they smiled at each other over her head.

Why have I never done anything like this with her before? Wesley was asking himself. He had enjoyed himself as much as she had.

'How would you and Fleur like to dine with me tonight?' he asked suddenly. He had had such a wonderful afternoon that he didn't want it to end.

Maryann's mouth dropped open with surprise. Then she answered, 'That would be lovely, sir. But I doubt Fleur would be able to stay awake long enough. She's had a very busy day and she's yawning already.'

'Oh yes, of course, how thoughtless of me. Then how about we all have lunch together tomorrow?'

Maryann nodded. 'We'd enjoy that,' she agreed readily.

It was then that he had another idea.

'Wouldn't it be wonderful if we could all dine together in the dining room on Christmas Day? I mean *everyone*, all of us together! It would save Nellie and Cissie an awful lot of work, and Fleur would love it. Do you think they'd agree to it? We could all open our presents together then and it would be so much more fun than me having to spend the day alone.' He had spent far too many Christmas Days alone since losing his wife, and suddenly he couldn't bear the thought of another one with only himself for company.

'I could certainly put the idea to Nellie for you,' she said, seeing how much it would mean to him. 'Leave it with me.' And he was more than happy to do just that.

They enjoyed a pleasant meal together on Christmas Eve when Fleur and Maryann joined Wesley in the dining room for the very first time. Her coordination was not brilliant but Wesley only smiled indulgently when she dropped the odd morsel of food onto the napkin that Maryann had tucked into the neck of her dress.

'Santa is coming tonight,' she told her father at least a dozen times. Maryann had told her lots of stories about Father Christmas and the little girl was so excited, Maryann was worried she was not going to be able to sleep a wink that night. 'We have to leave him a mince pie and some milk before we go to bed,' she informed him solemnly and keeping as straight a face as he could, he nodded in agreement.

'You certainly do. Perhaps I could come along at bedtime and help you?'

She nodded, her face aglow, and he found himself thinking what a pretty little thing she was.

'I don't suppose you've had time to put my idea about all dining together tomorrow to Nellie yet, have you?' he asked Maryann.

'Yes, I did – and everyone thinks it's a marvellous idea,' she informed him. And he found himself thinking that this was how Christmas should be.

That evening as promised he went along to Fleur's bedroom and helped her to lay out the mince pie and the saucer of milk. Then he tucked her into bed and kissed her goodnight. After he and Maryann had left the room, he chuckled, 'I think she's going to lie awake all night watching that mince pie.'

'Well, I think she'll try to,' Maryann grinned back. 'But she's so tired I don't think she'll be awake for long.' And sure enough, when she peeped back in at her half an hour later, the little girl was fast asleep with a smile on her face and her thumb jammed into her mouth.

Chapter Thirty-Four

'I still ain't sure about this,' Nellie told Maryann on Christmas morning when she went down to the kitchen to get Fleur's breakfast. Nellie had already been up for hours preparing the goose for the oven and peeling great mounds of vegetables.

Maryann instantly knew what she meant. Nellie had actually been very against the invitation to dine with the master, and it had taken all Maryann's persuasion to get her to agree to it – but she hadn't told him that, of course.

'It's crossin' a line,' Nellie had said. Much as she loved Mr Wesley, she was of the old school and believed that servants should know their place. In the end she had only agreed to it when Maryann pointed out how much it would mean to Fleur, but she still clearly wasn't happy about it, special occasion or not.

'It's just the once,' Maryann pleaded. 'Miss Florence will be back in a week's time and there'll be no chance of it happening again then, will there?'

'I suppose not,' Nellie admitted grudgingly. 'But I still don't think it's right.'

Maryann crossed to a large pan of creamy porridge simmering on the range and began to spoon some into a dish for Fleur before adding a large dollop of honey to it. The night before, she had bathed her and washed her hair then brushed it until it gleamed, and she was now looking forward to the day ahead, especially the afternoon when Toby would be coming to join them all for tea.

Once upstairs, she found Fleur in a fever of excitement. After the little girl had been persuaded to eat her breakfast they then chose an outfit for her to wear and Maryann helped her to dress before brushing her hair and tying it back with a red ribbon the same colour as her dress. She then set about trying to entertain Fleur until dinnertime.

When they finally entered the dining room Fleur clapped her hands with pleasure when she glimpsed the table. Cissie had laid it with the finest crystal and china and solid silver cutlery, and along the centre of it bowls of holly with bright red berries made a striking contrast to the snow-white linen cloth.

Wesley was already there with a broad smile on his face, and as soon as they entered he asked Maryann, 'Would you like a glass of sherry?'

She wavered uncertainly but he was already pouring one out for her so when he handed it to her she sipped at it cautiously. It was actually very nice and helped her to relax. Soon after, Cissie and Nellie began to carry in large silver tureens full of vegetables and all manner of delicious treats, and Benny and Ted joined them too, all dressed up in their Sunday best. They had worked all morning to see to the horses and get the chores done, and now they could relax for a few hours and had every intention of doing just that.

Maryann was pleased to see that Wesley insisted that Fleur should sit beside him at his right hand, and felt that this was just as it should be.

They all said Grace then Wesley carved the goose whilst Nellie loaded all their plates with sprouts, carrots, parsnips and crispy roast potatoes. The mood was light as the wine flowed freely and they all found themselves enjoying each other's company. At one stage, Maryann looked about the room and felt a wave of contentment as she realised just how much these people had come to mean to her. Glancing up, she caught Benny's eye and knew without any words being spoken that he too was thinking of Christmases past shared with their family. The loss of her siblings and her mother and father had left holes in Maryann's heart that no one else would ever be able to fill but these wonderful people had helped her to feel she belonged, and to start again. She had been at her lowest ebb when she had arrived at Windy Manor, but it struck her then just how far she had come.

On her last Sunday off she had bought a holly wreath from the market and had laid it on her parents' grave in Coton churchyard, and now she offered up a silent prayer that wherever they were, they might know that she was thinking of them. Had she been at home they would have been dining on the pig that the cottagers had reared between them throughout the year, and the meal would have been nowhere near as grand a spread as lay before her now. Even so, she knew that her mother and father would not have begrudged her and Benny enjoying it, and she determined to push the gloomy thoughts aside.

The first course was followed by the most enormous plum pudding that Maryann had ever seen, and Fleur ate so much of it that Maryann feared she might make herself ill. But then at last they were all sated and Wesley ordered,

'Now leave the dirty pots for a while, Nellie. It's time to go into the drawing room and open the presents.'

For a moment, Nellie looked apprehensive, but then as Fleur dragged on her hand, she grinned and gave in. 'All right then. I dare say they'll keep fer a time, seein' as it's such a special day.'

A large fire was roaring up the chimney in the drawing room and the tiny candles that Maryann had lit on the branches of the Christmas tree flickered, but Fleur barely noticed them. Her eyes were fastened on the pile of parcels beneath the tree.

'Right then,' Wesley said with a twinkle in his eye. 'I'll hand them all out, shall I?'

Everyone grinned when Fleur nodded eagerly, and lifting the first one he peered at the name written on it before saying, 'Hmm, this one appears to be for you, my dear.'

Much to everyone's amusement, Fleur snatched at it and began to tear at the paper. When her new dolly was revealed, her eyes widened with delight and she was content to cuddle it for a time as her father then began to hand round the gifts he had bought for them all. There was a fine new pipe for Ted and a warm scarf and gloves for Nellie, as well as a very pretty bonnet for Cissie, which made her sigh with ecstasy and insist that she must wear it straight away, even if they were indoors. For Benny there was a new cap and a warm muffler. And then as everyone admired their gifts he crossed the room and picked up a canvas, and after turning it about he handed it to Maryann, making her already rosy cheeks blush even pinker.

It was a painting of Fleur and was so lifelike that everyone exclaimed. Fleur herself giggled with delight.

'It's me!' she told them all unnecessarily, causing a ripple of laughter to echo about the room.

Wesley had thought long and hard about what to give

Maryann. He had longed to buy her a new gown, something frivolous and pretty to match the colour of her eyes, but had thought better of it, knowing that the rest of the staff might feel it was inappropriate.

'I hope you like it,' he said self-consciously. 'I wasn't sure what to get you.'

Maryann's hands trembled as she stared at the painting and knew that she would treasure it forever. It was such a personal gift and must have taken hours to paint.

'Oh!' She stared at the image so overcome that she barely knew what to say as everyone oohed and aahed and admired it.

'Thank you so much. I love it. In fact, it's the loveliest gift I've ever had,' she assured him eventually.

Wesley was clearly deeply embarrassed but then Benny offered, 'I'll carry it up to yer room and hang it for yer later on, if yer like, Maryann.'

'Thank you, that would be kind,' she agreed, and then the tricky moment passed as Fleur tugged on her father's hand and pointed at the remaining presents. Laughing, he pushed yet another large box towards her; it contained her new dolly's perambulator. The rest of the presents were then exchanged and Nellie and Cissie went to go and fetch a tray of tea and some mince pies, even though everyone insisted they couldn't eat another thing.

Maryann rose and went with them, and in the privacy of the kitchen she said worriedly, 'I'm not ungrateful, you understand, and I truly love the painting that Mr Marshall has given me. But what will Miss Florence say about it when she comes back?'

'Huh! Let's 'ope she never goes into yer room again after the last time, an' if that's the case she's hardly likely to see it, is she?' Nellie assured her. 'And why shouldn't yer have it, eh? That little girl 'as flourished in your care an' she clearly loves yer. That other one's heart is made of ice, I reckon. She ain't got a kind bone in the whole of her body.'

But even though Nellie's words were reassuring, the gift had confirmed what the old woman had suspected for some time. She had seen the way the master's eyes would follow Maryann when he thought no one was looking, and now more than ever, she was convinced that he was falling in love with her. Not that it would do him a ha'p'orth o' good, God bless his soul. Maryann's heart belonged solely to Toby and Nellie could only see heartache ahead. It was a shame, the way she saw it, for since Maryann had arrived, Windy Manor had been transformed. It was now a much happier place. She would have made a wonderful mistress for Windy Manor, be she a former mill girl or not, but then no one could help who they fell in love with and Maryann was clearly in love with young Toby – or at least she thought she was. To her mind, though he was a nice enough lad, he had let Maryann down when the girl had needed him most, but then it was not her place to interfere.

After pouring boiling water over the tea leaves she had measured into the silver teapot, she left it to mash as the two younger women bustled away with two large platefuls of mince pies. Life was a funny business, she thought philosophically. There were no two ways about it.

Mid-afternoon, Fleur began to yawn and Maryann rose and took her hand. 'I'm going to settle this young lady down for a little nap,' she told them.

'And will you be joining us afterwards?' Wesley asked hopefully.

'I'm afraid not. Toby is coming for tea so I really ought to be getting ready,' she reminded him.

'Oh, yes – of course. I'd quite forgotten.'

'Aye, an me an' our Cissie ought to be thinkin' o' clearin'

that table an' gettin' the washin'-up done an' all,' Nellie chimed in as she saw his face fall. The day had gone far better than she had dared hope, but she didn't want to push her luck. He was the master, after all.

As they all rose to leave, Wesley smiled at them. 'Thank you for making this such a lovely day and for your very good company,' he said sincerely, but once they had all gone he propped his elbow on the mantelpiece and stared down into the flames of the fire as loneliness the like of which he had never experienced before engulfed him.

Once Fleur was asleep, Maryann slipped back downstairs and insisted on helping Nellie and Cissie with the dirty dishes, then she scuttled back to her room to tidy herself for Toby's arrival. It had been such a wonderful day up to now, and once Toby arrived it was set to be even better.

When she was ready, she snatched up the gift she had lovingly chosen for him and skipped back downstairs, after stopping briefly to admire the master's gift which Benny had already hung on her wall for her. She had found a leather-bound volume of Shakespeare's Sonnets in the bookshop in town, and as Toby shared her love of poetry she was sure he would like it, even though it had cost her a substantial amount of the wages she had saved.

By the time she got back downstairs after checking that Fleur was still fast asleep, she found Benny helping Cissie and Nellie to prepare the Christmas tea. He looked relaxed and happy, and she found herself thinking yet again how well he and Cissie looked together. Their tea would be eaten in the kitchen this evening and she briefly thought of the master all alone but then pushed the thought away. No doubt he was used to his own company by now so she doubted it would be a hardship for him.

Ted had gone out to check on the horses and the light

was fast fading from the day as Maryann looked down the snowy drive for a sign of Toby. And then suddenly there he was, striding towards her with his head bent, and she rushed to the door and threw it open, causing the flames to lick up the chimney.

'Shut that damn door, pet,' Nellie ordered sternly. 'Yer lettin' all the cold in.'

Maryann giggled as Toby strode past her into the warmth, shaking the snow from his shoulders, wondering if the day could get any better. His cheeks were red and his hands were blue, but to her he was still as handsome as ever.

'Merry Christmas, lad,' Nellie greeted him and he returned her greeting as Maryann helped him off with his coat and slung it to dry across a large wooden clothes horse that stood at the side of the fire.

'Eeh, it's enough to freeze the hairs off a brass monkey out there.' He chuckled as he took a seat on the wooden settle and held his hands out to the fire. Maryann immediately sat down next to him.

Ted had followed him in, content that his beloved horses were fed and warm and now Cissie pulled her old coat on, telling them, 'I shall just go and see the chickens into their coops afore we start tea.'

'Would you like me to come with you?' Benny offered, but she shook her head as she pulled a scarf across her thick wavy hair.

'No, you stay here in the warm. I'll not be gone long.' And then she opened the door and the darkness and the snow seemed to swallow her up as Maryann pressed Toby's gift into his hands.

'Why, lass, that's beautiful,' he said, awed, as he stroked the fine leather. 'I'll have many a happy hour readin' this.' He then fumbled in his pocket and pulled out a small box which he placed in her hand, saying apologetically, 'I'm afraid it's not much what wi' the way things are at present, but I hope you'll like it.'

Maryann opened the box and saw a silver brooch in the shape of a heart, and she fell in love with it instantly. Fastening it to her dress, she vowed, 'I shall never take it off, *ever.* Thank you, Toby.'

Aware that everyone was watching them, he said then, 'So what sort o' day have you all had?'

'Wonderful,' Nellie answered as she cut a thick fruit cake into slices. 'We dined wi' the master in the dinin' room an' he gave Maryann the most beautiful portrait of Fleur that he's painted.'

Seeing the frown on Toby's face, Nellie could have cut her tongue out. Toby obviously wasn't happy about the master giving her such a personal gift, but Maryann whispered to him, 'I'll carry it down and show it to you later on, if you like. Mr Marshall really is a very talented artist.'

'Might be worth a few bob then,' he commented thoughtlessly, but when he saw Maryann's face drop he added quickly, 'I was only jokin'.' Slightly mollified, he then changed the subject when he asked, 'I don't suppose you've seen anythin' of our Hugo today, have you?'

'No – why? Should we have done?' Maryann asked.

'Not really, but I'm afraid him an' our mam had a bit of a ruckus this mornin',' Toby admitted sheepishly. 'Things are still a bit fragile between 'em since he took all me money then got it stolen. Mam is findin' it very hard to forgive him, although I have. After the tiff he stormed off wi'out even waitin' fer his Christmas dinner. Still, let's not spoil things talkin' about me daft brother, eh? He just don't stop to think o' what he's doin', that's Hugo's problem. There ain't no real harm in 'im.'

Maryann was sorely tempted to disagree with him on that score but then he said, 'Tell me how little Fleur's enjoyed the day.' And so they went on to talk and the happy atmosphere was restored.

'Here, chick, chick, chick, chick,' Cissie clucked as she entered the dark barn. She knew that at least two of the chickens had scampered into there while she was rounding them up, and she was reluctant to leave them outside all night in the bitter cold even if they were a nuisance.

Leaning on her crutch she strained her eyes into the darkness and listened intently, silently cursing them. It was so cold she couldn't wait to get back to the warmth of the kitchen. And then she became aware of footsteps to the side of her and she stifled a scream as a figure loomed up out of the gloom like a spectre.

'Havin' a nice cosy Christmas Day, are yer?'

'Hugo!' She recognised his voice instantly and her heart began to thud with alarm. 'What are you doin' here?'

'Well, seein' as Miss Florence has dumped me an' cleared off to London again, I thought I'd come and see you.'

'Why would you want to see me?' she asked as she began to inch her crutch towards the partially open door.

Reaching out, he twisted one of her curls about his finger and stroked her face.

'Now don't get playin' hard to get,' he said cajolingly 'You've got a nice cosy set-up 'ere an' I know yer want me. I saw it in yer face the last time I was 'ere so happen it's time yer showed me how nice yer can be, eh?'

'Get away from me, Hugo,' she said as she lifted her hand from the crutch to swat his hand away. 'I don't know where you got that idea, and to be honest, after stealing your brother's money I wouldn't spit on you even if you were on fire.'

'Huh! Yer should be grateful I'm botherin' with yer,' he snarled angrily. 'You ain't exactly got a queue of admirers wi' that gammy leg an' hand, have yer!' She swayed dangerously and seizing his opportunity, he pushed her sideways; she landed heavily on a haybale, knocking the breath from her lungs and winding herself.

She blinked, trying to get her breath back, aware that he was lifting her skirts. Shame and humiliation washed through her as she began to struggle against him. She heard the buttons on her Sunday-best dress pop. It was the one she had chosen that had belonged to Mistress Amélie and she and Nellie had worked on it for hours to remodel it. Now it was ruined in seconds and she knew that she might never own another like it. And then as he fell on her like a wild animal, biting and pinching her most private parts, helpless tears began to course down her cheeks. Seconds later, he thrust deeply into her, and pain the like of which she had never known before tore through her and she prayed for death to claim her.

Chapter Thirty-Five

The table was bulging beneath the Christmas fare that Nellie had been preparing for weeks before and the tray containing the master's solitary meal had been taken to the dining room when Nellie commented, 'Our Cissie's takin' her time, ain't she? I ain't never known her be so long puttin' the chickens away before, an' it's so cold out there. Maryann will be back down wi' young Fleur any minute now, an' then we're all ready to eat.'

Ted, who was in conversation with Toby, glanced up. 'Now you come to mention it she has been gone a while, ain't she? I reckon I'll just go an' check on her, eh?'

'No, don't bother, I'll go. You stay there by the fire,' Benny said kindly as he strode to the door and pulled his boots on. He then slipped his long arms into the sleeves of his coat and had just opened the door when a bloodcurdling scream reached them all – and for a moment he froze on the spot. But then he was off across the yard like a March hare in the direction the scream had come from as everyone stumbled through the deep snow after him.

At the door to the barn he paused. After the glare of the snow it was even darker in there but as his eyes became accustomed to the light he saw a couple seemingly fighting, and realising what was happening he let out a roar that would have done justice to a mad bull as he lunged towards them. In seconds he had hauled Hugo off Cissie by the scruff of his neck and was shaking him like a dog would shake a rat.

Cissie instantly curled herself into a ball and began to sob uncontrollably as Nellie raced across to her and pulling her shawl from her shoulders, hastily covered the lass up. And then as Ted and Toby appeared in the doorway, Benny began to pummel Hugo with his fists. With his trousers round his ankles Hugo was at a disadvantage and within seconds he had spat out a tooth and blood was pouring from his nose.

'You – dirty – stinking – bastard!'

Hugo had collapsed into a heap on the ground by now but still Benny wasn't done. Rage coursed through his veins and he continued to rain blows down on him until Ted and Toby came to either side of him and caught his arms, dragging him away.

'That's enough, man, you'll kill him,' Toby shouted, although he had the urge to finish the job himself. Then whilst Ted held Benny back, Toby hauled the attacker to his feet and dragged him towards the door, only to groan with horror when he saw that it was his brother.

'Oh Hugo, what have you done now?' he gasped. 'A roll in the hay with a willin' mistress is one thing, but to force yourself on an innocent young maid is another. I never dreamed that even *you* would stoop to this.' He pushed his brother away from him in disgust and shame then, and without his support Hugo toppled face forward into the deep snow, blood from his injuries staining the snow black in the gloom.

Meanwhile Benny had taken his coat off and wrapped it around Cissie, and he and Nellie were half-carrying her across the yard. Ted crossed to Hugo and kicked him in the side as hard as he could, saying harshly, 'You'd best get him away, lad, afore Benny comes back to finish the job he started.'

'Mr Carter, I'm so sorry . . .'

'T'ain't your fault,' the older man said generously, seeing how mortified Toby was. 'Yer can't choose yer family. But as I said, best get him away afore I start on him meself. There'll be time to sort things tomorrow.' Then, grim-faced, he strode away with his back as stiff as a broom-handle.

Maryann had just entered the kitchen with Fleur when Benny helped Cissie into the room, and seeing at once that something was badly wrong, she propelled the little girl back into the hallway, telling her, 'I know, how about you have your tea with your papa in the dining room, eh? I'm sure he would love to have your company.'

Having thrust the child rather unceremoniously into the said room, she then hurried across to Wesley, who was sitting in the chair at the side of the fire, and whispered urgently, 'There's trouble in the kitchen. Will you keep Fleur here with you while I find out what's wrong?' And then she was gone before he had even had time to question her.

Back in the kitchen again she saw Nellie helping Cissie into a chair. Benny's coat slid from the girl's shoulders, and what Maryann saw made her gasp in horror. The buttons on Cissie's dress had been ripped clean off right down to the waist, and already the dark shadows of bruises were appearing across her small naked breasts.

'Good God above, whatever's happened?' she whispered as her hand flew to her mouth.

Benny stood against the sink averting his eyes from Cissie and he ground out, 'It were that scum, Hugo. He attacked her in the barn.' His voice was heavy with unshed tears as Maryann stared back at him, hardly able to believe what she was hearing.

'B-but why?' she finally managed to ask.

Benny shrugged. 'Why does that idiot do anything? He were raring drunk if his breath was anything to go by – but that's no excuse.'

Nellie meanwhile was gently shaking Cissie's hands up and down as she asked softly, 'Did he enter yer, pet? Yer must try an' tell me. There could be consequences.'

Cissie appeared to be in deep shock as she stared sightlessly ahead, but then just as Nellie was beginning to think that her words were falling on deaf ears, Cissie turned to look at her and as she saw the despair in her granddaughter's eyes, Nellie had her answer and her heart broke.

'Should I send for the constable?' Maryann asked, and her words seemed to bring Cissie out of her trance-like state.

'No! No, *please*, you mustn't,' she gabbled hysterically. 'It would only be my word against his. He told me so and then everyone would know and I couldn't bear it.' And she broke into a fresh torrent of weeping.

'But, pet – should there be consequences from what he's done he'll have to marry yer,' Nellie told her.

'I would rather die than ever marry him,' Cissie said, her teeth chattering with cold and shock. 'And if I am with child then you'll have to put me in the workhouse. I'd rather that than a life tied to *him*!'

Nellie rubbed her cold hands. 'There's a good chance nothin' will come of it,' she soothed, afraid of Cissie's reaction.

The girl's lip wobbled. 'But even if there ain't, who will ever want me now? I wasn't much of a catch before wi'

306

me crippled arm an' leg but now I'm soiled goods into the bargain.'

Unable to bear to hear any more, Benny stamped out to his room above the stable block and as Cissie watched him go she bowed her head as all the dreams she had secretly harboured crumbled to dust.

Whilst Nellie was cleaning Cissie up and getting some warmth back into the girl, Maryann slipped away to the dining room where Wesley was playing with Fleur. One of the presents he had bought her was a lovely carved wooden jigsaw with a painting of a snowman on it, and Maryann found them working on it side by side at the end of the table.

'She's better than me at this,' Wesley grinned, but then drawing Maryann to one side he asked quietly, 'What's happened?'

Maryann chewed on her lip as she wondered if she should tell him, but then deciding that Cissie wouldn't want him to know, she answered lightly, 'Oh, it was just a bit of a flare-up. Nothing for you to trouble yourself about. I reckon they've all had a drop too much to drink. But now I really should be getting Fleur up to bed. She's had a long day. Thank you for sharing your tea with her.'

'It was an absolute pleasure,' he said sincerely. He watched as Maryann took the little girl's hand and led her towards the door, but then Fleur broke away from her and running happily back to her father, she planted a sloppy kiss on his cheek.

'Night night, Papa,' she said sweetly.

'Night night, my dear.' He watched her skip back to Maryann and when the door had closed behind them he quietly fingered the area she had kissed with a smile on his face.

*

For the next few days everyone tiptoed around Cissie, who looked as if she had been put in a ring with a pugilist. She went about her chores as best she could, but the sparkle seemed to have gone out of her and so Benny took on most of her jobs and insisted that she should rest. The festive spirit seemed to have flown and Maryann fretted about Toby, knowing how ashamed he would be of his brother's latest misdeed. Surely he would not be able to forgive what Hugo had done this time? She had not even been able to say goodbye to him on Christmas Day and now she just prayed for Sunday to come so that she could go and see him on her afternoon off.

When it finally rolled around and Maryann came downstairs in her warm cape and her boots, Nellie said stiffly, 'Off to see Toby, are yer?'

'Oh, Nellie. What happened wasn't Toby's fault,' Maryann answered, laying her hand gently on the woman's arm.

Nellie's shoulders sagged and she answered wearily, 'I know it wasn't, pet. I think I'm just worryin' about Cissie, that's all. I mean, what's to become of her now? She only speaks when she's spoken to an' she walks about as if she's had all the stuffin' knocked out of her.'

'She'll come through it. Cissie is stronger than you think,' Maryann reassured her, then inching towards the door she said apologetically, 'I ought to be getting off now. Mr Marshall is watching Fleur, but it gets dark so quickly . . .'

'Go on, you be on your way.' Nellie forced a smile and waved her towards the door but once Maryann was gone, the old lady's chin sank to her chest and her tears ran freely. What was to become of her lovely girl now? As if she hadn't already had enough to cope with in her young life, what with losing her parents and being born as she was. It just didn't seem fair!

Granny Addison welcomed Maryann as warmly as ever when she eventually arrived in the court. The journey had taken twice as long as it normally would because of the deep, still fast-falling snow, and Maryann was exhausted and frozen through.

'There's trouble at the Jacksons' again,' she told Maryann as she took her cape and ushered her towards the fire, where Archie sat having forty winks. 'Toby helped Hugo home on Christmas Day covered in blood. Looks like he's been in another fight.' She shook her head, setting her double chins wobbling. 'I feel sorry to me 'eart fer poor Tilly an' Matt,' she confided as she swung the kettle into the heart of the fire. 'They never know what that one's goin' to get up to next, an' them such law-abidin' folks an' all.'

Maryann made no comment. Cissie was terrified that what had happened would become common knowledge, so as much as she hated avoiding telling Granny the truth, she decided that the best thing she could do was say nothing. Poor Cissie was in a bad enough state as it was without having to put up with gossip. Maryann had no doubt that if Cissie thought everyone was aware of it, she would never show her face in the town again.

'Did you have a nice Christmas?' she asked, keen to change the subject.

Granny beamed. 'Oh, we did that, pet. Me old man bought us a whole turkey an' I had all the children an' the gran'children round fer Christmas dinner. It was a tight squeeze, I don't mind tellin' yer, but we enjoyed it. How about you? An' how's little Fleur goin' on?'

And so for the next fifteen minutes Maryann focused on telling her about the good things that had happened on Christmas Day, avoiding any mention of Hugo. Eventually she rose and draping her cape about her shoulders, she kissed Granny fondly, telling her, 'I'd best get round to see Toby then. It'll be time to set back off again before I know it.' She left after promising that she would visit again very soon, and minutes later she tapped at the Jacksons' door.

Toby opened it and drew her inside, saying, 'I was wondering if you'd make it in this weather. I wasn't sure if I'd be welcome up at the Manor.'

She glanced at his mother, who was darning at the side of the fire, and his father, who had his head buried in a newspaper, and was pleased to see that there was no sign of Hugo. They both seemed reluctant to look at her and she could only guess how bad they must be feeling.

'No one blames you for what happened,' Maryann said to him, deeply conscious of the other people present in the room.

'Why don't you two go into the front parlour?' Tilly quietly suggested, knowing that they would want some privacy. It was hardly the weather to be walking out. 'I'm afraid the fire ain't lit in there so it won't be very warm, but at least you'll be in the dry.' The woman looked pale and drawn, and Maryann felt sorry for her. She was clearly deeply concerned and ashamed of Hugo.

'Thank you, Mrs Jackson,' Maryann answered as she and Toby turned in that direction. Once inside, she shuddered. It was so cold in there that her breath hung in the air in front of her and she decided to keep her cape on.

'How is Cissie?' Toby asked immediately.

Maryann sighed. 'Not good to be honest,' she admitted sadly. 'She barely speaks to any of us any more, although physically she escaped with just cuts and bruises.'

'Hugo swears that Cissie were willin',' Toby told her and Maryann's temper flared.

'Oh yes? And do you *really* believe that Cissie would have been in the state she was in if that was the case?' she snapped in a rare show of temper. 'You saw for yourself what happened, Toby! You even heard her screaming. What will your brother have to do to make you stop finding excuses for him!'

'I can't begin to tell yer how upset about it I am,' he muttered with his eyes downcast. 'Me mam has been a nervous wreck waiting for the constables to knock on the door and arrest him.'

'I don't think that will happen. Cissie doesn't want anyone to know about the rape and she's refused to let Nellie or Ted inform the police.' Maryann was angry. It sounded as if they were all more worried about Hugo being arrested than about what had happened to Cissie.

Toby paced up and down. 'Well, at least Benny gave him a good pasting! He ain't been able to get out o' bed since he got home. What a way to end Christmas Day, eh?'

Maryann suddenly wanted to go home, and for the first time she looked at Toby through different eyes. He wasn't the man she had thought he was.

Chapter Thirty-Six

Violet lounged against her silken pillows and nibbled at the expensive chocolates one of her clients had given her for Christmas. None of the girls had worked since the day before Christmas Eve as most of the men who frequented the brothel were expected to spend the festive season with their families. But tonight she would be entertaining again, and she found that she was quite looking forward to it. She had missed being pampered and spoiled, and was only sorry that soon she would have to leave until after the baby was born. It was getting more difficult to hide her condition now, but because she was naturally plump, none of her clients had thought anything of her roundness. When she entertained now she insisted on keeping her lacy corset on and most of the men seemed to like it, but even that wouldn't suffice to hide the fact that she was with child much longer.

She sighed with regret, but then was cheered again as she looked towards the expensive array of French perfumes on her dressing table. She had her own little select clientèle now and the men always came bearing gifts. The beautiful mother-of-pearl jewellery box, yet another gift, was full of trinkets, all of which were made of solid gold. Some of them were set with precious stones – emeralds, sapphires, rubies, even diamonds courtesy of Judge Williams – and she never tired of looking at them and trying them on. Others bought her expensive lingerie and fripperies from the finest emporiums in London.

Violet was a happy girl and knew that this was the life she had been meant for. She and some of the other girls had spent Christmas Eve shopping in the most fashionable parts of London, and Violet was thrilled by the glittering displays in the shop windows and the brightly lit streets where carol singers stood in groups on the corners. The whole place was teeming with life and with exquisitely dressed ladies and gentlemen. It was certainly a far cry from her home town.

Christmas in the brothel had been a festive affair. The girls had all dined together with Ruby and Jed in the vast dining room, and the wine had flowed like water. In fact, Violet had drunk so much that Daisy had eventually had to help her to her room where she had promptly emptied the considerable contents of her stomach into the china chamber pot that was kept beneath her bed. Daisy had warned her that it wasn't good to drink whilst she was pregnant – she had heard that it wasn't healthy for the baby – but seeing as Violet had no intentions of keeping it anyway, she wasn't overly concerned. She just wished that it could all be over now so that she could resume the life she loved – but then it wouldn't be long now and it was that thought that kept her going.

New Year's Day was a sombre affair at Windy Manor and the mood further deteriorated two days later when Miss Florence and Miss Lord arrived home from London. From the second she set foot in the door it was evident that Florence was in an ill humour, and on hearing her aunt's voice in the hallway Fleur stubbornly refused to leave her room.

The mood below stairs was no easier either. Cissie still did everything she had done before the terrible rape on Christmas Day, but she rarely spoke and always retired to her room as soon as her chores were done. Benny was walking about with a face like a wet weekend too and Maryann had a sneaky suspicion that he was missing the old Cissie who had followed him about like a little shadow.

The following morning, Maryann took Fleur to the barn to see her kitten. Fleur had chosen a pure white one and could hardly wait for it to be old enough to leave its mother. It had taken some effort to persuade her from her room, for since her aunt's return Fleur had become slightly withdrawn but once away from the house she laughed and giggled as the kitten purred and licked her hand. Even so, all the while Maryann was looking out for Florence and was relieved when they could at last return to the sanctuary of the child's room. The whole atmosphere of the house had changed and not for the better.

Part Three
January 1851

Chapter Thirty-Seven

It was a cold blustery day towards the end of January 1851 when Nellie entered the kitchen one morning to light the fires and find one of the cats lying dead near the sink.

'Ted!' she shouted. 'Come and move this fer me, would yer?'

Ted snapped his braces into place as he came into the kitchen and learned what was to do. 'That's odd,' he remarked. 'Tabby couldn't 'ave been no more than two or three years old at t'most, an' there ain't a mark on her. What do you think could have killed her?'

Nellie's mind was working overtime. Something at the back of her mind had been bothering her for a while but she couldn't for the life of her put her finger on it. It was a shame about Tabby though; she'd been a placid little thing and Nellie would miss her. As Ted lifted the animal and carried it away, she sighed sadly and went on with her chores.

Later that morning, Florence informed her at breakfast:

317

'Miss Lord and I will be visiting my dressmaker in town before lunching with a friend, so you need not prepare us anything to eat at lunchtime, Carter.'

Nellie scowled and slammed a silver dish full of bacon onto the sideboard. *Carter* indeed! She'd known Florence since she was knee high to a grasshopper, and many a time she'd wiped the child's snotty nose or bathed a grazed knee for her, yet now the woman treated her like something that was stuck to the bottom of her shoe.

Benny arrived back at the house mid-morning after dropping Miss Florence and Miss Lord off at an address in Swan Lane. He had strict instructions to pick them up and transport them back to the Manor in plenty of time for the evening meal, but in the meantime he intended to clean the stables out and groom the horses – one of his very favourite jobs. As he drove the carriage through the back yard on his way to the stable block, he saw Cissie struggling to carry some logs into the kitchen. Leaping down from his seat, he left the reins dangling and the horses pawing at the frosty ground as he raced across to her. Fetching the logs in was a job he had taken on, but because he had been busy driving the ladies into town so early he hadn't had time to do it yet.

'Here, let me do that for you, Cissie,' he offered courteously but she barely looked at him.

'I can manage,' she answered curtly.

He stopped abruptly, feeling more hurt than he could say. Ever since Christmas night, she had said barely two words to him. He missed their cosy chats and all the little things she had used to do for him. He missed the hot brick that she would place in his bed for him each night, and seeing her easy smile; the way she had always made sure to get him a nice hot cup of tea the second he set foot in the kitchen and the way she had always sliced the tops off his boiled eggs. All very trivial things, but most of all he was shocked to realise that he missed *her*!

'Don't be so silly,' he scolded, snatching the heavy logs from her arms and almost overbalancing her. 'You shouldn't be out here on that crutch. It's slippery and you're likely to fall and break your leg.'

'And why should *you* care?' she responded angrily.

'Of course I care – we all care!'

They were nose to nose now, like sparring partners in a ring.

'Only because you all feel sorry for me!'

'Happen we do, but—'

'Well, you don't need to feel sorry for me,' she told him as her eyes filled with tears. 'I might be soiled goods but I still have my pride!'

She then limped away, leaving Benny to stare after her with a bemused expression on his face.

Much later that evening, after Benny had retired to his rooms and Ted had gone to bed, Cissie informed her grandmother, 'You can stop worrying now. I started to bleed earlier this evening.'

Nellie heaved a huge sigh of relief before squeezing the girl's hand. 'That's a blessin' then, ain't it, lass?' Then, peering at her, she asked, 'What were you an' Benny arguin' about in the yard this mornin'? I overheard yer when I were washin' the pots up.'

Cissie hung her head. 'He said he felt sorry fer me,' she muttered.

Nellie smiled. 'An' why shouldn't he be? We all feel fer you after what happened. Benny's a good lad an' happen he were only tryin' to be kind.'

Cissie tugged her hand away, a mutinous expression on

her face. 'Well, I don't need him to be kind or feel sorry fer me! I'm dirty now, ain't I?'

Nellie scowled at her. 'Of course you ain't dirty! It's the low-life that did that to you who's dirty. An' as fer Benny feelin' sorry fer you . . . well, I wouldn't be too sure about that, me girl! I've noticed the way his eyes foller yer about, an' if I ain't very much mistaken I think he has feelin's fer you. I thought he were goin' to kill that Hugo the night he— Anyway, I reckon you have feelin's fer him too, so don't let what happened spoil the rest o' yer life.'

Cissie grabbed for her crutch, then she was gone as Nellie fretted, wondering if she had been too hard on the girl. But then she had only been telling the truth, and sometimes you had to be cruel to be kind. What had happened to Cissie was awful, but she should not let it ruin the rest of her life.

And then the following evening, they all had yet another shock. Maryann had gone down to the kitchen for a cup of cocoa before retiring and they were all sitting about the fire when Benny suddenly entered the room and looking pointedly at Ted he said, 'I er . . . I've been meaning to have a word with you, Ted – about your Cissie.'

'Oh aye? What about her then, lad?' Ted smiled at him as he tapped his pipe out on the fender.

Cissie had been about to retire but now she paused to stare at him and after glancing shyly at her, Benny cleared his throat and blurted out, 'I was wondering . . . that is, what I want to ask you is, would you give me permission to ask your granddaughter to marry me, sir?'

Nellie almost choked on her cocoa and Ted's eyes stretched as he said weakly, 'Well, lad, this has come as a bit of a shock, I don't mind tellin' you. But what does young Cissie herself think about it?'

All eyes turned to the girl now and she amazed them when she said resentfully, 'Thanks very much for the offer,

Benny, but I ain't prepared to marry no one just 'cos they pity me. I could have been carryin' another man's child – an' how would yer have felt about that, eh?'

'I wouldn't have cared,' he declared stoutly. 'What happened wasn't your fault, so if a child had been the result of it, I'd have accepted it as my own, an' no one need have known that it wasn't.'

Cissie threw back her head, her lustrous hair dancing on her shoulders. 'That's very honourable of you, I'm sure, but thankfully I ain't with child. But as I said, my answer is still no, thank you. I'm not a charity case just yet!' And with that she wedged her crutch beneath her arm and limped off to her room without giving him a second glance.

For a moment there was a stunned silence in the room but then Benny stood up and after muttering a hasty good-night to them all, he fled from the room.

'Well, I'll be . . . What do yer make o' that then?' Nellie breathed. 'Yer could have knocked me down wi' a feather but I reckon our Cissie should have taken him up on the offer like a shot! There ain't many as would have offered to take her on after what's happened.'

'Yes, but she's still got her pride,' her husband pointed out sensibly. 'Although I have to say there's nowt would make me happier than to have young Benny join the family. He's a good lad, so he is.'

Feeling in the way, Maryann rose and after placing her empty mug on the table she beat a hasty retreat, wondering what on earth was going to happen next. Benny usually told her everything – so why hadn't he confided in her if he had feelings for Cissie, which he obviously had? He had clearly been hurt at Cissie's refusal and she felt sorry for him. It was all very disturbing.

Despite all the excitement of the night before of Benny's

proposal to Cissie, Nellie was concerned the following morning when she saw Mr Marshall leaving the dining room after breakfast. He looked pale and gaunt, and once again something began to niggle at the back of her mind. It had been there ever since she had found the cat dead in the kitchen, and as she hurried into the room and began to stack the dirty pots onto a tray, it suddenly hit her like a hammer blow. Mr Marshall was always so well whilst Florence was in London, and yet as soon as she returned he became unwell again. She thought back to the day before the cat had died when she'd been clearing the pots from the dining room following dinner. She had noticed the slice of beef that the master had left untouched on his plate and lifting it off, she had commented to Maryann in the kitchen that it smelled strange. Thinking no more of it, she had then dropped it into the cat's bowl before scraping the rest of the food into the rubbish sack and going about her chores.

Now she decided it was time to do some investigating as soon as the opportunity arose, and it came sooner than she had expected, for the following morning Florence informed her again at breakfast: 'Carter, Miss Lord and I will be visiting my dressmaker in town this morning before lunching with a friend in Swan Lane.'

Nellie didn't even bother to answer her.

Once Nellie had watched the carriage rattle away down the drive, she set off upstairs. She had left Cissie scouring the breakfast pots; Polly was busily sweeping the dining room; Ted and Dennis were in the tack room cleaning the horses' harnesses; Mr Marshall had left for the mill and Maryann was in Fleur's room – so she knew that she had little chance of being disturbed – which, if her suspicions proved to be correct, was just as well.

She entered Florence's room first and glanced around, wondering where she should start. Deciding on the drawers, she opened one after another, going through the contents carefully so that Florence would not realise they had been disturbed. She rifled through underwear and petticoats but found nothing amiss so next she opened the wardrobes, feeling in each of the pockets of the fine gowns and skirts hanging there – but again she found nothing. After half an hour she had searched the room thoroughly and was beginning to think that her imagination was playing tricks on her. But she wasn't quite finished yet, so after making sure that she had left the room exactly as she had found it, she crept out and hurried to Miss Lord's room.

Again she began the search in the drawers and in the fourth one she gave an exultant little cry as her fingers closed around a small glass vial. Carefully pulling the cork out, she sniffed at the clear contents, recoiling as the foul smell hit her nostrils. Then she gave a grim little smile of satisfaction. It was just as she had suspected but now the dilemma was, what should she do about it? If she revealed what she had discovered to the master, there would be serious trouble in the house, but if she kept what she had found to herself . . . She shuddered at the thought before concealing the vial in her pocket and tiptoeing from the room. She would decide what to do over the course of the day.

When the master arrived home late that afternoon and rang the servant's bell in the drawing room, Nellie insisted on going to see him herself. 'You prepare his tea tray,' she told Cissie.

'Hello, Nellie,' Wesley greeted her when she entered the room. 'I was expecting Cissie. She is well, isn't she? She's been very quiet of late, not her usual cheerful self at all.'

Nellie licked her dry lips as Wesley watched her curiously. There was clearly something troubling her but he didn't want to rush her.

'Cissie's just a little off-colour, that's all. But the thing is, I've noticed that you've been under the weather too – and off your food again lately, sir,' she said quietly.

He frowned. 'I suppose I have, but if you're going to nag me to go to the doctor's, Nellie I—'

'I weren't goin' to do that 'cos I have a funny feelin' I might just have discovered what's been causin' yer to feel as yer do.' As she spoke, she drew the glass vial from her apron pocket.

He stared at it. 'What's this then?'

'Well, the thing is, I got to noticin' that while Miss Florence an' Miss Lord are in London yer seem to get yer appetite back. Whilst they're here, Miss Lord allus dishes the food up instead o' Cissie. At least she used to, but since Miss Lord now eats in her room, Miss Florence does it.'

'So? What are you implying and what's that you're holding?' He looked totally confused now.

'Well, one evenin' recently when you sent most o' your meal back untouched, I noticed that your meat smelled a little strange afore I fed it to the cat. I knew I recognised the smell from somewhere, but couldn't put my finger on it. And then the next morning I got up to find the cat as stiff as a board at the side of her food bowl. And then this mornin' I suddenly remembered what the smell was.' She took a deep breath, praying that she was doing the right thing, before saying, 'It was arsenic.'

'*What!* You're telling me that someone has poisoned the cat and they are trying to poison *me*?' Wesley spluttered. 'Nellie, don't you think you are letting your imagination run away with you a little? That's simply preposterous!'

'Is it? Well, smell this – an' tell me why Miss Lord would have it hidden in her clothes drawer then?' She pulled the cork from the glass vial and handed it to him and just as she had done, he sniffed it and recoiled.

'Now explain *that* away,' she said smugly.

He shook his head in bewilderment. 'But why would Miss Lord or my sister wish to harm me? It doesn't make any kind of sense.'

'Perhaps yer should ask her that yerself,' Nellie said sagely as she pressed the vial into his hand. 'And perhaps it would also be as well if you serve yourself from the sideboard in future, or insist that our Cissie does so. They're up to somethin', I'm tellin' yer, as sure as eggs is eggs.'

'Very well, Nellie. Thank you, you can leave this with me now, and rest assured I shall serve myself this evening while I decide what to do about this.'

'Right y'are, sir.' Nellie shuffled away, vastly relieved. At least forewarned was forearmed and it would be interesting to see if the master started to feel better again now.

Once alone, Wesley stood by the mantelpiece and stared down into the flames licking up the chimney. Nellie's revelation had shaken him to the core and he felt sick to his stomach – even sicker than he'd been feeling of late. He didn't want to believe that his sister, or Miss Lord for that matter, could be capable of what she had suggested – and yet the evidence was there in front of his very eyes. But *why?* he asked himself over and over. He had always treated Florence fairly and given her everything she asked for, so why should she wish to harm him? One thing was for sure, he would be watching her very closely from now on.

Florence and Miss Lord arrived home mid-afternoon. They each retired to their rooms to change but it was only a matter of minutes before Elizabeth barged into Florence's room without knocking to tell her, 'The vial has gone from my drawer!'

'What do you mean, it's gone?'

325

Miss Lord wrung her hands. 'It's gone, I tell you. I've looked and looked again, but there's no sign of it!'

Florence had been resting on her bed but now she rose and began to pace up and down the room in a state of great agitation. Why would anyone have gone rifling through Elizabeth's chest of drawers? Could it be that someone had guessed what they were up to?

'You will have to get Benny to prepare the carriage and take you back to Swan Lane immediately,' she snapped as her skirts swirled about her. 'We must hope that the gentleman we met today will not have left for London yet. If you see him, you will tell him that we wish to conclude our business *as soon as possible.*'

Miss Lord instantly raced from the room, her heart thumping, to do as she was told as Florence crossed to the window and stared out across the grounds, her thoughts elsewhere.

Chapter Thirty-Eight

"Old yer 'orses, I'm comin', ain't I?' Granny Addison shouted one afternoon in early February. The bitterly cold weather had badly affected her arthritis and even the short walk from the chair at the side of the fire to the door seemed like a mammoth task to her. She couldn't think who it might be anyway; most people she knew simply tapped and barged in.

She opened the door a crack, reluctant to let the heat out, to find a finely dressed young piece standing there in a fancy hat covered in feathers and a thick velvet cape that looked as if it had cost more than her Archie could earn in a whole year.

'Yes? What can I be doin' fer yer?' she asked abruptly.

The young woman laughed. 'Don't you recognise me? It's me, Granny – Violet.'

'Good Lord! No, I didn't, an' that's a fact.' Granny was astonished. Violet's cheeks were rouged and her lips were painted, and she found herself wondering what her parents would have thought if they could see her now, God rest their souls.

'I was wondering why there are different people in our cottage,' Violet said then, gesturing across the yard. 'Have Father, Maryann and Benny moved?'

Granny gulped, hardly able to believe that Violet didn't know what had happened to John Meadows. But then she wouldn't, would she? she reasoned. Although the girl had written to them, she had never left a forwarding address so Maryann had had no way of informing her of their father's suicide.

She ushered the girl into the kitchen, where Violet appeared like an orchid on a dung heap, and after telling her as gently as she could about her father's untimely demise she ended, 'Maryann is workin' up at Windy Manor wi' Benny now. She got took on as the master's little girl's nanny an' she loves it. But how about I make yer a nice cup of tea, pet? What I've told yer must 'ave come as sommat of a shock.' She had never been fond of Violet but all the same she hadn't liked being the bearer of such bad news.

'Thank you,' Violet said shakily, 'but I have a carriage waiting at the end of the alley and I ought to be getting up to the Manor really, before it gets dark.'

'Aye, well, you do that then, pet. Happen Maryann or Nellie Carter who works there will find yer a bed fer the night.'

Violet embraced the old lady and then she was gone, leaving Granny to whistle in amazement as she wondered what Maryann would think of her dolled-up sister now.

Once the carriage bowled to a halt in front of the Manor, the driver helped Violet down and she marched up the steps and rang the bell as if she owned the place. Thankfully, the loose cape she was wearing completely concealed her swollen stomach, but she was painfully aware that once she took it off, her secret would be out. Still, one step at a time, she told herself. Best let Maryann get over the shock of seeing her first, before disclosing the reason she was there.

A fresh-faced young girl in a maid's apron opened the door and Violet asked, 'May I see Maryann Meadows, please?'

It hadn't occurred to her to go to the servants' entrance and the young girl looked slightly taken aback before she said, 'Yer'd best come in, miss. I'll try an' find out where Maryann is fer yer.' She left Violet standing in the hallway and scuttled away to the kitchen where she found Maryann preparing a tea tray for Fleur.

'There's a young woman 'ere to see yer,' Polly told her breathlessly.

'To see *me*? Are you quite sure?' Maryann had never had a visitor apart from Toby and couldn't begin to imagine who it might be. She was just glad that Miss Florence had gone to London again the day before or it would have been woe betide her, having visitors come to the main entrance.

'Go an' see who it is, lass,' Nellie urged. 'I'll finish the little 'un's tray fer yer.'

And so Maryann wiped her hands on a piece of huckabuck and followed Polly back down the hallway to see a young woman in a very fine bonnet and cape standing with her back to her admiring one of Wesley's paintings.

'Good afternoon. I believe you wished to see me,' Maryann said formally, and when the figure turned, the colour drained out of her and she had to clutch at the end of the banister rail for support.

'Violet! Is it really you?' And then she was laughing and crying all at the same time as she rushed towards the girl and hugged her as if she would never let her go.

Eventually Maryann held her sister at arm's length and the torrent of questions began.

'Why didn't you let us know where you were? Where have you been? Are you all right? Do you know what happened to Father? Did you—'

'Whoa, slow down, you're making me dizzy,' Violet giggled as she held up her hand and stopped Maryann mid-flow. 'I'll answer all your questions, but is there somewhere we could sit down first? I've travelled all through the night and all today, and to tell you the truth I'm feeling a bit done in. And my luggage is still out on the carriage too.'

Maryann was instantly contrite. Violet did look tired – but where could they go to talk in private?

And then it came to her. Wesley would not be home from the mill for at least another hour and as Polly had already lit the fire in the drawing room, it would be warm in there. She ushered her sister inside, then after asking Polly if she would go out and get the carriage driver to unload Violet's luggage, she rushed through to the kitchen to make her sister some tea and send word to Benny to carry her luggage into the kitchen. He would want to see her too, of course.

'It's my sister,' she told Nellie with a radiant smile on her face. 'The one that ran away from home after Mam died. She might need to stay for the night. Do you think the master will allow it?'

'Don't see why not, seein' as the miss is away,' Nellie answered. 'There's plenty of empty rooms up in the attic. An' take as long as yer like wi' her, pet. Cissie's gone up to Miss Fleur an' I've only the master's meal an' ours to see to, so everythin's in hand. You'll have a lot o' catchin' up to do.'

'Thanks, Nellie.' Maryann lifted the tray of tea-things and hurried back to the drawing room, where she found Violet mooching about stroking the fine china and admiring the furniture.

'Looks like you've dropped on your feet,' the girl said wryly.

'Well, I have a good position here,' Maryann answered as she placed the tray down and added sugar lumps to two cups. 'But I'm only a servant. Nanny to Miss Fleur actually.'

'I know. I went back to the court and Granny Addison told me about Dad and where you were. I . . . I'm so sorry I ran off like that, Maryann.'

'Aw well, you're back now,' the girl said. She was so pleased and relieved to see her sister that she would have forgiven her anything in that moment.

'Won't you take your bonnet and cloak off?' she suggested then, but for now Violet shook her head.

'No. You see, I need to talk to you first, and when you've heard what I have to tell you, you might not be so keen for me to stay,' she sighed.

'Go on then,' Maryann said, intrigued, sitting down opposite her.

Violet lowered her head. 'I don't know where to begin,' she said eventually.

'The beginning is usually a good place.'

'Well, the truth of it is, just after Mam died I met a man in the marketplace an' I grew fond of him,' Violet began. She had practised the lie until she was almost word-perfect. 'He turned my head good and proper, so when he asked me to run away with him and get married, I couldn't resist him. He was slightly older than me so I knew Dad wouldn't give his permission and I loved him so much that I couldn't bear to lose him.' She sniffed before going on. 'I don't think I was quite in my right mind at the time, what with just losing Mam and that, so I seized the opportunity and away we went. Jed – that was his name – took me to London and we were married in a little church there a few days later. It was *so* romantic.'

She held out her hand and Maryann saw a slim gold wedding band on the third finger of her left hand. She could have no way of knowing that Violet had only bought it the day before, nor that it was brass and would probably turn her finger green in no time.

'We were so in love and *so* happy,' Violet said dreamily. 'Jed treated me like a princess, and then . . .' she fumbled in the pocket of her cape and after producing a tiny lace handkerchief, she dabbed at her eyes . . . 'and then we discovered we were going to have a baby and everything was perfect. Until . . . until Jed was run over by a tram coming home from work one evening not long ago – and that's why I'm here.'

She stood then and dramatically dropped the cape from her shoulders, and as Maryann's eyes settled on her hugely swollen stomach she gasped. Violet looked as if she might give birth at any moment.

'I only have a few weeks left to go now,' Violet said pathetically, and her acting would have done justice to one of the actresses from the Drury Lane Theatre that she was so fond of visiting.

'Oh my poor, poor girl,' Maryann cried as she wrapped her arms about her distorted waist. 'I shall ask Wes— the master if you can stay here until after the baby is born and then we can try and find you a position somewhere.'

'Thank you,' Violet said meekly. 'I knew that you would help me. I didn't have anyone else to turn to or I would never have troubled you.'

'You could *never* be a trouble to me,' Maryann assured her heartily. 'But now drink your tea and then we'll go through to the kitchen and you can meet Nellie and the rest of the staff. I shall have a word with the master about you staying here as soon as he comes in.' She grinned then before adding, 'Just think yourself lucky the mistress is away. She's a real harridan, I don't mind telling you.'

Much later that evening, when Violet was tucked up in the small attic room that the master had said she might have, Nellie asked Maryann curiously, 'So what job did this husband o' your Violet's do then? Strange that he left her wi'out a penny, ain't it?'

There was something about Violet's story that didn't quite ring true to Nellie. The way she was dressed, for a start-off. She had turned up like a painted lady dressed in a gown that was so low-cut it was almost indecent. Hardly the clothes you would expect a penniless widow to be wearing, although Maryann had clearly fallen for her story hook, line and sinker.

'She didn't actually say,' Maryann admitted. 'But I believe it's very expensive to live in London so I dare say all his wages went on rent and food and bills.'

Not all of it, if Violet's fancy clothes were anythin' to go by, Nellie thought, but she kept her thoughts to herself for now. She would never have willingly hurt Maryann for the world.

Maryann herself was fretting about Violet's future. It would not be easy for her, a young widow with a child, but then both she and Benny were earning and had already agreed that they would help her all they could.

It was the immediate future that was the problem for now. Violet had been so worn out after her journey that Maryann had merely told Wesley that her sister had turned up and that she needed somewhere to stay for that night. She hadn't as yet had the courage to admit that Violet was widowed and with child, but she had promised herself that she would reveal all to him tomorrow and pray that he might agree to allow Violet to stay until after the birth.

At least she and Nellie would be on hand then to help her with the birthing before they had to worry about finding a position and somewhere for her to live.

Maryann was very aware that it wasn't going to be easy, but even so she was determined to do all she could for her sister. They would worry about tomorrow when it came. For now, the way she saw it, Violet was back where she belonged with her family and Maryann was determined that this was where she would stay.

Upstairs, could she have known it, Violet's thoughts were running along a very different track. Because of her fondness for her, Ruby had been wonderful to her over the last few months. She had allowed her to stay in the house out of sight right up until she felt that to leave it any longer to travel back to her home town might be detrimental to the girl. And so Violet had left, with promises from Ruby that she could return just as soon as the birthing was over and resume her position there ringing in her ears. It had all been so easy up to now, Violet thought with satisfaction. Maryann had always been so soft-hearted and gullible that she had believed every single lie that Violet had fed her, and now all she had to do was bring the bastard she was carrying into the world and then clear off and leave Maryann to care for it, which she had no doubt she would. Snuggling down into the bed, she fell into a deep sleep. Everything was going exactly to plan.

The following morning, Maryann caught Wesley as he left the dining room following breakfast and asked him, 'Might I have a word with you, please?' She had spent a sleepless night tossing and turning and had decided that the sooner she told Wesley the truth about Violet's situation, the better.

'Of course,' he answered amiably, turning back into the dining room. He was always happy to make time for

Maryann. She followed him in and as she told him the story Violet had relayed to her, his face creased in sympathy.

'The poor girl,' he said, instantly remembering how he had felt when he had lost his wife. 'Of course she must stay here until after the birth, at least. And then perhaps we could find her a position here if she wished to stay. Nellie is always telling me that many hands make light work, and I confess I have let the staff situation sadly lapse over the last few years. This is such a large house I am sure there is enough work here for at least one more pair of hands.'

Maryann could not hide her relief and had the urge to kiss him, although of course she didn't. But then as a problem reared its ugly head, her face became straight and she asked, 'But what will Miss Florence say about this when she returns?'

'You just leave my sister to me,' he said grimly. He was still watching her very closely after Nellie had shown him the arsenic and was not prepared to let her rule him, or the house for that matter, any longer.

'Thank you, sir. I really appreciate this,' Maryann told him sincerely and then on light feet she dashed away upstairs to tell Violet the good news.

'*What*? You mean he wants me to be a maid here or something?' Violet said incredulously when Maryann breathlessly passed the news on.

Maryann nodded happily and Violet forced a smile to her face. She couldn't think of a worse fate than having to skivvy after anyone. She was used to being waited on herself now but she couldn't tell her sister that so she pretended to be thrilled.

'Just think how lovely it will be, us all living together again under the same roof,' Maryann gushed. 'And of course we'll have the baby soon too. Oh, I can't wait to know what it is. Would you like a boy or a girl?'

'I don't mind really,' Violet said weakly.

'You could perhaps name it after Mam or Dad,' Maryann suggested, but then she said hastily, 'Of course, if it's a boy you'll probably want to name it after your late husband?'

'I hadn't really given it a lot of thought yet,' Violet muttered and Maryann felt guilty for talking so heartlessly. The last thing she wanted to do was cause her younger sister yet more heartache.

'Look, you must be tired. Why don't you spend the day in bed today and have a good rest?' she urged gently. 'I can bring your meals up on a tray.'

'That would be nice. I must admit I am a little fatigued,' Violet said, batting her eyelashes pathetically. This is more like it, she was thinking. Maryann was like putty in her hands and if she played her cards right she could have a nice easy time of it until the brat decided to put in an appearance – which hopefully shouldn't be too long now.

'That's decided then.' Maryann leaned over and kissed her forehead, then after straightening the blankets she went back downstairs to fetch Violet her breakfast. The girl lounged lazily back against the pillows. Suddenly it looked as if the next few weeks weren't going to be so bad, after all.

Chapter Thirty-Nine

When Florence and Miss Lord returned from London two weeks later, Florence's reaction to Violet's presence at Windy Manor was every bit as bad as Maryann had feared it would be.

'Have we become a home for waifs and strays? Isn't the workhouse the best place for people like her?' Maryann overheard her roar at Wesley as she passed the drawing room on her way to the kitchen. The atmosphere had been even more strained than usual between the pair ever since the day that Nellie had given the glass vial to Wesley, and this latest incident had only served to add fuel to the fire.

'She is *enceinte*, and seeing that she is Maryann's sister I feel that I should help her,' Wesley told her coldly.

'There you go again,' Florence ranted. '*Must* you insist on calling the servants by their first names? It gives them ideas above their station!'

Maryann didn't hang about long enough to hear any more, but she was happy to hear Wesley bravely defending her.

'Oh dear, I just heard Miss Florence bawling at the master about Violet being here,' she confided to Nellie as she closed the green baize door firmly behind her.

'Ah well, we expected that – and no doubt he'll show her who's in charge. At least he's putting his foot down with her now,' Nellie, who was rolling pastry at the table, said complacently.

Her words did nothing to reassure Maryann, however. Mention of the workhouse had sent chills down her spine, and she knew that as long as there was a breath left in her body, she would never allow Violet and her baby to end up there, even if it meant leaving the Manor and finding themselves somewhere where they could all live together. Since Violet's arrival she had gone into town on a few occasions and purchased the things that the baby would need when it arrived. Violet had made no offer to do so, and with the birth so imminent, Maryann was beginning to panic.

'Talk about adding coals to the fire,' Nellie had commented when Maryann had arrived home with all her purchases. 'Folk are already sayin' you an' the master are havin' a secret love affair, so what'll they say when they see you buyin' baby clothes?'

'Let them say what they want!' Maryann had retorted indignantly. 'People know that Toby and I have an agreement, and the master has never been anything other than a perfect gentleman to me.'

'It ain't *me* that you have to convince, pet,' the woman said gently and then seeing that Maryann was becoming upset she had let the subject drop. Now, however, they had the added problem of Florence being home and Nellie had no doubt whatsoever that she would make life even more uncomfortable for Maryann now, if she could.

They already had Granny Addison on the alert for when

Violet went into labour and the master had agreed that as soon as she was needed, Benny could take the carriage to fetch her. And so now all they had to do was wait. Secretly, Nellie hoped that the event would come sooner rather than later. She hadn't taken to Violet at all, if truth be told, and it annoyed her to see the way she had Maryann waiting on her hand and foot, not that the latter ever complained. The way Nellie saw it, pregnancy wasn't an illness. Most folk she knew worked right up to the birth; they had no choice, but not Violet. Anyone would think she was the only woman in the world who had ever been pregnant and she had her poor sister running around after her like a headless chicken. Still, she consoled herself, it wouldn't be long now and once the child was born Nellie intended to see to it that Violet pulled her weight about the place.

It was as Maryann was collecting some clean washing that was airing near the stove that Florence barged into the kitchen, a grim expression on her face. She was obviously het up after her confrontation with her brother.

'Is this true what I hear about your sister staying here after she's had her baby?'

When Maryann nodded numbly, the woman almost growled as she said, 'Then let's hope she earns her keep, otherwise she'll have her marching orders, brat and all!' And with that she flounced away, leaving Maryann to stare after her with a troubled look. Things had never been easy between the mistress and herself, but she had an awful feeling that they were now set to get even worse, if that was possible.

She glanced at Nellie, who shook her head solemnly, then hurried away to pop in on Violet, who had said that she was feeling too unwell to get up, before joining Fleur, who was playing with her kitten in her room.

*

Two days later, Polly answered the front door to find a handsome gentleman standing on the step. She gawped up at him. It was rare for them to have visitors.

'Would you kindly inform your mistress that Mr Nelson is here to see her, please?' he said pleasantly.

Polly gulped as she held the door wide for him to step inside.

'Would yer wait here, sir?' she said. 'I reckon Miss Florence is upstairs. I'll just go an' tell her you're here.' She scuttled away, passing Violet on the stairs. The girl was bored with lying in bed and as Polly raced past her, she wondered why she was in such a hurry.

She continued down the stairs and then as she saw who was standing in the hallway, she nearly fainted. *'Jed!'* she hissed. 'What are you doing here?'

It would have been hard to say who was the most shocked.

'I could ask you the same thing,' he said as he stared back at her in disbelief. 'But it's best that no one here knows that we are acquainted. Go about your business and we'll perhaps get a chance to talk later—' But just then they heard a door close upstairs and Jed clamped his mouth shut, while Violet hurried on her way.

Curiosity ate away at her. She turned the corner and paused in time to hear Florence descend before saying sharply, 'Haven't I told you never to come here, Jed! Whatever do you want? Come into the drawing room quickly and think yourself lucky that my brother is away at the mill.'

Violet heard their footsteps on the highly polished floor and then the sound of the drawing-room door closing behind them. Slipping noiselessly back round the corner, she went to press her ear to the door . . .

Florence was clearly angry. 'You'd better have a very good reason for coming here,' she said. 'How would I have

340

explained who you were to my brother, had he been at home?'

'It's Ruby,' Violet heard Jed say, coming straight to the point. 'I'm afraid she had a stroke last night and I came to tell you as soon as possible. She's in a bad way, poor darling.' He did not mention Violet, thank heavens. Florence was clearly in a bad enough humour as it was, and Violet dreaded to think how she would react, were she to know that she was harbouring a whore beneath her roof.

'Poor Ruby!' Violet's hand flew to her mouth. What would become of her if Ruby were to die? Would she still have a job to return to – and how did Jed know Florence, anyway? She could hear Florence pacing up and down the room like a caged animal. 'So who is taking charge of the house at the moment?' she asked then.

'Well, Daisy is for now.'

Unbeknownst to either Jed or Violet, Florence's mind was racing. Her first plan to get rid of Wesley and Fleur and inherit the Manor had been scotched, and now it seemed that her second plan might be in danger too.

If only I had got Ruby to sign the papers first, she thought now. How naïve she had been! But who could have envisaged this happening? The money that she and Miss Lord had leeched out of Wesley over the years had been poured into the brothel and made her a nice tidy profit, but nothing like she would make now that Ruby had agreed that Florence could own everything outright. The house alone was worth a small fortune and her share of the whores' fees would have kept her in comfort for years – but now it looked as if her future was in dire jeopardy.

'But if Ruby should die before we have signed the papers saying that I am now the lawful owner of the house and the business, I will have lost everything,' she cried. 'I paid what she was asking for her half of the house and the business

341

into her bank account last week, and we had agreed that I would return next week to sign the legal documents.'

'Don't worry. That's why *I* am here,' Jed reassured her then. 'I think Ruby realises how ill she is and she has sent me to get you to sign the papers. She has already signed her part, and once you have signed yours the agreement will be binding.'

There was a triumphant note in Florence's voice as she said, 'It's sad that your plans of her retiring and coming to live with you by the sea might come to nothing now.'

'I know,' Jed said gravely. 'Ruby and I go back a long way and I don't know what I shall do without her. But that's enough of my woes. It's imperative that I return this to the solicitor immediately for it to be binding before anything happens to Ruby.'

Inside the room he produced a thick legal-looking document from a small leather case he was carrying and Florence eyed it with dismay. It was pages thick and Wesley could be home at any moment. There was no way she would have time to read through it all.

'I assure you everything is in order,' Jed said sincerely. 'All you have to do is sign your name here, and then I shall make haste back to London and deposit it with the solicitor.'

'Very well.' Unseen by Violet, Florence hurried across to a small escritoire standing beside the window and signed her name on the document with a flourish. She then pushed it back to him, urging him, 'Do make haste! And I apologise for snapping at you when you arrived. I appreciate your coming, Jed. It's important that everything is signed and sealed. I would offer you refreshments, but time is of the essence.'

'Quite,' he agreed sombrely, folding the document neatly and placing it back in his bag. 'And now I will wish you good day.' And then after bowing he turned to take his leave as Florence paced up and down in a state of nervous excitement.

Violet scuttled away with her mind racing. Who would have thought it, eh? Miss Hoity Toity Florence the owner of a brothel. It beggared belief! And what would she think when she knew that Violet herself was one of the whores who would be working for her? One thing was for sure, if need be Violet could use this information to her benefit. After all, it stood to reason that Florence wouldn't want her brother to know that she was about to become a brothel-keeper.

Once outside and back in the carriage, Jed wiped his brow with relief. It had all been so much easier than he had hoped for. Could Florence have known it, she had actually just signed her half of the house and business over to him, which meant that from now on, he and Ruby need be beholden to no one. Better still, he knew that there was nothing that Florence could do about it. After all, she would hardly wish to involve the police and have everyone know that she had been the part-owner of a brothel. By the time she discovered their trickery, Daisy would be the Madame of the brothel and he and his beloved Ruby would be living in a lovely little cottage by the sea with not a worry in the world. From now on, without that bitch's involvement in the business, life would be sweet.

Congratulating himself, he took a cigar from his pocket and chuckling, leaned back to enjoy the ride.

Chapter Forty

It was late that evening when Violet came down into the kitchen to join everyone for a last drink. She often came down at this time knowing that all the jobs would be done.

Nellie smirked, knowing just what the little madam was at. 'Oh, feelin' well enough to get up fer a bit now, are yer?' she asked with a hint of sarcasm in her voice.

Violet smiled at her sweetly. 'Actually, I've had awful back-ache all afternoon.' That at least was the truth, although she doubted that Nellie would believe her. She knew that Nellie hadn't taken to her and the feeling was mutual, although they were both polite to each other for Maryann's sake.

'You do look a little pale,' Maryann fussed, getting up and giving Violet her chair by the fire. 'Come and sit over here and I'll get you a drink.'

Violet started towards her then suddenly stopped dead in her tracks clutching her stomach and staring down at the floor where a pool of water had appeared.

'Oh!' she gasped as embarrassment and panic took a hold. 'I think I've wet myself.'

'No, you ain't,' Nellie stated matter-of-factly. 'I'd say yer waters have just gone. Best get yourself back to bed, me girl. I reckon you'll be meetin' yer baby afore long.'

Violet looked terrified but before she could make a response a terrible pain seized her and she doubled over, screaming blue murder.

'What did I tell yer,' Nellie said, gripping Violet's elbow to support her through the contraction. Then taking control of the situation she told Benny, 'Go an' get Granny Addison in the carriage, would yer, lad? But tell her not to panic. First babies have a habit o' takin' their time. An' you, Cissie, boil some water an' fetch some towels and clean sheets upstairs. You help me get her back to her bed, Maryann.'

Maryann was in a panic, flapping about hardly knowing if she was coming or going, but Cissie was the picture of calm efficiency as she began to fill as many pans as she could with water before placing them on the range and the fire to boil. Between them, the two older women managed to get Violet back to the little room in the attic, which was no mean feat as the contractions were coming quite regularly and she had to keep stopping to hang on to the banister rail.

Once inside her room, Nellie laid some old sheets across the bed then helped Violet to undress and get into her nightgown before lying her down where she squealed loud enough to waken the dead.

'Try an' save all yer energy fer the birth,' Nellie advised, but she might as well have kept quiet. It was clear that Violet was not going to be an easy patient and Nellie had an idea it was going to be a very long night indeed.

Almost an hour later, Granny Addison huffed her way up to the attic, after leaving Archie tucked up in bed. 'Phew, them stairs'll be the death of me,' she grumbled, then rolling up her sleeves she felt around Violet's abdomen. 'Hmm, the pains are comin' nice an' regular so yer might be one o' the lucky ones an' 'ave this baby fairly quick,' she commented as Violet thrashed about the bed all in a sweat. Then turning to Maryann she grinned and said, 'Why don't yer go an' make us all a brew, pet? You look almost as bad as this 'un here.'

Once Maryann had gratefully escaped, Granny looked about the room approvingly, pleased to see that everything was in readiness. There was a bowl of water steaming on the table at the side of the bed and a large stack of clean towels. At the other side of the bed was the small wooden crib that Cissie had slept in as a baby and a tiny pile of baby clothes.

'All we need now is the babe to put in it,' she said to Nellie and they settled down to wait.

As the first fingers of dawn painted the sky in pale mauves and lilacs Violet fell into an exhausted sleep.

'She's worn out,' Granny said quietly. 'It's all that weepin' an' wailin' she's been doin'. Didn't I tell 'er to save her energy – but would she listen? Would she 'ell! It'll be God 'elp us when this baby does finally decide to put in an appearance.'

'Ah, but she's only young,' Maryann said defensively, and Granny patted her hand.

'Aye she is, pet. Happen I'm bein' a bit 'ard on her. I'm surprised she ain't called out for her man though. Most women do when they're birthin'.'

'Perhaps it's too painful for her to think of him,' Maryann suggested, and Nellie and Granny exchanged a glance, although they didn't comment.

Nellie bustled away soon after to start the day's chores and to begin preparing the breakfasts, promising

Maryann that she would send Cissie to attend to Fleur. Granny fell into a doze as Maryann watched her sister closely. She felt utterly helpless; there was nothing she could do to ease the girl's pain apart from pray that it would soon be over.

By mid-morning Violet's screams were not quite so loud. She was utterly exhausted, and as Granny bent over her to examine her yet again, she frowned. Going on how close together the contractions were, she judged that the baby should have been born hours ago – but there was still no sign of it happening and she was beginning to get worried.

'I reckon if nothin's happened within the next hour we ought to send for the doctor,' she said, then seeing the dread on Maryann's face she added quickly, 'Just to be on the safe side, like.'

There were huge dark circles beneath Maryann's eyes and she looked tired, but despite Granny urging her to go and lie down she stoutly refused to leave Violet's side.

'I shall have a rest when I've met my niece or nephew, and when I know that Violet is all right,' she said stubbornly, and nothing that Granny said could persuade her otherwise.

And then suddenly Violet let out a growl and leaned forward.

'That's more like it. She's started to push,' Granny said as she flipped Violet's nightdress up over her swollen stomach. 'That's a good girl. Now when I tell yer push fer all you're worth.'

Maryann swayed as she looked at the pool of blood forming on the bed between Violet's legs. Was this normal? She had no way of knowing and she tried to get a grip on herself. Violet needed her and this wasn't the time to go to pieces. The next twenty minutes were the most horrific of her life as she watched her sister battle to bring her baby

347

into the world – but then suddenly she saw a thatch of dark hair between Violet's legs and Granny shouted exultantly, 'That's it, gel! Now one more good 'un should do it! Go on . . . *push*!'

With a final effort Violet pushed as hard as she could and suddenly a tiny body propelled itself onto the bed and let out a mewling little cry.

'It's a little wench, a bit on the small side but a right bonny one at that.' Granny smiled as she quickly cut the cord and passed her to Maryann, who was waiting with a towel to wrap her in.

'Oh Violet, she's quite beautiful,' Maryann gasped. 'Would you like to hold her?'

But Violet was lying limply against her pillows and did not reply.

'Perhaps when I've bathed her and Granny has cleaned you up a bit then,' she said joyfully, staring in awe at the perfect little soul in her arms.

It was then that she noticed Granny's expression.

'Everything is all right now, isn't it?' she asked.

Granny had a towel pressed between Violet's legs and within seconds it was sodden with blood. She tossed it aside and reached for another one, saying over her shoulder, 'I reckon yer should get Benny to ride into town fer the doctor. I can't seem to stem this flow o' blood.'

The smile was gone now as Maryann clutched her niece to her and rushed towards the stairs to do her bidding. Violet seemed to be barely conscious, unaware of what was happening to her, and suddenly Maryann was mortally afraid. It was as she was re-entering the room some minutes later, still holding the newborn, that Violet's eyes suddenly fluttered open and she gave Maryann an angelic smile.

'I – I'm so sorry,' she whispered in a voice that was so

faint Maryann had to bend towards her to hear it. 'I – I wish I could have been good like you.'

'But you *are* good,' Maryann replied with a catch in her voice, but Violet's eyes had already closed again. Maryann had good cause to be afraid, for by the time the doctor arrived two hours later Violet had quietly slipped away, followed minutes later by her tiny daughter.

Violet had been washed and placed into a clean nightgown by Nellie and Granny, and she looked so peaceful that anyone could have been forgiven for thinking that she was merely sleeping. And still Maryann sat on at the side of the bed holding the tiny infant to her and refusing to let anyone take her away. Granny had tried and so had Nellie, but now they had departed for the warmth of the kitchen, at a loss as to what they should do. Benny had been in and cried as he had said his goodbyes, and then eventually the door opened again and Wesley appeared, his face solemn.

'My dear, why don't you come away now?' he said softly. 'There is nothing to be gained by sitting there. Violet is at peace now and so is the child, God rest their souls.'

Only much later would Maryann find out that Wesley had sat up all night waiting for news, but for now she just stared straight ahead, dry-eyed.

'I have taken the liberty of sending Ted for the vicar and the undertaker,' he went on. 'And you mustn't worry about anything. I shall make all the arrangements.'

'No!' His words seemed to jerk her out of her trance-like state. 'Benny and I will arrange the funeral. She was our sister.'

'We'll worry about that later,' he soothed. 'But why don't you give the baby to me now? She needs to lie with her mother.'

Maryann stared down at the perfectly formed little face and then reluctantly allowed Wesley to take her. And then, as he laid her gently on her mother's chest, the tears finally came. Hot burning tears that threatened to choke her.

Chapter Forty-One

'Won't you please change your mind and attend the service with us, Florence?' Wesley asked his sister on the day of the funeral.

Laying her napkin down, she answered heartlessly, 'Why should I? The girl was nothing to us. I don't even know why you are bothering to go! And anyway I shall be leaving for London mid-morning.'

There had been no word from Jed, but she could hardly wait to get to Greenwich and take possession of the brothel that was now solely hers, paid for with money that she had cheated from her brother over the years. She felt no shame at what she had done. The way she saw it, if Wesley had been more of a man he wouldn't have been so easy to take advantage of. Also, she felt entitled to half of the estate, so this was only fair, to her way of thinking. Now all she had to do was get rid of Elizabeth and then she could begin her new life. She would never set foot in Windy Manor again if she could help it, and she wouldn't miss it at all.

Wesley excused himself and went to get changed into his dark suit as Florence hurried to her room to supervise Elizabeth packing her things.

'Oh, isn't it exciting, dear,' the woman twittered. 'Just think what fun we shall have living in the capital.'

Florence forced a smile as she nodded in agreement. The carriage that was booked to take them to the railway station was due to arrive shortly after the funeral cortège had left for the church, and she was still nowhere near ready to go, so she ushered Elizabeth away to do her own packing and continued to load things she felt she might need into her trunks.

Downstairs, the Carters and Maryann were sitting quietly in the kitchen all dressed in the darkest clothes they had. Polly and Dennis, who would meet them at the church, had been given the day off, and Benny and Ted had been up since the crack of dawn seeing to the animals. Now all they could do was wait. Eventually they heard the knock on the front door sound and Nellie rushed away to answer it.

Outside, she saw the cart containing Violet's coffin drawn by two black stallions pawing at the ground, and behind it the master's carriage with Benny sitting aloft waiting to take the mourners to church. The mahogany coffin was the best that Maryann and Benny could afford, and atop it was a simple wreath. They had politely but steadfastly refused Mr Marshall's offer of help towards the cost.

'It's here,' Nellie told them all softly as she re-entered the kitchen, and without a word they all silently followed her outside as Cissie watched them leave from Fleur's bedroom window. She had willingly volunteered to look after the child, as she was still traumatised after her rape and found it difficult to venture far from the house. The master had sent a number of paints, brushes and paper up to Fleur's room to keep her amused while they were gone. The girl turned away from the sad sight and with a loving smile at her young charge they settled down and began to paint.

From the shadow of the barn, Hugo watched the solemn procession move away. He had learned from local gossip that Miss Florence had refused to attend the funeral because she was departing for London and now at last he intended to take his revenge on her. Many a time he had thought of the jewellery case standing on her dressing table, and believing the house to now be empty, he intended to fill his pockets with her valuable gewgaws. He rubbed his hands together gleefully as he thought of the new life they would bring him, and imagined how furious the unfeeling bitch would be when she returned to find them all gone. This time though, he would be more careful. He had heard that Newcastle was a nice place to live and he intended to make his way there. He would pawn the jewellery and live like a king.

Taking off his cap, he stuffed it into his pocket, and making sure that everyone had really gone, he sauntered across the yard and tried the back door. It was unlocked as he had hoped it would be, so now he made his way across the kitchen and into the hallway. He paused for a moment to listen and hearing nothing, he took the stairs noiselessly, two at a time. Within seconds he was inside Florence's bedroom and his eyes immediately went to the jewellery box. He strolled across the room without a care in the world and after lifting the lid he stared down admiringly at the gold and glittering gems that winked up at him. There was a fortune there, he was sure of it, and after tossing his cap aside he began to lift things out and stuff them into his pockets. And then suddenly the dressing-room door opened and Florence stood there in person; they stared at each other in shock.

'Just what the hell do you think you're doing?' she gasped eventually, and Hugo panicked. He started to back towards the door but in seconds she was on him like a wild cat, tugging at his pockets as she tried to snatch her jewels back.

'Get off me, yer silly cow,' he hissed as he tried to free himself, but she was hanging on to his coat for grim life.

'*Give – them – back– now!*' she growled, and he felt her nails rake the soft skin of his cheek.

She was surprisingly strong for a woman, and suddenly Hugo saw himself incarcerated in a prison cell for years and years, and he knew that he wouldn't be able to bear it. He heard the seam of his jacket tear and reached out blindly for something, anything to make her let go of him. And that was when his fingers closed around a heavy brass candlestick standing on a small table. He fumbled to get a grip on it, then lifting it high above his head, he brought it crashing down as hard as he could on her forehead. There was a sickening thud and she crumpled like a rag doll, hitting her head again on the edge of the dressing table as she fell. For a moment Hugo just stood there stupefied, watching as her life's blood collected in a pool about her. But then, realising the danger he was in, he looked about wildly.

He must make it look like a burglary, so again he crossed to the jewellery box and hastily crammed the rest of the contents into his pockets before charging from the room as if Old Nick himself was snapping at his heels. Hugo pelted down the stairs, out of the back door, and didn't stop running until he had reached a copse at least a mile away from the Manor. Here he sank down onto the ground and dropped his head into his hands as he tried to catch his breath. He had a terrible stitch in his side and he had never been so afraid in his life, but thankfully he didn't think anyone had seen him. Once again, everything had gone terribly wrong but there was nothing he could do about it now, although he realised he would have to delay his departure. If he were to disappear immediately, it would look suspicious and the coppers would be on to him in no time. Somehow he was going to have to go home and try to act normally until the heat had died down, and then he could escape – never to be seen again.

He waited until his heartbeat had returned to normal then straightening himself up as best he could, he headed for home.

His mother was scrubbing the kitchen floor when he got back and glancing up at him she asked, 'What have you done to your face now? Gone a bit too far with one of the lasses and got put in your place, have you?'

He knew that his mother still hadn't forgiven him for what he had done to Cissie but he brazened it out.

'Somethin' like that,' he replied vaguely, then, 'Where's Toby?'

'Yer know where he is. He's had a mornin' off to go up to the Manor to keep his eye on the place while they're all at the funeral. He should be there now.'

'Oh yes, o' course. I'd forgotten about that.' *Damn*, he silently cursed. *I'd forgotten about that but happen it wouldn't matter*. The chances of Toby having spotted him were slim.

'Huh, you would,' Tilly snorted, then returned to her scrubbing as he sidled past her and went upstairs to the room he shared with his brother. Once inside he closed the door and looked about wildly. He would have to hide the jewellery until he could get it away, but where?

And then it came to him. The hole beneath Toby's mattress. Since he had stolen his brother's savings his brother had been a lot more careful about where he hid his money. So careful, in fact, that as yet Hugo hadn't found

355

the new hiding place. But the old one was still there and it was doubtful that Toby would ever use it again. Dropping to his knees, Hugo began to cram the gems into the hole. Once he'd done, he stood back up to make quite sure that the bed looked exactly as he had found it. Satisfied then, he lay down on his own bed and squeezed his eyes tight shut as a figure of Florence dropping to the floor swam behind them. And it was only then that a sickening thought occurred to him. He had failed to retrieve his cap before leaving Florence's bedroom!

Judging that the carriage should be back from the funeral soon, Toby entered the kitchen and filled the kettle from the bucket at the side of the sink. Happen they would all be upset when they got back, so he would make them all a cup of tea before going on to work. And it was then that an ear-splitting scream rent the air and he nearly jumped out of his skin. It seemed to be coming from upstairs, so racing into the hall he was just in time to see a hysterical Miss Lord almost tumbling down the stairs.

'What is it?' he asked, catching her in his arms and shaking her gently.

As she pointed upstairs, he could feel her whole body trembling. 'It's Florence!' She collapsed against his chest and began to sob broken-heartedly.

'What's wrong with her?' he asked, baffled, but realising that he would get no sense from her, he gently pushed her aside and climbed the stairs two at a time. He was almost at the top when he heard horses' hooves on the drive and stopped where he was. The master strode through the front door, raising his eyebrows as he saw Toby staring down at him. He then looked at Miss Lord, who was babbling incoherently, and asked, 'Whatever has happened now?'

Toby spread his hands. 'I've no idea, sir. I came to check on the horses as I promised I would, then decided that I'd put the kettle on ready for when you all got back afore I set off for work. That was when I heard Miss Lord screaming, but I can't get any sense out o' her so I was just comin' up here to see what was wrong. She just keeps sayin' somethin' about Florence.'

'Then I'd better come up with you,' Wesley said, handing his black top hat to Cissie. He then mounted the stairs and Toby followed him in the direction of his sister's bedroom.

'My God,' Toby croaked in horrified disbelief as they saw Miss Florence lying there. He sprinted across the room and bent to feel for a pulse before turning to Wesley and saying hoarsely. 'I'm afraid she's dead, sir.'

Wesley swayed with shock, but after pulling himself together with an enormous effort he said, 'Would you mind going to ask Benny if he would fetch the constable, please?'

Within no time at all the house seemed to be swarming with police, but locked in her own grief for Violet and the baby, Maryann seemed oblivious to everything and sat huddled at the side of the kitchen fire.

'Eeh, I'd be a hypocrite to say I liked Miss Florence,' Nellie muttered to Ted as she went about her usual tasks. 'But to die like that in yer own home! It don't even bear thinkin' about.'

At that moment a constable was questioning Miss Lord in the drawing room, but it was an uphill task. She had been devoted to her mistress and was totally devastated that the life they had planned had been snatched away from her at the eleventh hour. Another law officer was questioning Toby in Master Wesley's library, but Toby wasn't able to tell them much. Cissie had already been questioned but insisted that she hadn't heard a thing.

And yet another officer was conducting a thorough search of Miss Florence's room, looking for clues, and it wasn't long before he came back downstairs brandishing Hugo's cap.

'This was lying on the floor at the side of the bed, sir,' he told the man who was questioning Toby, and as Toby looked towards him the colour drained from his face. He would have known that cap anywhere. His mother Tilly had bought him and Hugo identical ones for Christmas, and as it certainly wasn't his, it could only be his younger brother's. He gulped deep in his throat. He had known Hugo was heartless for some long time, even though he had always managed to make excuses for him. But surely even Hugo couldn't be capable of murder?

'Have you done with me now?' he asked shakily as the older man took the cap and began to turn it over in his hands. He had already told him all he knew at least half a dozen times.

'Yes, Mr Jackson. For now, you may go about your business.'

Toby thought his legs were going to let him down as he made his way into the hall, and there he leaned heavily against the wall just in time to see Nellie waddling towards him with a loaded tea tray. Bless her, Nellie thought tea was a cure for all ills, but it was going to take a lot more than tea to cure this one.

'Have a drink, lad. Yer look proper shaken up,' she offered kindly.

'I won't if you don't mind, Nellie,' he answered, dragging himself away from the wall. 'I reckon I'll head for home now. I'd not be able to concentrate on what I were doing if I turned in fer work. But I'll just go through to the kitchen and say goodbye to Maryann first, if yer don't mind.'

'O' course I don't. You go on, lad.' She watched him walk away with his shoulders stooped and then hurried on her way with the master's tea.

Chapter Forty-Two

Toby found Maryann still sitting in the chair at the side of the fire. Dropping to his hunkers, he took her hands in his, asking, 'Are you all right, pet?'

She was deathly pale but he was relieved to see that at least she wasn't crying any more. Maryann herself was sure that she didn't have a tear left in her whole body.

'Yes, Toby, I'm all right,' she said. 'This latest business with Miss Florence . . . it's dreadful, isn't it?'

'Aye, it is,' he agreed gravely.

'Do you think they'll find who did it?'

Toby cleared his throat before answering, 'I'm sure they will. But I'd best be off now. I'll see you on Sunday, shall I?'

When she nodded, he did a strange thing. In a rare show of affection he leaned forward and kissed her full on the lips then stroked her cheek . . . and then without another word he strode from the room leaving her to stare after him.

Soon after, the police began to depart too with promises

that they would be back. One went in to speak to the master, whilst another entered the kitchen where Nellie was trying to prepare a meal of sorts. It would be just cold cuts of meat today and pickles. No one was really hungry but she felt she had to produce something.

'Good afternoon, ladies,' the young constable said politely from the kitchen doorway. 'I just need to ask that none of you leave the area until the investigations are complete.'

'Well, where do yer reckon we'd go?' Nellie answered sarcastically as she spooned some pickled onions from a large jar into a dish.

The young man looked uncomfortable, but then Maryann pointed to the cap he was holding and gasped, 'Where did you get that cap?'

'Why?' He was alert now.

'Toby, who just left, and his brother Hugo had an identical one each for Christmas as a gift from their mother,' she answered innocently

'Are you quite sure of this?' The constable's heart started to race as visions of a promotion floated in front of his eyes.

'Of course I'm sure,' Maryann said as she turned back towards the fire. 'The pattern on them is quite distinctive, isn't it?'

The young policeman left without another word and hurried off to pass on the news to his superior, who was just about to leave.

'Well done, lad.' The man slapped him on the back before taking out his notebook and flicking through the pages. 'It all adds up, doesn't it? Toby Jackson was here whilst everyone else was at the funeral. There were no witnesses so he could easily have killed Miss Marshall and then pretended to find her body. And to think we sent him on his way . . . I heard from local gossip that he'd had all his savings stolen not so long ago, so that could have given him the motive too.

Perhaps Miss Marshall disturbed him while he was in her room, and things got out of hand? Still, I know the young man's address – he lives in the courts in Abbey Street – and I also happen to know of his brother, Hugo. Now *he's* always got his sticky fingers into something or another, but up to now he's always managed to give me the slip and I've never been able to pin anything on him. I've never heard owt bad about his brother though,' he said thoughtfully. 'Still, I reckon we should pay him a visit, don't you? An' there's no time like the present. Come on, we've work to do.' And with that they slammed out of the house.

Tilly was just adding dumplings to a *rabbit stew* simmering on the fire when Toby barged in. His mother looked up in surprise, saying, 'What are you doing here? I thought you were going to work this afternoon. It's never that time already, is it?'

'Where's Hugo?' he asked abruptly, ignoring her question.

'What? He's upstairs as it happens, but why do yer want him? An' who's upset yer?'

Without stopping to answer, he strode towards the stairs door, leaped up the narrow staircase and banged into the room he shared with his brother. Hugo was sprawled across his bed and when he saw the look on Toby's face he said in a faltering voice, 'What's up wi' you then?'

'I rather think *you* should be tellin' me that, don't you? You've really done it this time. Even I can't help yer wi' this one,' Toby said tonelessly.

Hugo hastily sat up and swung his feet onto the cold floorboards. 'I don't know what yer on about,' he blustered, but the truth was written on his face.

Toby sprang towards him and caught him by his collar. 'Where have yer been all day?' he shot at him.

362

'Err . . . 'ere an' there. Nowhere in particular.' But Hugo was sweating heavily.

'*Liar!*' Toby shook him until his teeth rattled then crossing to the chest, he took out his best cap and wagged it at Hugo, saying, 'Where's yours, eh? Yer wouldn't have left it up at the Manor by any chance, would yer?'

Hugo had paled to the colour of bleached bone now but still he tried to bluff it out as he choked, 'I don't know what yer on about, man!'

Slinging the cap down onto Hugo's bed, Toby hissed, 'Where did yer hide the jewellery yer stole afore yer caved Miss Florence's head in?'

'Wh-what jewellery? I tell yer, I've not a clue what yer on about.'

Terror was pumping through Hugo's veins like iced water now, but before he could say any more they heard a commotion downstairs followed by an alarmed cry from their mother and then the sound of heavy footsteps pounding up the stairs. Seconds later the room seemed to be heaving as uniformed law officers flooded into the room and grasped both of them firmly.

'Toby Jackson, we have reason to believe that this afternoon you robbed Miss Florence Marshall up at Windy Manor, killing her in the process,' a grim-faced officer said.

Toby shook his head in distress. 'No, I *didn't*,' he cried, but his words fell on deaf ears as the officers began a thorough search of the room. The contents of the drawers were tipped out onto the floor and they heaved the mattress from Hugo's bed and began to examine it as the two young men looked helplessly on.

'There's nothin' here,' one of them said eventually, leaving the pillows and blankets in a tangle on the floor. He then crossed to Toby's bed and the process started again. And then suddenly he found the hole in the base of Toby's horsehair mattress, and as he delved inside it, his fingers closed around some of the jewels.

'I reckon I've got summat here!' he crowed triumphantly. He withdrew his hand and the weak sunshine filtering through the tiny leaded windows sparkled on the jewels, reflecting all the colours of the rainbow about the lime-washed walls.

Tilly had fought her way through the officers on the stairs like a cat trying to protect her kittens, and now as she looked at the gems her mouth fell open and she gasped, 'Where in God's name did they come from?'

Completely ignoring her, the man in charge looked at Toby and demanded, 'So what do you have to say for yourself then? Do you deny that this is your cap?' He waved the hat in front of him, but then another officer pounced on the cap that Toby had flung onto Hugo's bed.

'Here's the other cap, sir.' He brandished it in the air. 'So the one we found up at the Manor must have been his!'

Suddenly a lawman was arresting Toby for murder and theft as his mother started to sob.

Toby glared at Hugo, waiting for him to confess – but his brother merely bowed his head to avoid his eyes – and in that moment Toby knew that he was done for.

There was a stunned silence for a while. Tilly knew her oldest son inside out and she couldn't believe that he would be capable of such vile acts. Hugo was staring at him open-mouthed too now, but being the coward he was, he didn't say a word.

'Toby wouldn't harm a fly,' Tilly wept. 'Get yer hands off 'im!'

'You're coming with us, my lad,' Toby was told as they hauled him away, and Tilly ranted and raved in desperation while Hugo looked on with his hands clenched into fists.

*

It was late that evening and almost bedtime when Nellie answered the front door of the Manor to find the officer in charge standing there once again.

'Lordy, don't you men never go home?' she asked amiably as the man removed his hat and stepped into the hall. 'Was it the master you was wantin'?'

He nodded, and after she had shown him into the library she shot back to the kitchen to tell them all breathlessly, 'The officer is 'ere again to see Master Wesley. Do yer reckon they've caught the bugger that's killed the mistress?'

'I can't see why else he'd be callin' at this time o' night,' Ted answered as he puffed on his pipe. It had been a rare old day, there was no doubt about it. 'But I dare say we'll find out soon enough.'

And find out they did, for when the visitor left a short while later, the servants' bell in the library rang and Nellie scuttled away to answer it.

'Nellie, do you know where Maryann is?' the master asked when she entered the room.

'Aye, I do. She settled Miss Fleur then went off fer an early night. It's been a bit of a day fer her one way or another, but then it has fer all of us.'

'It has,' he agreed, for he had been very shaken by his sister's gruesome murder. 'I wonder if you would ask her to join me, please. I wouldn't ask if it wasn't important.'

'I'll do it now.' Nellie was already heading for the door and once it had closed behind her, Wesley stared sightlessly at the dark window, wishing that he could be a million miles away.

'But why would the master want to see me at this time of night?' Maryann asked when Nellie entered her room. She had just been about to blow out her candle.

'I've no idea, pet, but he does, so get a move on.' Nellie held her dressing gown out to her.

'But I can't go down in my nightclothes, and I haven't done my hair,' Maryann protested. Her eyes were still swollen with grief from her sister and baby niece's funeral.

'There ain't time fer that,' Nellie said. 'Now come along, young lady!'

And so Maryann shrugged her arms into her robe and after hastily shoving her feet into her slippers, she followed Nellie back downstairs, wondering what on earth could be so important that it couldn't wait until the morning.

Wesley was pacing up and down the library when she entered and she stood there, very conscious that her hair was loose about her shoulders and that she was in a state of undress.

He looked across at her, his face haggard, and said, 'Won't you sit down? I'm afraid I have some rather bad news for you, my dear.'

She moved across the room and perched on the edge of the fireside chair, her hands clasped primly in her lap.

He came to stand in front of her and she noted that he seemed to be struggling for words before he eventually blurted out, 'They have charged someone with my sister's murder.'

'Oh!' She stared at him blankly.

'The thing is . . .' He swiped his hand across his brow. 'They have charged Toby. You see, Florence's jewels were found hidden in his mattress.'

Maryann stared at him uncomprehendingly for a moment. Her head began to swim. She surely must have misheard him! Toby was a gentle person – he wouldn't hurt a fly. But then as she looked into Wesley Marshall's face she saw that he had spoken the truth, and for the first time in her life she slithered to the floor in a dead faint.

Chapter Forty-Three

A few days later, Elizabeth Lord clutched the letter that had arrived just that morning, a look of shock on her face. She felt as if she had had all the breath knocked from her body – and yet the facts were there in black and white. She had been betrayed! The day after Florence had died, she had written to the solicitor in London, asking if everything was in order for her to take over the property in Greenwich in Florence's place. With her own eyes, she had seen Jed arrive, carrying the papers for Florence to sign. Once that was done, Florence should have legally owned Ruby's half-share of the business as well as her own. Elizabeth and Florence had had an agreement that, should anything happen to Florence, the whole business and the house would become hers – but according to the solicitor, *Ruby* was now the sole owner of the property.

Ruby, it was clear, had tricked Florence – and Florence in turn had tricked *her*! But what was she to do now? Wesley had already warned her that now that his sister had died, she would no longer be required – and Elizabeth had a strong feeling that as soon as the funeral was over, she would get her marching orders. But where would she go? She had absolutely nothing. Florence had always handled all the money they had swindled out of her brother over the years, and trusting her lover implicitly, Elizabeth had made no objection, believing that her future was secure. But now . . .

Hot tears spurted from her eyes at this final injustice. How could Florence have done this to her, after all they had been to each other? And then anger set in. She would not take this lying down! Perhaps it was time for Wesley to know just how much his sister had despised him and there was no time like the present!

Marching from the room with the letter still clutched in her hand, she stormed downstairs to the library and went in without knocking.

'I need to speak to you – about Florence,' she burst out.

Wesley had been painting. He said, 'I really don't feel inclined to discuss my sister with you, Miss Lord. And now if you would kindly leave . . .'

'No, I won't leave,' she spat, and he saw that she was trembling from head to foot, In fact, she looked almost unhinged – as if she were teetering on the brink of insanity.

'Were you aware that your sister always felt that your father should have left the Manor jointly between you?' she demanded.

He nodded. 'Of course. But Florence knew that the oldest son always inherits, and I had told her that I was happy to sign the townhouse in London over to her if she didn't wish to live here. In fact I was in the process of doing just that. Not that this is any business of yours, mind. You are simply a servant, in case you've forgotten, Miss Lord.'

'Well, she wasn't happy with just that,' Elizabeth said hotly. 'And I was so much more than a servant to your sister.

We were lovers – and Florence *hated* you! In fact, she hated you so much that she wished you and Fleur dead! She was sending me into the apothecary's in Bedworth each month to buy arsenic with which she was lacing your food, so what do you think of that?'

It was only then that she thought of her own guilty part in this sorry mess, and she gulped deeply in her throat.

'You knew of this and yet you did nothing to prevent it,' Wesley said coldly. 'That, I believe, makes you an accessory to attempted murder, Miss Lord.' He thought of Nellie's suspicions, of the small vial of clear poison and the many times he had felt ill whilst Florence was in residence . . . and everything finally fell into place. He had tried not to think of it; tried not to believe it – but now he could no longer deny it. And Florence and Elizabeth lovers! How had he not noticed? Wesley thought of the way he had behaved for far too long – selfishly shut off from others, including his own, precious daughter. Now more than ever, he realised that it was time to make a stand, take control and become the master of his own house again.

Moving to the bell-pull hanging at the side of the fireplace, he rang it. When Nellie breathlessly entered the room, he said, 'Please tell Benny to have the carriage brought round to the front of the house within the hour. Miss Lord is leaving Windy Manor and I would like him to drive her to the railway station.'

'B-but where will I go?' Miss Lord sobbed, already regretting her impulsiveness. Why oh why hadn't she just kept her mouth shut? She had made things a million times worse now, if that was possible.

'That is really not my concern,' Wesley answered as Nellie scuttled away to do as she was told. 'The truth of the matter is, I should really be handing you over to the authorities to get your just deserts. Think yourself lucky that I am being so lenient! And now I would like you to go and pack your things. If you are not ready to leave by the time Benny has the carriage at the door, I shall have you escorted from the premises and you can walk to the station for all I care. It would certainly be no more than you deserve. Goodbye, Miss Lord!' He then turned his back on her as the woman staggered in shock.

'No, please, you can't send me away,' she begged. 'I didn't mean what I said. I was distraught after losing Florence.'

'Just *go*.' He practically shouted at her. She had never seen Wesley like this before. Florence had always been able to manipulate him, but now he appeared to have awoken after a long sleep and was very much in charge again.

She wrung her hands as tears streamed down her ashen cheeks but he remained unmoved, and finally she stumbled from the room.

An hour later, Nellie and Wesley watched from the library window as Benny loaded Miss Lord's trunks onto the top of the carriage before helping her inside. The woman looked deathly pale, and just once she turned her head to lock eyes with Wesley. The look she cast at him made his blood run cold. If looks could kill, he knew that he would have dropped dead on the spot, it was loaded with so much venom, but he steeled himself and turned away. Miss Lord could do him no more harm now.

'Good riddance to bad rubbish, that's what I say,' Nellie muttered. 'I knew her an' Miss Florence were cookin' sommat up, but to try an' kill yer!'

Once the carriage had rattled away, Nellie turned to go back to her chores but she paused when Wesley asked, 'How is Maryann doing, Nellie? I haven't seen her for the last couple of days.'

'As well as can be expected,' Nellie answered sadly.

'They've moved Toby to that new prison in Birmingham till the trial. Winson Green, I think it's called, an' she's hopin' to be able to go an' see him shortly. She don't believe that Toby did it, and atween you an' me, I don't neither. Toby always seemed like such a nice young chap whereas we know all too well that that brother of his has no morals whatsoever. Problem is, although Toby ain't admitted it, he ain't said who he thinks did it either.'

Wesley shrugged helplessly. He too had grave doubts about whether Toby was capable of committing so horrendous a crime, but the evidence was compelling.

'Give Maryann her due, she's still lookin' after Miss Fleur an' tryin' to get on wi' things,' Nellie went on. 'Which is all credit to her under the circumstances, ain't it?'

'It certainly is,' Wesley agreed. 'Would you mind telling her that I'd like a word with her this evening after dinner, please, Nellie?'

'I certainly will.' She went back to the kitchen with a heavy heart, hoping that Wesley wasn't going to dismiss Maryann too.

The same thought had obviously occurred to Maryann, for when she had settled Fleur for the night she went to her room and tidied her hair before heading for the library.

'Come in,' Wesley called when she tapped at the door, and squaring her shoulders she entered the room.

'Before you dismiss me, sir, I would like to tell you that I have come to tender my resignation,' she told him primly.

'You've come to do *what*?' he repeated incredulously. Maryann faltered. Perhaps he hadn't been about to dismiss her, after all?

'W-well . . . I just thought that seeing as it was my young man who . . . who . . . Well, I just thought that you wouldn't want me in the house any more,' she ended lamely.

'Then you thought wrong,' Wesley admonished her. 'And

371

furthermore, I don't mind telling you that I don't believe that Toby killed my sister, despite all the evidence pointing that way.'

'You don't?' She was staring at him wide-eyed, hope stamped on her face.

'No, I don't – and what I wanted to say to you was that I will provide him with the best barrister that I can, and the best character reference.'

'Oh!' Maryann hastily sat down on the nearest chair, afraid that her legs might let her down. They had turned to jelly and she suddenly felt tearful.

'I also wanted to thank you for the way you've taken over the care of Fleur again,' he went on. 'Not many who have been through what you have recently had to endure would have done that, and I'm very grateful. You must know that the child dotes on you, Maryann? It would destroy her if you were to leave, so please, no more talk of resigning, eh?'

'Very well, sir,' she answered meekly. 'But aren't you afraid of what people will say? To them you are employing the intended of the man they believe murdered your sister.'

'They can say what they like,' Wesley said tiredly. 'You and Benny belong here and that remains the same. Nellie tells me that you are hoping to be able to go and see Toby. Would you like me to come with you?'

'Oh no, thank you,' she said hastily. 'I shall catch a train and will be perfectly all right going alone.'

'Very well, but should you change your mind the offer stands. And don't forget to tell him what I said. It may not be too late.'

She was so choked with emotion that she could only nod as she rose and stumbled blindly towards the door. Oh, he was a good man through and through was the master, there was no doubt about it – and she would never forget his kind words. For the first time since she had known him he appeared to be taking control of things. She finally also had a glimmer of hope for Toby. All she had to do was convince him to tell the truth now, for deep down she was convinced that Hugo was the murderer.

Nellie tapped at the door of the library and carried a tray of supper in for the master, placing it silently down on the side table before the fire. Wesley was sitting with his hands clasped beneath his knees and she stifled the urge to go to him and give him a hug, as she had done when he was a little boy. Miss Florence's funeral, which had taken place the day before, had been a sombre affair with few mourners and she was glad that it was over. There had been too many funerals of late. It was more than a body could bear.

'Try an' eat somethin',' she urged, and lifting his head he gave her a weak smile.

'Thank you, Nellie. I will.'

She slipped away, sensing that the master needed his privacy, and once he was alone again he buried his face in his hands. There had been so much heartache. First the death of his wife and now his sister, but he knew it was time to move on. There was a little girl upstairs who needed him and from this day forward he intended to do right by her.

Chapter Forty-Four

'Are you quite sure that you don't want me to come with you?' Benny offered as he stood with Maryann outside the railway station early in April. She was finally going to see Toby, and the master had insisted that Benny should drive her to the station in the carriage.

'I shall be fine, honestly,' she promised him, although her emotions were all over the place. One part of her could hardly wait to see Toby, whilst another part dreaded what it would be like to see him in the grim confines of the prison. His trial had been set for the following week, and she knew that this would be the only chance she would have to speak to him before he faced the judge.

'I should be going,' she said then. 'I don't want to miss my train.'

He nodded and then leaned down to kiss her cheek. 'All right, sis. I shall be here to meet you at half past five when you get back. Make sure you take a cab to the prison from New Street when you get into Birmingham. I don't like the thought of you wandering about there on your own.'

She promised him that she would, before hurrying onto the platform. She was only just in time for the train was already drawing into the station.

Some time later she stood in front of the prison and suppressed a shudder. It looked dark and forbidding, but then she supposed that she shouldn't really have expected it to be otherwise. It was a gaol, after all.

At exactly two o'clock the gates were opened and she and the other visitors were ushered inside by a grim-faced janitor. They were shown to a lime-washed waiting room where she sat and fiddled with the brooch Toby had given her. She had rarely taken it off and she never intended to. If only she could make him see sense! The visitors were led away one by one to see the people they had come to visit, and at last it was her turn. A portly officer in uniform asked her sternly, 'You here to see Toby Jackson?'

She nodded numbly, too terrified to speak, and he beckoned her to follow him. They passed through a maze of long cold corridors that all looked the same until at last he paused outside a door and told her, 'He's in there. You've got half an hour.'

'Thank you.' The door was opened by someone from inside, a guard who was as thin as the other had been portly.

She found herself in a small room. The only light was from a tiny barred window set high in the wall, and the only furniture was a plain table with a chair placed either side of it. Toby was sitting in one and her heart sank at the sight of him. He had lost a great deal of weight and he had large dark circles beneath his eyes. His hands were handcuffed but his eyes lit up when he saw her and he made to rise, only to be told to sit down again by the gaoler who had locked the door behind her and now stood in the corner of the room.

'Oh Toby!' she choked as tears stung the back of her eyes. 'Are you all right?' What a stupid question that was. How could anyone be all right in this place? And was that guard really going to stand there for the duration of her visit and listen to everything they said? It appeared that he was.

She sat down and went to reach out to him but the officer insisted, 'No touching, if you please.' She quickly withdrew her hands as she stared at Toby miserably.

'Toby, no one believes that you killed Miss Florence,' she told him in a lowered voice. 'And I *know* that you didn't. Mr Marshall has told me to tell you that he's going to get you the best barrister in the country. Won't you please tell them who really did it? For me? It needn't be too late.'

He saw the plea in her eye and lowered his head for a moment before slowly raising it again and saying, 'I wish things could have been different, Maryann. I realise now that I should have married you when you lost your dad, but I was too pig-headed. I wanted the dream. Huh! And look how it's turned out. The only reason I allowed you to come today was to say goodbye. I owe you that at least. We both know that when I stand before the judge next week he's going to don a black cap before he passes sentence – unless the person who really did it comes forward, that is.'

'No!' She was sobbing now. 'Surely you will tell the truth for *me*? Don't I and the life we were planning together mean anything to you?'

'Of course they do, but sometimes things happen that are difficult to change.'

She wondered how he could look so calm and accepting, as if the sentence had already been passed.

'I want you to promise me that you will never come here again,' he went on in a low voice. 'Not even to the trial. Promise me, Maryann, *please*. And when you go away, I want you to try and remember me fondly . . . just in case.'

She wiped her eyes, unable to see him for tears. 'But it needn't be like this,' she wept. 'Mr Marshall will help you all he can, but you have to help yourself!'

Toby gave a ghost of a smile before saying, 'He's a good man and it gives me comfort to know that you have him to look out for you.'

'But why are you doing this?' she asked in anguish. 'We both know who really did it and Hugo is never going to come forward – so why are you protecting him?'

'Because of what it would do to my parents and because he is my brother,' Toby told her.

'And all of them mean more to you than I do?'

He rose then and looking towards the prison guard he told him, 'I'm ready to go back to my cell now.'

The man looked at him with a new-found respect. 'Right you are, sir.' And in that moment Maryann realised that he too knew that Toby was innocent of the crime, just as she did.

Toby paused at the door and when she looked at him she saw that his cheeks were wet.

'Goodbye, my love,' he said softly. 'Have a happy life and remember, Mr Marshall is a good man.' And then he was gone and Maryann sobbed unrestrainedly until another officer came to escort her from the building.

She had no idea how she got back to New Street station. She had a vague recollection of hailing a Hackney cab and boarding the train, and then she was in her home town – but there was no sign of Benny waiting for her. She was there much earlier than they had anticipated so she hailed yet another cab to take her back to the Manor.

The moment Wesley saw it draw up from his library window he rushed outside to meet her, and paid the cabman. He then led her back inside and into the library before ringing the bell for Nellie. Maryann certainly looked as if she could do with a drink, if her reddened eyes were anything to go by.

'Ah, Nellie,' he said when she appeared, glancing anxiously at Maryann. 'Would you mind bringing us a glass of sherry through?'

'O' course not,' she said obligingly, and hurried away to inform Benny that his sister was already back. He had been just about to set off for the station to meet her.

'How did the visit go?' Wesley probed gently.

'Toby asked me not to visit him again nor even to attend his trial,' Maryann answered dully. 'He has obviously decided to take the blame and I don't think there is anything we can do to change his mind now. I truly believe that Hugo murdered Florence, but Toby wants to protect him and seems accepting of his fate.'

'Then *I* shall attend the trial,' Wesley decided. 'He didn't say that I shouldn't go, did he?'

She shook her head. Somehow it gave her a little comfort to know that at least one person he knew would be there. She couldn't bear the thought of him facing the trial alone. She twiddled with the little brooch pinned to her dress then as her mind drifted back to happier times, and Wesley watched her anxiously.

And yet deep inside her, something had subtly changed. For the first time, Maryann felt resentful towards Toby, for as he had said, things could have been so different if he had married her when she had asked him to. She had been almost homeless and penniless, on the verge of starving, and yet still he had put his dreams before her. It came as a little shock to realise that he was doing the same thing again now – and she suddenly wondered if they would ever have come together. Unless Hugo stepped forward and admitted his guilt she would never know, and she had little hope of that happening. All she could do now was pray that Toby would see sense and speak the truth, for once again he was putting other people before herself.

Wesley had already left for the courts on the day of the trial by the time Maryann had dressed Fleur and given her her breakfast. Then, unable to settle, she asked the little girl, 'Would you like to come outside and play in the garden for a while?'

Fleur nodded eagerly. It was a beautiful late-spring day with a cloudless blue sky and soon Fleur was plodding across the lawn as she chased her kitten while Maryann watched, her mind far away.

Wesley had warned her the day before that it would likely be very late before he returned. The trial might even run into the next day, and if it did he intended to stay in a hotel in Birmingham for the night. So now all she could do was wait for the verdict and pray for a miracle or for Toby to see sense – and every minute felt like an hour.

As darkness fell with still no sign of the master returning, her spirits sank. It looked as if the trial had run on. She settled Fleur for the night and joined the Carters and Benny in the kitchen. Polly and Dennis were there too and it was clear to them all that the couple were now very much in love just as Nellie had prophesied. But tonight they were all subdued as they waited for news of Toby, and when the creak of carriage wheels sounded outside, they all looked nervously towards each other.

Nellie hurried into the hall to help the master off with his hat and coat and then they all stood up respectfully as he followed her back to the kitchen, his face set in grave lines.

'Would you come into the library, please, Maryann?' he said and she went with him like a lamb to slaughter, fearful of the news he was about to impart.

Once inside, he stared at her for a moment before saying,

'I am afraid it isn't good news. Hugo has apparently disappeared and Toby was found guilty of murder. He will be hanged within the prison on 1 May at ten o'clock in the morning. I'm so sorry, my dear. If there was anything I could have done . . .'

'I understand,' she said remarkably calmly. Somehow she had known since the day she had visited him that there could be no other outcome now. Toby had always protected his younger brother and now he would pay for Hugo's life with his own.

'Thank you for attending the trial,' she went on. 'At least I know what's happening now. Goodnight, sir.' And with that she turned and went upstairs, where she shut herself away for the rest of the night.

During the following days, Maryann walked about like a shadow of her former self as they waited for Toby's execution. Although she never failed in her duty to Fleur, she took to eating her meals in her charge's room and distanced herself from everyone, even her brother. But no one minded. They could only begin to guess what agony she must be going through and they all went out of their way to be nice to her, which somehow only seemed to make things worse. Maryann longed for normality, for the ease that had once existed between them all, but now she wondered if it was gone forever. She felt strangely detached from everyone and everything, and sometimes when she went to sleep she prayed that she might not wake up. Then she would be in heaven waiting for Toby to join her as he surely would, for she knew that Toby was a good person. But each morning she did wake up until at last the dreaded day was upon them. She rose at six as she always did and washed, dressed and tidied her room before going down to the kitchen to fetch Fleur's breakfast tray.

'I didn't expect to see you up an' about so early today, pet,' Nellie greeted her. 'Why don't you go on back to bed an' have yerself a bit of a lie-in? Me an' Cissie can see to Miss Fleur this morning.'

'Thank you but I prefer to keep to my normal routine,' Maryann said tightly as she began to prepare the child's breakfast, and then suddenly she could hold her feelings in no longer and she crumpled to the floor as tears spurted from her eyes. Nellie knelt down and held her tightly.

'There, there, me lass,' she crooned as she rocked Maryann to and fro. 'You just have a good cry now. It's better out than in, so it is!'

Nellie glanced at Benny helplessly, but he was at a loss. He too was feeling sick at heart. Toby had been his good friend for as long as he could remember, and he would never believe that Toby was capable of robbing and killing anyone. But now the terrible day was upon them and he felt completely impotent.

Maryann pulled herself together with a great effort and Nellie and Benny both helped her to her feet. Today her brother had expected tantrums from her, and God knew she could have been forgiven for them, but she quietly resumed preparing Fleur's breakfast.

'I could do that,' Nellie offered again, but Maryann shook her head and gave a wobbly smile.

'Thank you, Nellie, but I'm better if I can keep busy really.'

'Will yer be comin' down to join us fer breakfast when you've settled Miss Fleur, pet?' Nellie asked then as Maryann lifted the loaded tray and headed back to the hall door without a word. 'I could fry yer a nice bit o' bacon up if you like.'

'Thank you, Nellie, but I'll miss breakfast today if you don't mind,' Maryann answered. 'I'm not really hungry.'

And with that she was gone, leaving Nellie and Benny to glance at each other anxiously.

Just before ten o'clock, Maryann made sure that Fleur was occupied with her painting before going out onto the landing. She then went to stand at the top of the stairs. She would hear the grandfather clock in the hall strike from there, and strike it did, each chime marking away the seconds of Toby's life.

And then there was only silence and she dragged air into her lungs and allowed herself to breathe again as she fingered the brooch he had bought her. It was done, and as she stood there, loneliness the like of which she had never felt before settled about her like a cloak.

Chapter Forty-Five

At that moment, Cissie was hunting for eggs in the barn. She knew most of the chickens' hiding places and Nellie had asked her to find some for the cakes she was going to bake that morning.

She already had more than ample but decided that she would just check behind the haybales before going back to the kitchen. That was when the sound of muffled sobbing reached her and she paused, leaning heavily on her crutch.

Yes, the sound was definitely coming from behind the bales, she decided, and limped over to find Benny sitting on the straw with his face in his hands, sobbing bitterly.

'Aw, Benny, don't cry, man,' she urged kind-heartedly. There had never been the same ease between them as formerly before he had asked her to marry him after the rape, but that was forgotten for now as she dropped her crutch and sank down beside him. She wrapped her arms about his shaking frame and just held him for a while.

There was no need to ask what was wrong for she already knew how much he had been dreading this day.

'It ain't fair, lass!' he cried. 'Toby were a good, kind chap. He'd never have hurt a fly. Everyone that knew him feels the same, but he always covered up for his brother from when they were little. I don't think he ever really believed that Hugo would let him hang for him though.'

'I know, I know,' Cissie soothed, feeling his pain. 'But there's nothing to be done about it now. We just have to go on.'

Benny had been torturing himself all morning with visions of Toby being led from his cell and having the noose placed about his neck. And then of him jerking like a puppet at the end of the rope as he dropped into space. But at least it was over now and Benny could only pray that his friend's end had come swiftly, and that he was now in Heaven where he belonged.

'I'm sorry, lass. You must think I'm a right cry-baby,' he apologised as he swiped the tears from his cheeks with the back of his hand.

And then suddenly he turned to her and they found that they were almost nose to nose in the sweet-smelling hay.

'Why did you turn me down when I asked you to marry me?' he demanded, completely out of the blue, and he watched the colour flame into her cheeks.

'I suppose it were 'cos I knew you were only askin' 'cos yer felt sorry fer me,' she mumbled.

And suddenly as he stared into her beautiful face he felt as if he had been struck by a bolt of lightning and everything was crystal clear.

'To tell the truth, I reckon I was at the time.' Benny was nothing if not honest. 'But the thing is . . . since then I've found I've missed our chats an' the little things you used to

384

do for me, like putting a hot brick in me bed each night and cutting the tops off me boiled eggs.'

She shrugged with embarrassment. It was like a physical pain being so close to him, for she had been forced to admit to herself a long time ago that she had loved Benny since the very first second she had clapped eyes on him. Even so, she had her pride and had always maintained that if ever she married, it would be to a man who loved her as much as she loved him.

'Well, I suppose we could always try to go back to bein' good friends again,' she said shyly, but he shook his head.

'No, you don't understand what I'm trying to tell you,' he choked.

She raised an eyebrow as his hand lifted to tenderly stroke her cheek.

'The night that vile creature raped you, I wanted to kill him!' Benny's eyes were blazing as he remembered. 'And I thought I was being kind by saying I'd be willing to marry you. But the thing is, Cissie, it was really because I loved you but hadn't realised it. Do you hear what I'm saying? *I love you*, girl, more than life itself. You're beautiful both inside and out but I just didn't see it until now.'

Suddenly he laughed as he pulled her into his arms and planted a big warm kiss smack on her lips.

'What I'm trying to say – and not very well – is that I really and truly do want to marry you, Cissie. I want you to be the mother of me children and I want us to grow old together. So what do you say? Will you marry me and make me the happiest man on earth?'

Cissie stared at him in disbelief. 'But what about me arm and me bad leg? You could have anyone you wanted, Benny. Surely you don't want to saddle yourself with a cripple. And don't forget . . . Hugo took me maidenhead. I'm no longer a virgin.'

For answer, he lifted her withered hand and kissed it gently. 'You're beautiful, every single inch of you, and I wouldn't change you for the world.'

He spoke with such sincerity that he brought tears to her eyes, and she joked cautiously, 'In that case, I suppose I shall have to marry you!' But she didn't get the chance to say any more because his lips were tight on hers then and she gave herself up to the pure pleasure of the moment.

Sometime later, as they sat in a contented silence wrapped in each other's arms, she said, 'I don't think we should say anything to anyone else about this just yet, Benny – especially not today.'

'I reckon you're right,' he agreed, but then he was smiling again as he helped her to her feet and brushed the hay from her skirts. 'But it's going to be really hard to keep quiet. I want to shout it from the rooftops – *I'm gonna marry the most beautiful girl in the world!*'

She giggled as he handed her the crutch, her face glowing with happiness. But out of respect for Maryann they both agreed that for now at least, they would keep their secret. They then reluctantly parted to go about their chores.

The couple waited for four weeks before sharing their good news with Nellie, upon which she beamed from ear to ear.

'Well, it's about time an' all,' she told them. 'Anyone with half an eye could see that you two were made fer each other.'

'We've known for a while,' Benny admitted as he stared at Cissie adoringly, 'but we felt it was too soon to say anything with all that's gone on.'

'I know,' Nellie said stoically. 'But happen a bit o' good news will cheer everyone up, so let's share it, eh?' And so they did and everyone, especially Maryann, offered their sincere congratulations.

The master was also thrilled for them and promptly told the couple they were welcome to live in the vacant cottage on the estate once they were wed if they wished to, which they most certainly did. The place would need some work doing on it, of course, as it had stood empty for some time but neither Cissie nor Bennie minded that. So the wedding was set for December. Cissie couldn't help but feel guilty as Maryann had no wedding of her own to look forward to. The poor girl was so quiet nowadays and rarely ventured out of Fleur's room. But then they all knew how much she had loved Toby so they did not expect too much of her too soon. Every spare minute Benny and Dennis had was now spent working on the cottage, and the master kindly donated all the materials they would need to make it watertight and habitable again. The happy couple nattered away non-stop about what sort of curtains they would have and how they would like to furnish it.

'Everythin's worked out so well for 'em,' Nellie commented to Ted one balmy July evening as they sat out in the yard enjoying a jug of ale. It was too hot for tea, even for Nellie. 'I just wish we could bring a bit o' joy into the master and Maryann's lives now. They both seem so sad.'

'Aye, they do,' Ted agreed, puffing away contentedly on his pipe.

'I noticed that the master has hung that paintin' he did o' Maryann up in his bedroom when I went in to clean it today. It were the only one he wouldn't sell when he had his exhibition,' Nellie confided with a deep sigh. 'If only the girl would open her eyes she'd see he has feelin's for her, but she's too stuck in the past. Trouble is, she can't bring Toby back, can she?'

'Now don't you go interferin' in that direction, woman!' Ted warned her and she grinned.

'Oh, don't worry, I ain't about to go stickin' me oar in,'

387

she assured him. 'But I just wish she'd come out of her shell a bit. It's been three whole months now.'

'That ain't so long in the greater scheme o' things,' Ted said placidly. 'Look how long it took the master to get over losin' the mistress. Different folks grieve in different ways, an' there's a process to be gone through afore they move on. Things'll work out in the end, you'll see if yer patient.'

'Aye, I dare say yer right but I wish I could hurry things along a bit, that's all.' And Nellie then lifted up her knitting and they sat in a compatible silence.

'She's actually remarkably good for her age, isn't she?' Wesley commented to Maryann the next morning as he looked at the latest paintings Fleur had done. 'She's got a real eye for colour.'

'She must take after her father,' Maryann answered as she stood folding Fleur's clean clothes and putting them away in her cupboards.

He flushed with pleasure at the praise as he looked towards his daughter, who was busily chasing her cat about the room. 'Now don't go getting yourself over-excited, my dear,' he said fondly. 'I want you to rest this morning because I have a big surprise for you coming this afternoon and I want you all bright-eyed and bushy-tailed to enjoy it.'

'What is it, Papa?' Fleur asked as she skidded to a halt in front of him.

'Ah, now if I told you, it wouldn't be a surprise, would it?' he teased. 'But I want you to be down in the stableyard at three o'clock prompt. Can you do that for me?'

She nodded eagerly before skipping away to resume her game as he watched her affectionately.

'You have made such a difference to that child's life,' he said.

Maryann's hands became still as she paused to look at

him. It did her heart good to see the love that had blossomed between father and daughter. Wesley was also continuing to do lots of good things for his workers too, if the reports she was getting from Granny Addison were anything to go by. The child workers at the mill had not only had their working conditions improved and their hours shortened, but he had also insisted that they all attend school now, for at least two mornings a week. He was even making the living conditions in the cottages he owned better too. And it had all stemmed from the day she had dared to confront him about little Tommy Briggs's accident. Thankfully, Tommy had made a full recovery. But how things had changed for her since then, she thought morosely. From Granny she had learned that Tilly and Matt Jackson had now gone to live in Newcastle, near Tilly's sister. Now that Toby was dead and his brother had disappeared, the poor woman had suffered a severe breakdown and Matt had felt that a new environment might be better for her. There was certainly nothing to keep her in the Midlands any more.

She had also been shocked when Granny informed her that Elizabeth Lord was now living in the workhouse. It appeared that after Benny had taken her to the railway station on the day the master had dismissed her, the woman had chosen to stay in Nuneaton. She had pawned everything she owned eventually, apart from the clothes on her back, before taking to the streets. And then with not a penny left to her name she had had no alternative but to admit herself into the workhouse. Just the thought of having to live in that dark dreary place made Maryann's blood run cold, and yet she found it difficult to feel any sympathy for the woman. She had willingly gone along with Florence's plan to kill the master – and the common opinion was that she deserved nothing more.

Maryann's thoughts were dragged sharply back to the

present then as she became aware of Fleur tugging on her skirts, saying, 'Can we go for a walk, Maryann? Puss wants to go outside.'

'All right then,' Maryann answered indulgently. 'But only for a little while. I want you to have a rest after lunch, ready for your papa's surprise.'

She and Wesley smiled at each other as she led Fleur from the room, with him following closely behind, but he noticed that the smile did not quite reach her eyes any more.

They were almost at the bottom of the stairs when he suddenly plucked up the courage to say, 'I don't suppose you'd care to have dinner with me this evening, would you? It seems such a long time since we all dined together.'

She opened her mouth to refuse but then seeing the pleading in his eyes she answered quietly, 'Very well then, thank you. That would be very nice.'

They had not dined together since the last time Florence had returned from London, and suddenly that seemed an awfully long time ago. And so the date was set and he went off to his library with a spring in his step whilst she took Fleur outside into the sunshine.

That afternoon at three o'clock sharp Maryann led Fleur to the stable block to find the master waiting for them.

'Your surprise is in there. Would you like to open the door and see what it is?' he asked his daughter.

Intrigued, Fleur stood on tiptoe to open the latch then gasped with delight as a tiny pony nuzzled her hand.

'He is for you, so you'll have to decide what you want to call him,' her father told her. 'I thought I might teach you to ride. How would you like that?'

Fleur grinned ecstatically as she stroked the white pony's soft mane. And then Ted appeared carrying a tiny saddle that the master had had especially made.

'We'll give you your first lesson tomorrow,' Wesley promised, and Fleur could hardly wait.

'She's decided to call him Horse, much as she insisted on calling her cat Puss,' Maryann informed him that evening when they were all sitting down to dinner. 'I'm afraid she isn't the best in the world when it comes to choosing names.'

Highly amused, Wesley winked at Fleur as he answered, 'Well, that's fine as long as she's happy with it, and I think it's a grand name.' He felt as if he were walking on eggshells. Such a lot had happened since they had spent any time together and he found he was choosing what he should say with care.

The meal continued but Wesley found that most of the conversation took place between himself and Fleur; often he would glance towards Maryann to see her staring off into space, a faraway look on her face. But then it was early days yet. He thought back to how long it had taken him to get over the death of his wife and he had all the patience in the world.

Chapter Forty-Six

The following morning when Maryann entered Fleur's room, she was alarmed. Usually Fleur was sitting up in bed bright as a button waiting for her, but today she lay silent beneath the sheets. When Maryann crossed to her she found the child was burning up with fever and shaking, so gathering her skirts she raced downstairs hoping to catch Wesley before he left for the mill.

'I think we ought to send for the doctor,' she told him as she burst into the dining room without knocking. 'Fleur is running a fever and doesn't seem well at all.'

'Of course,' Wesley agreed instantly. 'I'll get Benny to go into town and ask him to call as soon as possible.' His face was a mask of concern and in that instant, Maryann realised how much his daughter had come to mean to him. He hurried away then to find Benny whilst Maryann returned to the little girl and tried to tempt her to eat some breakfast. But it was useless; Fleur just turned her face away and refused everything but a sip of water.

Wesley had joined them by then, having decided not to go into the mill that day. He sat at the side of Fleur's bed holding her hand and sponging her brow with cool water.

The doctor arrived mid-afternoon, by which time Fleur was more feverish than ever. Maryann and Wesley waited nervously out on the landing whilst he went in to examine her. The doctor seemed to be in there for a very long time, and when he eventually came out carrying his black bag, Wesley took him downstairs to the drawing room whilst Maryann hurried back to watch over Fleur.

It was half an hour later before Wesley reappeared. Maryann crept out onto the landing, where he told her, 'Dr Piper thinks that Fleur is suffering from a chill as we feared, but he also said that he felt her heart was not as strong as it was.'

Maryann could see the strain in Wesley's face as he told her, 'As you know, it is very common for children like Fleur to have heart defects, and Dr Piper is going to ask a friend of his who specialises in this subject to come from London to examine her. There might be something he can do to help her.'

His voice was so full of hope, but Maryann could not help but remember the child from the courts who had resembled Fleur so strongly and who had died at a very tender age.

'And what do we do about the chill?' she asked, and was gratified to see him smile weakly.

'Exactly what you're doing. Give her sips of drink and keep sponging her with cool water to try and bring the temperature down. And Maryann . . . thank you. I know my daughter could not be in better hands. You've made such a change to her life since you came here . . . and mine too, if it comes to that.'

Maryann blushed at the praise and turned hastily back to the bedroom door. 'I am only doing what I am paid to do,' she said faintly as she disappeared inside. But standing there, Wesley disagreed. She had done so much more than that if only she could have known it, but he would never tell her. Maryann's heart still belonged to Toby, and his own feelings for her would have to stay hidden away forever.

Despite all Maryann's best efforts, Fleur continued to deteriorate over the next few days and when the doctor paid his daily visits he would look very grave. But still Maryann worked on doggedly, sponging the child down continuously and speaking to her all the time. 'Come on, little one, you can overcome this, for me. Puss and Horse are missing you, so get better and you can stroke them again and give Horse an apple!'

Wesley made Maryann take short naps in the chair whilst he took over, seeing how exhausted she was, and finally late one morning, Fleur opened her eyes and smiled at them tremulously before croaking, 'Papa, I'm thirsty.'

Laughing and crying all at the same time, Maryann dribbled a tiny drop of water into her mouth and seconds later the child was sleeping again, but peacefully this time.

'Thank God,' Maryann whimpered as tears sprang to her eyes, and suddenly Wesley's arms were about her and just for a moment she leaned against him as if it were the most natural thing in the world. But then suddenly remembering herself, she jerked away, then felt strangely bereft.

Wesley too was shaken, saying chokily, 'My dear Maryann, I think my daughter has turned the corner now, so I insist you go to your room and get some rest. You look fit to drop, and I don't want your health to suffer. I shall stay with her tonight.'

Maryann thanked him and scuttled away without another word.

Over the next week, Fleur continued to improve although Maryann was concerned to note that the child tended to tire much more easily than she had before her illness. Still, she consoled herself that it was still her convalescence and tempted her with tasty tit-bits that Nellie prepared, to try and encourage her to eat. Wesley now came to the little girl's room each evening to read her a bedtime story, as well as devoting large parts of each day to her. The doctor from Harley Street – a middle-aged and beautifully dressed man with a rather red, bulbous nose – arrived as promised, and after spending a long time examining Fleur he closeted himself away in the drawing room with Wesley to tell him his prognosis.

Maryann waited anxiously for the specialist doctor to leave, and when she looked through Fleur's bedroom window and saw him depart, she hurried downstairs and tapped on the drawing-room door, eager to hear what he had said.

She entered to see Wesley restlessly pacing the room.

'I'm afraid Dr Wigmore's prognosis was not good,' he said immediately. 'After studying Dr Piper's notes he was able to inform me that Fleur's heart condition has deteriorated slightly,' he told her.

'Oh, I see.' Maryann felt as if someone had slapped her in the face. She couldn't bear to try and imagine life without her.

'It seems,' Wesley went on with a catch in his voice, 'that there is little to be done for the condition so he told me to just take it one day at a time. Fleur could live for a number of years, or on the other hand her heart could just stop at any moment.'

Their eyes locked and she said softly, 'Then it is up to us to make sure that every single day is as precious and happy as possible for her, isn't it, sir?' And with that she bobbed her knee and fumbled her way from the room as tears blinded her.

Later that day, when Maryann informed Nellie of what the doctor had told Wesley, the woman mopped at her eyes before asking worriedly, 'But what will become of you if anything should happen to Fleur, pet?'

'I suppose I would have to find another post,' Maryann answered, although the thought of leaving tore her apart. The Carters had become more and more like family to her. 'I'm sure Mr Marshall would give me a good reference. But let's just hope that it won't come to that for a very long time. Nothing is going to happen to Fleur if I have my way.'

Nellie sighed. What with one thing and another, she didn't know if she was coming or going lately.

Maryann meantime was forced to realise that Fleur and the Carters were not the only ones she would miss, should she be forced to leave. During Fleur's illness she and Wesley had grown very close, and she had been impressed to witness the tender way he had cared for his child. Their relationship had undergone a subtle change, and surprisingly she had found herself not thinking of Toby so much – but then she supposed that this was natural, because she and Wesley had both been so concerned about Fleur. Still, for now at least Fleur was out of the woods; no doubt Wesley would return to the mill and life would resume some sort of normality. But yes, she would miss him.

Over the summer months Wesley spent more and more time with Maryann and Fleur, taking them on picnics and coaching Fleur on her pony, Horse. On the day that they ventured beyond the grounds of Windy Manor, Fleur was almost beside herself with excitement at her first glimpse of the big wide world, and everything she saw held wonder for her.

396

'Look at the church,' she gasped in awe as the carriage rattled through Hartshill on their way to Hartshill Hayes, a large country park which was mainly woodland. The church did look very pretty with its towering spire and the sun reflecting off its stained-glass windows and Wesley felt guilty about all that his child had missed while locked away at Windy Manor, and determined there and then that he would take her out more often. He might even suggest a trip to the seaside at some point if the doctor felt that she was strong enough to withstand the journey. Fleur's mouth gaped with pleasure at the little cottages and the people they passed. The sheep and cows in the meadows all had her exclaiming in delight as Wesley and Maryann looked on indulgently.

The little girl was realising that the world was a big place. Once at the Hayes she scampered amongst the trees and bushes shrieking with joy, and Maryann became concerned that she might over-exert herself, yet didn't have the heart to stop her. It was wonderful to see the child enjoying herself so much and she could clearly see that Wesley was happy too. When they came to a brook, Fleur and her father kicked off their shoes and socks and splodged in the water like two children as Maryann set up their picnic. They then sat beneath the shade of a huge old oak tree to eat the treats that Nellie had packed for them, and Maryann felt happier than she had for some long time. It was to be the first of many such outings, and with each one she and Wesley became easier in each other's presence.

It was towards the end of August when Wesley tentatively asked Maryann if she would like to accompany him and Fleur on a trip to the seaside, but as much as she had enjoyed their days out, she politely declined the invitation. It was one thing to go out for day trips, but quite another for a young unmarried woman to accompany her employer on a trip away from home. Maryann was quite aware that Nellie would see it as a complete breach of etiquette and she shuddered to imagine what the gossips would have to say about it. Wesley was still merely her employer, after all, and for no reason that she could explain, the reminder of this fact saddened her.

A few days later, as she tied the ribbons of a pretty new bonnet her father had treated her to beneath the little girl's chin, Fleur leaned forwards unexpectedly and planted a sloppy kiss on Maryann's cheek, saying, 'I love you, Maryann.'

'And I love you too, pet,' Maryann replied with a large lump in her throat. And it was true. She could not envisage life without the child now, and when she thought of what the doctor had said she was filled with dread.

Since Maryann had taken over all the household accounts, with Nellie's help, Wesley had been shocked to see the difference in the bills. His sister had clearly been milking him of a very large amount of money each week. But Maryann still considered that her main role was that of a nanny. Now that they had Polly's extra pair of hands to help, the women had the house running like clockwork, but Maryann was always painfully aware that if anything happened to Fleur she would be surplus to requirements.

The future seemed so uncertain, but after everything she had been through, Maryann had learned to see the wisdom in, like Fleur, living one day at a time, and in making that day as happy and fulfilling as possible.

Chapter Forty-Seven

'Are yer sure I look all right?' Cissie asked anxiously as she adjusted her veil in the mirror.

'Yer look better than all right, pet,' Nellie answered croakily. Then turning to Polly who was to act as bridesmaid at the wedding she told her, 'An you look lovely an' all!'

Polly was dressed in a pale green gown of soft satin. Cissie's was an ivory colour that matched the lace veil that Nellie had just placed across her head. She had refused to wear white and Nellie had been staying up late sewing the outfits for weeks, with Maryann's help. Upstairs, Maryann was getting Fleur into a smaller version of the dress that Polly was wearing, for much to her delight she was to be the flower girl.

Cissie had asked Maryann to be one of her attendants too, but she had quietly refused, using the excuse that she preferred to be in the wings in case Fleur needed her. She had, however, treated herself to a new gown with some of her wages. It felt strange wearing it, after being used to wearing plain grey ones. The dress was made of a pale blue watermarked silk material, trimmed with navy ribbons and with a jaunty little matching fur stole and muff. She had even managed to find a very becoming blue bonnet trimmed with pale blue silk flowers around the brim that was a perfect match. Maryann was pleased with it, although she still winced to think of how much it had cost.

Polly and Dennis had recently announced that they too planned to wed the following year, but today everyone's attention was focused on Cissie, which was just as it should be.

The little cottage in the grounds, which was to be the happy couple's home after today, had now been completely transformed, and Cissie could hardly wait to move in. Benny, Dennis and Ted had been working on it every spare minute they had throughout the summer, and now all Nellie could do was pray that they would be happy there. If the besotted way they looked at each other was anything to go by, she suspected that they would be. Nellie reminded herself then that she must remember to pop over there early in the evening to light the fire that she had laid ready in the grate for them.

Ted would be giving Cissie away and the master had insisted that they should travel to church in the carriage. It had been decorated with little silver bells made by Fleur and Maryann. The master's gift to them had been an astounding five guineas, with which to start married life. He'd been as good as gold, had the master, Nellie reflected as she stared at the vision that was her granddaughter. Cissie was the most beautiful bride that Nellie had ever seen, but where was Ted? That husband of hers should be ready by now, surely.

'Ted, where are yer?' she hollered from the doorway, and he appeared looking as smart as a new pin but decidedly uncomfortable in his new togs.

'Phew, I shan't be sorry to get this damn thing off,' he grumbled, running his finger around his neck to loosen his stiff collar. But then as he caught sight of Cissie, his eyes grew moist as he muttered, 'Why, lass, yer a sight fer sore eyes, so you are.'

The dress she was wearing was heavily trimmed with lace and just like Nellie he was sure he had never seen a lovelier bride – apart from his Nellie, of course.

'Now don't you dare get goin' all weepy on me,' Nellie scolded as she straightened his cravat and smoothed his grey hair down. No amount of Macassar oil seemed to tame it for long, but then she supposed he'd have to do. She just wished that Cissie's parents could have been there to see her on this special day and then it would have been really perfect. She hoped they were looking down on her from Heaven.

But then the sad thoughts were banished when Fleur bounded into the room, looking a picture in all her finery. She was waving her posy about excitedly and Nellie wondered if the flowers would have any heads on by the time they got to church. But then what did it matter? She didn't want anything to spoil today and was determined that Cissie and Benny should have a day they would never forget.

'Fleur pretty!' the child whooped as she twizzled about, setting her full skirts dancing, and they all agreed with her.

Maryann came into the room then and after telling Cissie sincerely how beautiful she looked, she confided with a grin, 'Benny was a complete bag of nerves when he left for the church with Dennis a while back! I'm sure he's convinced himself that Cissie is going to stand him up at the altar.'

'Aye, well, she may do if we don't get a move on,' Nellie said bossily as the women all reached for their warm cloaks. The wedding finery was all very well but it was only two weeks before Christmas and outside, the ground and the trees were coated with a thick hoar frost. Thankfully the snow had held off until now, although Ted had insisted that the sky was full of it. Nellie hustled them all outside and soon they were on their way, Ted and Cissie in the first carriage with the rest of them rattling behind in a second one that the master had hired especially for the occasion.

The guests and the groom with Dennis standing as Benny's best man were already inside when they arrived, but the vicar was waiting at the church door to greet them.

Nellie and Maryann hurried past him to take their seats, smiling at Granny Addison and Archie who were all decked out in their Sunday best, whilst Polly quickly helped them off with their cloaks. Fleur was sitting with her father, her face aglow at the excitement of it all, and many other people who Maryann knew were friends of the Carters were also there. But then the wedding party were all in position and as the organist began to play, Cissie floated down the aisle on the arm of her grandfather clutching the posy of paper roses and greenery that Fleur and Maryann had painstakingly made for her, feeling like the happiest girl on earth.

The church was full, but from the moment Benny turned to watch Cissie coming towards him, there might have been no one else but the two of them in the whole church, and those who attended the service said for a long time afterwards that they had never been to such a joyous affair.

Once they had been declared man and wife, Benny kissed his wife soundly on the lips and they left the church in a shower of rice as the church bells pealed.

Outside, the holly bushes that surrounded the churchyard were full of red berries and as Maryann looked towards the gravestones her face became sad as she thought of all the people she had loved and lost: her parents, her little brother Joe and her sister Gertie, her sister Violet and her baby niece, and of course Toby. Mr Marshall was watching her and his heart ached for her as he guessed at what she must be feeling. When she had first walked into the church and he had seen her in all her finery, he had been deeply shaken for he had never seen her in anything other than the rags she had worn when he first met her, and her plain grey dresses. She could quite easily have been a lady born and bred, a natural aristocrat, whereas he and his family had made their fortune from trade. He found it hard to tear his eyes away from her.

Unaware of his scrutiny, Maryann forced a smile to her face as the jubilant newlyweds rode back to Windy Manor where the real celebrations would begin. The master had insisted that the reception should be held there, and had even offered to bring in another cook and more servants so that Nellie could enjoy the day too. However, in her usual proud, independent way she had politely declined his offer, telling him that it wouldn't be proper, and so she had done all the catering herself. After all, as she had pointed out, it wasn't every day that your granddaughter got married and she certainly didn't want a lot of strangers taking over her kitchen! However, she had agreed after a lot of persuasion to allow the master to take on a couple of maids brought in especially for the occasion to serve the guests. And when they all arrived back at the house, she had to grudgingly admit that it was nice to be met at the door with a glass of champagne and to be waited on for a change.

The meal Nellie had prepared was delicious too and she beamed, highly gratified, when everyone remarked on it and complimented her. There were huge game pies, fresh baked bread and a selection of pickles and pastries, and they all tucked in, hungry after being out in the cold crisp air. Once the meal was eaten, the cake had been duly cut by the newlyweds, and the speeches were over, everyone headed for the drawing room where a small orchestra formed of men from the village was tuning up. Chairs had been placed around the walls, the rugs had been rolled up and soon everyone was dancing, and for the first time in years Windy Manor was alive with the sound of music and laughter.

'Takes me back to when the old master an' mistress were alive an' we were newlyweds recently employed here,' Nellie reminisced to Ted, and he nodded in agreement. They had been happy days back then. Nellie had her feet tucked beneath her skirt as she had kicked her new shoes off because they were killing her, but she didn't have time to sit for long, for soon the young master approached her and asked formally, 'May I have this dance, please, Nellie?'

She feigned reluctance but she was soon up and dancing, and for the rest of the evening she barely sat down again.

'Ooh, I'll suffer fer this tomorrer,' she winked at Maryann at one stage as she whirled past on Dennis's arm, and the girl chuckled. The wine, cider and beer were flowing like water and everyone was having a wonderful time – but eventually Maryann saw that Fleur was beginning to flag, so taking her hand, she led her from the room. It had been a lovely day but she didn't want the child to overdo things.

She had just got her into her nightclothes when Fleur's bedroom door opened and the master appeared.

'Oh, go back to the guests,' Maryann urged him. 'I can read Fleur her bedtime story this evening.'

But he shook his head. 'I'm quite happy up here with you and Fleur,' he assured her. 'And from what I saw on my way up, I'm sure I shan't be missed.' He grinned. He then tucked the blankets around Fleur and sitting at the side of the bed he began to read to her as Maryann silently went about tidying the room and hanging Fleur's clothes away. He had barely read two pages when he glanced at the child to see that she was already fast asleep with her thumb jammed tight in her mouth and a little smile on her face.

Maryann came to stand beside him, and as they looked down on Fleur she said softly, 'She's really enjoyed today, hasn't she?'

'Yes, I think she has,' he agreed. 'And I hope you have too?'

'How could anybody not enjoy it?' she answered. 'I think the whole town will be talking about this wedding for weeks. You've really given them a day to remember.'

'I hope so,' he said. 'They deserve it. But the day isn't over yet, so perhaps when you've finished in here you might come back down and dance with me. And by the way, may I say how charming you are looking today.' And then he leaned over to plant a gentle kiss on Fleur's cheek and silently padded from the room, leaving Maryann to stare thoughtfully after him.

She did go back downstairs and she did dance with the master – not once but several times – and she found that she quite enjoyed it. Yet underlying her pleasure was a sense of guilt that she was having a good time whilst Toby was lying in an unmarked grave within the confines of the prison. Even so she put on a brave face, and when Ted eventually drew the cart around to the front door she was there with the rest of the merrymakers to see Cissie and Benny off to their new home. The cottage was no more than half a mile from the Manor but just for tonight they would travel in style.

Benny paused on the steps and hugging her, he said, 'Don't get worrying, sis. I'm still here for you even if I do have a wife now, and we'll still see each other every day when I turn into work.'

'Of course we will.' She smiled bravely but he glimpsed the loneliness underneath and his heart went out to her. But then people were nudging him down the steps to join his wife and amidst cheers from the onlookers he swung the new Mrs Meadows up into his arms and lifted her onto the cart as if she weighed no more than a feather.

Cissie balanced precariously for a second as she turned her back on the small crowd and threw her bouquet across her shoulder – and when it landed smack in Maryann's arms, a great roar went up.

'There yer are then,' Nellie laughed. 'Looks like you'll be the next.'

Very conscious of the master's eyes on her, Maryann blushed and then Ted shook the reins and Bracken trotted away. Some of the wedding party had tied a number of old shoes to the back of the cart and they rattled across the ground as people ran alongside it for a while throwing yet more rice and dried rose petals up at the happy couple.

'They'll curse me when they get into bed,' Nellie confided with a naughty chuckle. 'I filled it wi' rice when I popped over to light the fire for 'em earlier on.' She had also taken a laden basket of food left over from the meal as well as one of the master's finest bottles of wine that he had insisted they should have, and she was content in the knowledge that before they retired they could eat like a king and queen.

'It'll be odd, not seein' our Cissie fer a couple o' days,' she said musingly. Wesley had also insisted that the newlyweds should take a short honeymoon, and all in all Nellie felt that they had all done them proud. She just wished that she could see the master himself settled now.

Chapter Forty-Eight

'Benny gone to the cottage, has he?' Maryann asked one evening when she went down to the kitchen to fetch a cup of warm milk for Fleur.

'Aye, both him and Cissie were off like greased lightning the second their chores were done,' Nellie said. 'I reckon they're busy paintin' the spare room ready for when the baby comes.'

It was a good few months after the wedding, and everyone at Windy Manor was delighted when Cissie had shyly informed them that she and Benny were expecting a new arrival. Everyone was looking forward to having a baby about the place, although it had made Maryann think sadly of the little girl that Violet had given birth to. She would have been toddling about the place now, had she lived . . . But Maryann had learned to look forward rather than backwards these days.

'I hardly get to see Benny any more, only in passing,' she remarked, but she didn't really mind. It was lovely to see her brother so happy and settled, and she just hoped that it would continue that way. All in all, it had been a peaceful time.

The only dark spot on the horizon was Fleur's health. As the autumn had rolled in and the weather turned colder, she had developed a hacking cough that no amount of medicine seemed able to shift. Dr Piper was concerned about her.

'Should we call the doctor from London back in to see her?' Wesley asked him.

Gideon Piper sighed. 'You could, but it would only be for your peace of mind,' he told him kindly. 'I'm afraid there is nothing that he could do that I am not already doing.' He could have added that Fleur's heart condition was worsening, but did not wish to add to Wesley's misery. And so everyone fussed over the little girl. Nellie took great care over her meals, and Maryann restricted her to very short walks outside, terrified that the cold air would do more harm than good.

And then came the day in early October when Maryann entered her room one morning to find Fleur flushed and lethargic. The child had had a very restless night and Maryann had spent most of it sitting in the chair at the side of the bed with her.

'Want Papa,' Fleur said in a breathy little voice and Maryann instantly flew downstairs to fetch him. Wesley was in the dining room as she had known he would be, but he took the stairs two at a time and sent word to Nellie that he would not be requiring breakfast that morning. Nor would he be going into the mill. Instead he spent the whole day at the side of Fleur's bed reading stories to her and, as before, gently stroking her brow with a damp cloth in an effort to bring her temperature down.

Nellie fetched up bowl after bowl of steaming water with Friar's Balsam in it, insisting that the vapour would do Fleur's chest good, and Wesley was grateful, only too pleased to try anything that might help. But still the terrible cough persisted, and mid-afternoon, Wesley asked Benny to ride into town for the doctor.

When he arrived, Dr Piper listened to her heaving chest as Wesley and Maryann looked fearfully on. Then putting his stethoscope away he turned to Wesley and said, 'Perhaps we might have a word outside?'

'Of course.' Wesley followed him downstairs whilst Maryann sat at the side of the bed stroking Fleur's hot little hand.

'I'm afraid her heart-rate is slowing,' the doctor informed him once they were in the privacy of the library, but Wesley would not accept it.

'There must be *something* you can do!' he thundered.

The doctor's silence was his answer and Wesley's hands balled into fists.

'I will give you another note for the apothecary for some linctus that might make her more comfortable,' the doctor said and Wesley nodded eagerly. He was willing to try anything at all that might help. And so the doctor wrote on his notepad and after passing the paper to Wesley he wished him good day and left the house with a sad shake of his head.

'Benny is going in to the market shortly,' Maryann told Wesley when he returned to Fleur's bedroom a short time later. 'If you wouldn't mind staying with Fleur, I could go in with him and fetch the medicine.'

He accepted gratefully and she hurried away to find her cape and race downstairs before Benny left.

'I need to go into town with Benny. He hasn't left yet, has he?' Maryann asked Nellie breathlessly as she barged into the kitchen.

Nellie glanced up from the vegetables she was rinsing.

'No, lass, he ain't as far as I know. If yer hurry yer may just catch him.'

Benny had just climbed up into the cart when he saw his sister running towards him. When she gasped out what she needed, he hauled her up onto the seat beside him and urged the horse into a trot.

'I'll get you into town and then bring you straight back,' he promised. 'I can always go back and collect the feed for the horses in the morning, if need be.'

And so Maryann clung to the edge of the seat as Benny urged the horse on and they made the town in record time.

As soon as he drew the horse to a halt in Queen's Road, Maryann leaped down and raced off to the apothecary's, frustrated to see that there were already two people in front of her waiting to be served.

She stood there tapping her foot and seconds later two more women entered to stand behind her. She recognised them from one of the courts in Abbey Street but she was in no mood to make small talk so she kept her eyes straight ahead as she waited impatiently for her turn.

And then one of them spoke in a voice loud enough to be heard and Maryann was instantly alert.

'Well, would yer just look at that,' the fatter of the two women said. 'It's that whore from up at the Manor who's paradin' as Mr Marshall's nanny to his halfwit, if I ain't very much mistaken! Huh! Nanny indeed. Since when 'as it been the job of a nanny to keep her master's bed warm, eh?'

The shop became silent and Maryann just prayed for the ground to open up and swallow her as her cheeks flamed with humiliation.

'It's no wonder the chap's never married again when he's gorrit on tap, is it?' the other woman chortled – a scrawny, smelly little thing who was crawling with headlice. 'But then I 'eard tell 'er sister weren't no better. Yer know, the one that run away. My old man were talkin' to a bloke in the Red Lion who reckoned she run off to a knockin' shop in London.'

Maryann could hold her tongue no longer and she whirled about, her eyes flashing.

'It's Mrs Pickett, isn't it?' she asked, addressing the thin woman.

The woman eyed her warily. 'Wharrif it is?'

'Well, I'd just like to inform you that Mr Marshall's daughter is a dear little thing and certainly no halfwit! The child has more intelligence than you two rumour-mongers put together! And as for my sister, I'll have you know that she was respectably married in London. Also, before you go calling other folks, you might do well to look closer to home.'

'An' just what is that supposed to mean?'

'Why don't you ask your husband where he goes each week when he tells you he's going for a game of dominoes? Or better still, why don't you ask Hilda Mainwright? It's common knowledge that he's just about worn a hole in the path leading to her door, he's been visiting her for so long.'

The fat woman's lips twitched into a sneer and now Maryann turned her wrath on her. 'And I shouldn't laugh too much if I were you, 'cos *your* husband is a regular visitor there too – if the rumours are true!'

Hilda Mainwright was shunned by the women of the town, for it was a well-known fact that she made her living lying flat on her back, taking money from other women's husbands. Both women looked totally flabbergasted but thankfully they remained tight-lipped then and soon after, Maryann stormed out of the shop clutching the linctus, glaring at them as she passed.

But once outside her anger fled and her shoulders sagged as she fought back tears. She had hoped that the rumours about her and Wesley might have died down by now, but it was clear that they hadn't: she doubted that they ever would whilst she remained at the Manor. And the awful things they had said about Violet! Unbidden a picture of Violet's low-cut dress and her rouged cheeks flashed in front of Maryann's eyes but she blinked it away. She must try to remember Violet as her innocent younger sister; the things the women had implied were just too awful to contemplate. But then the reason for her trip into town came back to her and pushing her upset aside, she lifted her skirts in a most unladylike manner and raced back to where Benny was waiting for her in the cart. She was keen to get back to Fleur.

The linctus did indeed seem to help and as the week progressed Fleur seemed to improve a little, to the point that she felt well enough to get up and sit in the chair by the window with her cat on her lap.

Maryann had taken to sleeping in the chair by the side of the bed, although Wesley had offered to have another bed brought into the room for her.

'There's really no need,' she assured him although she appreciated the offer. 'Fleur seems to be rallying round again, thank goodness, so no doubt I'll be back in my own bed in a few days anyway.'

Wesley was spending a lot of time in the room himself, coaxing Fleur to eat and drink, and playing games with her, so sometimes Maryann was able to slip away to her own room for a few hours and catch up on some much-needed rest.

Often he would place a small table in front of the child and encourage her to paint, and one day she produced a delightful picture of three people, all holding hands in the garden.

'That's Papa, Fleur and Maryann,' she told him solemnly, and as he stared down at the stick-like figures he felt a lump

412

form in his throat. She had depicted them as a little family.

'It's beautiful,' he told her softly. 'In fact, I think I shall have it framed and hang it on the wall in my library.'

Maryann's heart skipped a beat and she could have cried with despair as she gazed at the innocent little scene. All she could ever be was Fleur's nanny, and yet the child clearly saw her as much more than that.

Nellie bustled in then with a tray and she too admired the little painting before telling her, 'Right, miss, I've made you a lovely strawberry jelly – look – an' there's some cream in the jug to go on it an' all. Will you eat a little bit just for me, eh?'

She coaxed and cajoled her, going away some minutes later feeling satisfied that she had managed to encourage the child to eat a little at least. *I'll make her a nice soft-boiled egg fer her tea*, she said to herself as she descended the stairs. *An' I'll find time to do a batch o' jam tarts an' all. It ain't often she refuses them.* In fact, Fleur was usually waiting for them to come out of the oven and had burned her mouth more than once because she couldn't wait for them to cool.

Much to everyone's relief Fleur continued to improve, and the next time Dr Piper came to visit her he told Wesley truthfully, 'The fact is, I feared for her life last week, but it appears that this little girl is determined to live – and long may it last.'

Maryann was able to return to sleep in her own room, although she still got up regularly during the night to check on Fleur, for since the confrontation with the two women in the apothecary's she had found it difficult to sleep. Their words kept springing to mind. *That whore from up at the Manor*, they had called her and the hurt went deep, not just for herself but also for Wesley. He was such a good, gentle man and it did her heart good to see the closeness that now existed between himself and his daughter. Perhaps her job

413

at the Manor was done and it would be fairer to all of them if she moved on, for whilst she remained there, the gossips would continue to talk. Benny and Cissie were clearly devoted to each other and the house was now running smoothly. Truthfully, she felt that she was no longer needed, and once she realised that, Maryann began to think of her future. As long as Fleur had her father she was sure that the little girl would soon adapt to another nanny.

The thought of leaving all the people she had become so fond of was painful, but there were other jobs in other parts of the country, surely? The more she thought of it, the more of a solution it appeared to be, so early one morning she summoned up every ounce of courage she had and tapped on the library door.

'Oh, good morning.' Wesley was doing some paperwork at his desk and he greeted her with a wide smile. 'I thought it was Nellie bringing me my morning tea. There's nothing like a good cuppa to set you up for the day, is there?' But then seeing the expression on her face he asked immediately, 'There's nothing wrong with Fleur again, is there?' Although Fleur had rallied from her last illness, they were both now only too aware that the next time, she might not.

'Oh no, sir,' Maryann assured him. 'She's playing with Puss and ready for her breakfast, but I wondered if I might have a word with you first?'

'Of course,' he said, solicitously rising from his seat and leading her to a chair. 'What can I do for you?'

She cleared her throat before beginning. 'The thing is . . . Well, there's no easy way to say this so I may as well just come straight out with it. The fact is, I've come to resign from my position as Fleur's nanny. I will of course stay until you appoint another one, and then I was hoping you might kindly give me a reference so that I could apply for a position elsewhere.'

He stared at her in shocked disbelief for a moment before gasping, 'But *why*, Maryann? Have we done something to upset you? Are the wages not adequate? I would quite happily give you a pay increase, just name your price—'

'It's nothing like that,' she stated uncomfortably. 'I . . . I just feel that it is time to move away and get on with my life. There are so many memories here . . .'

As her voice trailed away he swiped a lock of hair from his forehead. 'I see,' he said quietly. 'Of course I cannot force you to stay, but should you choose to go you will be sorely missed.'

This was proving to be much harder than she had thought it would be, and she quickly looked away from the hurt in his eyes as she rose quickly and turned to the door. And then she was out in the corridor and hurrying to the kitchen. She must tell Nellie of her decision now.

Chapter Forty-Nine

As she had thought, Nellie was preparing breakfast for Wesley and she looked up and smiled as Maryann entered the room.

'Good morning, lass. Why, whatever's the matter with you? Is summat wrong wi' young Fleur?'

'No,' Maryann said awkwardly, then: 'I've just been in to the master and resigned from my position as Fleur's nanny.'

Nellie almost dropped the teapot she had just filled, but then slamming it onto the table she said brusquely, 'What did you just say? You've done *what*?'

Maryann told Nellie what the two women had said in the apothecary's, ending lamely, 'I realised that the rumours will never die down while I remain here, so I thought of trying to get another position in another part of the country. But of course I shall stay until the master has found someone suitable to replace me.'

She was shocked to see Nellie bristle before she said explosively, 'So you'd just clear off, would yer, without a second thought, an' leave that little mite upstairs that loves yer like her mother? An' what about the master, eh? Ain't yer got eyes in yer head, girl? A blind man on a gallopin' hoss could see how much he loves yer, but yer too wrapped up in yer memories o' Toby to give him a chance!'

'I *loved* Toby. We were going to be married until . . . until . . .'

'Until *what?*' Nellie shouted at her. 'Until he put that rotten-to-the-core brother o' his afore you, an' took the rap fer sommat he didn't do! Why, girl, open yer eyes an' look at the facts. Some might say it were commendable to do what he did, but the way I see it he were downright selfish – an' there you have it! He destroyed his parents so much that they had to move away, an' did he give a thought to what might happen to you, eh? No, he bloody well *didn't*! All he thought about were that no-good brother o' his an' he put him afore those that loved him. An' where were he when yer lost yer mam an' dad, eh? Even then he were prepared to see yer go into the workhouse rather than delay his dream of ownin' his own house for a while an' put you first. You always came second to his dreams o' betterin' hisself. I reckon it's time yer saw things as they really are, lass, an' got on wi' yer life, before it's too late. The master an' Miss Fleur have been different people since you arrived an' yet yer prepared to walk away from 'em just 'cos o' some gossip. It's downright cruel, to my way o' thinkin'. Well, I'm shocked at yer, I really am – but you do what you think best, miss! It's clear no one here means a jot to yer, an' now if you'll excuse me I'm goin' to get this through to the master.' And with that she turned her back on Maryann and marched from the room pointedly ignoring her.

Cissie waddled cheerfully into the room seconds later to find Maryann standing exactly where Nellie had left her, as if rooted to the spot.

'Why whatever is wrong, pet? Cissie asked. 'Yer look as if you've seen a ghost.'

'C-could you take Fleur's breakfast up to her for me?' Maryann gasped and then she fled from the room, leaving her sister-in-law to stare after her head in bewilderment.

Maryann pounded up the stairs and into her room, slamming the door behind her so loudly that the hinges almost cracked; only then did she give way to the tears that were threatening to choke her. Later, wiping her eyes, she placed her hands flat on the windowsill and peered out. She saw the master heading for the stable block. His head was down and he looked as if he had the weight of the world on his shoulders. Guilt, sharp as a knife, pierced through her. She had expected understanding and sympathy from Nellie, certainly not the terrible tongue-lashing she had received, and she was shocked to the core. Surely Nellie could understand how she felt? Moving to the bed, she lay upon it and sobbed again until eventually the door inched open and Cissie appeared with a steaming mug of tea in her hand.

'I thought you might like a drink,' she said quietly, and after placing it down on the bedside table she went on, 'Gran just told me that you're gonna be leavin' an' I feel sick to me stomach thinkin' of it. Benny will be too – he was so lookin' forward to you bein' here fer the birth of our baby. But then if you ain't happy here, I dare say I shouldn't blame yer.'

'It's not that I'm not happy here,' Maryann answered thickly. 'It's just that . . . oh, I don't know. Everything is such a mess and I'm all confused.'

Cissie shrugged. 'Well, you've knocked the master fer six, that's fer sure. He's been over to the stables to tell Benny that he won't be needin' the horse saddlin' today 'cos he ain't goin' into the mill, an' now he's locked hisself away in the library. Still, that ain't your problem at the end o' the

418

day, I don't suppose. It's just such a shame that you got his life back fer him an' then you decide to leave. He's been like a different man since you arrived an' I've no need to tell yer how much he thinks of you. We're all just hopin' he don't go back into his shell again after you've gone, that's all.'

'What's that supposed to mean?' Maryann leaned up on her elbow as Cissie flushed.

'Aw, don't tell me yer don't know how he feels about yer? But anyway, I must get back to work. You have a day off if yer like, an' I'll see to Fleur.' And with that she was gone, leaving Maryann to stare thoughtfully after her.

For the rest of the day Nellie and Cissie's words rang in her ears as she paced restlessly up and down her room. More than once she remembered the closeness that had sprung up between her and Wesley when they were nursing Fleur, and the easy way he would take her hand as they sat with the child watching her sleep. She remembered the way she had felt when he had taken her in his arms, the day when they had realised that Fleur was going to get well – more peaceful than she had ever felt in her whole life before, almost as if in his arms was where she was meant to be. At the time she had ignored her emotions because they had made her feel disloyal to Toby's memory. But as the day wore on she was forced to admit to herself that there was an element of truth in what Nellie had said.

Toby *had* always put his own dreams before hers. She remembered the utter despair she had felt on the night they had found her father dangling from a rope in the stairwell. At one stage after the tallyman's visit when he had given her notice to quit the cottage, she had felt that there was no alternative for her but to go into the workhouse. But even then, Toby had not offered to marry her. Even when she had secured the post of Fleur's nanny he had raised

419

no objections because it meant that he would not have to become responsible for her until it suited him.

As the hours passed, and Maryann had time to really think, she acknowledged that she did have feelings for the master. Feelings that she had held at bay because of her misguided loyalty to Toby. And now when she analysed her love for Toby in the cold light of day, it hit her that theirs had always been an understanding rather than a passionate love affair. They had never even shared more than a chaste kiss on the lips.

Deciding that she couldn't hide in her room forever she washed her face and tidied herself, then resolutely made for the kitchen. It was time to try and put things right with Nellie, who was clearly very disappointed in her.

She had almost reached the bottom of the stairs when she frowned. The front door was wide open, allowing the freezing wind to gust into the hall. As she made her way towards it, intending to close it, a figure suddenly jumped out from behind the coat-rack and Maryann skidded to a halt.

'Remember me, do you?'

It was Elizabeth Lord, although she looked nothing like she used to. She was stick-thin and there were huge dark circles beneath her eyes, which were gleaming with hatred. Her lank hair was unpinned and straggled about her shoulders like rats' tails, and she was dressed in the uniform of the workhouse – a coarse brown garment that hung from her skinny frame like a sack.

'Thought you'd seen the last of me, didn't you?' the woman spat, and in that moment Maryann realised that she was quite mad. Terror coursed through her, especially when the light caught and reflected from a lethal-looking knife that Miss Lord was clutching in her hand.

The woman advanced on her slowly as Maryann tried

to back away, but her legs were shaking so much that she could barely move.

'I was happy here till *you* turned up. Florence and I loved each other but you spoiled everything and now I've got nothing left to live for.' Tears began to course down Elizabeth's pale cheeks as from the corner of her eye Maryann saw the library door open.

'And now you have to pay for destroying our dreams,' the woman said softly – and before Maryann knew what was happening, Elizabeth had lunged towards her and she felt a sharp pain in her chest.

Her hand dropped to where she felt the pain and she was shocked to find that the knife was embedded in her and that her fingers were sticky with blood. And then everything seemed to happen at once as she heard someone running towards her from the kitchen, while Wesley leaped out from the library, emitting a scream that would have wakened the dead as he threw himself on Elizabeth Lord, dragging her to the ground.

Suddenly arms were about her and she found herself staring into Nellie's face. The woman was groaning as she tried to hold Maryann upright but then a welcoming darkness came to claim her and she knew no more.

'Ah, yer awake at last,' someone said tenderly as Maryann struggled to open her eyes. The voice sounded a long way away, but she thought it was Nellie's. Then she heard her say, 'Cissie, run an' tell the master she's comin' round, pet.'

She heard the sound of Cissie's crutch tapping across the floor before she sank back into silence again.

The next time she came to, she was aware that someone was gently holding her hand. She tried to open her eyes once more but it was so difficult. Her lids felt heavy and her chest felt as if a horse had trampled over it.

'Come on, sweetheart. You *must* come back to us,'

she heard someone say and she thought it sounded like Wesley's voice. But who was he talking to? And then finally she managed to open her eyes and as a face floated in front of her she saw that it was him.

He began to cry as he stroked the hair back from her brow and told her, 'Goodness, you gave us a terrible scare, Maryann; we thought we'd lost you for a time.'

Why was she lying there, she wondered. And why was the master talking to her like that? And then suddenly she started to remember and she panicked and thrashed around, but kindly hands held her down.

Nellie and the doctor entered the room, and Wesley discreetly stepped away from the bed as Dr Piper leaned over her and listened to her chest.

'You've been a very lucky young lady,' he smiled at her. 'Had that knife gone an inch the other way, it would have pierced your heart. But you'll be good as new in no time now if you do as you're told. There is no infection and the wound is healing nicely.'

'M-Miss Lord,' she muttered through dry, cracked lips.

'You have nothing to fear from her any more,' he said. 'She won't hurt anyone ever again. She's safely locked away in Hatter's Hall and I doubt she'll ever get out of there alive. I'm afraid she's totally insane now; you could almost feel sorry for her if it wasn't for what she tried to do to you. But now I want you to rest and follow my instructions and I shall be back to check on you in a couple of days.'

As the doctor left the room Nellie and Wesley closed in on her again with relieved smiles on their faces.

'How long have I been lying here?' Maryann managed to ask.

'For over a week – an' there were times when we feared yer weren't goin' to wake up,' Nellie told her with a little catch in her voice.

422

Maryann was shocked as she realised how close she must have come to death, but she had little time to dwell on it, for Nellie was heading for the door again, saying, 'I'm goin' to go an' make you a nice cup o' beef tea.'

When they were alone, Wesley approached the bed again but now that she was awake he made no attempt to touch her.

'I should go now and let you rest,' he whispered bashfully, and then he turned and left without another word.

When next she woke, Maryann was surprised to see that the room was full of flowers and there was a large bowl of peaches on the bedside table. She wondered where they had come from, since peaches were not easy to come by at this time of year – but then she was asleep again; it seemed that she couldn't stay awake for more than a few minutes at a time. She didn't mind, for when she was asleep she was in no pain. Each time she woke, Wesley was there and she found his presence comforting before she drifted off again.

And then one evening she was finally allowed to sit in the chair at the side of her bed and he offered to stay and keep her company. She willingly agreed. Cissie had just taken Fleur away to get her ready for bed and she could not face the thought of another evening alone. Everyone had been wonderful but they still had their chores to attend to as well as looking after her, so her evenings were usually very solitary.

'The doctor says I am allowed to get up and get dressed tomorrow, so I should be able to resume my duties soon – unless you have already found someone to replace me, that is?' she said falteringly.

'Of course I haven't – how could I?' Wesley said more sharply than he had intended to. In a softer voice he confided, 'I am very concerned about how Fleur is going to react when she finds out you are leaving, Maryann.

You are the closest thing to a mother she has ever known.' And suddenly he knew that he must share the secret he had been forced to keep for so many years and he went on sadly, 'I'm afraid my marriage was not all it appeared to be to the outside world. You see – Amélie did not care for the intimate side of marriage from the day I brought her here as a bride. She wanted to go home to her parents but I thought after a time she would grow to accept it and so I ignored her pleas. She was devastated when she discovered that she was with child, and even more so when Fleur was born. Everything had to be perfect in Amélie's little world and, of course, Fleur was not perfect. I should have sought medical help for her then, for she started to become more and more withdrawn from the world until the night she . . . Well, until she died. Ever since then, not a day has gone by when I haven't blamed myself for her death. I should have allowed her to leave, knowing how unhappy she was, but I kept thinking that things would improve.'

'Oh, Wesley.' Maryann reached out to him and took his hand in her own – it felt like the most natural thing in the world to do. 'But you shouldn't blame yourself. Amélie was clearly mentally unbalanced, poor soul, and there was nothing you could have done apart from have her locked away. But you didn't do that. You cared for her and were kind to her and so you must stop blaming yourself.'

'Do you really think so?'

She nodded. 'Yes I do.' And she was gratified to see the look of relief in his eyes. Maybe now that he had shared his burden, he would be able to put the past behind him.

Just then, the door burst open and Fleur spilled into the room rosy-cheeked from her bath, wearing a clean nightdress and a pretty little pink dressing gown.

'I've come to say goodnight to you both,' she gabbled with a broad smile, and she tripped over to them and embraced them all at once with an arm round each of them as she planted wet kisses first on one cheek and then another.

Maryann's and Wesley's arms both instinctively closed about her and as their fingers touched Maryann felt heat start to rise in her.

'Leave her here, Cissie,' Wesley said pleasantly. 'I shall take her up and tuck her in in a minute when she's tired.'

'Right y'are, sir,' Cissie said obligingly before swinging her crutch about and leaving the room.

Fleur promptly clambered onto her father's lap, and looking at Maryann she shocked them both when she suddenly announced, 'I don't have a mama, you know, Maryann. She's gone to be an angel, so could you be my mama?'

There was a stunned silence, but the moment was saved by Wesley, who rose and swung Fleur up into his arms, saying, 'Now, Fleur, Maryann still isn't properly better yet. Say goodnight, there's a good girl.'

Fleur did as she was told and then her father smiled at Maryann apologetically before carrying the child from the room, leaving her to stare pensively at the door.

Chapter Fifty

'Eeh, it's good to see you up and about again, lass,' Nellie commented when Maryann walked into the kitchen one blustery November morning. She, Ted and Cissie were sitting at the table enjoying a drink before starting their chores and Maryann joined them at the table.

'Aye, it is,' Cissie agreed. 'But yer still look a bit peaky to me so you must take yer time fer a while.'

Maryann reached to lift the heavy teapot but Ted immediately grabbed it first and poured a mugful out for her, saying, 'That pot's 'eavy when it's full an' we don't want yer overdoin' things fer a while, do we now, else we'll be back to square one. Master Wesley told us that the doctor said you're to take yer time.'

Maryann sighed, but she knew that Ted was only trying to be kind. They had all been kind to her and treated her as if she were family, nursing her with love and tenderness.

As she spooned sugar into her tea, Cissie's hand dropped to her swollen stomach and she said, 'The baby keeps moving. We were lyin' in bed last night and I woke Benny so he could feel it too. He were right excited.'

'That's wonderful.' Maryann was thrilled for them both and yet she also felt strangely envious. It must be nice to be carrying the child of the man you loved.

Ted broke her chain of thought then when he rose from the table and plonked his mug down, saying, 'That's me done then. I'd best go an' give Benny a hand rubbin' the horses down.' Then crossing to Nellie, he pecked her on the cheek before saying, 'And make sure as you have that pot full again at eleven for me, woman!'

'Yer cheeky old bugger,' Nellie retaliated and again Maryann felt a pang of envy. For all their teasing there was another couple who deeply loved each other.

Cissie meanwhile was making for the green baize door on her way to get Fleur dressed, and Nellie went to sit by Maryann for her second cup of tea of the day. It was then she broached the subject that was constantly on Maryann's mind when she asked, 'So are yer still plannin' on leavin' us then?'

Maryann had learned long ago that you could always rely on Nellie to come straight to the point.

'I – I'm not quite sure,' she answered indecisively.

Nellie clucked her disapproval. 'Then happen it's time yer were, pet. T'ain't fair on the master, him not knowin' from one day to the next where he stands.'

Maryann nodded in agreement, knowing that Nellie was right – and that afternoon when she had retired to her room for a short rest her thoughts turned to Wesley and she felt butterflies flutter to life in the pit of her stomach. She found herself thinking of the many times she had fought the urge to reach out and stroke the wayward lock of hair that had a habit of flopping across his forehead and the warm feeling she had experienced when she saw the lovely portrait of her which he had painted. There were so many little things to recall: the closeness they had shared as they sat at the bedside throughout Fleur's illnesses; the many kind things he had done for her and the way his face would light up when she came into a room . . . eventually she berated herself for a fool as she finally acknowledged her feelings for him. But was it too late? Had the damage been done, when she had told him she was leaving? Would he ever be able to trust her again? Yet even if this were so, surely she could leave on a happy note?

She fingered the tiny brooch that was pinned to her gown and then very slowly she removed it, and after staring at it long and hard she placed it away in a drawer. She would never wear it again.

Some minutes later she made her way down to the kitchen to ask Nellie timidly, 'Did the master happen to say what time he would be back from the mill today, Nellie?' She knew that he had already left because she had heard his horse gallop away down the drive as she was getting dressed.

Nellie blinked with surprise as she looked up from the pastry she was rolling. 'As a matter o' fact he poked his head in an' told me he'd be back mid-afternoon.'

Maryann thanked her then went back upstairs to see Fleur. She felt she had neglected her lately, but when she entered the child's room and the little girl tottered over to her with outstretched arms, the enormity of what she had done when she had tendered her resignation hit her afresh. She loved the child; how could she ever have thought that she could walk away from her and never see her again? The little girl's life might well be limited, but now she knew that she longed to be a part of it.

Cissie had been entertaining Fleur while Maryann rested, but now she told her, 'Look, if you're sure you're all right, I'll get back down to the kitchen now an' help Gran get the

428

dinner ready. I'll be back in no time an' then you're to go and have a lie-down.'

'Yes, ma'am,' Maryann grinned, and then turned her attention to Fleur. After lunch, at Cissie's insistence she went to her room and despite the fact that she didn't feel at all tired, she was asleep in no time.

She woke, just as the sky was beginning to darken, to the sound of laughter floating through her bedroom window. She crossed to the window and twitched the curtains aside. Fleur and her father were out in the garden, and the sight of them brought a smile to her face. She quickly tidied her hair in the mirror, shook out the skirts of her plain grey gown, and hurriedly throwing her cloak on, she went down to the front door. Once out on the steps she paused as she watched Fleur and her father on the front lawns examining some of the fallen leaves with great interest. The whole lawn was covered with them and they made a pretty picture: a patchwork quilt of russet, gold and browns. The leaves scrunched beneath her feet and floated into the air as she strode towards them, and both their faces lit up as she approached them.

'Should you be out?' Wesley queried anxiously. 'I just brought Fleur out for a little fresh air before it gets dark, but I don't want you over-tiring yourself.'

'I'm fine,' Maryann assured him but then Fleur was waving a particularly pretty leaf at her and Maryann had to stoop to admire it. The child then scooted away in search of more treasures.

The atmosphere was slightly fraught between them to begin with as they watched Fleur's antics, but Maryann knew that it was time to say what she had come to say, so taking a deep breath she began quietly, 'I was wondering . . . is it too late to retract my resignation? I find that I really don't want to leave after all.'

429

'I see.'

She held her breath as she caught him looking pointedly towards Fleur with his hands clasped behind his back.

'May I ask what has brought about this sudden change of heart?'

'I . . . I suppose it's a number of things,' she stuttered. 'Fleur is such a lovely little girl and I've grown very fond of her. And then there are the Carters, of course – they've been like a second family to me and I can't imagine leaving them. I've actually realised that I'm very happy here.'

'And?'

He certainly wasn't making this easy for her, and she felt herself squirm with embarrassment. 'And . . . I've grown very fond of you too,' she squeaked. 'So please may I keep my job?'

His answer made her heart skip a beat.

'I'm rather afraid you can't, Maryann,' he said calmly. 'You see, I find that if you were to stay there is another role I would wish you to take on – that of my wife. I think I have loved you from the very first moment I set eyes on you in the mill, with your hair thick with cotton and clogs on your feet. And then when Elizabeth Lord attacked you and we thought you were going to die, I knew that I couldn't bear it . . . so what do you say? Will you marry me, Maryann?'

Her mouth opened and shut before she croaked, 'But you can't marry me, Wesley. As you just said, I was a mill girl. What would people say? It would cause a scandal, to say the very least.'

'They can say what they damn well like,' Wesley retorted. 'You are more of a lady than any I have ever met. More to the point, you are the lady I happen to love – so what's your answer to be?'

As Maryann looked back at this man her heart swelled with love for him and she knew in that instant that she had found her soulmate, the man with whom she wanted to spend the rest of her life. It was a powerful, all-consuming love that she knew would last a lifetime and beyond. She would never forget Toby, but she realised now that what she had felt for him was nothing compared to what she felt for Wesley. The townsfolk had branded her his whore – and if that was all she could ever have been to him she would have accepted it gladly – but here he was asking her to be his wife.

Now it was he watching her closely, but to his dismay she said nothing – but then standing on tiptoe, she kissed him on the lips, and as their arms wrapped about each other he had his answer and he thought his heart was going to burst with joy.

Fleur meantime had turned, and seeing her father and Maryann locked in an embrace, she was off like a hare across the lawn bursting into the kitchen to tell Nellie breathlessly, with a radiant smile on her face, 'Nellie, Nellie, Papa an' Maryann are kissin' in the garden. Do you think Maryann is going to be my mama?'

Nellie's hands became still for a moment as she leaned on the pastry she was rolling. But then she sniffed to blink back her happy tears and turning to the child she told her with a smile, 'I reckon it does, pet. An' about time too, eh? Now 'ow about a nice glass o' lemonade?'

Acknowledgements

Many thanks to Rebecca, Kate, Florence, Hannah and all the team at Little, Brown for making me feel so welcome.

Not forgetting my brilliant agent, Sheila Crowley, and my lovely copy-editor, Joan Deitch.

About Rosie . . .

Looking back I can't remember a time when I didn't love writing. Even as a very young child I was always making up stories, and this pastime continued when I had my own children. I never imagined that any of my stories would be publishable, though, so it was wonderfully exciting when my first novel, *The Bad Apple*, was published in 2004.

I suppose part of the charm of writing, for me, is being able to create different characters and to travel all over the world without leaving my office. I love it when my characters come to life: I grow to love them and then feel a bit sad when the book is finished, but not for long! Usually another story is already forming and then I'm off again. People often ask me which of my books is my favourite and I can always truthfully tell them: the one I am writing now. After all, if I don't strive to make each one better than the last then I would be letting my readers down.

Before becoming a full-time author I worked for Social Services, both as a foster mum and a Placement Support

Worker. Our own daughter had been an only child for seven years, which is one of the things that motivated us to foster, and over the years many children have joined our family. Some came as babies and others were as old as eighteen; some of them stayed for just a short time and some for a number of years. Many of my foster children still keep in touch, and it's so lovely when you can watch them grow up into confident adults and hope that you helped them, just a little bit, at a time when they really needed support. I think this is one of the reasons I am never short of ideas for stories.

Becoming an author has opened up yet another new world to me, as I am now the patron of three establishments for which I fundraise. One of these is a children's holiday scheme which each year aims to send underprivileged children for a break to the seaside (CHYPS (Camp Hill Young People's Holiday Scheme), community.office@prideincamphill.co.uk); another is the Bulkington Community Library, where a willing team of volunteers work tirelessly to keep the village library running smoothly and open for the public (bulkingtoncommunitylibrary@btconnect.com); and finally I am a patron of the local Mary Ann Evans Hospice, who do a wonderful job working with people who have life-threatening illnesses (www.maryannevans.org.uk).

Of course, an author's life is far from glamorous. Much of my time is spent locked away in my office with my imaginary characters, but I can truthfully say I love it. I have been lucky enough to meet a number of fellow authors whose books I have always enjoyed, and am now able to call many of them friends. I also get to spend lots of time with my children and grandchildren, who are wonderful; not that I am biased, of course!

Almost three years ago my husband and I moved into a wonderful, old, character-filled house, and we have been in our element making it into our own. I love getting my hands dirty and working in my garden. In fact, I find I am much better at knuckling down to writing in the winter when the nights are dark and I can't get outside.

Another huge part of my life is my three dogs: Lilibet, Tallulah and Sassy. They are all Shih Tzus, affectionately known as 'the shitties' to us, and they come everywhere with us, even sharing our bedroom. We have a holiday home on the East Coast and rarely go abroad as we don't like to leave them behind; we are never happier than when wandering along the beach with them on a nice evening.

This year, I was delighted to discover that I had climbed well into the Top 100 of the UK's most borrowed library authors, so I must say a huge thank you to all of my wonderful readers. I love to hear from you all via Twitter, Facebook and my website, so do keep your messages coming, they always make my day. Finally, do sign up for my newsletter if you're interested – I promise I'll try to keep you up to date with everything that's going on in my life!

With love
Rosie x

Dilly's Sacrifice

A moving and uplifting story of a young mother's love, loyalty and determination – from the streets of the Midlands to the fields of Ireland.

With her husband unable to work and four children already at home, Dilly cannot afford to feed her new-born baby. Heartbroken, she secretly delivers her daughter to the Farthing family at the big house for adoption. This act of desperation will change the lives of both families irrevocably – and the onset of WWI even more so . . .

The Mill Girl

A warm and captivating story of fighting for love in the face of adversity.

Life is tough on the cobbled courtyards of Warwickshire in the 1840s, but Maryann is happy there, until her mother dies. Struggling to cope, she is finally offered a lifeline: a job as nanny to the daughter of the mill owner, Mr Marshall. To Maryann's surprise she grows close to him. But their relationship threatens to unleash a world of problems on them all . . .

The Soldier's Daughter

A compelling and wonderfully authentic portrait of family life amongst the perils of WWII.

For as long as Briony Valentine can remember she has been soft on Eddie, the boy next door. But their chance of romance is stifled when the Luftwaffe begin dropping bombs on the Midlands. Eddie is called up to serve, as is Briony's father, tearing her world apart. As the Valentine children make for the safety of Cornwall, all Briony can do is pray.

A Mother's Shame

From the corridors of a mental asylum, to the plains of Australia, for the sake of two unborn babies . . .

One dismal day in 1857 Maria Mundy arrives at Hatter's Hall, the local mental asylum, not as an inmate but as a worker. She is ordered to care for Isabelle Montgomery, the daughter of an influential land-owner. But Isabelle is not insane; she has been banished here by her family. Hatter's Hall serves to hide unmarried women in the family way from prying eyes.

Home Front Girls

A gripping and emotional WWII drama about three women who kept the country moving during its darkest hours.

Dotty has never known a life outside of the orphanage where she grew up; Lucy is the sole carer of her little sister now that her brother has gone to war; Annabelle's life of privilege is stalled now that war is here. For the three girls adjusting to life on the shop-floor of Coventry's only department store is hard enough, but then the bombs begin to fall . . .

The Empty Cradle

Charlotte is the privileged daughter of the local vicar, but behind closed doors she is his prisoner.

Naïve, lonely and craving freedom, Charlotte is sent to Ireland to hide a shameful pregnancy and forced into a convent's harsh, humiliating regime. Returning to England older than her years, she flees her father's grasp and chooses to become a London midwife. But her longing to prevent others from suffering the same horrors as her leads her into danger . . .

The Misfit

An abandoned baby. A damaged child. Can Rebecca escape her broken past?

Abandoned outside a hospital, baby Rebecca didn't have a good start. When her adoptive mother dies, her greedy aunt takes her in, but it is not a happy home and soon Rebecca's life is worse than ever. She longs to escape to the circus that visits her town, with its carefree life and freedom from her past – but will she ever find happiness?

Whispers

Sometimes the past really does come back to haunt you.

When Jess Beddows steps inside a rotting, old manor house, she feels she has come home. Against her family's wishes she buys the house, and later finds a journal – untouched for over a century. It holds the heartbreaking tale of Martha, and the entangled lives of the servants and masters of the house from nearly two hundred years ago. As Jess is drawn into their tragedy, the whispers begin and everything she loves will be threatened by long-kept secrets . . .

The Ribbon Weaver

A baby rescued from the snow. A wealthy family's tragic secret. A girl determined to make her mark.

One winter's night a baby is rescued from the snow and changes two families for ever. The tiny girl grows into a gifted young woman, Amy, with far-reaching ambitions. She dreams of designing hats and clothes, but as more secrets are revealed, Amy is caught between two worlds, until she must choose where her heart truly belongs.

Don't let the story stop here

Join

ROSIE GOODWIN

and her readers